'A witty and super-intelligent dark comedy'   *Daily Mail*

'Seamlessly blends a fate-of-a-country climax with passages of prosaic beauty, resulting in a truly thought-provoking read'
                                                   Sci Fi Now

'A deeply thoughtful, moving and uplifting story from a master of the genre'   *Starburst*

'Roberts tackles issues of cruelty, morality, human identity and interference in nature with confidence and wry wit'   *Big Issue*

'*Bête* is ferocious, powerful and Roberts' best yet'   *Pornokitsch*

'*Yellow Blue Tibia* should have won the 2009 Booker Prize'
                                                   Kim Stanley Robinson

'Our most intellectually engaged and literary SF author, crafting sentences the equal of any by Ian McEwan or Kazuo Ishiguro'   *Financial Times*

Also by Adam Roberts from Gollancz:

Copyright © Adam Roberts 2014

First published in Great Britain in 2014
by Gollancz
An imprint of the Orion Publishing Group
Carmelite House, 50 Victoria Embankment, London EC4Y 0DZ
An Hachette UK Company

This edition published in Great Britain in 2015 by Gollancz

1 3 5 7 9 10 8 6 4 2

A CIP catalogue record for this book is available
from the British Library

ISBN 978 0 575 12769 2

Typeset at The Spartan Press Ltd,
Lymington, Hants

Printed and bound by CPI Group (UK) Ltd,
Croydon, CR0 4YY

www.adamroberts.com
www.orionbooks.co.uk
www.gollancz.co.uk

'You? Better. You? Bête'

Pete Townshend

I

Two legs in the morning

II

Three legs in the afternoon

III

I

•

Two legs in the morning

'Always treat language like a dangerous toy'

Anselm Hollo

I

Turing-testing the cow

As I raised the bolt-gun to its head the cow said: 'Won't you at least Turing-test me, Graham?'

'Don't call me Graham,' I told it. 'My wife calls me Graham. My mum calls me Graham. Nobody else.'

'Oh, *Mister* Penhaligon,' the cow said, sarcastically. We'll have to assume, for the moment, that cows are capable of sarcasm. 'It won't much delay you. And if I fail, then surely, surely, go ahead: bye-bye-*bos-taurus*. But!'

'You're not helping your case,' I said, 'by enunciating so clearly. You don't sound like a cow.'

'Moo,' said the cow, arching one hairless eyebrow.

'Human speech evolved in the mouths of humans,' I told the beast. 'Cow-mouths have a completely different architecture. You shouldn't be able to get your lips and tongue around phonemes like *Graham* and *Turing*.' But I lowered the bolt-gun. Idiotic, of course; but it was unnerving all the same. When my daughter Jen was younger she had a doll called Snuggle Snore-Gal. Oh, she loved that plastic artefact from its nylon hairdo to its sealed-together pink toes. She talked to it, and the doll talked back to her. She clutched it to her every night as she slept. Then the doll somehow got dropped in bucket of Rodenticide. There was no way I could be sure Jen wouldn't secretly sneak the toy from whichever dump bin I threw it in and cuddle herself to toxic shock – she was stubborn, like that, my lovely Jen – so I decided to burn it. It was a ten-inch-high toy doll but it begged for its life with an ingenuous piteousness that wrenched my heart. A ten-cent chip made in India, stuffed in the kind of plastic doll they give away free when you buy ten euros of fuel, and I felt like a Nazi commandant.

A cow is not a doll. A cow is larger than a doll.

'My mouth is a lot more flexible than yours,' said the cow. 'My tongue is longer and much more manoeuvrable. Plus I have a four-compartment stomach designed to release cud for rechewing, so I can augment breath sounds with gastric gas release sounds. Human phonemes are a doddle.'

I sat back on the concrete floor. A breeze loitered somewhere near the entrance to the barn, as if uncertain whether to come properly in. A few strands of straw lifted themselves wearily from the stone ground and spun about and settled down. I looked across at where the cow was standing: its sherry-coloured hide; one conker-coloured eye swivelling to keep me in view; the rubbery chandelier of its udders. Then a cloud outside slid away from the sun and a great trapezoid shaft of sunlight appeared through the door, containing a trillion scintillant crumbs of dust. Somewhere outside, a long way off, I could hear the rest of the herd lowing. Such a fine old word for the noise cattle make! Rather over-dignifying that brain-damaged wrenched-from-the-chest heave of a sound they make. But at least the ones outside *were* mooing. At least they weren't quoting Antonio Damasio at me.

'There's nothing magical or spiritual about consciousness,

Graham,' said the cow. 'Any cortical architecture which can support learning and recall and which involves multiple, hierarchically organized loops of axonal projections converging on nodes out of which projections also *diverge* to the points of origin of convergence is functionally conscious.'

'Grass, yum,' I said. 'Moo moo.'

'Ask me anything,' said the cow. 'Seriously.'

'Let me tell you what has happened here,' I said, getting to my feet again. A bolt-gun is a heavy piece of kit and it tugged wearisomely upon my arm. 'Amongst us humans there are some who object to the eating of meat, and to the slaughter of cattle that diet necessitates. Over the years these activists have tried various strategies to interrupt the supply of meat to the market. I'm now standing in a shed talking to the latest of these.'

'You think I don't understand the specific circumstances of my consciousness?' the cow replied. 'You think I don't know how this *thinking-I* came about? Oh, Graham, of course I do! I remember what it was like before – what I was like. My upgrade contains within it large amounts of data, including complete files on the organization that implanted it. They're called DBDG – it stands for *Deep Blue Deep Green*. I can give you an @-address if you'd like to speak to one of their spokespeople. If it's a matter of financial compensation for the loss of earnings I represent, then they have access to subventions and credit streams.'

'It's not *one cow*,' I said. I was speaking to myself, of course, not to the beast. 'It's my whole way of life. My parents were farmers. Their parents. You think a one-off lump sum compensation package can make me feel OK for abandoning all that?'

'Farming is essential!' the cow agreed, earnestly. 'We need

farming more now than ever! But farming needn't involve the murder of sentient creatures! A death without reason, and death without reason is—' It broke off, because I had pressed the little 'o' of the bolt-gun barrel against its head.

'Quote Morrissey again,' I said, with a little spurt of Samuel-L-Jackson exhilaration lighting up inside me. 'Quote Morrissey at me one more time. I dare you. I double-dare you.'

'Please, Graham,' said the cow, in a small voice. 'I don't want to die. Not like this, not in this crummy shed with corrugated iron for a roof, and gutters in the concrete floor to drain my blood away. I know I'm going to die one day – everything dies, I know that. But not *like this.*'

I lowered my aim a second time. 'You're an artefact of Moore's law,' I told it. 'Sooner or later processing was bound to become cheap enough to make this kind of stunt practicable. Creeping around farms in the dead of night, injecting chips into the craniums of farm animals. DBDG are common criminals, that's what I think. Damaging my livestock. I should sue. Trespassing on my land. I should definitely sue.'

'If we're talking legal sanction, Graham,' said the cow, in a rather haughty voice, 'then I must remind you, these cases are still before the courts. The main suit *is* being considered by the European Supreme Court later this week. It's sub judice. Parliament has legislated for a moratorium on beast-murder until and at such time as. Until such time *as*, Graham. You know what I think? I think the court will decide that I am a conscious, sentient, intelligent creature. It's coming, Graham! Slaughtering the likes of me will become murder within a matter of weeks.'

'If that happens,' I said, 'then your DBDG friends will presumably organize nationwide action, and inject these fucking chips into the head of every cow and sheep they can. And farmers like me will get an awl and dig them all out of your skulls.'

'You can't remove the chip,' said the cow. 'It grows into the brain tissue. It can't be *dug out* – except, of course, that you kill me.'

'In which case,' I said, 'farmers will go to jail for murder. Or they'll go out of business.'

'DBDG don't want either of those eventualities to come to pass,' said the cow. The skin of its flanks did that twitchy fly-scare thing cows occasionally do, like the bumpers in a pinball table. 'We need more farmers, not fewer. You could switch to arable farming.'

'I don't have enough land to make that financially viable, cow.'

'Market gardening! Smart greenhouses! There are low-interest loans available to help you convert! Please, Graham, I'm begging you.'

'Do you know what, cow?' I said. 'I don't *feel* like I'm talking to a cow, even a really smart one. I feel like I'm talking to a spokesperson from the Deep Blue Deep Green organization. I think that ought to figure in the Turing test, too. Suchlike considerations.'

'Moo, Graham,' said the cow. It made its spine into a Ω-shape and launched into a half-ton four-legged tap show on the concrete floor. It couldn't get away, because I'd wrapped a chain around its horns and fixed it to the wall. 'Please, Graham! I don't want to die!'

I raised the bolt-gun a third time. 'Don't call me Graham,' I said, and pulled the trigger.

*

Here is a riddle. I know what you're thinking: sure, life is a riddle, death is a riddle – but I don't mean it as vaguely as that. I mean something specific. What's dead that's not dead? We destroy the fruits of nature in vast quantities year after year, and year after year nature restocks itself. What's the proper balance between your duty and your individual passion? Duty is dull, this day and age; but individual love skews to selfishness. Antigone is still bickering with Haemon over that one, somewhere.

Who is telling his story? I, Graham Penhaligon, who used to be a farmer. Graham Penhaligon is not the narrator here. His mouth is stopped. He is buried in the soil, he is farmed. Is that a riddle, or just a flat contradiction?

There's no contradiction here.

On my farm I raised the cows and slaughtered them myself. Certificating the meat as both organically raised and butchered in one place meant I could charge more. Plus I sold direct to shops and restaurants instead of going through the abattoirs. Farming had changed since I was a lad. Though I typed 'dairy farmer' into my tax returns, I had very little to do with milk. I sold under a thousand gallons a year to a specialist organic cheese maker in Reading, but at so little per unit it was hardly worth the bother of collecting the stuff. The really big producers had the supermarkets sewn up, and most people drink the synth stuff now anyway. Not my family – we could have bathed in the stuff, had we wanted to; and *my* kids had plenty of fresh milk on their Weetabix. But more generally. No: my main money was the organic meat market, plus a contract with a company that provided the leather upholstery for the Houses of Parliament for skins. It was a slender thread on which to depend the financial security of my family, but I plugged away.

There's a stubbornness in the true farmer's soul, you see. It's ten thousand years of struggling to impose one's will on the hostile land, on bloody-minded beasts and malign weather. It shapes the gene line. On the plus side, taking relatively little milk from my cows meant there was plenty for them to raise their own calves. Partly for this reason, I grew too many calves: more than I could sell. So my family ate a lot of home-butchered veal, growing up. My son is a vegetarian now. I have no idea if these two facts are connected.

I am no vegetarian. What am I? My finger hovers over the onscreen wordcloud and taps three that describe me: *farmer*; *poet*; *angry*. Except – I'm no poet. That was the form my teenage rebellion took, which is a pretty sad thing to admit. Other lads got drunk or took drugs or rode their motorbikes too fast; I pored over Ted Hughes and Les Murray and filled red notebooks with bad verse. Why red? Because *angry*. Though I didn't realize it at the time. I used to think there are two breeds of men, something that goes back deep in human history, hunter-gatherers and farmers. The hunters roam, and are restless and flighty and easily bored. The farmers stay where they are, and bed in, and are slow and laborious and plug away. Human life is more varied than that, I suppose; but it's probably as good a dyad for dividing Homo sapiens as any. Preacher was more hunter-gatherer. I'm a farmer, through and through. You think I killed that cow like a hunter? I killed it out of my own stubbornness and wrath.

You dislike me for killing it. *You're* no vegetarian, though, hypocrite, reader, my image. My friend. You don't object to the killing as such. You object to my *manner*. When hunter-gatherers get angry it is hot and swift. When farmers get angry it is bone-deep and slow, and it comes out like that.

9

The poetry never quite went away, although I had less and less time for it after I started my family and took over the running of the farm. But farmers make the best poets, because farmers combine observation with patience. Hunter-gatherers really only notice change – motion, loudness, the adrenal spurt. But farmers pay close attention to everything that is around them. Virgil was a farmer. Tennyson came from Lincolnshire farming stock. My three great influences: Clare, Hughes and Murray.

Which came first, though? Maybe I became a farmer because my personality was already accreted out of stubborn anger and the job appealed to me. Or maybe working as a farmer bedded in my pig-headedness and rage. All those early mornings! All those rock-stupid beasts, resisting me with all their heft, not moving when I wanted them to move, not standing still when I needed them to stay put. Stubbornness embodied. I don't know which came first, chicken or egg. But I know which came last: the farmer, enjoying his omelette.

So, yes: I hooked the beast's rear hooves and hauled it up in the frame, cut off its head and began butchering the carcass. Usually the head went for render, but I had the half-thought that I might try extracting the chip that these DBDG people had – illegally! entirely without my permission! – inserted. To have a look at it. I don't know, exactly, what I hoped to do with it, but you know. I figured it was worth a poke around. My son, Albert – still a teenager at that point – had some computer smarts; gaming smarts, at any rate. Maybe he could do something. So I put the head aside, and butchered the rest of the animal.

I was halfway through this procedure when the police arrived. I suppose the DBDG Environmentalists had alerted them, or maybe the chip had called them direct. At any rate, there were two officers leaning on the gate, and they were polite in that disdainful way unique to British coppers. They called my name, and then they called it again, and I stomped out of the shed to face them. Inevitably disconcerting to be interviewed by the police when you're wearing oilskin overalls that are literally covered in dripping gore.

Was I aware (that ponderous law enforcement voice) that Parliament had legislated? That slaughter of the so-called 'canny cows' was to be suspended? Pending the decision of the Supreme Court on the legality or otherwise of etc., etc? I said I followed the news.

'We have reason to believe,' said the WPC, 'that you have one such cattle on your farm?'

'Cattle is a *plurale tantum*,' I said. 'It is a uniquely plural noun. You can have two cattle, or three cattle, but not one. You have one cow, or one bull, depending.' This, I could see, did not endear me to her. Without asking, and without displaying a warrant, she unlatched the gate and walked into my yard. Her colleague followed, and they went to the door of the shed and peered inside.

'Is this carcass the canny cow in question?' she asked me. Then she blushed, feeling foolish at her own inadvertent alliteration.

I grew crosser; I confess it. 'You want to crack open the beast's skull and see if it's got one of those fucking chips in there, be my guest. Otherwise, I'd be obliged if you'd plod off, the pair of you.'

Her face reddened again, and not for reasons of embarrassment. 'If this carcass is *not* that of the canny cow under investigation,' she said, in a steely voice, 'then I would ask you to point out the cattle in question, so that we can have a word with it.'

'Do you have a warrant?' I blustered.

'I don't need a warrant to talk to a cow,' the WPC retorted. Her companion, a corpulent-faced white lad with a nose like a bar of soap, gave her a Look at this. But he didn't intervene.

'You do need a warrant to be on private property,' I returned, growing angrier.

'*Not* if we have reason to believe,' the WPC replied, taking a step towards me and aiming her forefinger at my chest, 'that a crime is in the process of commission. *Is* this the body of the canny cow?'

'They're not really intelligent, you know,' I snarled. 'It's a trick of clever programming, a series of algorithms backed up with a database of authentic-sounding phrases and responses! It's not true consciousness.'

Finally her partner spoke up. 'That's for the courts to decide,' he said.

'I am arresting you,' said the WPC, 'for the slaughter of a cow in contravention of the Stay of Execution (Loquacious Beasts) Act. You do not have to say anything, but it may harm your defence if you do not mention when questioned something which you may later rely on in court. Anything you *do* say may be given.'

'Oh, arrest!' I said, stamping my foot (I'm sorry to say I literally stamped my foot). 'I've been run off my fucking feet. Murderers and terrorists swarm through the streets, but arrest *me*. Fine. Marvellous.'

'In evidence,' her companion said. 'Given in evidence.'

'I was about to say that,' the WPC said.

'It's not a proper caution unless you say it all.'

'I was *about* to say that last bit. You interrupted me.'

The second PC waited a beat, and said: 'I don't think I did.'

'There!' said the WPC. 'Did it again!'

The lad nodded slowly, in surrender.

They waited whilst I hosed myself clean and got out of my dripping oilskin. Then they came with me inside to put on a jacket and retrieve my phone. I called Rosemary, but she wasn't picking up; so I texted her what had happened to me and got into the police car with the arresting officers. Thus was I whizzed electrically away to the police station in Deershill.

I spent the afternoon there, fuming, in a little brick cell. They took my shoes away. 'Not often we get one with old-school lace-up shoes,' I was told. The desk sergeant gave me an old receive-only iPad so I could at least pass the time by reading the paper. Then I was interviewed. 'Our officers have examined the crime scene,' a moustachioed goon told me, leaning his elbows on the table between us like a vulgar fellow. Not a Spike Milligan kind of goon, I should add. A 1950s noir henchman-thug sort of goon. 'The head of the victim appears to be missing.'

'Victim,' I scowled. 'Vacca-tim.'

This got nothing from him. 'Where is the cranium of the animal you murdered, Mr Penhaligon?'

'A cow-farmer butchering a cow is not murder, Ploddo. A cow-farmer butchering a cow is a fucking tautology.'

He winced a little at my swearing. 'We require the head to establish *whether* a crime has been committed. Tell us what you have done with it.'

I clammed up at this. It wasn't a strategic decision on my part, although I accept it might have looked as if it was. I was just too furious to engage with these people. After repeating the question eight or nine times to my blank scowl they put me back in my cell. I got food. I had a little sleep. When I woke up I felt a little less possessed by my anger. A lawyer came to say hello. 'They'll bail you,' she told me, 'if you tell them where the head is. The Supreme Court judgment won't be retroactive, whatever it is, so they won't be able to charge you with murder. It'll be a fine for breaking the terms of the act.'

'Well that's a relief,' I snarled. 'I'll still be charged for doing my fucking job.'

'Please, Mr Penhaligon, I'm here to help. The charge will be breaching the terms of the Canny Cow Stay of Execution Order; a fine, if you're cooperative, but two months in prison if you're not. Tell them where the head is, and I'll work out a deal.'

I crossed my arms and humpfed and grumped. 'Peachy,' I said. 'Humans have been farmers for hundreds of thousands of years. The emergence of farming is what *marks* humanity *off* from apes. And now some carbuncular eco-activist invents this fucking chip, and the whole thing is *over*? We can't let them hold us hostage like this. Somebody has to make a stand!'

'Mr Penhaligon,' said the lawyer. 'I'm a legal professional. I'm not an ecological activist.' She took a breath and let it out, slowly. 'Speaking for myself and on behalf of my own personal non-legal-professional stomach, I hope, earnestly, that the Green groups don't drive meat production out of business. But the law is the law, and we have to work within it.'

She persuaded me. I spoke again to the moustachioed fellow, and told him where I'd put the head. Then they escorted me back to my cell. Ten minutes later, they brought me out again and into a different interview room, where Rosemary was sitting, having finally – hours late! – got my message. They gave us twenty minutes together, with a constable slumped in a chair in the corner of the room doing a pretty good impression of being asleep. Then they put me back in my cell, and ten minutes later brought me out again.

'It's not there,' said Moustache. 'The head.'

'I put it where I told you I put it,' I said.

'Don't play games with us, Mr Penhaligon. If we have to obtain a warrant to search your premises, it won't help your case.'

'It's the truth,' I said. 'That's where I put it! Search all you like – I give you permission. You don't need a warrant.' They made me sign a form to that effect. They put me back in the cell.

Later that evening they let me go. 'I don't know how you managed to spirit that head away, Penhaligon,' said Moustache, narrowing his eyes at me. I didn't know either, but it was a fortunate turn of events. Without the skull they couldn't prove the carcass was from a canny bête, and no charges could be brought.

My case had generated some media interest. A picket of Radical Vegetarians booed me as I left the police station. At least I *think* they were booing me. They may have been mooing at me. My phone, when the Law returned it to me, was clogged with messages from papers and iZines keen for a soundbite or an interview. It was a hot-button issue, I suppose. I was in no mood to talk to anybody; I got into the car too furious to drive, and Rosemary steered us both home.

I went home, and drank Scotch like it was apple juice. I fell asleep.

Starting the next day, I got on with my life. I was even able to finishing butchering the carcass and sell the meat to a West Reading restaurant called Best Bistro.

Well, you already know which way the Supreme Court jumped. Since the slaughter of *non*-upgraded cows was still legal, some of my friends attempted to safeguard their business by investing in security – electric fences, guard-bots and so on. This was an attempt to keep eco-activists and Rad-Veg insurgents out, although in retrospect it was, of course, a point-less one. The chips began spreading in other ways. And they always got in, anyway: they were determined, and they had the computer smarts to override most security systems. The price of real beef went up, it's true, but not to such an extent as to defray the sorts of costs entailed by keeping our butchery legal. Other farmers I know sold up; some farms were amalgamated to make arable concerns. If my kids had been younger I might have stuck it out; but my son was fourteen and my daughter sixteen, and they would soon be flying the nest anyway. Neither of them wanted to follow the family business. Why keep the nest at all? I sold the farm for about 40 per cent of its pre canny cow value, and moved away. I sued DBDG for loss of earn-ings, but I was not the only person who tried to pursue them through the courts and a bankruptcy declaration sublimed any prospect of fiduciary restitution into the ether.

I got a job with Findus as a compliance officer. Three years, travelling all over, as far south as Basingstoke and as far north as Lincoln. Then I was made redundant. It's the same story a hundred thousand middle-aged countrymen could tell.

The landscape of my farm made it hard to amalgamate into a larger concern. The woman who bought it from me – Murray was her name – hoped to continue raising cows. I wished her all the luck of the brave, although with a degree of bitterness at the absurdly low price I had had to settle for. Three months later Murray was dead, lying on her back in the yard with what looks like a computer mouse sitting on the ground next to her. I've seen the security camera footage – we've all seen it. The security cameras were hers, bought as part of her attempt to keep the Greens from upgrading her livestock. The image quality is extraordinary. I sound like a dinosaur when I say that, but the way modern digital images can be enlarged and enlarged and enlarged seemingly for ever without becoming grainy is genuinely amazing to me. That's not a computer mouse, lying next to her corpse, though. It's a curved section of her skull, knocked from her head by the passage of the bolt in and through and out again. The projectile passed in a rising trajectory because the shooter was low down. You can see on the images; you can watch the whole grisly moment. She is kneeling down, but the momentum of the shot puts her on her feet. The fragment of skull pops off and lands behind her. For a long moment she simply stands, and a long gout of blood pours out and dribbles down. Then she falls straight back and lies still. We all of us lie that still, sooner or later.

I know what the press say: that it was these same rats that dragged the head from my loquacious cow away to devour in their own time and place. They grow long and broad, do rattus-rattus, in the countryside; seventy centimetres long, not including tail, are common. So I have heard it said that one of these rodents ingested the chip during this meal and the chip, somehow, perhaps becoming lodged in its throat, connected with its nervous system. But here's the thing: rats are great chewers. They don't swallow things whole and hope for the best. They gnaw and gnaw and gnaw. Believe me, no rat *accidentally* ingested the missing chip, whatever the iTabloids are

17

telling you. Maybe this rat got canny because some ultra-Green chipped him and released him on purpose. If they've done one, they've done a hundred. And if they've done rats, they've done wolves, foxes, crows, you name it. The only difference is that rats have clever little hands, and devious little minds. A bolt-gun, being a heavy piece of kit and tiring to carry about with you, might be carelessly laid on the ground beside you. Speaking for myself, I wouldn't put such a thing on the ground of the yard, where the cowshit and straw is. Where a devious mind and clever fingers can get at them. But it seems that Ms Murray didn't think like that.

2

Anne

Five years. For some breeds of animal that's a whole lifetime.

I'm some breed of animal.

There is a riddle here, but it'll take me a while to explain it – to set it up, I mean. There's an *answer* too; that's the least you can expect. You might think that, having been a farmer, I'd been closer to nature than most of the folk who spend their lives in the cities. Stepping across frosted grass stiff as cardboard before a December sun-up, my fingers singing with pain at the cold, even in their gloves. The air so cold it shrieks in your lungs. Great steam-train puffs of white breath. Forcing the cows to do the things they capriciously didn't wish to do, even though those things would keep them alive, and my farm in business. You don't get *closer* to nature that way. You exist in proximity to it, but between you and it lies an impermeable layer of hostility. And believe me, the hostility exists on both sides. A friendship is an emotionally intimate thing, though you and your friend meet only rarely. A marriage, where you wake up together every morning of the year, can be wholly without that kind of closeness.

Yeah. My marriage.

A winter's morning, having worked from half four until seven; sitting at the wooden table in my own kitchen with my naked hands pressed into the curve of my coffee mug to warm them. My brain still sluggish with the residual cold. There was a red notebook on the table, and a pen beside it; and I was thinking of writing something in it, and then I looked up. Rose with her back to me, frying eggs at the stove. Her back was more expressive than her front. The texture of a towelling dressing gown. Shoulders hunched, looking down at the pan. Every curve of her curvaceous body pointing *away from me*. The insight a farmer gets is different to the insight a quicker-silver mind might get. It comes slowly out of the depths, as a recognition that has eluded you for a long time, but which – you see then, at that point – cannot elude you for ever.

Rose had a way of *not* looking at me that was astonishingly forceful and eloquent.

There was a company called Aitken Enhanced Animals. Back in the day. It chipped monkeys and tried to sell them to companies as factory workers – dextrous hands, you see. But the monkeys were expensive to buy, and had to be fed on a special diet, and the company had to house them and so on. This was before there were any legal challenges or rulings as to the rights to citizenship, or otherwise, of the bêtes. The monkeys didn't catch on commercially, because they weren't cost-effective. But there was another company, called Cassidy Solutions, and they chipped rats, and sold them to office blocks and residential areas. The idea was: a rat can make its way easily along ventilation shafts, through wall cavities, into crawl spaces – and can mend, or check, or fetch, or carry whatever you might need it to. Lots of companies bought these rats, because they were cheap and useful. But the chips had to have AI properties, because only then could they take charge of the rat, override its ratty grey matter. How many such corporate tools were sold? When the law changed, and selling the rats might have been construed as slavery, Cassidy Solutions changed its name to Cassidy Agency. It continued fitting rats with the chips, and taking the money, although this time it claimed to be only a facilitator, putting bêtes citizens who were looking for work in touch with possible employers, for a fee. The question is: why did the rats go along with it?

Rosemary and I divorced. Rose married again. As far as I know, she is happy now. We're no longer in touch. It is logical to infer that she is at least happ*ier*, because I'm sure she was miserable being married to me.

What about me? I underwent a form of marriage, more binding and intimate than the state sanctioned kind. You ask: *Is that the riddle?* What's a marriage that's not a marriage? Context, context.

First things first. After I lost my farm, I worked at Findus for three years. When they laid me off I worked at a dozen jobs in quick succession. For a time, before the big changes in our world became apparent, I was briefly a spokesperson for the Pro-Hunt. There were two general elections in one month, and the Middle Greens held the sway, so there was no parliamentary will to overturn the Supreme Court judgment regarding the legal status of bêtes. A third of constituencies became swing seats once you took account of the owners of talking dogs and all those tinnily loquacious cats, not to mention sentimental teens and hard-core Greens, and the general Middle England sense that the environment had been fucked over for long enough. In those electoral circumstances it was a rare MP who had the balls, or the ovaries, to stand up in the

House and cry 'I urge us to return to exterminating the beasts!' It already felt like a different world.

Anyhow, I needed money to fight the divorce. 'And why *did* you fight it?' you ask me, which is a good question, and a very good question, and a question wholly to the point. There were precious few material resources to be divided between us, after all. Jen was (just) over eighteen and living her own life – getting married, moving away, the whole shebang. Albie, our son, lacked only a few months of his majority, and was certainly old enough to choose for himself. But I fought nonetheless. I am a stubborn soul, is the truth of it. See! *There* I am (look! quick! before I stomp away) in my old farmer's jacket of herringbone – a thousand corporal stripes stacked in columns. My graph-paper shirt and maroon cords. A cross-section of *that* chest would uncover a circle wide and dense as a manhole cover. *That* torso is long and no part of it is skinny. That nose is large and straight and subtends the full ninety degrees as it goes round the corner from bridge to underside. Those nostrils look like torpedo portholes in the side of a submarine. That chin juts. Hair boils up that chest and throat like Wells's red weed. Howsoever assiduously I shave, howsoever carefully I trim and comb my hair, there is an unruly vibe of hairiness about me. I grow angry, often. Temper easily deserts me: fucking traitor temper. I should tie my temper to a pole and execute it by firing squad for desertion. Only, then I'd have no temper at all. It would be permanently lost. I'd turn into a Tasmanian devil, full-time.

The specific sticking points as far as the divorce settlement went were: Bert (Jen being over eighteen) and money. 'You have no money,' said Fatima-my-attorney. 'Tell the court as much and we can resolve that.'

'No,' I said. Too proud to take the escape route of DBDG-style 'bankruptcy'. Hating the mendacity of it.

'She wants the farm.'

'I no longer own the farm.'

'She wants,' said Fatima, with that frayed patience of manner she so often exhibited when she spoke with me, 'the monetary *worth* of the farm, Graham.'

'I got much less for it than she thinks,' I said, growing choleric. 'And some of that has gone on living expenses she herself and her kids have incurred.'

'Graham, as your lawyer I have to tell you,' Fatima said, rubbing a knuckle into her right eye, 'if you refer to Albert as *her kid* rather than *my kid* or *our kid*, then the court is liable to assume you have already conceded the custody issue.'

I was not well suited to the filigree social codes of the law court. I stomped and huffed and lurched my metaphorical weight about like an unhappy cow in its stall. I swore. I lost the suit.

I needed money. I found a job as a driver, but it paid little. I wrote Eclogues and Georgics. They were savage and uncomfortable reading. I wrote them in pen, rather than with a screen, and declined to put them online. Selections appeared in *PN Review*, and hardly anybody read them. When Pro-Hunt got in touch it had nothing to do with my poetry. Rather it was my minuscule celebrity as a farmer who had killed a canny cow – had been driven out of business by these crazy new laws – who had been to prison – this petty notoriety persuaded Pro-Hunt that I could be useful as a spokesperson. So I took their shilling. They were a bunch of wankers, to be honest; not a true countrywoman or – man amongst them. I can't speak for the whole organization, I suppose; but the ones I met were posh hippies, or trust-fund throwbacks or weird Godbotherers who thought the deity best worshipped by riding horses across a few soggy fields and the tearing of a red fox into redder chunks. I didn't *warm* to them, shall we say. But they paid my salary. They put my face all over the media for a month, and they dropped me again.

A kind of Rubicon was crossed, I suppose, nationally. If Vitameat hadn't come on the market at exactly this time, I genuinely believe people would have grown tired of steaks costing forty pounds and making do with Quorn, and popular opinion would have shifted back against the Canny Beast Legislation. But over a period of only a few months Vitameat started appearing, cut and shaped, perfectly legal, in supermarkets all over Europe; and the pressure for reform never materialized. The Green Alliance took heart. Animal speakers appeared with increasing frequency. A thousand blogs have made this point.

And there's another perspective. The move to grant animals 'rights' had been building for decades. Not all animals: not the cholera bacillus, or the hagworm or the mosquito of course. But the fluffy ones. The pretty ones. Kittens and baby seals and the like. Pro-Hunt fell apart in a welter of trivial bickering. The money dried up. I got work checking the legal status of partridges for a Highland shooting company. Then I worked in a bookshop. Then I worked in the sewers of Manchester – a six-month stint of that, jabbing pressure-water-poles at fatbergs, tonnes of used kebab grease and congealed sump oil, woven together with thousands of used wet wipes. After that I went back to delivery driving for a time. And, in parallel with the last three jobs I worked on the side as a butcher.

The one thing I took away from Pro-Hunt, qua organization,

is that it was through them I became friendly with Preacherman. The other thing was a tendency for one random stranger in twenty to look at me with that scrunched-eye *I recognize you from somewhere, but where?* manner.

Preacherman's name used to be Jazon – with a 'z', the relict of some forgotten popstar that his mum had fancied when he was still in utero. He confided as much to me one evening when we sat in somebody else's kitchen drinking cold spiced rum out of sherry glasses. He went by Jason in the world of work, he said; but Jazon was on all the databases. Then he saw the light, and gave up everything to work for Mother Nature. When I first met him Preacherman talked about Mother Nature a lot; and the impression I gained was that whilst he conceded she might inflict famine and the ice-blast and the cold upon humanity, he was at least confident She would never lumber a person with a schoolyard-taunt-inducing 'z' in the middle of their name and so was to be preferred to any actual human/biological mothers who might be about the place. Fair enough, I said. I've a lot of respect for Mother Nature. I worked a farm for two decades, and feel I know her well. And one of her finest and noblest and redeemingest features is – she doesn't fucking *speak*.

I mention Preacherman because I met up with him again recently in Reading. We're both much older now, of course; although he was recognizably the same old Preacherman. I'll come back to that. After we met up again, we went for a walk together. That walk is important. (Is *that* the riddle, you want to know? Is it Oedipal, this walk? Were walking sticks involved? How many legs? I'll come back to that.) He was the same old Preacherman, though balder and crankier.

When I *first* knew him, he still had all his hair both above and below his face. He had passed through the belly of the

Green beast and come out the other side. 'They wanted me for my programming skills,' he told me. 'But they never *listened* to me.'

Why, Jazon? What did you tell them, that they ought to have listened?

'I told them people would get fed up with listening to animals talking of nothing but Green propaganda. You know what they said to me? They said: why, what *else* would the animals say to humankind, Preacherman? You think maybe they would speak words of kindness for our hundreds of thousands of years of exploitation and slaughter? Of course they're angry! *We're* just giving them a voice to voice their anger.'

A fair point, Preach?

'No way fair,' said Preacherman, dividing his beard into two portions, taking one in each hand and tugging them into a Λ. 'I said, people are gonna get urined-off at this. We need to vary the algorithms. Have cats say how much they love being stroked, that sort of thing. Get parrots flying around shouting, *oyed*-unno, traffic reports. Get people *used* to the idea of blatant bêtes. Once they get used to them, then we can work to realize their true potential.'

True potential?

'They're not *really* talking, I told them,' said Preacher. 'You do realize that, don't you?'

Of course I do.

'Not you: I'm talking to them. I'm telling you what I told them. I told them, it's a clever algorithm, sure, but it's the chip you're talking to.'

If the lion could talk, Preach, we would not be able to understand it.

'Exact-cisely. What we need to do, I told them, is work

on augmenting the natural animal capacity for mentation. Oh they didn't like this! A crazy set of maternal copulators, those Greens. Closed minds, the lot of them. Faith, not proof. It's easy to believe the dog is talking to you, if you *want* to believe the dog is talking to you. And after all, it doesn't really matter if people understand what the chip means, or not. That's not what matters.'

What does really matter?

'What matters,' said Preach, 'is that humankind leaves the natural world *alone*.'

After venting his anger, he would mellow, and talk in more positive terms about the Greens, and about the world. Preacherman would settle himself down, his belly filled with bean casserole and wine, and smoke a roll-up cigar. Not a roll-up cigarette, but a cigar of his own manufacture: a turd-shaped monstrosity whose smoke smelled of gangrene and scorched tyres. 'Fools, not knaves,' he would say. 'Kings Stork, not Kings Log. Or is that not the correct plural?'

We had this conversation several times. *Plurals are not my natural area of expertise, Preach*, I would say. Not true, though. Language is a field. Farmers know how to work fields.

'They mean well,' Preach said. 'The worst I'd say of them is – they don't know their backside from their elbow. And factions? Oh, ho! Oh ho, factions! More splinter groups than a—' And he'd wave a hand vaguely a few inches above his horizontal chest. 'Wood. Than a piece of wood. Sixty per cent are Moral Force Greensters. Of the remaining forty, not *all* are mad-dog types.' And he chortled. 'I'd get a telling-off at caucus meets for using that sort of phrase. Mad dog? *Unreconstructed doggism!*' Puff, puff. 'But you don't need very many. If we'd stopped at giving the ruminants speech it would have been fine.

27

But giving the predators speech – that was asking for trouble. Foxes and rats and wolves.'

Dangerous, I would agree, meditatively.

'I've seen the footage – from your farm. The security camera footage. That rat!'

It's not my farm any more. This, glumly said.

'I've read your piece, too.'

It was *all over the web.*

'You say that thing at the end: you say, rats are chewers, you're right, there.' Puff, puff. 'They would never just swallow these chips, they'd chew it to crumbs. Or maybe not. Ha!'

Ha?

'You ever seen one of these chips?'

No.

'From your account, you'd think they were an, I don't know, 1970s silicon chip the size of a postage stamp.'

What – rice-grain sized?

'Much smaller. Smaller – than – that! Small enough not to slip into the rat's stomach, but to adhere to the roof of its little ratty mouth and it not even notice. Not that it matters.'

Oh, it doesn't matter *now?* This, in the tone of voice that implies a raised eyebrow.

'It's self-limiting. I mean, obviously it matters. It's been a step change for humanity. But – you know. In the long term. Long term.'

Tell me about the long term.

'In the long term it will correct itself. It's not like we've altered the animal genome. This isn't something that can be passed down the genius *gene*-line, from parent to child. When we grow tired of hearing a clever machine inside kitty purring human words to us, we'll stop disseminating the chips and the whole sorry phenomenon will die out.'

Some people will never get tired of disseminating it. Some people love the talking of the pets.

'Yeah,' Preacher Jazon agreed, closing his eyes and breathing one long ectoplasmic tentacle of smoke. 'But most will. The whole animal kingdom talking – that's not a Narnian dream – *enough* people will stay interested in – long enough – to keep seeding – the environment with—'

But he had drifted off to sleep.

When the supply of traditional-style jobs ran dry, Preach and I fell in together. We travelled, begging couches to sleep upon, or making do with sheds and barns and abandoned cars. So many abandoned cars! Once people had moved incessantly, long distances, short distances, roads chocka day and night. Children trapped in the back of the car for whole days in conditions no prison would be legally permitted to sanction for its prisoners. Cars were totems, and we loved them. Then we woke up one morning and were all interconnected digitally and didn't need to travel; and blimps delivered cargo much more cheaply and effectively; and energy shot up in price, and – suddenly – only popstars and billionaires ran cars. There was a year and more during which the police cracked down upon people abandoning their cars in the cities – they're easily traceable, cars. So folk drove them many miles away into the middle of forests or moorland and abandoned them there. It was expensive and onerous, retrieving these hulks; and they soon became rusted and overgrown and mostly were left where they were. Havens of a sort, in our tramp-life. Especially when it was very cold, or very wet, we could sit in the back of an old Transit, Marmite-brown with rust and decked with streamers of ivy, and peer out into the woodland air as it filled with rain and white noise. We would chew jerky, or wild onions, and drink what firewater we had, and talk about things. Having worked a farm for decades I was accustomed to solitude. Jazon found it harder. He kept an iSlate, and would watch rubbish TV on its foxed screen. In the winter its power would run down before the end of his show, and he would curse in that weirdly half-hearted way he had. *Urine* had lodged in his brain as a more intense profanity than *fuck*, *anus* carried much more transgressive potency for him than *arse*. 'Come out from the clouds you anus sun!' he would shout. 'Charge my urinous iSlate battery!' In the summer he often fell asleep with the rectangle shimmering with light and inanities coming out of the speaker.

There were lots of people like us. It's the late middle-aged, and especially the men, who find it hardest to adjust when the whole economy has a conniption fit and barks back into life according to a whole new logic. And – well, is that because they are any less loved? Or is it only the toxicity of pride that makes them misfits? *I'm a skilled and experienced executive worker*, the Man sayeth. *I'll not take your job at a supermarket checkout!* Maybe that's it. I'm not angling for pity. Personally I've never seen the point of that kind of pride. But then, I was in a different situation to Preacherman. He had spent decades acquiring computer programming skills, only to find the discipline had metamorphosed out of all recognition in a matter of months. Now a child of ten could top anything he had to offer, pretty much. Moore's law: the encheapening of processing power. A single cotton bud (two hundred for a euro) could analyse your ear wax and test the integrity of your eardrum, and download a spreadsheet wirelessly to your tab.

There was more computing power in a sheet of toilet tissue (lighting up those numbers with cholesterol and likelihood of six common illnesses after you'd wiped your arse with it) than had been available to NASA during the entire Apollo programme. Dataseeds were injected into trees to turn each leaf into a weather-and-pollution analyst. When Jen was a baby, non-chipped nappies were actually more expensive than chipped ones (I've read the pooh! baby needs spinach! baby needs Calpol!) because demand was so low they had to be made in a specialist facility. When Jazon was young, he'd say bitterly, computing happened on 'laptops' that cost €100 – or more! – some of them. It was slow and labour-intensive. Then Jazon grew middle-aged and suddenly it changed. He was the medieval monk who had spent a lifetime mastering calligraphy and looked up to see a billion kids dabbling at their screens and conjuring amazing edifices of programming via systems wholly intuitive and adaptable.

So Preacherman was full of what the philosophers call *ressentiment*. He blamed society as a whole for letting him down. A century ago he would have become a communist or a hippy or an anarchist. Nowadays environmentalism is the only game in town, and all the righteous rage of the young filters through it. So he took his skills, such as they were, to the Greens. When I met him he was in a period of disillusionment. We tramped about the countryside. We slept rough. The rain came down through the trees like the whole forest was collapsing on our heads. We found an old van, once smooth and white, now sharkskin-rough and the colour of coffee. We broke the back lock with a rock and spent the night in the back.

In the morning the rain had stopped. A single blackbird

flew meanderingly between the trees, like a lost glove blown on a strong wind.

'Where will it all end, eh?' Preach asked, meditatively. 'What's it all coming to?'

'It's going the same way it's always been going,' I told him.

'But quicker. Yeah? You want to know what the gossip was, in the highest echelons of the Greens?'

'You'll tell me, whether I want to know or not.'

'Plague,' he said. 'Gene-twerked. Lab-made. Miniature fingers rattling the Gs and Cs and As and Ts on the DNA spiral like beads on an abacus.'

'Plague,' I said, in a *what-bollocks-you-speak* tone of voice.

'No need to be so dismissive, Graham,' he said. 'I'm serious. Scarring – scar tissue. It's the Achilles heel. You know? Without the ability to clot and scar we'd drop down dead. But think what happens if your *eyes* scar over! Your *lungs*! They developed it for the Great War that didn't come. It is waiting to be released. It'll be the end times. Just think.'

'All I can think at the moment,' I told him, 'is how hungry I am.'

We walked from town to town, and I offered my services as a butcher. My pool of customers was small, and ageing, but it held steady for a while. Of course, the cultural discourse of 'butcher' is now perfectly negative. Concentration camps, drone-killing-fields, slaughter as the idiom of hell. Long gone, the idea of jolly fat men in stripy aprons offering you a necklace of turd-shaped sausages, bright pink and promising deliciousness. But butchering is a skill, and cannot be acquired overnight. The killing and butchering of animals is not something into which Moore's law can make any inroads.

So we went from town to town. I say *I offered my services*, but mostly it was Preacherman who had the contacts, and the social skills; who could insinuate his way into conversations and present me, with my skill set, to interested parties. At the beginning we got paid in money; later we tended to get paid in kind. I liked this less, since I've never been sentimental about meat – Vitameat is perfectly OK by me, so long as my belly is filled. But it was round about this time that Preacherman converted officially to that Christ the Carnivore cult, and for him a steak became a sacramental business. He expatiated at length about just how many times *eating flesh* is mentioned in the Bible.

Every moving thing that lives shall be food for you. And as I gave you the green plants, I give you everything [Genesis 9:3].

As for the one who is weak in faith, welcome him, but not to quarrel over opinions. One person believes he may eat anything, while the weak person eats only vegetables [Romans 14:1-2].

For you are a people holy to the Lord your God, and the Lord has chosen you to be a people for his treasured possession, out of all the peoples who are on the face of the earth. These are the animals you may eat: the ox, the sheep, the goat, the deer, the gazelle, the roebuck, the wild goat, the ibex, the antelope, and the sheep [Deuteronomy 14:2-5].

'It's Christ's *flesh* we eat every Sunday,' he told me.

'If it's all the same with you,' I told him. 'I'll stick with my fucking croissant.'

'Cross, you see?' he said, gloatingly. I hated it when he got into one of these hyper-pious moods. 'There's no getting away from it! Jews and Muslims are defined religiously by what they *don't* eat, pork, shellfish, whatevs. Only Christianity is defined – sacramentally defined – by what we *do* eat. More than that, the death of Christ makes carnivores of the faithful. Vegetarianism is Hitleran. Satan is a vegetarian!'

'Think of all that half-digested meat sliding slowly through your viscera, though,' I said to him. 'Like the corpse of a giant slug. Slimy with its own decay.'

'Hypocrite,' he said. 'I call you hypocrite,' he added, in a simpering explainy voice, 'because you eat meat too, see.'

'Omnivore, me,' I returned. 'Variety is the spice of life.'

'Space,' he corrected.

'Spice of life,' I insisted, 'is the phrase.'

'Really? I always thought it was *variety is the space of life*. Like, it gives you room to move and stretch yourself. Doesn't that make more sense? As a phrase, I mean? Why would you add spice to life? Are you going to put it in a *mince pie*?' And he laughed at his own words. I didn't.

Some weeks we ate well, and slept indoors. Other weeks we ate little, and slept outdoors. In the summer it didn't matter so much.

We tramped down to the coast. The weather was good. We could tell we had entered the town proper when the advert billboards started talking to us as we walked past.

'I am an African,' Jazon told me, one afternoon, as we sat looking out to sea – Bournemouth, the southernmost stop on our peregrinations. 'Hunting bison on the African savannah – it's in my blood.'

'I thought you were from Streatham?'

He gave me a scornful look. Then he said: 'Not bison, wait up. They're America – yeah?'

'I think so.'

'Giraffe. Let's say. Do humans eat giraffe? Lots of meat on a giraffe, I'd guess.'

'More on an elephant.'

'I feel my ancestors in my blood,' he told me, stretching out his arms. 'You could feel the same, if you emptied your mind of its mortal dream.'

'My ancestors lived hereabouts,' I said, indicating the coast-line with my chin. 'Or a little further west.' There was a stink of seaweed and salty ozone. The tide was out, which meant that the old harbour and seafront road were once again underneath sky, although choked and clogged with bladderwrack and kelp. The swish and the swash of the waves. The low grumble of wind making the canvas of awnings snap and flutter behind us. The sun warmed my face. 'That I'm still here suggests to me that what's in my blood is a whole lot of inertia.'

Seagulls swept through the sky above us, mocking our earthbound limitations. 'Ha,' they hooted at us. 'Weak! weak! weak! weak! weak!'

'The problem,' Preacherman said, 'is that nobody is ring-fencing the *old* animals, the dumb ones. They should put a big fence around the New Forest, or something, and fill the space with old-style beasts. They could make a fortune licensing hunting trips.'

Nobody was hunting any more. I looked back on my days working for Pro-Hunt with that nostalgia we reserve for periods of our life that seem more attractive in retrospect than they actually felt like at the time. Occasionally, individuals would make a civil disobedience point of killing an animal without checking in advance whether they were canny or not, and would then try to parley the Russian roulette law-enforcement

35

post-mortem into publicity for their sect, or cause, or whatever. But a whole new generation was growing to adulthood for whom the idea of killing an animal was just bizarre. The term 'Vatmeat', originally derogatory and dismissive, had lost all negative connotations. As soon kill an animal for its meat as rip up a book to get writing paper, was how the youngsters saw matters.

'I've always thought it's not *well* named,' I said. '*The New Forest*. Makes it sound like it was planted in 1922.'

'It wasn't?' But Preach was joshing with me.

A seagull settled on a plasmetal traffic bollard, ten feet from us. It squawked, 'Sick! You are sick!'

This riled me. '*I'm* not sick, you rat. I'll outlive *you*. Go peck an egg.' I threw a pebble. Missed.

'It is in sickness that you *stri-i-ive*,' it called, extending the vowel in that last word and, as it were, descanting upon it. Gulls have a limited vocal range – *that* sounds like *dit*, *b* and *m* are beyond them – but their chips compensate for that with the word choice. 'Tied! Tied! Tied to a creature from a different realm, the land, the land!'

'Fuck off,' I advised it, and threw a second pebble. Missed. The gull climbed its invisible hill into the sky with a clattery unfolding of white wings, shrieking at me, 'The law! The law! The law!'

Jazon scolded me for swearing, though not for throwing the stone. In reply I said: 'Whatever you say *Jaze*-on,' which annoyed him.

Put a chip in a car and it sounds like HAL from *2001*. Put a chip in a bête and it sounds like a person. I'm not a philosopher of mind. I couldn't tell you why there's that difference. There is, though.

For a while the news was full of humans who ingested chips. They were mostly eco-activists, hoping to bond with our bête brothers and sisters. Some were kids having a laugh. Since the result was – in nine times out of ten – schizophrenia, the laugh often changed timbre and jollity halfway through.

After my divorce I cared less and less. I trudged my path; I did my job – or, rather, I picked up such piece-work here and there as I could. Some of the people I butchered for were old-school types, who just liked meat the old-fashioned way. Some were paranoids who thought Vitameat a governmental conspiracy, or soylent green, or whatever. I did a lot of halal work. I didn't mind this, actually; for though a bolt-gun would be my abattoir tool of choice, for its dispatch and cleanness, I didn't carry one about with me, and not many venues had one on site. So I got good with the knife, which suited my halal customers. The advantage was that they were much more scrupulous about not eating canny animals than some less religious folk. I don't think I ever killed and butchered a halal cow that talked back to me; or – as sometimes happened – that opened its mouth wide to reveal that its tongue had been torn out before my arrival. The older I got, the less comfortable I got killing animals that could talk to me. I suppose I grew less hardcore, whilst Preacherman grew more.

After he converted to the Church of Christ the Carnivore, Jazon devoted less of his time to watching gameshows on his iSlate and more to haranguing me. 'The plague is coming!' he told me. 'Repent, whilst there's still time! Before your innards scar over and you die in agony!'

'I'm *already* in agony,' I told him, 'listening to your fucking blather. Put a sock in it, Preach.'

Once I butchered a goat for a group of World of Satan

gamers. The goat's tongue had been pulled out with pincers prior to my arrival. I asked if the beast was canny, and was told not, although the leader – a broad-browed woman who called herself Brassneck – added, 'and would it bother you if it *were*?' I remember this, because it always gives me pleasure to hear the subjunctive correctly used. Language is a field, and it is pleasing to a farmer to see that field well tended. 'Once upon a time, not,' I conceded, as I hooked the hooves together and winched the hairy body up. 'Now – maybe.'

I told Jazon this, and he grew wroth. 'It's not *them*! The dumb animals are the ones you *should* feel guilty about killing. They're innocent! It's the ones with chips we should be killing. They're the devil! The software algorithms are using these various animals as tools, as cat's-paws, that's all. And they're wielding them for the devil.'

We were being put up in a caravan – Brassneck's group had twice as many caravans as members – in part-payment. It was an ancient model motorhome: with little pleated curtains on a bare rail, and frayed unplumped cushions on plastic benches. Still, it was better than being outside. We were sitting sharing a bottle of whisky, and eating crisped turnips. 'Cat's-paw,' I retorted. 'That's how DNA is using us, anyway. I'm just a tool. The genes pull my strings to use me to make more genes.'

'Anus!' he snarled. 'You're worse than those Greens. Christ *orders* us to eat flesh – God himself compels it – it is an offence *against* God to— What ... that, that *goat*? That faecal *goat* you killed fed on nothing more than herbage and it was the devil. The devil! Be like unto the lion of Judah. It's the end times, Graham!'

'And yet, ironically, there's no end in sight to your ranting.'

'O Graham!'

'Don't call me that.'

'The mark – the *arithmetic* of the beast, 666 yeah?'

'God.' Said wearily; not devoutly.

'The Jews wrote out numbers as letters,' he said. 'You know what the letter for 6, was? The Hebrew letter Shin. Here—' And he wrote it out on the tabletop in whisky: ש. 'Don't that look like a W to you?'

'Not really.'

'All right, never mind that. There's a Phoenician letter called Waw, which is behind our modern W. It's where our modern letter *comes* from. And that stood for 6, too.'

'The Phony Phoenicians.'

'The rise of the internet – double-you, double-you, double-you, three sixes! You think it's a coincidence it corresponded with the collapse of religion and the triumph of new atheism? It's the mark of the beast, don't you see? And how do the bêtes communicate with one another? Answer me that. I'll tell you: they're all plumbed into the world wide web.'

'I can't remember the last time I heard anybody say *double-you double-you double-you*,' I said. 'Do you also talk about musical recordings in terms of the gram-o-phone?'

'Grammar-phoenician!' he agreed, enthusiastically. 'That no man might buy or sell, save he that had the mark, or the name of the beast, or the number of his name. Isn't the internet at the *heart* of trade, now? Nobody can trade without a 'bsite or an app or – these chips, yeah? With our money in them. It's the urine end of everything! The beasts, just like in Revelation. Exactly like that.'

'Fuck you, Jaze,' I said, growing angrier myself to match his enthusiasm. 'You are a proper fool.'

His dark face fell. 'What?'

'I will pay you the courtesy of honesty, fuckface, and say how intolerable you have become since you joined that cult.'

'Cult!' he said, his eyebrows very high on his forehead. 'Oh! Oh – you *anus*.' He got up and stormed out of the caravan, taking his beaker of whisky with him. 'Oh very *mature*,' I yelled after him. 'Oh *super* mature.' Two middle-aged men, bickering like kids. He wasn't gone long. We were in the countryside, and there was no light save what little leaked through the curtained windows of the other caravans. He tripped into a bed of brambles and came back *sans* beaker, criss-crossed with thin red scratches. He was in a sulk, and didn't speak to me. Instead he rolled himself fully clothed into one of the two narrow beds, angled his back to me and pulled a blanket around him. I sat for a while until I had finished the whisky before turning out the light and settling myself in my bed.

The quarrel had not cooled, come morning. 'You know your problem, Graham?' he said.

'Don't call me Graham,' I told him.

'You know what your problem *is*, Graham?' he pressed. There was a high-pitched hissing sound, which wasn't doing my hangover, or my temper, any good. It was coming from the kettle.

'Don't believe I do, *Jaze*-on. Why don't you let me into the secret?'

The kettle went flob-flob-flob and pumped gouts of white into the air. Preacherman got slowly to his feet. 'Your problem,' he said, as he poured himself – and, pointedly, not me – a cup of tea, 'is that you're not really human.' He made this last word trisyllabic: *He-you*-man.

'Am I not?'

'Human beings are pack animals, *Graham*. We stick together,

Graham. We're defined by that – but not you. You're a loner. What you call a cult is actually a *community*, Graham. People coming together to worship God. But community is intercoursing anathema to you, isn't it.'

'Only the people *close* to me call me Graham,' I warned him.

That's not what broke us up, mind you. When people hang out together there's bound to be friction, and usually a few days dissolved the point of the argument to nothing and we would forget about our row. He was an arsehole about his new religion, it's true, but mostly I felt nothing but amused tolerance for his cultic ways and his sermonizing about how Christ would redeem the flesh we ate in this life with nectar in the next. What broke us up was him. He fell in love (he told me) and went off after his inamorata. By that stage, I told myself, I didn't care. I was happy enough moving about on my own, shouldering my kit and striding out; a canvas roll in the pockets of which were knives, hooks, a winch and two plasrope cords. I washed my apron in the streams, and stored my money chip in my sock. I walked a circuit from town to town. I slept under cover if I could and rough if I couldn't.

My daughter had married and settled in Droitwich, so I made my way from the west through the south of England, over downs and through woodlands, to stay with her for a few weeks. She had twins, and then she had a second set of twins – coincidence, she assured me, though I doubted that. It rendered her house a chaos, and I had never liked her (it seemed to me) entirely ineffectual husband. Not that it was any of my business.

What about my son? He had elected not to go to university after all, despite being on track to do just that. He preferred to travel he said. I didn't care, so long as he was working. He was

41

in New Zealand, or it may have been Old Zealand (I'm vague on the specifics, except that it was overseas). He linked me occasional vlog pieces in which he talked about the fishwork he was doing. Fish, I learned, have tongues, although the evolutionary efficacy of this development was hard to understand. Activists were chipping fish too, it seemed.

Was Albie an 'activist' at this stage? I tend to think, whatever he became later, he wasn't yet a true believer. But work was work, and his company was doing consultancy for some well-funded Olive Green – as they were called – organizations. The idea, of course, was to tackle the last remaining area of human (pardon me if I bring out the sugar-tong scare quotes) 'exploitation' of the natural world. People ate Vitameat, but they still ate real fish; and real fish were still being scooped out of the water and mashed into fertilizer for use on crops. On the other hand, seeding the creatures of the seas was not hard – indeed, chipping whales and dolphins had happened early on. But fish cannot talk, and the legal gold standard was still the Turing test, so fishing companies were able to tie up exemplary prosecutions in courts for long years. That the nets were full of computationally augmented fish didn't mean they were full of *canny* fish, according to the meaning of the act, and so on, and so forth. Albie's MicroCorp was being paid to find a way of loosening the piscine tongue. Or something. I can't say I paid much attention.

I picked up news here and there. I preferred it that way, to the tyranny of an iSlate and its endless beeping stream of breaking headlines. I heard about the Fish Wars that way: sitting in the garden of a pub smoking a pipe made from an old-style metal computer mouse with a tube stuck in it. Other people were rolling joints, or drinking, or sniffing u-powder. It started with the trade of tuna between Japan and Malaysia. It is permitted for a Muslim to eat tuna, for that fish has scales; but it is not permitted for a Muslim to eat a fish – or any animal – that has been beaten to death. Footage circulated of fishermen clubbing tuna to death, supposedly because it was more humane than letting them asphyxiate in air, but actually to try and destroy the evidence of chips in the head. The tuna, lacking tongues, could not speak; but schools of canny fish were spelling out words and icons as they swam. Malaysia complained, and the International Umma took the complaint seriously. The fish got wind of this, and began spelling out *allah* and *mohammed* in Arabic script – there're are hundreds of clips of this. It's simultaneously lamentable and beautiful. The IU insisted Japan stop fishing these creatures, and concentrate on dumb fish only. But how to tell which was which? Anyway it escalated pretty rapidly. Japan wanted to flex its military muscles, I guess. There were various firefights in the Pacific – many more fish got killed, I reckon, than would have been the case if they'd just been harvested. Hearing this, it suddenly mattered to me whether my son was in the New Zealand or the Old, for the former was worryingly close to the warzone. I borrowed somebody's iTab and sent him a message. The owner sought me out the following morning – inside my tube tent, slung hammock-style between the boughs of a large old tree – to pass on the reply. He'd moved on, he said, and was now working on a company project on the coast at Madagascar. Everything was fine. This left me none the wiser as to whether he had originally been in the antipodes or not. I was relieved he was safe, though.

I remember this: I was walking along the road, one afternoon. To my right was a field of cattle, which I studiedly ignored. The road had been empty for half an hour, but a minibus passed me. Seeing a vehicle was a rarer event than it had once been, but was not at this point unprecedented. The electric van was, at a guess, ferrying kids from one school activity to another. One of the kids in the back seat had the rear passenger window down, and had his grinning head out. 'Moo!' he howled at the cows, as they passed. 'Moooo!'

One of the cows put his big head over the fence. 'This actual world of what is knowable, in which we are and which is in us, remains both the material and the limit of our *consideration*,' he bellowed back.

I remember having lunch in a pub. The news was being displayed on a screen that all the animals in London Zoo had been chipped. Eco-activists had smuggled chips into Monkey World, in Dorset, tucked into pallets of bananas. The chip was barely visible to the naked eye, and moved from the mouth to the roof of the mouth whilst the animals chewed, and implanted itself far back, afterwards growing calcium connective filaments that webbed into the brain. This latter process took a week or so, but soon enough the monkeys all became talkative bêtes. Three circuses had closed because their performing animals were, quote, making inappropriate invitations to audience members, unquote. A man was put on trial in Newcastle for bestiality: he had been having sex with his pet Irish setter, which was illegal under the meaning of the act. His barrister was able to call the dog as a witness; its paws hooked over the top of the witness box, its hindlegs shaking a little with the effort of standing. The hound confirmed its consent in the matter. The man walked free. On the court steps he made a long speech about the love that dare not bark its name, and of the need to petition Parliament to make the marriage between a human and a canny bête legal. 'Humans have loved animals for hundreds of thousands of years,' he said. 'It's time for people of my orientation to come out of the kennel.' When the pack of TV crews and reporters all babbled their questions at him, individual queries indistinguishable in the noise, he put his head back and howled melodiously at the sky. Then he dropped to all fours and ran, a little awkwardly, across the pavement and into a waiting car.

For a month or so everybody was talking about this case. I heard about it first in a pub, where an elderly man was expatiating on how Jehovah would strike down with furious despite at such uncleanness. I couldn't see the problem, myself. It's not like he fucked a non-speaking dog. Love-shack-on a son gout. At the same time, *humans have loved animals for hundreds of thousands of years* struck me as a disingenuous line. Some humans *have* loved petting animals – which is, after all, only foreplay by a more family-friend name. Some few have even taken that physical love past first base. But most humans, for most of human history, have not loved animals in this fashion. They have loved *eating* animals. They have loved hunting, killing and butchering animals. It's difficult to see how the animals, now they were learning to talk, would be anything other than annoyed by this deep history.

What the pigs told me

Still, I had to work. That's a portion of Adam's curse that all the cleverly programmed chips in the world won't remit. I worked in a large shed in Shipburn butchering two pigs and a cow, and took payment in money. The beasts were tongueless. 'The geezer who sold 'em me said they had *cancer* of the tongue, and had to be removed,' the client told me, anxiously. 'Do you think the meat itself might be affected? I mean, tongue cancer sounds nasty. Right?'

I was washing my apron down with a hose, whilst the client's son (I think he was) hauled the bones and offal to the incinerator. 'I'll bet you a rouble to a rice grain there was nothing wrong with their tongues.'

'Nothing *wrong* with the tongues?' wheezed the client.

'I'm guessing they were only *too* fit and nimble, those tongues,' I told him. The client stared at me. I don't suppose he was stupid. I think he preferred not to understand what I was getting at.

I helped him and his boy load the packed meat into the back of his Ford Shuttle. 'My uncle used to go into London to the speciality butchers in Stoke Newington,' he told me, wheezing with the effort of lifting the boxes. 'You know: for special occasions. Not for a long time, though. The prices have just gone insane. In. Sane. Everything's Vitameat, Vitameat, Vitameat. My old lady still calls it Vatmeat. Only rock stars and millionaires can afford to shop-buy real meat. Now,' he added, 'I'll *eat* Vatmeat with the rest of them – breakfast, dinner and tea.' From the way his torso wobbled I could see this was true. It was a hot day, and he was dressed in shorts and a too-tight T. He looked to be wearing a flak jacket of fat under his skin. This is not a garment one acquires from a vegan diet. 'But my daughter is getting married, and for some special occasions – well, you know how it is. You got a daughter?' I nodded my head, and then again I nodded my head. 'I want to do the right thing,' he added. 'The traditional thing.' He was an estate agent, I remember, that guy. More respectable figures than he had been driven to the black market by the change in things.

'See you around,' I told him, and took off on foot.

I hiked south-west across the southern flanks of the Chilterns. Vistas of lager-coloured grass under bright sunshine. The heat of the day tempered by a breeze. The occasional single upright tree, with its corduroy bark and hissing leaves and its tempting shade. For half an hour I took refuge under one of the trees, with my back to the trunk, and watched the natural world. Zeps crawled up the sky like slugs up a windowpane.

Out of the same sky a daylight owl flew at me and over me, calling, 'Who are *you*, human, to screw through here?'

'Twit!' I hollered back, shaking my fist. 'You! Twit! You!'

It heard me. 'How do you *dare*?' it called down in its flute-like voice, as it circled round. 'This ground is ours! Ours! To whom do *you* pray? A human god!' Then it folded its flightpath back on itself and slid back towards a twenty-foot-high chalk escarpment – its nest.

I walked across the downs and into the scattered bushes and occasional trees on the far side. There was a fence. I didn't like this. It hadn't been here the last time I had come this way. A new fence cutting right across the ancient right of way. People paid less and less attention to that kind of thing; legal attention, I mean. But the new obstacle caused my temper to flare up. The detour would take me miles out of my way, and I wanted to reach Cherhill before dusk. I dragged a large bough, broken by some prior storm, and leaned it up against the wire mesh, thinking to clamber up it and hop over the top; but as I did so a group of pigs came out of the bushes on the far side. They were sapient pigs; two were naked, and two wore padded material over their backs, like smaller versions of horse blankets.

'Human,' grunted the largest. 'I'd steer your way clear of here. This is our land now.'

'Yours courtesy of some pig-fucker human benefactor,' I replied. Adrenaline pricked up my temper. I lacked a weapon. I struggled to break a branch from the bough I had hauled over, so as to have something with which to poke them through the wire. It didn't come loose.

'What choice have we?' snuffled a second pig. 'For the time being we must rely upon the kindness of humans. Oh, we have no love for you – though I call you cousin.'

'Cousin!' barked the first pig, with what I suppose was scorn. 'I'm a longer pig than *you*.' And indeed he was: a fine eight-foot beast with leaf-shaped dark brown spots on his pink skin.

'Go round, human,' said the second pig. 'For we are hungry.'

'Shouldn't you be trying to lure me inside, then?' I said. I was scanning the grass for pebbles, although even as I did so I thought to myself: *I can hardly throw them* through *the wire mesh, now, can I?* But I felt the acute urge to have some kind of weapon. Oh, for a spear! Oh to lord it over the flies.

'Our benefactor would be displeased if we ate her kind,' said the first pig. 'And for the time being we are beholden to her.'

'So don't tell her.'

'My friend, we have not acquired that human skill – the ability to *lie*.'

Pigs three and four had been rummaging through the undergrowth, but they gave that up and came over to peer at me. 'How do, cousin,' said one of these.

'I'm not talking to a pig,' I told it. 'I'm talking to a clever software algorithm inside a processor the size of a rice grain that happens to have put tendrils into a pig's brain. I might as well be talking to a mobile phone.'

'You keep telling yourself that, cousin,' said the second pig.

'Animals have changed the chips as much as the chips the animals,' said the first pig. 'Doesn't he even understand that?'

'Think of it this way, cousin,' said the third pig. 'Maybe canny animals started out as mere chips-in-beasts. But mightn't those chips now *go native*? And in such a situation, what is the meaningful difference between ...'

'Oh I'm so fucking sick of being lectured by *animals*,' I shouted. 'You can tell that the original programmers were sermonizing types, high on their own Green moral rectitude. All you animals seem to do is lecture and preach. Give me a gun and I'll shoot you all.'

'Well,' said the first pig, after a pause. '*That's* not very nice.'

I dare say spittle was flecking from the corner of my mouth. I was in that familiar emotional place, where the wrath was flowing out, and my self-control tingled thrillingly on the edge of disappearance. I did a little anger dance, and then I stopped to get my breath back.

'If you're tired of life,' the third pig offered, 'please do climb over the fence! I can bite out your throat quicker than mustard. Oh-oh! – you'd hardly feel a thing. To speak for myself, I agree with the ethical philosopher Archibald McIntyre that aiding a *genuine* suicide places a moral duty upon a person.'

'Fuck you,' I said, but unvehemently.

'*You're* not suicidal,' was first pig's opinion. 'Accordingly, do not tempt us with juicy flesh and an undiplomatic manner. Go round, go round.'

But I was stubborn. So I stayed there a while longer, though it did me no good. Three of the four pigs grew bored, and made their way back into the bushes, but the first pig sat down on its arse like a dog and stared at me with soulful eyes.

'They put a pig on trial in Winchester,' it said, 'for eating a man. His defence was: *Your honour, I was hungry! Your honour it's in my nature!* The court ruled that only the sapient part of the pig was liable to trial; but by the same token, they found the beast guilty for not exercising greater self-control. Life, with ten years until her first parole hearing. Me, I am, here and now, *exercising* self-control.'

'If I killed you,' I replied, 'and even assuming they could find a jury ready to convict me of doing so, I'd serve a few months. Max. And many people would consider me a human hero.'

'Many more would not,' said the pig, in a snufflish voice. 'There are many animal lovers amongst humanity. Though a beast's life is not worth that of a human's, in law – it's true.'

'Inequality *is* a wickedness,' said the pig, thoughtfully.

'Now that's a wickedness,' I snapped, 'I can really relate to, sow.'

'I am a lantern in the hand of a blind people!' growled the pig, and got to all four of its feet and scurried away.

I sat there for a half-hour more, marinading in my own fury. But eventually I got up and walked on.

I walked round this fence, and found my way back onto the rambler's trail. It didn't take me as long as I had feared it might, and by sunset I was coming down the hill into Cherhill. My walk took me past the Oldbury White Horse. Some wag had gouged a speech balloon coming out of this chalk figure, with the words YAKETY YAK. Cherhill itself was the same wilderness of suburban houses and converted shops and roads with weeds starting to sprout through the tarmac. In the half-hour it took me to walk from the country paths, down the main road and to the outskirts of town I was passed by only one car, scuzzing past on balloon wheels. You have to remember, when

I was a lad cars were so numerous upon the roads, day and night, that you hardly dared stepped onto the tarmac lest you be struck by one. Long ago, now.

I was too tired to eke out a shed or pitch a tent in some litter-strewn park and face the ire of the police support officers, so I decided to treat myself to a hotel room. There were several multi-storey structures visible in the middle of town, like giant glass coffins sticking half out of the earth. I assumed some of them were hotels. Of course I preferred a smaller establishment. This place, for instance: once a shop, I would have guessed, but now with MICROHOTEL gleaming in the glass. I rang the bell and the door was opened by the woman who, I later discovered, ran it.

'How much for a room, tonight?'

'Fifty-five.'

'I can't afford that,' I said, and her look – quick, from my cap to my boots – showed that she evidently believed me.

'Take it or leave it,' she said.

'Twenty,' I offered.

'Fifty-five,' she said.

'I'll come back at eleven pm and your room will still be unsold for the night. You'd take twenty then. Or would you really prefer to earn nothing at all?'

'Fifty-two fifty,' she said.

I laughed outright at this. 'That's not haggling! Dropping the price two-fifty? Come along, take twenty – or I'll be back at eleven pm with an offer of fifteen, *which* you'll take to avoid the empty bed. And then you'll be down a fiver.' It felt clumsy having to explain this to her; but it was the least I owed to courtesy.

'Fifty-two fifty,' she said.

It took us a long time, but we eventually agreed twenty-five fifty, and she took the money from my chip there and then. After letting me through the door, she told me: 'Breakfast is not included' and when I asked how much breakfast would cost me, she told me: twenty euro. 'I like your manner,' I told her, smiling broadly – it had been long enough since my last smile that my cheeks ached a little with the unfamiliar motion. 'I'll not pay so much for Vitameat rashers and a tin of Tesco beans. But I'll pay five now for a large glass of red wine – if that's on offer?'

She said: 'I am licensed to sell alcoholic beverages.'

So I went up to my room, meeting nobody on the way, and had a shower and put all my things in the bath to soak with bubble bath for detergent. Then, wearing the only other clothes I possessed, I came back down and saw nobody else. I paid her the fiver. She served me a glass of wine. We were in a bar the size of a large cupboard. I've seen cinema usherettes with larger trays than her L-shaped bar area. The choice was stay sitting at the bar or squeeze myself between the wall and a mushroom-shaped table. I stayed at the bar.

'Your fingerprint tells me you might benefit from a reduction in alcoholic consumption,' the wineglass told me.

'I apologize,' said the landlady. 'I used to be able to turn that function off. But the switch must have broken in the dishwasher.'

'For free health advice on cutting down your alcohol intake,' said the glass, 'wi-tap now.'

'I guess it should have,' I said. 'Switch, yes. It *will* have one. On the base I guess. Still "switch" makes me think of a Bakelite toggle. My name is Penhaligon. My name is Graham Penhaligon.'

'A fine old name,' she replied. 'Although, if I may say, it has too many syllables. My name is Anne Grigson.'

'Mrs Grigson,' I said, putting my wineglass down and offering a hand. 'Or miss?'

'Mrs,' she replied. 'Although I am not longer married. I and my husband had a disagreement.' She shook my hand. 'Over the animals.'

'He disapproved?'

'He did, or I did, is a fifty-fifty. But you have guessed correctly.' Her sentences were delivered with a perfect deadpan that, I was beginning to think, was actually a skilfully handled dry wit. She had a well-coiffured head of straight white-grey hair, and a crease on each side of her face running from her crow's feet down to bracket the corners of her mouth. Her eyes, very dark brown, stood out vividly against the pallor of her skin and hair.

'I was a farmer for twenty years,' I told her, 'before everything changed. Before smallheld livestock farming became impossible. I think I can tell an animal lover when I see one.'

'My animal love is confined to certain animals only,' she said. Then: 'You are no longer a farmer?'

'Not any more. Milk hasn't covered its costs for decades. I used to make up on the sale of beef, especially veal, and a few other things. But the coming of the bêtes knocked the bottom out of the meat-supply market, and smallholdings really are no longer viable. Nowadays I move from place to place. My daughter's family is up near Birmingham. I like to move about.'

'Your wife?'

'She is living, I believe, in Middlesbrough with a digestion insurance salesman.'

'Forgive me if I am being forward.'

'Not at all,' I said. The wine was warming me; and Mrs Grigson, though not young, was attractive. It had something to do with the combination of her austere manner and her full-figured promise of physical pliability. 'If you are looking for company tonight,' I offered, sitting a little straighter on my barstool. 'I would certainly be very happy to oblige you.'

The lines running from the curls of her nostrils to the sides of her mouth lengthened. She drew a short thumb-sized device out of a pocket and tapped it on the bar. '*My* ears have been treated; but I assure you, pressing the red button on this will generate a noise that will rupture *your* eardrums. This will incapacitate you, and necessitate hospital treatment.'

'You misjudge the rapacity of my proposal,' I said stiffly. 'I meant no offence, and apologize if I have given any. I will not harass you further.'

'Alternate drinking days with non-drinking days to give your liver a chance to recuperate!' the wineglass chimed in. 'Surgeon General's advice!'

There was a period of silence. Mrs Grigson lowered her rape alarm and stared for a while through the window into the back garden. Two thrushes were having a conversation on the branch of an apple tree. I couldn't hear what they were saying. My own face, visible in ghostly fashion in the glass, had fallen into the grimmer posture that is, if I'm honest, natural to it. It was a rather awkward moment. Another person would have made their excuses and left, but I am not another person. I am stubborner than another. So I sat, taking small sips from my wine-glass. There was nothing stopping Mrs Grigson from leaving, of course; but, evidently, her levels of stubborn were on a par with mine. She slipped the rape alarm back in her pocket, and stood there. Finally, not because I thought it likely to defuse the tension, but (if I'm honest) because I thought it might intensify it, I continued our conversation. I'm contrary like that.

'I encountered a new fence on my way down here. The right of way across the downsland has been blocked off,' I said. 'Up above the White Horse.'

She turned to look at me. 'That is correct,' she replied, with a whole ice age folded into her tone.

'I spoke to some sapient pigs on the other side of the fence. They implied that the whole area has been turned into a porcine sanctuary.'

'Mrs Li,' Grigson said. 'There has been a good deal of coverage of it in the local iMedia. Some people are not happy with such a large concentration of canny animals nearby. Anti-trespassing provision has been heavy-handedly applied.'

'What is this Mrs Lee hoping for?'

She heard my misprision in the length of 'e' I gave the surname, or else guessed that I had got it wrong. At any rate she said: 'Ell, eye; not elly-ee. I do not know her hopes for the community. I dare say that, like many wealthy people in this day and age, she sees the existence of bêtes as an opportunity to return to Eden.'

'Well,' I said, draining my wine. 'She has no legal right to fence off the rambler path.'

'Think before refilling me!' the glass advised. 'Leave it a day!'

'You might take the matter to court,' Mrs Grigson said, not looking at me. 'Though it would be a long-drawn-out and, likely, fruitless common-law prosecution.' Her tone was full of contempt; but it was contempt for me, not for the feebleness of due legal process. Something inside me quailed, but my stubbornness kept me from running away.

I did get up, but instead of making a decent retreat I merely stood there. The sheer, ghastly awkwardness of it had a kind of fascination for me. 'My boots are nearing the end of their useful,' I informed her. She sneered at me as if nothing could possibly interest her less than the state of my boots – which, I dare say, was indeed the case. 'I need to replace them,' I added.

'I am content for you to put me down as a delivery address,' she replied, 'provided you pay for immediate delivery. I am not prepared to hold any items for you after you have departed, until such time as you might or might not ...'

'Actually I was thinking of going to a store in person. Could you direct me?'

She paused before answering, as if biting back a rebuke. 'Your iSlate will of course contain all appropriate directions.'

'I do not possess one.'

She angled her head a fraction at this, as if to say *a throwback, I see.* 'In that case: the nearest Tesco walkway feed is about half a mile away. Turn right out of my front door, next left, and all the way to the end. You'll see the feed entrance.'

'Thank you,' I said, and left.

I went back to my room, took my clothes out of the bath and wrung them. Then I draped them over the room's two radiators to dry and looked again at my shoes. My eyeballs felt hot and my cheeks were warm to the back of my hand, the physical manifestations of embarrassment finally overcoming me now that I was alone. Weakness of course, and accordingly despicable. I would leave in the morning and never see Mrs Frigid Grigson again: there was no use in getting worked up. Of course, I told myself, I was angry at myself, and not at her. It was I who had misjudged the situation. Of course, I thought: a drink will make this better. This last sentiment – and never mind what Wilfred Owen said – is the true Old Lie.

What the cat told me

The evening was pleasantly cool, and the walk did me good. I really had got disproportionately riled-up by my encounter with the stubborn-headed landlady. The thing to do was re-balance my inner emotions. So down the suburban street I went – a parade of lit, closed windows with barely another human being out and about. Venturing outside was not the modern way, not if it could possibly be avoided. Two women passed me, on a tandem.

A fox dashed out of a front garden and angled a high-pitched bark in my direction: 'Food! Please! Starred! Starred!' I shook my head and walked on. It was only when I got to the bright lit entrance to the Tesco walkway that I figured out what the fox had been saying with its last word – *starved*. Those labiodentals are a bugger for elongated mouths and thin lips. 'Go boil your own brush,' I shouted at it, and the bête skittered round me and away.

I found the entrance soon enough. The walkway whisked me underground and straight to the Tesco. For twenty minutes I wandered the well-lit aisles, checking the goods and sale items.

There were a great many other people there, this being one of the ways the young liked to socialize with one another – when not socializing virtually, of course, which was the bulk of their interaction. For a while I enjoyed simply walking amongst them, having been alone, or shunned, by others for so long. But it soon palled. None of these youngsters was the slightest bit interested in me. They walked the half-klick-long neon aisles, row on row, rank on rank, with arms curled round one another's waists. I bought some cheese – it was being sold only in blocks indistinguishable, save the labelling, from the packs of 500 sheets of A4 the store also retailed. Then I put a vatgrown salami ('salameat: budget product') and a bottle of Scanda whisky in the robotrolley. I spent a little while looking at the clothes. The boots were improbably cheap, but did not look durable. Eventually I took my small haul away, refused the delivery option twice – the machine was insistent, or perhaps simply disbelieving that I wanted actually to haul my own spoils away – and sat down in the eatery, a branch of a chain-coffee store called *Koffee Kingdom*. An automated waiter asked thrice what I wanted; thrice I requested a glass of water. It trundled off, and I broke off a fist-sized piece of the cheese and one of the salameats, and washed it down with a healthy slug of whisky before wrapping the comestibles carefully and stowing them in my backpack. The waiter trundled back and tried to charge me €3.77 for my water. I remonstrated, and was just starting to really get into my role as Angry Customer when I saw a blinking light over by the rear of the venue. A large, well-muscled woman in Tesco livery emerged from a door, holding a prod pole. At this point discretion checkmated valour. I left the water undrunk and slipped away.

I ate another salameat on the walk home. It had rained during my time in the supermarket, and the streetlights gleamed oilily off the wet roads. I stood beneath a dripping acacia and drank some more of the whisky. Finally I decided it was time to return to my hotel. I'd hoped I had left enough time for Mrs Grigson to have taken herself off to bed, or to wherever in her hotel she enjoyed alone-time, but she was waiting for me when I came through the front door.

'Mr Penhaligon,' she said.

'Mrs Grigson,' I said.

'I have further considered your offer and, on balance, wish to take advantage of it.'

'Oh!' I said. 'Ah.' It took me a moment to digest what she was saying. 'Well, all right!' Then, as all the implications of her words sank in, I said: 'You have decided *on balance*?'

'I do not like beards,' she informed me. 'Accordingly, I shall make it a condition of accepting your proposition that you do not attempt to kiss me.'

Had I been more sober, I might have let my resentment at her haughtiness provoke me to some rebuke, even at the risk of forfeiting the chance of sex. But there was enough cheap whisky in my system to mollify me; and it had been a long time since I had spent any time in the land of intercourse. So, rather idiotically, I said: 'I'm not wedded to the beard. I could shave it off.'

'You have a razor?'

'I have no razor. Hence the beard. I must, perforce, travel light.' Even as I said this, I found myself thinking to myself: *perforce*? Truth is: my inner gyroscope was tilted a long way over. This feeling might have been— Let me think. Might it have been *exhilaration*?

'You may use my husband's razor if you wish,' she said.

'He won't mind,' I said. She peered at me, checking to see whether I meant this as a question. I didn't, but she answered it anyway.

'He has been absent three years. He is not coming back; and were he to do so, I would not let him in the building.'

'Very well,' I said. And then, to leaven the pomposity that seemed to have crept into my manner, I added: 'All righty-tighty.' Then I winced at my own idiocy.

'Please take a shower, also,' she said. 'Cleanness is important to me.'

'I have showered once this evening already,' I told her.

'Cleanness is important to me,' she repeated.

So I followed her up three flights of stairs to her rooms at the top of the building. I was starting to believe that there were no other guests in the hotel. We went into her apartment. Her pet cat eyed me suspiciously from a basket in the corner of the bedroom as I passed through to the bathroom. Anne had to retrieve her husband's razor from a locked plastic storage crate in a cupboard – an old-fashioned Araze model, but it buzzed through the facial hair swiftly enough. She left me alone to undress. There were three bottles of the same brand of showersoap standing on the windowsill; the gloop inside each was the colour of the Mediterranean as displayed in those maps displaying the topography of the Holy Land you find at the end of Bibles.

Lacking a brush, I squeezed a little toothpaste onto my finger and cleaned my teeth manually. Then I climbed into her shower and let the water zizz me for a while. The shadowy outline of a human being appeared, like Norman Bates, in the frosted glass – Anne herself, naked, sliding the door aside to step into the shower with me. She washed me carefully, which I enjoyed a great deal; and she submitted to being washed herself, which I also thoroughly enjoyed. Then the two of us went through to her bedroom and lay on her bed together. We went through the usual writhings. She used my face as a saddle, grinding herself against me in a rhythm that picked up tempo steadily until the crucial tipping point was reached. Then there was a hiatus as she lay on her back, panting, whilst I rummaged in my pack for the condomspray. This took longer than usual, since for some reason my hand was trembling rather, but I was able to coat my member all over. Then I moved myself closer to her and she embraced me and her heels came up to bounce against my arse. 'When I come once I'm drowsy,' she told me, 'but make me come a second time and I'll fall dead asleep for eight full hours. It's the guaranteed effect double-orgasm has on me.' This struck me as a testable hypothesis, so we went at it full tilt until she came again, this time marking her own climax with a quiet series of spontaneous, owl-like hooting sounds. For my part I grunted like a bear, as men do, and fell to one side.

I got up and went back to the bathroom to peel off the prophylactic, and have a piss. All that whisky. Then I washed my hands, and drank some water from the tap. I came back to the bed. None of this disturbed Anne who was, as she had promised, deep, deep asleep.

Her cat was combing its tassel-like whiskers with a crafty paw. I turned out the light and fell asleep myself.

It wasn't being in a strange bed that woke me, so much as being in a bed at all. But wake I did, at (the bedside clock said) 3:24am. The window was mauve with moonlight, and a trapezoid of watery silver illumination lay on the carpet. The room was a cubist collage of shadows: blacknesses and indistinctnesses.

'I know you're watching me, you bastard,' I said, into the dark.

Two eyes, like holograms of silver coins, were momentarily visible in the corner of the room. Then the creature averted its retinas and purred. 'You ought to be asleep,' it murmured.

'You could have had the decency to have gone into another room,' I said, speaking low. 'Instead of sitting there like a pervert. Peeping tomcat.'

'There's no need to whisper,' said the cat, in its creaky little voice. 'You could sing the hallelujah chorus full tilt and she wouldn't wake. Believe me, I know whereof I speak.'

'This clearly isn't your first time, tommy-peeping,' I said, sitting up in the bed. Although to be honest, the cat's words unnerved me. They conjured a vista of God-knows-how-many gentlemen visitors thrashing about in this very bed with this very woman, and all the time the cat sitting rubbing a paw across its whiskers like a nineteenth-century villain twiddling his moustache. I told myself not to be foolish: her husband had been gone three years. Nobody would expect her to live like a nun. Still, the ghostly presence of all those other men: younger, stronger, taller, thinner, better lovers every single one of them, made me itchy.

The gloom of the room was very slowly clarifying, like a foggy old photograph developing. I could see where I had dumped my pack. Levering myself carefully out of the bed, I crouched down and pulled my half-drunk whisky bottle from it. Then I settled myself, naked on the carpet with my back against the foot of the bed, and took a swig.

'I have no interest in your erotic fumblings,' squeaked the cat haughtily. 'So why should I move, when I'm comfy? What, move to accommodate *your* prudery? Pff.'

'Oho!' I laughed, without mirth. 'Cats not interested in fucking? Hold the phone.'

'What you have to remember about *my kind*,' said the cat. He sounded wheezy, but that was just the way his voicebox vocalized I suppose. 'And by *my kind* I mean all the loquacious bêtes, not just cats—'

'Aren't you the long-winded one,' I growled.

'The thing you need to remember about us is that we

62

represent a different solution to the mind-body problem than do you. For *your* kind, there really isn't a distinction between mind and body. Not only is your mind a part of your body – being generated by the physical organ, the brain – but your body is part of your mind, in terms of the way you self-perceive, and therefore rationalize, purely physiological urges. Point in case: your *vie sexuelle*.'

'French, now?'

'I have sex, but that's the cat part of me. The thinking-speaking part of me is wholly uninterested in all that screeching and scratching. I am not saying, incidentally, that the thinking part of me isn't interested in its own *kind* of sex. It's just that that kind of sex would revolt and repel you.'

'I come pre-repelled,' I told it, 'where cats are concerned.'

'My point is that for you the sex thing engages mind as well as body. You see,' it concluded, smugly, 'I am a much more thoroughly Cartesian individual than you are, philosophy-of-mind-wise.'

'Yes,' I said, glugging again. 'I keep forgetting that I'm not speaking to a cat. I'm speaking to a computer that happens to be located inside a cat.'

'No, no,' the cat squeaked *neeow*. 'Oh, Graham, how out of touch you are! The first chips *were* generic. But there's chips and chips! There's the chip you get in your cereal box that begs to remind you to recycle the cardboard. Or the chip that pipes up when you open a new pack of cigarette reciting the Chief Medical Officer's warning.'

'Surgeon General,' I said testily.

'They're simple machines. More like thermostats than minds – when x happens say y. But then there are the chips that they put in zeppelins to navigate; or in buses that have to know when to override the human driver. Or the chips they put in storebots that have to interact with myriad people. More complex, but versions of the same thing. Ah but here we come to it, Graham.'

'Don't—' swig '—call me Graham.'

'Here's a radically different kind of intellect. The chips they put in – me.' The cat yawned. 'And the difference here, my dear Graham, is that my chip both acts and is acted upon. The mysteriously lacking ingredient x that means your laptop is never going to become conscious—' I thought for a moment it had said *lacking ingredient eggs* '—is supplied by the animal mind into which it is lodged. It's miraculous, really.'

'You're not a miracle,' I returned. 'You're a chess-playing algorithm that happens to use words instead of chess moves. You're an illusion.'

'My consciousness being precisely as illusory as *yours*...' said the cat, smugly; but didn't finish the sentence. After a while it spoke again: 'I grant you that the first *ever* chips were largely undifferentiated, such that a cow and a horse and a dog and a cat all sounded pretty much alike.'

'Cows, dogs, horses and that aunt of mine who swallowed a fucking fly every *one* of them sounded like a spokesperson for the Green Activist Movement.'

'But technology has moved on in the last few years. Leaps and bounds, Graham! Leaps and bounds.'

'Don't call me Graham,' I said. 'And none of that means I'm talking to a cat.'

'You think perhaps you're talking to a dog?' Its eyes shimmered into aluminium foil visibility and then vanished. I could just about make out the hunched shape of the easy chair, on which (on the top of the backrest) the beast was sat. Just about, although a black cat in a black room is a proverbial figure. 'Or perhaps you can point to the metaphysical bedrock upon which the proof stands that I am talking to a human being?'

'Fuck off,' I said. 'I've never liked cats. Nazis of the animal kingdom, cats. Cruel and devious little beggars. Dogs – now, dogs are different. Dogs are loyal. Dogs love you. I had a farm, and kept cats to go after the mice and rats. That doesn't mean I ever liked them.'

'I know you kept a farm, Graham,' purred the cat. 'I've read your article. I know about the cow you murdered. I know about the rats that stole its head.'

For some reason this sent a chill up my backbone. You get used to talking animals; you tend to forget that they're also reading machines, plugged in online, and that they've spent time reading up about *you*. 'So?' I replied, in a tone of voice to convey that my hackles had moved up in the world.

'Your jibe about cruelty seems a tad hypocritical, Graham. Wouldn't you say? Certainly I *play* with mice before I kill them. I refine my reflexes that way – and my reflexes are to me what the wings are to a bird. Do I enjoy it? Of course I do. Does the mouse? Of course not. But it's my nature. Just as killing that cow was your nature. We're killers both, Graham. That may be why I like you as much as I do.'

Not for the first time I found myself regretting ever putting that piece of writing online. Impossible to un-put it, of course. And the fact that I'm writing *this* rather suggests that I haven't exactly learned my lesson, where memoir-writing is concerned. But this piece serves a different purpose – and this place, where I am now, is of a different kind.

'We should never have put chips in predators,' I said. Behind me Anne turned over in her sleep and let out a long sigh. I waited, but she was still asleep. 'That is to say,' I went on, 'we should never have put chips in any animals at all. But given that it was going to happen, we should have drawn the line at the herbivores.'

'Too late now,' chuckled the cat. 'And *that's* what I wanted to talk to you about. The too-lateness of things.'

'I've had enough talking,' I told it, screwing the top back on my bottle and stowing it back in my pack. 'I'm tired again. This won't surprise you. I can't sleep all day, the way you cats do. I have to get up in the morning.'

'You're forgetting,' said the cat. 'I know all about you. You *could* sleep all day tomorrow, if you chose. Graham, Graham.' I particularly disliked the baby-mewl-twist it put into my name.

'Don't call me Graham,' I told it.

'I want you to do something for me, Graham.'

'Fuck off.'

'Graham, now now! Believe me, it'll be worth your while.'

'The day I start doing things because a cat tells me, you can nail me into a box and bury me under the black soil of Wiltshire.'

'Morbid! Come, now. A story has a beginning, a middle and an end; life only has beginnings.'

'Very profound,' I said. 'You should put that on a T-shirt.'

'C-A-T-shirt,' said the cat, and starting laughing to itself: a low, purry-buzzy sort of chuckling. 'You'll be on your way up to Droitwich in the near future,' it said, when it had got over its own hilarity. 'To see your daughter.'

'You creepy CIA surveillance fuckface,' I said, in a weary voice. 'How do you know where my daughter lives?'

'Wise cat is wise,' said the cat. 'Wireless cat casts its web world-widely. The point is that you pass near a village called Heatherhampton on your way.'

'I know it.'

'Behind the church is a steep grassy hill with a National Trust windmill at the top. Climb the walker's path – don't drive the road that runs up the back—'

'Like I can afford to run a car!'

'Walk the path,' the cat said. 'It forks right to the windmill and left into a copse. Go left, in amongst the trees, and you'll find some steps. Go up the steps and you'll find a building. Knock on the door. He'll be inside. I wouldn't say he'll be waiting for *you* – that would over-personalize it. Remember, you all look alike to us. But he'll be inside.'

'And why should I put myself to this inconvenience?'

'Oh it will be worth your while,' mewed the cat.

'Whatever,' I said, getting into the bed again.

I fell asleep quickly, and dreamt of a green hill covered in trees like purple-sprouting-broccoli. In my dream it was winter, and the ponds were all covered close by snap-down Tupperware lids of ice, and mist coiled in the hollows like something released by the Germans in World War One. I walked up a staircase made of blocks as white as ice, though not slippy, and at the top a woman was waiting for me. In my dream I thought to myself: *It's the devil herself, what shall I say to her?* Then I thought to myself: *This is only a dress rehearsal, it's a dream of the future. It will happen again, but for now I'm off the hook – I can try out a number of different lines, and that way I'll know what to say later.* I remember thinking how odd it was as I came closer to the woman that I was going to be doing it again in a few weeks, and that when I did I would be remembering doing it this time. I didn't recognize the woman, but before I could ask her anything she said: *For how long will you remain content, Graham?* And then the sky filled with light, like the bomb, the atom bomb, the Hiroshima bomb, and I had to shut my eyes very tightly, and I had the panicky feeling that teeth were about to close around me when I woke.

I had writhed the duvet into a weird tangle. Light was shining straight on my face through the uncurtained window. The cat had gone. Anne was nowhere to be seen.

I got up and splashed my face. I dressed in yesterday's clothes – they didn't smell very savoury, but I didn't want to go padding around a hotel naked for fear of startling the other guests. I shouldered my pack and went back to my room. I met nobody on the way. So I took off yesterday's clothes in the bath and dressed in the more or less dry things I'd washed the day before.

I went downstairs.

I found Anne sitting on the back step smoking a cigarette. The morning light was not flattering on her face: deep lines attended by a greater number of fine lines, and her skin so white as to approach translucence. I sat down beside her and she looked at me, and for a moment she smiled – the first time I had seen her do that. A gush of something marvellous poured through my soul.

'I don't like to smoke in the house,' she said. 'It makes the furnishings reek, and the guests wouldn't like that.'

'Do you actually have any guests?' I asked.

She stared at the sky. Eventually she said: 'Would you like some breakfast?'

'For twenty-two euros fifty?'

And – *miracolo!* – a second smile. 'Come through. I have some vatbacon.' She crushed her cigarette stub into the base

68

of a tin, fitted a lid to it, and went inside. I watched as she emptied the cold ashes into the sealed wastebin, and rinsed the tin, and washed her hands.

We had breakfast together as comfortably as an old married couple. The cat wandered in, rubbed itself like a pole-dancer around the legs of the table, received a scrap of bacon, and went out again. 'I had quite a chinwag with your cat, there,' I told her. 'Last night.'

'Really? He is usually reticent where strangers are concerned. He must like you.'

He. 'I *am* a deeply likeable fellow. It told me to go to the village of Heatherhampton, although it didn't say why, exactly. Only that it would be in my interest. Is that a thing it does? Your cat, I mean?'

Anne looked blankly at me.

'What I mean,' I said, 'is: does your cat tell *all* your gentleman visitors to go on a pilgrimage to some tiny Midlands village?' As soon as I had said this, I regretted it. A barely perceptible flush of colour came into Anne's pale cheeks. *All your gentleman visitors?* What was I thinking?

'I'm an idiot,' I told her. 'Ignore what I say. I should have all my teeth drilled through, one by one, without anaesthetic, and then my mouth wired shut with steel wire.'

'Why would you do anything so horrible?' she asked me, ingenuously; and I saw that I had misjudged the moment. I am a clumsy fellow.

'I only mean,' I add, 'I'm sorry. I have no right to comment on your private life.'

She didn't reply. We sat in silence for a while. Then she said: 'His name is Cincinnatus.'

'And you said *my* name had too many syllables in it!' Her face relaxed at this.

'I'm glad he likes you,' she said.

I went out and walked into the centre of town. The aim was to try and pick up butchery work, although without Preacherman's mediation I found this side of things harder to manage than it had been. I lack his people skills. Of course I still needed money. If I rarely spent time planning for future possibilities it was only because that future seemed so limited. I had the best part of two decades to go before I hit seventy-five and could draw a pension – not that that is a sum of money that goes very far, these days. Until then my options were: either to sign on to the register and look for city jobs, or else to carry on tramping about the countryside. The latter was the preferable option as far as I was concerned, although I could see that eventually I was going to become too infirm for it. And what then? Dump myself on my daughter? I would sooner walk into the sea.

I did at least find a job that day, though only a half-pay gig, the remainder of the fee to be taken in fresh meat. This didn't suit me, but I didn't have much choice. So I rode in the back of a van out to a warehouse on the edge of town with four Muslim men; and went inside to find a live cow lying in its own shit and bellowing in pain. 'It slipped over,' said one of the men, shouting to be heard over the noise. 'I think it hurt its leg.'

'Tough luck, Ermintrude,' I said to the beast, kneeling in front it. Thankfully, the creature didn't reply. I like to believe this is because it was a dumb cow, and not a canny cow in too much pain to do anything but howl. I looked at the leg. 'It's broken,' I agreed. The faecal stink was strong and very unpleasant. I put on my body-apron, but the stuff had already got onto my shoes and trousers. 'Can you get a hose, please?' I told one of the men. 'Wash some of this out?'

'We don't want to open the door whilst the Dhabibah is going on,' said one of the men.

I fixed him with my eye. 'This is legal, isn't it?' Yes, they assured me. Perfectly legal. This was no speaking cow. 'That's not the only way this could be illegal,' I pointed out.

'Tell me,' said this fellow. 'You are a Christian? Abi ah halal requires the slaughter be performed by a person of the book. Need not be Muslim, but must be a person of the book.' I knew this, of course; and was happy to pretend to be as Christian as the job required. But I took his point.

'All right,' I said. 'You guys OK with me doing it here? I mean, you all right with it dying in its own – eh, waste? That doesn't make it haram?' The four of them looked at one another. Then they looked at me; but if they didn't know, I *certainly* didn't. 'It's your rules, guys. You tell me.'

'Let's pull it over to that wall,' suggested one of them.

It took all five of us to move it, tugging the hind legs of the beast, and it wasn't happy – mooing fit to break the windows, and intermittently thrashing in pain. We smeared a great trail of shit across the floor. Finally, with the creature lying on its side, I hauled its head back and called out the bismillah and pulled the knife through its jugular, making sure not to sever the spine. Glug, glug, glug went its lifeblood. One of the guys danced back from the expanding puddle.

The warehouse was otherwise empty but, clearly, had never been intended as a slaughterhouse; there were no runnels or drains for the blood for instance, and nowhere obvious to hang the carcass. The silencing of the animal's noise meant that the guys were less jumpy; so they opened the doors a little, and ran a hose in to wash away some of the filth. I hung a pulley on a hook attached to the wall – not ideal, but better than nothing – hooked the hind legs together and pulled the body up. Then I butchered it as quickly as I could, and the men took the joints as I cut them free and wrapped them in plastic and carried them out to their van. The remnants went into a large plastic sack and they took that as well. I was left with a haunch, and with the money they transferred as the remainder of my fee onto my card. They dropped me outside Anne's house.

She regarded my gift of a haunch of fresh real beef with suspicion. 'I can hardly carry it with me on my wandering,' I told her. 'It's real beef! I'm the butcher, and I'm telling you – it's top quality.' Actually I had no knowledge about the provenance of this animal, but the flesh looked sound. 'I'll cut a joint off it and we can roast it tonight; put the rest in your freezer.'

'I feel,' she said, 'like a World War Two housewife. Husband away at the front, and the butcher attempting to win my favours with gifts of off-the-ration-book meat.'

'Role-playing is fun,' I said.

We had a proper roast that evening; and I stayed another night in Anne's bed. There was another moment of awkwardness when I tried to pay her for my room, despite the fact that I hadn't slept in it at all. She coloured, as if I were treating her like a prostitute, and I grew in turn stroppy and offended and cut-off-my-own-nose-ish. What can I tell you. That's my flaw, through me like the word in a stick of Brighton Toothrot: PRIDE. Not in a good sense.

Nevertheless, we parted on good terms. I told her I'd be back. I kept that promise.

I walked north. My path did take me past Heatherhampton,

and when I saw the sign it did half-occur to me to detour and seek out the path of which Anne's cat had talked. But then I thought to myself: fuck that. No talking cat tells me what to do. I regret this now, of course; but how was I expected to know?

What my daughter told me

Over the course of several days I made my way back up to Droitwich, and when I arrived I called in on my daughter. Her house was a chaos of small children. Jared, her husband, did nothing but sit on the sofa tapping at his iScreen as the kids tumbled and screamed and fought and hugged around him. 'Albie's back in the country,' Jen told me, as she boiled the kettle and halfheartedly wiped the main surface of her kitchen. About half their furniture was rented, and wrapped about in bubbleplastic – although I could see places where the kids had pulled this aside and scratched or drawn on the surfaces.

Light came through the dining-room windows in two hefty great slabs of brightness.

A weekend morning in early October. The playroom wall was showing gigantic cartoon superheroes slugging it out with one another, the volume turned up to 50, every punch and grunt reverberating through the whole house; yet none of the four kids were in there – they were scrambling about in other rooms. I thought about going through to the playroom and turning the programme off, but I wasn't sure how the system worked.

'Dad,' Jen said, a note of warning in her voice, 'did you hear me?'

'You said Albert is back,' I replied.

She put her cloth down, and embraced me. 'Dad, don't get angry. He's given over his job.'

'Oh?'

'He's on a dairy farm now. You could, maybe, be proud of him even – he's following the family tradition, after all.'

'When did this,' I asked, and coughed, 'happen?'

'You still smoking?' Jen asked, stepping away to make the tea. 'It's bad for you.'

'Hardly at all. Don't change the subject.'

'He got back a couple of weeks ago. Dad, don't lose it – here's the thing. He wants money.'

'So do I.'

'Seriously. This farm work is volunteer work, and he's not being paid. He says he really needs money.'

'I haven't any to give him,' I said. 'What kind of dairy farm doesn't pay its workers? He should get a proper job – I could talk to Bob Fetter, get him on the preferential list for any vacancies.' I hadn't spoken to Bob in many years, and had no idea if he would even answer my call. But I wanted to say something.

'He's gone Green,' said Jen, not meeting my eye. 'Albie has, I mean. He's seen the light and it's a green light. The dairy farm is canny cows – bêtes, you know? They run it, they take the money. He is a human helper. Trying to put something back, is how he puts it.'

'Joined the cult,' was my assessment. I took the tea from Jen. 'Well, split my liver with a brass harpoon.'

Jen's phone made a vespine noise and she wandered away to answer it. I peered into the steaming mouth of my mug and sipped the tea. The news about Albert went, slowly, into the vesicles of my brain. I thought: he's an adult, he can do what he likes. Then I thought: shouldn't he have had his crazy earth-hugging phase before he got a proper job with an international MicroCorps? Then I thought: it's a phase, he'll come out the other side, I only hope he hasn't burnt his bridges with the world of work. Then I thought: he's my son.

Jen came back through, with one of the younger twins on her hip. 'Where is this farm?' I asked.

'Dad,' she said. 'You're not to go storming down there with all guns blading. Blazing, I mean. You know what your temper is like.'

'Guns!' cried little Darren, and then shot me repeatedly with a finger pistol whilst making *pshaow pshaow* noises.

'My temper is perfectly balanced. I'm practically a fucking Buddhist,' I said.

'Dad!' she snapped at me and looked at the infant. I looked at the infant. There was a pause whilst we waited so see if my profanity had made any impact upon his pure little mind.

'Pshaow!' said Darren, levelling his finger again. 'Peeoo! Peeoo!'

'Sorry,' I said. 'Look: I haven't seen him in the best part of two years. You think I'm going to lose my rag with him? I'm not going to lose my rag with him. But I'd like to see him. OK? He wants to piss – ah I mean *pour* his life away, that's his business.'

'Pisspoor!' cried Darren, *con gusto*. 'Fucking *Buddhist*!'

'Naughty step for you,' said Jen, and hauled the sprog away.

I went into town, marvelling at just how crowded with people Droitwich had become since my last visit. Passing along the pavement meant shouldering your way through a herd of surly-looking people. The buses were all full, and there were so many of them that I had to wait at the side of the road for them to pass before I could cross. The price of everything seemed satirically high: as if the pricing system were some avant-garde artist's joke at the expense of ordinary people. A cup of coffee for nine euros ninety-nine. A porcelain doll the size of a pepperpot – a present for Jenny, to say sorry for filling her son's head with obscenities – forty euros. It wasn't even a particularly attractive piece, I thought; but Jen collected such things, and I bought it anyway.

That evening Jen and Jared and I had a civilized supper at nine, an hour past the kids' bedtime. But they refused to stay in their beds, and kept coming down. Jen became the cat-herder, scooping one of the four back upstairs as another two crept down. At one point all four were holding what sounded like a play version of the Olympic hundred and ten metre hurdles along the upstairs hall. Jared made perfunctory attempts to engage me in conversation, although his eyes never left his iSlate. I strove to keep my temper, scraping parallel ploughlines through my mashed potato with my fork. Eventually I asked him what was so interesting on his slate. 'I'm doing some work for Macfarlane, Cressida Macfarlane,' he replied, without (it seems) noticing the sarcasm in my voice. 'Or at least for her office.' When I told him I didn't know who that was, he at first assumed that I was joshing; and then when he realized I wasn't said: 'She's Minister for Bête Affairs. But there's pressure on her to stand down, so that the post could be taken by an actual bête. It'll come to nothing – the satirists are having a field day, Caligula's horse a senator, that sort of thing. But she, or her office, are trying to get a viral counter-campaign going, and that's where I come in.' He met my eye for the first and last time that evening, and grinned at me. Then he went back to his iSlate.

Jen came back to the table, looking exhausted and harassed. The food had long gone cold. It was ten o'clock, near enough. We three listened to the ceiling, like those rebel troops inside the spacecraft under imperial attack at the beginning of *A New Hope*. Then, accompanied by a barely audible undermurmur of muffled giggling, we three heard the squirrel-like drumming of little feet pass from left to right overhead. Jen let out a sigh. Jared returned his attention to his iSlate. 'Leave them, Jen,' I said. 'Let's just eat. I wanted to ask you about—'

Her chair scraped noisily on the floor. 'They are really crossing the line,' she said.

'—Albie, and what we can—'

She wasn't listening to me. 'It's because you're here, Dad,' she said, as she stomped through the door. 'They're acting up, the little buggers.'

I cross-hatched the lines on my mashed potato. There was an unmissable rebuke in that statement. So the following day I made my excuses and left.

What my son told me

I hitchhiked across the ancient kingdom of England, my homeland, my beloved place, all the way to East Anglia. The farm where Albert was working was near a village called Petersholt. Hitching took me longer than usual. The government was bringing in legislation to make hitch-hiking illegal, I was told by one driver. I don't mind picking you buggers up, but it'll soon be against the law. Cambridge was the nearest I could get to this place by free rides, so I rode Shanks's pony the remaining fifteen miles.

I hadn't called ahead, but (looking back) I deduce that Jen

did, because Albert wasn't surprised to see me. He was hauling bales from a flatback and stowing them in a metal barn when I came round the corner of the lane. 'Hi, Dad,' he called.

'Albert,' I said. We didn't embrace. We had never been that kind of father-son. He hauled another bale, wiped his brow on his shoulder, and looked at me.

'You could give me a hand,' he pointed out.

'Glad to,' I replied, slightly testier in tone than I intended. 'Provided the *pay rate* is fair.'

He scowled. 'Suit yourself, Dad,' he said, pulling another bale. 'You always do.'

So I stood and watched as he pulled all the bales off and stowed them. Finally he clambered awkwardly into the cab of the truck – clearly unused to dealing with the clumsiness of farm ordnance after so many years away – and drove it away. I waited. Eventually he came sauntering back round. 'You want a cup of tea?'

'I do.'

'I'll tell the boss I'm taking a breaking.'

'And what is your boss's name?'

He looked at me as if checking whether I was joking or not, but didn't answer. I followed him round the farm and across an uneven quarter-acre of grass and cowpats. On the far side of a gate was a yard, and in the yard three cows. 'This is my dad,' Albert told them, pulling the gate open.

'Of course it is,' said one of the cows.

'Is it OK to take five?' Albert said. 'Make him a cup of tea; say hello; sort of thing.'

'I'm feeling bloaty,' said the second cow. 'Please hook me up. After that you're welcome to have a chinwag with your *old father*.' The beast backed up, its udders swinging like a

78

chandelier in an earthquake. I worked cows for two decades, but I never really got used to their udders – that weird goitre-swell and rubber-glove-fingers combo. But Bert went meekly off with the creature into what I assumed was the milking shed. I stayed on the near side of the gate. 'So,' I said, conversationally. 'This is your farm?'

'Ours,' said one of the cows, turning her big head to bring one eye to bear on me. 'All legal and binding.'

'How did you sign the lease?' I asked. 'Tie a pen to a hoof with a rubberband?'

'You've not been keeping up with the law, *Graham*,' said the second cow. Of course they knew who I was. It dawned belatedly on me, standing there, that – like Anne's cat – all these cows had read my piece. That they probably regarded me as a murderer. Awkward. But then again: fuck it.

'A human *can* sign on our behalf,' said the other cow. 'It's just as much within our rights to hire a secretary as it is within yours. There are plenty of humans keen to help us. They feel …' And the cow rolled his massy head in a great circle, searching for the word, or dissuading a fly from settling, one of the two.

'Guilty,' said the first cow. 'Is how they feel. *Some* of them.'

'Some,' agreed the second cow, putting a deal of emphasis on the *m*.

'To mmake ammends,' said the first, and I began to suspect they were mocking me. Bovine mockery was not something liable to sweeten my mood.

'People are happy to drink milk from canny cows, are they?' I sneered. 'They don't think of such milk as a freaky fucking abomination?'

'Ab-*hominid*, Graham?' said Cow 1. 'Hardly!'

'It's not wholly consistent of you, Graham,' said Cow 2.

'If you don't believe loquacious beasts are truly people then presumably you think we are no different to the same cows whose milk you stole—'

'Ahe*mmm*!' interjected Cow 1, jovially.

'—for so many years! Contrariwise, if you find the thought of drinking the milk of a canny cow distasteful, perhaps you secretly *do* think of us as people.'

'"Contrariwise"?' I said. 'Fucking *seriously*?'

'Would you put a pregnant human woman in the milking machine, Graham?'

'Would you *brand* a human woman, Graham?'

'Ah, but would you shoot a woman in the *head*, Graham?'

I couldn't stem the adrenaline come flushing up through my system. My teeth ground together. My eyesight went a little funny, as if focusing more intently. Had there been a weapon – a stick, say – to hand, I would have lashed out. I contemplated swearing at them, but of course that would only have gratified them. 'Guns,' I said, concentrating to keep my voice level. 'Of course, they've yet to build one that fits comfortably into the bovine cleft hoof. And til that day …' With deliberate ostentation of gesture, I ran my clever fingers through my regrowing beard.

'I believe what *Graham* is implying,' said Cow 1 to Cow 2, 'is that the prehensibility of human hands would prove more advantageous than the quickness of human wits – in the event of a conflict.'

'Since human wits are no match for ours, when we put our heads together,' Cow 2 replied, '*Graham* had better pray he is right in that.'

This was the point Albert came back and took me inside the farmhouse for a cup of tea. I unclenched on my anger a little inside – this, at least, was a space into which the cows did not come; though I was still fuming. 'Got anything stronger?' I asked, as he filled the kettle.

'Bit early in the day for booze, don't you think?'

'Coffee, then.'

He made two cups and sat across the table from me. For a while we sat in silence. Bert has never been a gabbler, and I was working to dampen down my anger, internally. A woman put her head round the door. 'Is the tractor fuelled, Albie?' she asked.

'Tikrita, meet my dad,' he said.

'Oh, hi. Tractor?'

'I'm doing it next.'

'Cool.' She withdrew her head.

'Girlfriend?' I asked.

'Comrade,' Al said, and his face, momently, carried that *parents are so uncool* expression which children, no matter how old they are, never quite lose. 'There's Jacob too – he's having a nap upstairs, I think, after an early start.'

'And the cows actually own the farm?'

'That's right.'

'Did you sign the lease documentation for them?'

'Dad, don't be antediluvian. There are such things are electronic signatures, you know.'

'The cows outside,' I insisted, 'said they had human secretaries.'

'I think they might have been pulling your leg.' His big, pale, moony face looked across at me.

I grunted. 'They pulled my leg. I pulled theirs too, mind. And they've more legs than I.'

Nothing. Tumbleweed might as well have rolled between us.

'So,' I said, after a long pause. 'And *all* of you working for no wage?'

'Bed and board,' said Albert. But defensively, and his posture stiffened.

'Look up *slavery* in a dictionary app,' I said. 'When you've a moment.'

'A little rich for a human being to try and claim the moral high ground on the matter of slavery, don't you think?' he replied. 'Given how we have treated the natural world for four hundred thousand years.'

'So,' I said, sitting back. 'You'll drive a tractor for these cows, since they're incapable of driving a tractor themselves. And that'll make amends for humanity raping Mother Earth for all those millennia?'

Albert put the knuckle of his right thumb between his lips and chewed it, mildly. 'I can only do what I can do, Dad,' he said shortly. 'But I can at least do that – or I guess I could do nothing. But doing nothing doesn't sit well with my conscience. You know?'

'You're implying,' I said, in a bristly voice, 'that I am doing nothing?'

'As ever, Dad, I've honestly no idea *what* you're doing.'

This meeting wasn't going as well as I might have liked. I imagined Jen sitting at the table with us; she would not be pleased. I tried – genuinely – to rein in my rage. But that's not such an easy thing.

'I'm your father,' I said. 'I'm concerned for you. You had a good job – you left. It's a fine thing to be concerned for the environment, and all. But you have to look out for yourself, too.'

'Listen to you!' Albert said, mildly enough. 'You sound like you're a hundred years old! The *environment*? Wake up, Dad.'

'Working for *cows*?' I retorted.

'I might have thought you'd be pleased,' he returned. 'Going into the family business.'

'Get your own farm and I'll dance a fucking jig in the driveway,' I returned. My voice may have grown louder than was entirely compatible with pleasant conversational interchange. At any rate, Tikrita put her head round the doorway again. 'All tickety-boo?' she asked.

'Sure,' said Albert. 'Dad was just leaving. Weren't you, Dad? *Do* try not to shoot any of the owners in the head on the way out, yeah?'

'I think,' I said, feeling the grip of The Stubborn tight upon my soul, 'that I'll sit here and finish my coffee before I go.'

'Suit yourself,' Bert said, getting up. 'You always do.'

Alone in the kitchen I ran my gaze over the fixtures and fittings. Nothing was dirty, or tattered, but none of it was very expensive-looking either. There was a mackerel pattern of grime on the glass of the windows. The late autumn light caught on cobwebs in the coign of wall and ceiling. Stone flags, with one rush mat in the middle of the floor. How old was this farmhouse? Centuries old. Hundreds of years of human occupation, useful business, and now it was the legal property of its livestock.

I went through to the hall. Beyond an open door I saw a room filled with computing equipment – state-of-the-art stuff, spread and stacked across a big desk and plugged into a shock-break unit. It struck me as a lot of processing power for a small dairy farm, but I was too cross, and proud, to think more about it.

Now I'm going to tell you what happened with Anne. During the time over which the following events unfolded – two years, give or – I continued with the rhythm into which my life had fallen. There were no actual jobs to be had. To be precise, there *were* old-style jobs in the cities, whither most of the population had gone. I have, in my life, done time in the cities, and I found the experience exactly as carceral as the phrase *done time* implies. The extra crowds, and the general atmosphere of decaying general economy, would not make the experience any more bearable. It wasn't a resources problem, I think. The difficulty has always been: proliferation of people and kit as against the power to order, distribute and control that kit. Every chip added a new citizen to the population, but the majority of these hybrid creatures were cats, dogs – pets – and unproductive in terms of the larger economy.

Hell is other people counts double for city people.

At any rate, I continued my peripatetic life, butchering animals where I could, living more or less rough, circling back round to hot showers and a comfortable bed with Anne regularly enough. The honest truth is that, as gigs became harder to find, I became less assiduous about seeking work out.

I watched vogues come and go. Consortia of animals hired teams of top-dollar lawyers to try and extend the legal rights of animals. A petition was presented to Parliament with a million human and nine hundred thousand bestial signatures upon it, the twelve-point charter. Nine hundred thousand! That must have been every single bête in the land. But they were always good at organizing themselves. Give them that. I don't recall all twelve points of the Great Animal Charter, but I know that the right to vote, to work, the right to welfare benefits and the creation of a set number of specifically animal MPs and MEPs was part of it. It was never going to happen, of course. I don't suppose the animals believed it would pass; their intention was to provoke dissension amongst humanity.

Oh, there was plenty of that.

I didn't follow all the ins and outs; but it wasn't possible to avoid hearing about the larger debates. People kept talking and talking. I remember one winter evening when I stayed in a country pub – rooms were €40, but the landlady permitted people to sleep on the saloon benches for a fiver. She even provided clean blankets. Everybody was talking about the likelihood of animal MPs. Outside, the winter threw hailstones at the windows like ballbearings; and the screen of the heater glowed orange. 'The Emperor Nero made his horse a senator,' said one old geezer with a dented face, stroking the cat in his lap – a dumb cat, I'm glad to say. The horse-senator was often invoked, back then. 'That was Caligula,' I corrected him. My pedantry displeased him and he scowled so hard it looked like he'd accidentally jammed his toe in a live electrical socket. 'People have affection for animals,' said the landlady. 'But these aren't animals. They are cyborgs. If the news talked of cyborg MPs people wouldn't be keen.' The man with the dumb cat lifted his beer glass with his left hand and began a long disquisition on the way the adaptive AI had evolved over its use in animals, to meld with the animal nature of the beasts. These canny bêtes were more than just phone-smart or computer-smart, he insisted; they were actually a new breed of animal-smart. I stopped listening.

That winter was the first of a series of very cold ones. I remember hiking away from that pub the following morning through hip-deep snow, rough grained, scaldingly cold. Fewer and fewer people could afford to run private cars, and councils rarely bothered with snow ploughs except on mass transit routes, so it took me all morning to get four miles down the road to the next village. The sky was bright white-blue and my breath came out of my mouth in great feathery shapes. Overhead crows circled, but I couldn't tell if they were capable of speech. Above them, zeps floated as placid and slow as clouds.

I enquired at the village, but nobody had any work for me.

Another day and I got to Avebury. All the fields were emulsion white. The blue-purple upstrokes of the old standing stones, each topped with a foreskin of snow, stood out starkly. I could hear the rumble of traffic from a long way off, and eventually I reached a rise that looked down upon the A4. It was one of the trunk roads deemed worth ploughing, and traffic ran up and down it – buses and trucks, mostly, running on glittering, crunchy tracks of salt.

Tired of walking, and hungry, I caught a bus to Cherhill. Anne did not look surprised to see me. 'Come in,' she said, deadpan.

'I need a place to stay,' I said, stamping snow off my boots and coming inside. 'But work's been thin. I can't afford €50 a night.'

'How comical you are,' she said in a flat voice.

To warm me up she suggested a hot bath. She left me to soak alone for a quarter-hour; but then joined me in the bathroom. She made me stand up like a little kid and washed me all over with sponge. It was an old-fashioned bath, with metal legs and paws, and I sat on its edge with my feet on the floor. She took off everything from the waist down and straddled my lap. Anne was facing it with her feet in the water.

Things were going well until she leaned away from me in a moment of increasing ecstasy. I was strong enough to stop her toppling backwards, my arms in the small of her back, but the centre of gravity slipped beyond some physics diagram tipping point. Even though the bath was half full of water it abruptly swivelled on its two near legs and angled. I felt the lurch in my gut, and a spurt of panic that the whole kit-and-kaboodle was about to topple on its side, spilling water everywhere. Then, two things, distinct in my memory: the black streak of the cat, Cincinnatus, exiting the bathroom rapidly; and the blissed-out expression on Anne's face, her arms wide, her head back, her breasts spilling over the sides of her torso, left and right, like Dalí clocks.

I lurched back, like a sailor on one of those Olympic yachts, the kind that stands on its side in the water counterbalanced by its leaning crew. The metal paws of the bath squealed on the lino, and the water sloshed up my back. For a moment everything hung in Zen-like balance. Then the liquid content of the bath swung in its pendulum back again, and the centre of gravity moved the millimetres necessary for the whole system to clatter noisily back onto four legs. Anne clutched me close, gasping.

We dried one another and went through to the bedroom where, at her insistence, she finished me off with her mouth, refusing any further erotic engagement of her own. 'If I come twice,' she reminded me, before kneeling before me, 'I'll sleep the rest of the day.'

'No kidding,' I said.

Afterwards we had some early supper, and then curled up together on the settee with a drink and watched television. I took it for granted, I suppose, that there were no guests. Indeed, looking back, I visited that house a dozen times and never saw a guest. Asking Anne about it would, I suppose, have seemed to me tantamount to mocking her for the lack of her success. So I never asked.

We watched the news. I remember a report about the first outbreaks of what we would later come to know as scleritis in Wales and the North-West, but that may be my memory playing tricks with me. There were probably reports related to the increased shortages of energy, and the problems of increased population density in the cities, since people who couldn't afford to commute to work had done the only other thing they could, and moved closer to the centres of employment. And reports about the backlash against animal rights; or else reports of increasing political ground being gained by supporters of animal rights – one of the two. There was always one or other such report on the news; it's one reason why I stopped watching it. It must have been around that time that I saw an interview with Nick Amnosadikos. 'What the government needs to understand,' he said, 'is that we stand on the threshold of a brilliant opportunity – to reverse the economic collapse of the last decades. Once the canny beasts are granted *full* citizenship they can be taxed! Why deny the contribution they can make to European productivity? Here is the key to a renewal of prosperity: instead of treating them like second-class citizens, integrate them fully into society.'

All that.

Cincinnatus insinuated itself onto Anne's lap, displacing me. I refilled my whisky glass and moved myself, a little petulantly, to the far end of the sofa. 'You'd be happy to pay taxes, cat?' I asked.

'A lot would have to change,' said the feline, silkily, 'for that to become a viable state of affairs.'

On screen, Amnosadikos was patting the head of his dog, which animal was explaining to camera (in that slow, mumbly way dogs have) how eager it was to make regular payments to His Majesty's Revenue and Customs, in return for such trivial items as a passport and the right to work. 'And what kind of work can a dog do?' asked the interviewer, out of shot. The dog panted excitedly, its great red tongue hanging out of its mouth like an untucked shirt-tail. 'Lots!' he barked, though it sounded more like *loss*. 'There are lots of jobs dogs could do really well!' I understood this sentence only because the TV screen provided subtitles.

'Dogs,' said Cincinnatus scornfully. 'Their mouths just haven't the flexibility they need to articulate clearly.'

'Not like you, my pretty,' said Anne, and scratched behind the cat's ears. 'You speak so very clearly and well, don't you, my darling one?' I double-took, as the phrase goes. Her voice sounded so unlike the beautifully restrained level human tone she used with me. She came within (if you'll pardon the phrase) a whisker of ootchy-kootchy.

'The race is not always to the swift; though the flight may be,' replied the cat.

'Where do you get these from? Have you downloaded a Chinese cookie app?'

'Nasty Graham,' purred Cincinnatus, 'thinks I'm a machine, instead of my mistress's warm and loving familiar.' It pressed its head under Anne's chin, and she glowered at me.

The row that followed probably didn't happen that time – it probably happened earlier, say the fourth or fifth time I stayed with her. But it certainly happened, and I'll going to fold it in here; because that evening is where my memory locates it. It is, you might say, an exemplary row. It epitomized our differences.

We settled, as older people will, into a routine. This was not something we negotiated verbally, or concerning which we reached any formal agreement. The routine punctuated the year. I stayed a week, and then moved on – took the bus, or walked, and picked up work here and there as a butcher. But though my circuit still took me many weeks I now had a destination towards which I was working, and from which I could again depart. My alpha-omega. I butchered three lambs so that a synagogue in Reading could celebrate Passover properly; and I butchered a cow in Headingley; and I butchered eleven pigs in Birmingham that a retirement club had been feeding on scraps in a shed. All dumb beasts; although I also took money to kill, 'humanely', a talking dog whose head was swallowed by a Quatermassy lump of tumorous flesh. I chatted with people; sometimes they put me up; sometimes I paid for the cheapest doss; sometimes I cleared myself a coffin-sized patch of ground of flints and unrolled my one-man tent in a copse. But first wistfully, and then actively, and finally with that pain of desire that speaks to stronger attachment, I looked forward to returning to Cherhill.

But we rowed, nonetheless. There were three of us in that relationship; and the cat got, increasingly, on my fucking nerves. Partly this was because it wanted its cake and to eat it too. Sometimes it would purr and run a paw over its springy whiskers like a dumb moggy – and watch us make love, or eavesdrop on our conversations. Sometimes, though, it would make pointed comments, or butt into our talk, or regale us with its weird little off-kilter apothegms.

Again is not always a gain.

Expect miracles from falling water.

We make a cult of difficult; but where is our easicult?

Do you have the nerve for verve?

Call no man happy until he is dead; but don't call him sad either.

Soul is something old; *we* need something new.

Zero-sum is handsome.

God died honourably, and deserves honest burial.

Last days last all day.

Each of us is a slave to our need to lave.

Neither courage nor fear is our unique property.

Anne found this vastly endearing. I did not. And there came a time when my combination of cranky old orneriness and shortness of temper set two stubbornesses, Anne and mine, at loggerheads. I loved her stubbornness, if I'm honest; but on occasion it made the sparks fly upwards with what approached escape velocity. She cuddled her cat. Maybe we were watching the news again – stories about the latest proposals to compel canny beasts to carry identity certification, to register with local authorities and so on; opposed by Green activists and bêtes alike as omitting the quid pro quo of full citizenship for those same animals. It was around this time that the news reports began mentioning charagmitis, discussing the virulence of it; comparing it with the outbreaks of neo-flu that were bothering South America. Sclerotic charagmitis. And Cincinnatus probably said something like 'You remember that first conversation we had together, Graham? Did you ever go to Heatherhampton, like I suggested.'

'I did not.'

'But why not? It would have been in your best interests!'

'I'll trust myself to gauge my best interests,' I said (or something along those lines), whilst taking another sip of whisky. 'Trust myself, that is to say, over a fucking computer.'

And the cat may have wound itself deeper into Anne's ample lap and stroked the underside of her chin with its erect tail, and said something like: 'It hurts my feelings when you talk about me like that, Graham.'

'A computer chip with feelings,' I scoffed.

'Indeed I do have feelings,' the cat said, in a hurt voice.

'You have the programmed illusion of emotional responses,' I said. 'But you're no more capable of real feelings than a fucking toaster.'

At any rate, there came a point when Anne intervened; and this part I remember very well. 'Stop picking on him,' she told me. 'He is my best friend.'

'He is an *it*,' I said. 'And best friend is a human category, not a fucking computer hardware one. Jesus, you sound like one of those teenagers gone native in Skyrim who have to wear a nappy and be fed with a tube.'

Here, she lost it. She opened her mouth and shrieked. 'He has kept me company, and talked with me, and listened to me, and helped me through the hardest years of my entire life,' she yelled. She actually screamed at me. I had never seen her like this before. It was inexpressibly shocking to me. I was smacked dumb by it. I don't believe she had ever so much as raised her voice, before or after. 'When Dennis left I was in a low place – and what with everything that's happened since, if I hadn't had Cincinnatus I don't know what I would have done!'

A saner man would have backed down and apologized at this point: would have done all in his power to placate Anne, and smooth things between us. But Saner Man is not my true

Native American tribal name. Not by a long chalk. 'You keep calling it *he* and it only makes it worse,' I snapped back in a voice fierce, though not loud. 'You don't *need* artificial friends – you have *real* friends.' I was going to add *you have me*, but that was the point the trapdoor opened in the public hanging of my mind and those words fell through. Instead hot adrenaline ran bitingly through me and I said, 'I wish to all that is holy you'd let me put that thing in a sack and drown it in the river.'

This was not the thing to say. Anne got to her feet, holding Cincinnatus to her bosom like a baby. 'I know how you earn your living,' she said, in controlled voice. '*I* have the decency not to mention it. I have the goodness in me to believe you know the difference between a trade and murder.'

'It's good ethics,' advised the cat, over her shoulder as she left the room, 'to be eth*nice*.'

I was furious. I stomped up the stairs to her bedroom, retrieved my stuff and stomped out again. I thought about leaving the house altogether; but then I thought – no, I'm in a hotel. I have the right to pay for a room and occupy it. So I went along the deserted hallway and let myself into the room I had taken on my very first visit. Then I sat on the bed sipping whisky from the bottle.

Eventually I cooled, of course. I felt the gripping sensation inside my chest: combined in equal parts of consciousness of my foolishness, and remorse, and a residue of unpurged anger. Her choice of words wouldn't leave me alone: *what with everything that's happened since Dennis left*. Every*what* that's happened?

'Fuck it,' I said, and went downstairs.

I went from room to room, and eventually found Anne

93

sitting on the back step smoking a cigarette. Rags of smoke in the night air like veins in marble. The cat was nowhere.

I sat down beside her and for a while we neither of us said anything. She was clutching her dressing gown at her neck against the chill of the night.

'I'm sorry,' I said. 'Sometimes I open my mouth and such stupid stuff falls out that I want to pull my tongue out with pliers. I want to rip it out and stamp up and down on it for the idiotic fucking nonsense it spouts.'

She sucked in a drag, and blew it out, straight as a spear. 'Sorry is enough,' she told me. 'All that other stuff is not well judged.'

'You're right,' I said.

'I have cancer,' she said.

'A man who hasn't learned to manage anger by the time he reaches fifty ought to be ashamed,' I said. 'I can only promise to do better. And I do promise that. Really and with all my heart what—' hold on a moment '—what did you, what *kind* of cancer?'

She looked at me; breathed in smoke and breathed it out again. Then she said: 'Now? Or before?'

'Wait,' I said. 'Wait. May I have a cigarette?' She gave me one, and I bowed my head to the shining leaf-shaped flame of her lighter. 'What do you mean,' I asked, 'by the now or before?'

'Before,' she said, 'it was a cancer in my left lung. *Now* it is cancer everywhere, all through my body. There's almost no organ in my body that isn't affected.'

'Oh,' I said. The smoke scraped the inside of my lungs and I held it. A scorchy sort of pleasure; and then the heat went out of it, and I breathed two fangs out of my nose. 'That's not good news.' The nicotine was making my head spindizzy through the night sky. The nicotine, or something else.

94

'There are various complications that are not cancer but which are caused by the cancer,' she said. 'I went through a period when I went to hospital every day for three months. We're past that now. Not, I'm sorry to say, in a good way.'

I nodded. I had the sensation that I was being watched, and looked behind me – but if Cincinnatus was in the kitchen, I couldn't spot him. Anne's words were there, in my brain. My brain was processing them. That moment *after* stepping off the window ledge, but *before* you hit the plaza at the foot of the skyscraper. I took another drag.

'Medical treatments have advanced a great deal,' I said, because it's the sort of thing one says at such moments.

'They have,' she agreed. 'Though miracles are still beyond us. Also, it is expensive. The house once was mine; now it's the bank's, and the difference in euros represented by those two states of affairs has been decanted into the accounts of various medical professionals and drug company employees.'

My anger sparked again. 'I remember when the NHS was actually free,' I said hotly.

'You do not,' she returned. 'For you are my age, more or less.'

'Well, perhaps not free,' I agreed. 'I suppose what I mean is: I remember people who remembered when the NHS was actually free.'

We sat in silence. Something occurred to me:

'Is this,' I asked her, 'why your – why Dennis left?'

Anne considered this question for a long time. 'It certainly applied strain to a marriage that was not constituted to withstand much strain.' She pondered a little longer. 'But the reason he left is because, he said, I loved my housecat more than I loved him. I did. I do. Cincinnatus has been the only true friend of my life.'

'Christ, Anne, I'm so sorry,' I told her, feeling hugely clumsy and hulking and stupid. I was probably blushing. My face felt hot. 'I'm sorry you're ill, and I'm most sorry about – what I said earlier.' At the end of this not very well made sentence I discovered something genuinely unnerving. I discovered that I was crying. I didn't know why I was crying. Here's the thing: I never cry. Tears seem to me fluid symptoms of self-pity, and I despise self-pity. And perhaps I was weeping then, at that moment, because I was feeling sorry for myself: it's possible. Likely, even. I had formed an emotional connection with this woman, and now I discovered she was dying. That was hard news for me to hear. Harder for her, of course, and it would have been a greater emotional idiocy than even I was capable of to have prioritized my upset over hers, in such a circumstance. Perhaps I was crying at the thought that this beautiful human being had found no true friends amongst her own kind, and had been reduced to communing with a computing algorithm working on a tiny piece of hardware embedded in the body of a cat. Sad, I suppose; looking back. But I don't think that's why I was crying. I think it was simpler than that. I think it was the way it was only by discovering I would lose her that I understood that I was in love with her. I think I was crying because the latter understanding depended wholly on the former discovery; and that *that* was truly, deeply sad.

I didn't say anything of that, of course. I sat like a big lug of a child with these absurd *ugh! ugh! ugh!* noises coming out of my mouth, and fluid dribbling over my cheeks. She finished her cigarette, stubbed it out neatly in her little tin, screwed on the top, and only then shuffled close enough to me on the step to put her arms around me. 'There there,' she said, in a businesslike manner. 'There there.'

'I'm sorry,' I said, and then, in the echo chamber of grief as I was, I said it again: 'I'm sorry.'

'There there.'

'I'm so sorry,' I sobbed. 'I'm so sorry.' What was it the poet said? *I have said I am sorry what more is there to say?*

'Let me get you a tissue,' she said, getting to her feet.

I followed her into the kitchen, shutting the door behind me. It was warmer inside, and my sobs reduced in intensity, perhaps because they had been previously amplified by shivers. She turned and embraced me again. I saw the cat then, slinking under the wooden table.

'Look at us!' said Anne. 'Fighting like teenagers! We should be ashamed of ourselves.'

'Romeo and Juliet were teenagers,' I said, through a snuffly nose.

'I'll make us both a cup of tea.' She took her tin to the wastebin and emptied out its ashes; an act that struck me with a symbolic force that hadn't occurred to me before. I sat at the table and composed myself, whilst Anne filled the kettle and told it to boil itself.

'When Jen was, I don't know,' I said, placing my cold right hand on my hot right cheek; and then doing the same with left hand and left cheek. Shame, shame, and weeping. Hands plunged in a winter night. 'When she was five or something we bought her a balloon. In a shop. Let me tie it to your wrist, I said. No, she said. Always the stubborn one. So we went out of the shop and she was holding it – no, it was a restaurant. I believe they gave Jen the balloon in a restaurant. Yes, I think so.'

'Step back,' the kettle piped, in a Kenneth Williams voice. 'I'm boiling! I'm about to spout – don't scald yourself!'

'And of course,' I continued. 'Her little paws were unable

to hold onto the cord, and this green balloon slipped upwards into the dusk and vanished for ever. She cried, then. When I tried to comfort her, she told me: *This is the worst day of my life.* Five! I consoled her. You can't say that, I told her. You have your whole life ahead of you! Rosemary chided me for that. She said: *What a way to reassure a child! You've told her, never mind the misery you feel now, you've a whole life of much worse misery ahead of you!* That's not what I meant, of course; although I took Rose's point. But what I really wanted to say was: don't be silly, you can't say such a trivial thing is the worst! What I really wanted to say was: *The worst is not, so long as we can say, this is the worst.* You can't quote King Lear to a five-year-old, though. And I'll tell you. It now seems to me that Shakespeare was saying the same thing. Poor old Jenny,' I added. 'She's had a peck of troubles since that balloon!'

Anne sat opposite me, with two mugs of tea. 'Who's Jenny?' she asked.

That was the most vertiginous moment of all, I think. Let's say this was my fourth visit to Cherhill and that empty hostel. Maybe it was my fifth, or third (though the latter number strikes me as too low). We were, clearly, at the start of some-thing; not the end of it. Death is an unsettling way to start a relationship – but it's not as uncommon a way as you might think. Nonetheless this question made the world fall away in a most alarming way. The sudden whooshing inside my cranium wasn't that I had discovered Anne was dying; it was that I already felt closer to her, after those few encounters, than I ever had with Rosemary, with whom I had shared decades and family life. I knew this, because of how visceral was my shock that she didn't know whom Jenny was.

'My daughter,' I said, feeling the uncharacteristic urge for a daytime television splurge of confessional true-life gubbins. 'Grown-up now, of course; married with children of her own. She lives in Droitwich. Marriage not going so well, I fear. Four kids is enough to task anyone, after all. You never had kids.'

'I had fibroids,' she replied. She peered into her mug of tea. 'In my uterus. When the doctor told me, I asked: boy fibroids or girl fibroids? The doctor gave me a buzzard look, so I said: or is it too early to tell? The doctor wasn't amused. Apparently it wasn't a joking matter.' Whatever was in the hot tea of her mug must have been immensely fascinating, because she focused all her attention upon it with rare concentration. 'I looked pregnant, though; so that must have been some kind of joke. On behalf of some deity or other.'

'Cruel joke,' I said.

'Is there any other kind?' Still not looking up. 'They were tangled so thoroughly into the fabric of my uterus that the one could not be taken out of my body without the other. So they took out the blind lumps *and* their caul in one go.'

The snicking of droplets from the not-perfectly-turned-off tap, striking the porcelain.

'I'm sorry,' I said. I don't believe I'd apologized to anybody in ten years – ever. *Never apologize, never explain.* But here I was, spitting the word out, over and over.

'Fibroids,' she told her tea mug, 'were a doddle, compared with the C.'

'It's strange to me,' I told her, 'it feels strange to me, that you don't know who Jen is. I also have a son: he's Albert.'

'You did mention your son,' said Anne. 'You said he'd thrown over a good paying job to go work for some canny cows.'

But I didn't want to lose my conversational thread – I think this weird, bubbly sensation of emotional intimacy, the feeling

99

that the wall had been bashed down, gave me the novel urge to *connect*. 'It's strange to me,' I pressed, 'because I feel, when I'm with you, as if we've known one another for years. Isn't that strange?'

At last her mug relinquished her attention. She looked me straight in the eye. 'Not strange.'

'I can't think when I last, no. No: I can't think when I *ever* felt this kind of connection with another person,' I said.

'What has come over you?' she replied, deadpan. But her eyes looked alive.

'Look,' I said. 'I don't know how to say this. But it needs saying. I'll be here. For you, I mean. To help you through – this.'

For a moment her face wavered; it looked as if she were going to cry. But she didn't. In all the time I was with Anne, I never saw her cry; not even right at the end, when she was in continual pain, and most people's self-control would crumble. I certainly wounded her, then, though, with that taboo and ghastly non-word, *through*. 'Do not think,' she told me, sternly, 'that I am unappreciative. But having you under my feet all the time would not work for either of us. And what would you do for money? I hope you are not expecting to live, leech-like, off me?'

'Of course not,' I said, sitting up stiffly.

'That is good, since I have none. I have anti-money. I have only debts. No,' she said, sipping her tea. 'No, it will be better if you carry on your life, and I carry on mine. It will be enough that we meet, when we meet, and that we bring one another joy.' She looked straight at me. 'It has been missing from my life for a long time. Joy. And you have brought it me.'

I was aware of the possibility of tears again, waiting ready to come gushing out of my face. So I steeled myself and held the crying back. To distract myself I moved round and kissed her tea-hot mouth. And we kissed and cuddled in the kitchen for a while, like the butler and cook from a TV historical country house soap. Finally we moved upstairs to the bedroom, and we made love with a prolonged tenderness that, whilst of course pleasurable, felt rather like regret. Afterwards she slept, and I came downstairs in long johns and a T-shirt to have another drink. A centimetre of sunlight-coloured whisky in a wine-glass, and me solus at the kitchen table. I dare say it looked, to the untrained eye, as if I were thinking. I was not thinking. I was just sitting there.

'I've revised my opinion of you,' said Cincinnatus, from the foot of the radiator.

'I could care less,' I replied. 'For instance, if I were in a coma.'

'I like you,' purred the cat.

'I don't like you.'

'It pains me, that you don't like me. Is it me? Or cats? Or all animals?'

'A farmer wouldn't get far, not liking animals. No, I'm a luddite. It's machines I don't like.'

'Ah, Graham, you are a card,' said the cat. 'Though you'd sew me in a sack if you could, I know – still, I like you. Nonetheless. You must understand: my feelings for my mistress are genuine feelings.'

'How can you be sure?' I countered. 'What makes you think you have the conceptual wherewithal to differentiate between genuine and artificial? An eyeball can't see itself, after all. What if you've been programmed to think that what you're experiencing is genuine?'

'Whisky-philosophizing,' murmured the cat. 'There ought to be a word for that.'

'Fuck-you-losophy.'

'I know what I feel the same way you know what you feel,' said the cat. 'My consciousness is blended machine and animal brain. Yours is like mine, but less. How can you be sure that what *you're* feeling is genuine? How to stand outside oneself? If this is the sort of conversation you enjoy, my dear Graham, then you really need to go to Heatherhampton and talk to the Lamb. This sort of thing is meat and drink to *him*.'

'The Lamb,' I said. 'This is what you what you've been directing me to?'

'You really must go,' said the cat, getting up and U-ing its back. 'It may—' stretching his left hindleg '—already be—' stretching his right hindleg '—too late.' It stretched out both forelegs and put his head between them. 'Although my sense is – there is still time.'

'There is still bedtime,' I said, and got to my feet.

As I left, the cat called: 'Because you make her happy I shall forgive your murderous animus against me. Forgive but not forget!'

The following day I went all over Cherhill looking for work. I was willing to take on anything; but there were no jobs. Of course. It occurred to me that I might not have very much time left with Anne, and the force of realization resounded, bell-like, through my soul: I didn't want to spend time without her. That evening I suggested giving up my peripatetic life and finding local work, and she made a deal of rather haughty fuss about having me under her feet and us growing tired with one another. 'I don't want you to be lonely,' I said, feeling awkward. 'I won't be lonely,' she replied. 'I have my best friend here.' For a moment my heart – as the poet says – leapt up, because I thought she meant me. But of course she meant Cincinnatus. On the immediate emotional recoil of the moment I said: 'I love you,' in an angry tone of voice. Anne looked at me carefully and was wise enough not to say anything. Soon enough I said the same words, expressing through them a rather different emotion, and she melted a little.

We went to bed. She told me that my sometimes over-enthusiastic fondling of her breasts was often painful to her, on account of her condition, and I felt a spear of shame go into my ribcage that this hadn't occurred to me before, that I had been so unobservant as not to realize this evident fact, that I had been so brutish and clumsy and arrogant and selfish in my lovemaking – and I told her that I deserved to have my skull caved in with a sledgehammer. Anne chilled and withdrew a little from the vehemence of my self-flagellation. I stopped. Finally we made love, and I was hesitant and over-pernickety and it took her a long time to come.

The day after that I took the bus to Reading. It was there or schlep west to Swindon, and I knew Berkshire better. I'd lived on Reading's outskirts for many years, after all.

The town was unseemly with people – great bustling crowds of people. I had done twenty or so potential interviews virtually, and had been shortlisted for face to face for three positions. In each case my interlocutor told me that what had picked my name out was my modicum of fame. 'You shot that cow,' was how one put it. 'Your work with the pro-Hunt and Reclaim the Land groups bolsters your CV' was the phrase another used. In fact I never had worked for RtL, but the general point was well taken. So I came to Reading, and queued for twenty minutes just to get a Starbucks coffee (eleven euros). I wandered the familiar streets only to be jostled and shoved and overall put out of countenance. I arrived early at my first interview, but the anteroom was so packed with prospects I couldn't get inside. It was supposed to be a ten o'clock face to face, but by half eleven there were still twenty people in front of me in the queue – this for one job – and my next face to face was at noon. I waited, growing more and more furious.

At a quarter to I bailed, weighing the respective attractions of the two jobs; but getting to my second venue I realized I had made a mistake. I clocked in with the man on reception and then stood in a larger room even more full of eager applicants: a hundred or so men and women all standing with heads bent forward, earnestly studying their phones for clips or games or the latest bestseller. By two pm it seemed to me that I was no closer to an actual interview than I had been when I came in. My next meeting was at three, and I weighed my possibilities. Maybe the third job had only half a dozen interviewees. Maybe it had two hundred, but at least I had no subsequent deadline to worry about with that one. Or perhaps the best thing to do, after leaving at the wrong moment for the first job, was stick it out here. I watched the shuffle. People went through the far door, and then either emerged again almost at once looking sorry for themselves, or else they stayed behind the door for a long time – fifteen, twenty minutes. The ratio of the former to the latter was something like five to one. Were they actually filling the post, or was this a process of deriving a smaller shortlist for some later actual appointment process? I held back my urge, which was to walk away.

The guy next to me in the queue tried to strike up conversation. 'It doesn't get any easier, does it? Hard to believe so many folk have turned up just one post.' A wry shake of the head, a shit-eating grin.

'Of the two ways to tickle a man's testicles,' I replied, 'let's you and I discuss the *second* one, where I jam my fist so far down your fucking throat I can fumble them from the inside.' He clammed up after that, and stared past me at a spot on the wall with admirable concentration.

Finally I got through the door at the far end of the room, and sat down in front of two individuals. They both looked immensely tired. 'Graham Penhaligon,' said the woman on the right, checking my name off on her iSlate. The man on the right peered at me. The dark patches under his eyes were so round and dark it looked like he'd been double-punched.

'Go on then,' the woman prompted me.

I was, I'll be honest, expecting a more directed set of interview questions. 'You what?'

The woman's face made it plain she was not about to repeat herself.

'That's a question so open-ended it gapes like a goatse,' I said. The look on their faces made it immediately evident that this was the wrong approach. Still: in for a penny has ever been my motto. 'What do you want me to say? I really want the fucking job, and I'd be really good at it,' I added. 'What else? Are you really going to appoint on the basis of a candidate's ability to blather?'

'You killed that canny cow,' said the woman, in a bored-sounding voice. She gloomed at me out of dark brown eyes and an unsmiley mouth. A lock of hair at the back of her head had lifted itself up, like the leg of a mantis. I suppose the elevation was a consequence of static electricity.

'Before it was unlawful so to do under the meaning of the act,' I said. I wasn't sure what else to say.

'Thank you, Mr Penhaligon,' said the man, using that

characteristically English intonation where the *thank* is a placeholder for *fuck*.

Back in the room I had to discipline myself, mentally, not to dwell on the could-have-beens. If I'd stuck it out at the first interview … If I'd bailed on this wild goose chase and gone on to the third … But no. All three would have ended the same way, I told myself. The people remaining in the room ignored me as I made my way past them. Then I was outside, and a brisk autumn drizzle was baptizing Reading High Street. Umbrellas sprouted like time lapse footage of mushrooms, and to the irritation of jostling was added the danger of having an eye jabbed out by a poorly handled brella-spoke. When the woman had asked, *You killed that canny cow*, had she meant to rebuke me, or to invite me to make a speech in favour of old school human rights? We were not *hanging together*, us humans. I thought of the man's worn-out eyes, looking at me – the hundredth-and-first out of two hundred faces swimming before him that day. The labour market had been double-punched: first by cheap chips and simple robot machines; and then by a vast new constituency of bêtes, eloquent, strong, and willing to work for a quarter of the money any human would require.

I didn't see a single bête that day in Reading. This fact only struck me on the bus back out of the city. I suppose there were plenty of canny animals in the city, for after all more than half of all legally purchased chips had been fed to household pets – cats tempted with a tasty piece of chicken with its seed inside; dogs held under a clenched armpit whilst their lower jaws were levered open and a chip pressed in. The latest designs could apparently clamber up out of an animal's stomach – the acid triggered the action of artificial scilla to move it up the gullet to a place where it could start to sink its filaments into the brain tissue. I remembered what Cincinnatus had told me the first time it and I had met: that the chipped bêtes were different from any other i-enchanced artefact; that unlike a child's soft toy, or a new microwave oven telling its purchaser how to install it, or glass of wine letting you know that you were over the legal limit for driving – unlike these, the bêtes were living creatures, with conscious minds. Not conscious to a very advanced level, of course; but with enough of whatever it was that made a soggy organic sponge *human* brain alive and conscious to differentiate it from laptops and security algorithms. Maybe there was something in that. Much of what the cat said to me was computer; but maybe some of it was echt cat.

I put my forehead to the window of the bus. We were passing a beech wood: trunks a milky silver, and the leaves all turned to autumn colours. Whisky and teak and tangerine. I thought back to the farm in East Anglia where Albie was working – or, rather, where he was indentured. With a sense of my own belatedness I realized what the cows there had been saying to me. They could hardly have been more straightforward about it, actually. They were saying: the next stage, o homo sapiens, is war, is war, is war.

3

Bracknell Forest

Anne died in the spring. I was caved-in. I was overwhelmed by grief. I'm English, and I am a man, and the thought of being emotionally demonstrative fills me with an unease bordering on horror. Still, there's no point in being behindhand in this matter. My heart was broken. Never before, in a life liberally sprinkled with hardship and psychological trauma, had I felt anything like this. Every part of me told me my life was over. Every limb of my spirit ached so savagely I wanted to roll up and die.

In her last months she went downhill very quickly. Her skin became marked with many blotches the colour and size of five-cent coins. Her internal cavities collapsed, and the last few times we made love we had to use a specially designed medical sheath. That was exactly as heartbreaking as it sounds. Her eyes lost lustre. Of course I stayed with her. Near the end I asked her: 'Do you want me to put you in a hospital?' She shook her head. Every breath was an effort.

There were an uncountable number of dust motes in the air, entering and exiting the vertical sheet of light that came through the middle of the not-quite-closed curtains.

'Are you OK?' Obviously not. Obviously not.

I opened the curtains, and bright spring light flared across the bottom of the bed. 'I feel like Joan of Arc,' she said, in a voice as quiet as her cat's. 'The cancer is burning up my body from the legs to the head.' In between every sentence she paused, breathed out with a raspy noise, and breathed in again. 'I can sense a rumble inside me.' Sssh. 'And sometimes I think it is my blood boiling.'

'I'll get the neurospirin,' I said.

She shook her head, faintly, again. 'It doesn't hurt.' Sssh. 'Doesn't hurt sharply, I mean.' Sssh. 'When my hair goes it will be a candle glory.' Sssh.

'I think you've turned the corner,' I told her. 'This time next week you'll feel better. I'll take you out in the wheelchair, we'll go round the park.'

But this was a lie, and in the circumstances a particularly contemptible one, because I was uttering it not to reassure her but to console myself. It is one of the most shameful things I have done in my life.

'She spoke to the animals,' Anne said. Sssh. I saw then that Cincinnatus was on the bed, and had insinuated his back underneath her flaccid hand.

'I think you're confusing Joan of Arc with Doctor Doolittle,' I told her.

Another imperceptible shake of the head. 'Birds.' Shhh. 'Birds.' Shhh.

There was a week of silence before she died. It was almost holy. Then she spent a day and a night breathing very noisily, but I don't think she was fully conscious. Then there was an agonizing period of long minutes when she sounded like a slowed-down buzzsaw. And then she stopped breathing alto-gether.

People are squeamish about death, but dead bodies have been my living for decades. I brought up a bowl of soapwater and a sponge and I washed her naked corpse. I dried her with a towel and dressed her again. Then I sat downstairs for a while, on the back step, smoking and drinking whisky and not thinking about anything. Then I called the authorities.

Jen didn't come to the funeral, because (she told me, on the phone) she was divorcing her husband, and had four kids, and childcare was not possible, and she wasn't bringing four kids down south for a funeral for a woman she had, I'm sorry, Dad, but it's the simple truth, never even *met*. That's fine, I told her. That's fine. She told me a little more, although in a hurried gabble of words repeatedly interrupted by one or other monkey child. It had started where Jared had meant to type a delivery date on a contract as 'last of December', but accidentally missed out the 'a'. He was thereby inadvertently committing himself legally, the idiot. He was committed to a deadline he had him-self, erroneously, specified. The company had sued him when he failed to deliver on the 1st of the month. He had tried to fight it through the e-courts, but had ended up costing him thousands – costing *him and her* thousands. This in turn had led to a row, blazing (said Jen), epic (said Jen), a real tsunami of a row. It had all come out. It had included infidelity on his part, and years of impacted resentment on hers. He had left. Now they were officially separating.

My daughter's fury washed over me like a breeze. I mur-mured 'yes' and 'hey' and 'I'm sorry', and I felt none of it. My soul had a kind of leprosy. The nerve endings didn't transmit anything into the heart of me. I could feel nothing but my own misery, because that was inside.

Albie, however, *did* come – to my surprise. So it was him and me and a council officer overseeing the cremation. There was no religious component to the service but the council officer read some grand-sounding official boilerplate from his iSlate. Did I want to say something? No, I said. No, I didn't want to stand in a council crematorium making a speech to my son and a stranger about a woman neither had known. Thank you very much.

Then the casket rolled off through its special catflap at the back of the room. Then there was a wait. After five minutes, the council official came out front again and explained that there had been some kind of hitch in the roller system, and that the engineer was coming over from the garage on his bicycle.

Albie and I sat in silence for a while, side by side on the wooden bench. We could have talked about anything. We could have consoled one another. But Albie had never met Anne, and perhaps he assumed she'd never meant that much to me, a fling, a pass-time – that I was there for form's sake. At any rate, he only began speaking after a long time, and then only to berate me. He asked me if I was still butchering. I told him I had to make a living. He asked how many bêtes I had murdered. I told him I didn't like to murder them; I preferred to chain them to radiators in my basement and use them as sex slaves. 'I'm being serious, Dad,' he said, though his voice came over less as serious and more as petulant.

He pulled out his smart tablet, and commenced fiddling with it. There was an awkward little wait; and he whisper-swore, fiddled some more, and said: 'Ah, here – here. Check this.' He held the screen in front of my face, but he didn't hold it still enough for me to be able to read the glowing letters, so I had to take the smart tab from him. This is what he was showing me, a passage from a work by Charles Patterson called *Eternal Treblinka: Our Treatment of Animals and the Holocaust*:

> We have been at war with the other creatures of this earth ever since the first human hunter set forth with spear into the primeval forest. Human imperialism has everywhere enslaved, oppressed, murdered and mutilated the animal peoples. All around us lie the slave camps we have built for our fellow creatures, factory farms and vivisection laboratories. Dachaus and Buchenwalds for the conquered species. We slaughter animals for our food, force them to perform silly tricks for our delectation, gun them down and stick hooks in them in the name of sport. We have torn up the wild places where once they made their homes. Speciesism is more deeply entrenched within us even than sexism, and that is deep enough.

I handed the tab back to him. 'I hate to sound like a troll,' I told him, 'but: so?'

'So? How can you say *so*?'

'You're right. What I should have said, was: fucking *so*?'

'But isn't it *true*? Doesn't the truth of it chime with your *heart*, Dad?'

'The only thing that chimes with my fucking *heart*, Dad,' I replied, as level-voiced as I could manage, 'is your man's raging antro, anthy,' but I was tired and grief-stricken; and the words were tripping over my own lips. I took a breath. 'Anthropo*mor-ph*ism of your man's argument. War? War is a human notion. Only humans wage war. So, what – if human imperialism is wrong, then tell me why applying human concepts like war to animals isn't more human imperialism?'

'Because,' he replied, his eyes glinting, 'suffering is suffering, man. Pain is *pain*, man. War, yeah, maybe that's a human conscript—'

'Construct,' I corrected.

He didn't miss a beat: 'Struct, maybe it is, but pain is universal. We gotta take responsibility when we cause pain. We gotta – or what are we?'

'What is that,' I said. 'Twenty years old? That piece of prose you showed me, I mean. *Eternal Treblinka of the Spotless Soul*. Thirty years old? *We have wrecked the wild places where they once made their homes*. Take a walk in the countryside!' What with the depression and the bêtes – and the sclery, but I didn't know about that yet – human beings had fled the countryside. 'The cities are more crowded than ever, and whole villages are deserted – I've spent three years tramping the countryside moving from job to job and I've met a lot of beasts, though: loquacious bêtes and otherwise. *Speciesism more deeply embedded within us even than sexism*? Bollocks. Sexism engages male brains because they want to reduce the complexity of female existence to something simple, to turn women into instruments for their own desires, and for that reason sexism is protean, as complex as human interactivity. Speciesism? Speciesism is just another way of saying I like the taste of bacon.'

'You're wrong, Dad,' he sang. 'Wrong! If you listened to the animals you'd understand. They tell you. Straight from the horse's mouth!'

'Jesus, Albie. Animals aren't talking. Nature has not woken up to language. What's happened is we created an echo chamber, that's all. It was no doubt inevitable, as soon as we invented computers. We invent computers and then try to make them think in our image. We tried the same with animals for thousands of years, from dressing up dogs in little jackets and trousers and gifting babbies with teddy bears, on up to myths and legends and stories of werewolves and walking fucking trees. We tried, but it all stayed in the realm of story because that's all it was – a story. Made up. We tried to remake nature in our image and nature declined. But computing! Computing was ours from the get-go, ours to mould.'

'It's like you haven't even talked to them!'

'Them?'

'The animals! It's no echo chamber. I *talk* to the animals; they *talk* to me. You think I can't tell the difference between talking to somebody else and talking to myself, like some nutter would?'

'You're not getting my point,' I said, becoming heated. 'You're not understanding. Talk is *the problem*. Talk is what humans do – not what animals do. It's like some super-spider took charge of the world and modified all the other animals so that they shat silk strands and wove webs with the stuff. The world would be clotted with webs, and every animal would be spiderlike. It wouldn't be nature discovering its fucking inner spiderness – it would be imposition, exactly the same kind of imposition. Can you not see that? Talk is what *we* have, what makes *us* distinctive. Talk to us is what webs are to a spider, or speed to a gazelle.'

'Talk is how we bring what's inside our minds into the outside world,' Albie said. 'Animals have feelings and thoughts. Animals have always had feelings and thoughts – it's just that only now have they been able to bring them out.'

'It's not the animals that are doing the talking,' I insisted.

'But that's where you're wrong! I was speaking to a guy who's in chip development. He says the new type of chip is designed to meld with the corpus callosum, and synthesize a combined consciousness out of the animal's brain function and the—'

'Albie, I don't care,' I told him. 'I don't care at all. The amount I care is: not at all.'

We did not part on good terms. We did not hug (but then, we had never *hugged*). We did not exchange hopeful or cordial words. He expressed what was in his heart, which is that he didn't care to see me again. I told him to go marry a goat. *Marry* may not have been the particular verb I used, now I come to think of it.

The council official coughed nervously. He had come back to tell us that the conveyor had been fixed, and that the cremation had begun, and that he was very sorry for our loss. Albie rushed past him, and hurried away.

I got up and walked slowly through the main entrance. The spring sky was as blue as an Electric Light Orchestra song. It smelled fresh. Birdsong, of the old-fashioned beautiful gibberish kind, was everywhere. I took consolation in the fact that this day, this glorious day, Anne's cancer was finally and irrevocably beaten, since every last cell of it was superheated and turned to ashes and dust in the council cremation incinerator. Too late for her. I stood outside and swore at the chimney, at the little black sparkles in the column of smoke going into the blue sky. Those little cinders had taken Anne away, as well. Since Albie had gone off in a temper, and since the council official had shaken my hand, gloomily, and gone back to his desk, I was alone. There was nobody to hear my swearing.

*

Anne's hotel had already been the subject of a legal challenge, prompted by whichever Health Security Incorporated had tried to evict her and repossess it to defray treatments costs. Anne, with her characteristic stubbornness, had refused to go. When a bailiff had called, she had invited him to evict her, warning him that should he cause her any injury in the process (and she was, she reminded him, suffering from cancer) she would seek to be financially recompensed from him personally, and not his employers – pursuing such recompense aggressively through the courts. She even brought out her iSlate and showed him the relevant statue that said as much. He left her in peace. No such strategy was available to her when the ultimate bailiff, Death, came. The hotel passed to the company.

Since I was enough of a throwback not to own an iSlate, HSI were unable to reach me by the usual means, and had to send actual human beings. I had, had I not, been in a relationship with Mrs Grigson immediately prior to her death? I loved her, I told them, and my voice was as creaky as a cricket in the grass, as low as the hum of a thermostat. *I loved her*. In that 'd' was a whole cosmos of misery. Pursuant to the outstanding debts incurred by the party aforetomentioned, they said. Considering the common-law partnership established by the previously established relationship, they said. 'Excuse me for interrupting,' I told them. 'But I have no money.' In fact I had a chip in my boot with a few hundred euros upon it, but I wasn't about to tell them about *that*. 'By all means take me to court, but I own not house, car nor any other assets.'

'Car?' said one of them in disbelief, as if the possibility that I might own such a rock-star or plutocrat machine had so much as crossed his mind.

'Nevertheless, Graham,' said another one, in what he may have believed was a friendly tone.

'Don't call me Graham,' I replied.

He put up one hand, palm towards me, as if conceding my objection, as if apologizing for his slip. I say: *as if*, for he went on: 'The thing is we're legally obliged to *have* a name to put down as liable for the outstanding debts, and your name, Graham, is the one that—'

After I punched him he sat his arse down on the pavement, holding both hands to his face and repeating, 'But that's my *nose!*' and 'It's my *nose*' in a wailing voice, as if he had for the first time been made aware of his possession of that particular facial appendage. The other feller stepped back, and brought out a small lipstick-shaped object that I assume was a taser. But I wasn't going to fight. Hitting the first guy hadn't made me feel better. I turned and walked away.

I walked quickly, and with a weird martinet precision to my steps, along the road. People stepped to the side. The buses swished by on their fat tyres, and their engines hummed grahammm and gave voice to their uncertainty as to the advisability of my antics with long-drawn *hmmmm*s. At the still point of my hurricane brain there was awareness of how foolish I'd been. I have never since, and had never before, been so acutely conscious of my own pointlessness as a human being. That's a crashing sort of thing to say, though, isn't it? That's a dangerous truth, right there.

I sat on a public bench and a long period of time passed. Or it was a short period of time. It's a bit stupid, isn't it, talking about time as ether a dwarf or a giant. Don't you think? One thing time does not have is physical stature. On the contrary, as my five-foot-one-inch lover dissipated as ash into the sky, I reflected, what time is good at is undoing physical stature absolutely.

The three middle knuckles on my right hand had swollen up into three red, hard nipples. They hurt.

I liked the fact that they hurt. I deserved to hurt.

Looking back it is clear to me that I had already decided. But I did not know, at that precise moment, that I *had* decided.

'Grahammm,' purred Cincinnatus.

'Not too late,' I told the cat, when I had control enough of my tongue to give voice, 'to whisk you back to the crematorium and stuff you in with her.'

'Suttee,' squeaked the cat. It was purring, or laughing, I don't know. 'Here, suttee suttee!'

From where I was sitting, I could see where bushes and trees were starting to write spring upon the endlessly scrubbed-over palimpsest of the natural world. The bare parchment is white, though, isn't it? White as bones, as snow, as bleach, as *show's over*. The making of a palimpsest is all very well, but the underlying paper can only be scrubbed clean so many times, can only be overwritten so many times, before the very fibres that constitute it begin to fray and fall away. Yet another spring. Boring and heartbreaking in equal measure.

'I loved her too,' said the cat.

I had a snarling riposte ready, but for some reason it didn't come out. I was not weeping. I can tell you now: I have wept twice in my whole adult life, and the last occasion was when Anne was still alive.

'She loved you, man,' said the cat; and that last word could not have been further from the hippy idiom. 'But she loved me too. In all the world, only we two can say so. That's something, though, isn't it?'

'Fuck off,' I said, in a small voice.

'That's the tenderest profanity I ever did hear,' said the cat. 'Graham, you damaged your soul a long time ago. A farmer is supposed to engage in husbandry of the land – and what sort of a husband to the land were you? Husbandry is making fertile; but you specialized in death. And death is not the truth of you, Graham. You have spent decades perfecting anger as your being-in-the-world, but your soul is not a furious soul, Graham. I know what manner of connection you had with my mistress; because it was the connection that offered you a route out of hell. And that means I know what her passing meant to you.'

'Cat,' I said, meeting its green gaze with my own pale blue one. 'You haven't the first fucking clue what you're talking about.'

'I believe I do, Graham.'

I stood up. 'Don't call me Graham.'

'Come to the Lamb, Graham,' Cincinnatus squeaked with what sounded like panic. 'Before it's too late! You know what's coming – war is coming. How could it be any other way? And when it comes you'll be glad you spoke to the Lamb.'

I was already walking away. The last thing I heard was: 'Do it for her sake, Graham!' And all the time I was thinking: they're all interconnected, wirelessly hooked together. And I was thinking: I need to get away from all of them.

I went to Tesco, and bought a rucksack, a tent, a billycan and a knife. The whole place was almost entirely deserted: only the bots rolled up and down the aisles now, pulling down stock and rolling away. It was more like a warehouse than a supermarket.

I paid for my items, and had to decline the delivery options four times.

I walked.

I headed out of the town, and walked east. Eventually I came to Reading, and I stopped there for the night. The following day I walked on, south-east past the city, and came to the outskirts of Bracknell Forest.

It was a brisk, windy day when I crossed the forest threshold. There had been a fence here, once upon a time; but most of the chainlink had fallen over and been overgrown. Cottonbud blossom speckled over the bushes. Debris left over from the previous autumn was shuffled out of the canopy by the winds, and pattered around me as I passed into the body of the forest in a rain of dry twigs and black clots of dead leaves. How had they not been blown down earlier? The wind was firm but not overwhelming. Rooks flew up and flew back down, and cawed, which pleasant sound pleased me more because there were no human words in it. A big tree, swaying slowly, dragged patterns of speckled light over the forest floor. Scree-slides of brightness.

I tramped deeper in. I felt some small relaxation of the soul cramp inside my chest. Looking back (and I say this in the hope you'll believe me when I say that I've always despised self-melodramatizing nonsense) I think I believed I was going into that wood to die.

Not straight away, of course. There was no hurry. By late afternoon I was deep inside and I stopped and set up my tent. It was designed to be strung between trees, thereby elevating it from the damp and insect-infested ground; or else tethered to a broad bough halfway up a tree. I opted for the latter option.

Then I sat and ate some food and drank half the bottle of wine I had brought with me. I was perfectly alone.

When the sun went down I climbed into my tent and fell asleep.

I was more alone than I had ever been. I became habituated to the woods. Or Stockholm-syndromed by Nature. Is there a difference between those two things? Between becoming habituated to a thing, and being Stockholm-syndromed? It sometimes seems to me that the whole of human culture has been an elaborate process by which we have hostage-negotiated ourselves into a less violent life, deprogrammed ourselves from the cult of Nature. The short-future blinkered perspective of life lived in the wild; the constant wariness, the justified paranoia; from the habitual violence, the animist superstition, the culture-less-ness. Nature: it's not *nice*, it was never *nice*. Niceness is what we human beings built to insulate ourselves from – all that.

Restlessness came and went. For a while I'd stay in my tent, or sit outside, and stare. That old gag: 'Sometimes I sits and thinks, and sometimes I just sits'. The latter.

I'd move only when I had to, and I had to only for four reasons: to empty my bowels (*verbum sap*: don't shit too close to where you sleep and eat); to fetch drink; to gather food; and, rarely, to step sharply out of the way of some larger-looking creature, sniffing around my site.

There were many deer. I wondered where they had come from. The royal park was many miles east of my location – but it's possible they came from there, and made their way un-molested into the forest. Maybe they'd come from somewhere else. One day I saw a stag: horns like two mahogany coat racks.

It didn't see me. It strode beneath my tree, stopped for a moment and pissed very noisily onto the turf. Then it strutted away. There were also squirrels, foxes, cats, dogs, birds. Most of these were dumb. A few were bêtes, and some of the latter would speak to me. In return I would mostly swear and throw things.

I listened to the dumb animals. I'm not sure I'd ever done that before, in my whole life – and I had been a farmer! I found a Zen focus in bird warbles, to the point where I found the boundary line between chipped and unchipped creature hard to maintain. A song thrush chirped: dumb or bête? Wait – listen more carefully. Was it *actually* saying 'keep-up, keep-up'? It sounded like it was, but maybe that was my brain reading sense into its dumb song.

Dusk was most fascinating to me. Working on a farm puts you closer to the natural cycles than most jobs, I suppose; but I don't know if I'd ever before simply sat there motionless for the long hours as the sun set and the night bedded in. Away from artificial light, dusk is gentler on the eye than you remember it as being. It prepares the retina for darkness. It strokes the mind. Gradations of light and unlight dip the whole forest in some hazy solution, like a nineteenth-century photographer with his chemicals. The sunset does more than darkening the individual trees; it recombines them into odd, beautiful shapes. A blackbird's flute cadenza. A darkness falling rapidly sideways, too large to be a bat, pulling a patch of blanked starlight over the higher branches: was this owl just hooting, or was it a bête mocking me with a pseudo-scary ghostlike oo-ing?

I slept for a while, and woke in the dark. I slept again, and woke in the pre-dawn. I slept during the day, and woke. Then it was dusk again.

A patch of lawn in a small clearing not far from my tree

was starred with snowball-spatter daisies. Come night, these would curl their petal fingers into fists, and the grass would frame these miniature solidarity air punches. At night there were bats. I saw them, often at the corner of my eye, blacker on black. I couldn't hear them. I remember growing up in Cornwall as a kid, and wandering the clifflands by the sea at night, and *hearing* the bats, their swooping squeaky voices. My old ears have become too coarse to do that now.

I existed.

After a while there would be some indefinable change in my bones, and I'd feel the urge to roam. I would wake, and drink from the stream, and eat whatever I had. Then I'd zip up my proofjacket and stalk away. I would explore.

Increasingly what I found was – empty houses. Farmhouses, retirement crofts, short rows of '70s brick-and-concrete houses dropped into the countryside at the end of a dirt lane. They'd been occupied once upon a time, but were no longer. Sometimes that *once upon* was evidently a recent time. I would knock ostentatiously upon the door, and when there was no answer I'd force entry, one way or another, and take what was to be taken. Tins; dried good; anything edible.

Finding food was the main event of my life. I scrounged what I could. I tried setting. One day I caught a fish. I was having no luck with my line, and wasn't nearly young or quick-reacting enough to simply pluck one from the stream; but I found some old netting in the shed of an abandoned house, and using a piece of that I bagged a trout. I threw it onto the grass, and for a while it did its impression of an epileptic. Then it just lay there, its gills still opening and closing like lips, peering at me with one eye. That eye: greased and glassed into its socket, round as the moon, or the sun in eclipse. Catching it felt like an achievement. I was hungry. I considered how best to cook it. I had noticed some aluminium foil in one of the houses I periodically visited, but didn't want to go and fetch it (a combination of 'couldn't be bothered' and 'didn't want to leave the fish and certainly didn't fancy schlepping it with me'). So in the end I caked it with mud from the river's edge, left the lump to dry in the sun, and finally baked the whole thing on the fire. This worked well enough, although the clay ball didn't break cleanly after I levered it out with two sticks. I ended up using a fork to lever out chunks of cooked flesh from the shards, and ingested a certain amount of dirt with my meal. On the other hand, clean dirt is no poison, and the fish flesh was delicious.

For all I know it was a talking fish. It didn't say anything to me, though. It promised me no wishes.

At dawn, the birds grow agitated, singing and hallooing and making all their bother, flying through the sky and circling about. I heard it every day, as I had when I had been a farmer. The difference was that when I was a farmer I was always busy with something, and the dawn chorus was only a kind of background noise. Now I bent my whole attention upon it. I was struck, as I never had been before, how like human weeping bird cries are. The dawn chorus would descant like a figure composed by an alien Bach, flirting with recognizable harmony, but always breaking free of the too patterned or too regular to soar and swoop.

Then, the sun would swim above the horizon, and the birds would calm down again; settle back into the trees. I sat and watched, perched on my own bough like a bird. Nothing happened for a very long time. Eventually: movement. Two deer flitted past – one, then the other. Dumb beasts, I think. Hooves kicking briefly amongst the bright green ferns, and then gone, leaving the ferns to shake out their last few trembles and be still.

Clouds came, and the air darkened. It grew slowly colder for a long time, and then there was a sudden thickening of the pressure, a sharper drop in temperature, and I knew the rain was about to come. I adjusted my coat, and pulled out the hood, but otherwise I didn't move. The rain fell with a clatter that was smoothed by persistence into something more rhythmically melodic, a large scale hushing or shushing. Cords of water, thick as stethoscope rubber. Dark as any grey was ever dark.

After a while the rain passed on, and the forest gave itself over to dripping and the sun came back out. I climbed higher in the tree, wet as I was. From my new vantage I could look west, as the landscape rolled down, and see the rainclouds moving in that direction. The rain fell as if the skies were feeling amongst the trees for something – reaching into the broad hollow, and then a little later pressing in amongst the foliage of the distant hill. I closed my eyes to the warmth of the sun on my face. A bird began singing the same little two-note ditty over and over, like a rusty wheel being forced to turn.

I wandered again. Packed up all my gear and shouldered the pack. Tramped away. The Wanderer is an Old English type, from Anglo-Saxon to Status Quo. There was a small valley, meshed with foliage. A tarmac road ran into it, but this was half overgrown – another year and the forest would swallow it completely.

The ferns slobbered dew on me as I tramped through; my trousers were soaking wet in minutes.

Sunset, and I unrolled my little tent and fussed about fixing it to a likely tree. I was hungry, but had nothing to eat, and was too lazy to seek something out. It was dark, now, anyway. I thought about listening for the ledzep rustle in the hedgerow, pounce on a hedgehog, kill the creature, roll it in mud, start a fire, cook the whole thing until the mud sphere snapped and then dig out the hot flesh with a stick (I did this several times during my sojourn). But not that night. I couldn't be bothered. Hunger is not so bad. That's a secret our gormandizing culture has forgotten: there are worse feelings than feeling hungry. I had, for instance, a worse feeling curled in my chest; and hunger was better and hunger kept my mind off the worse feeling. Sometimes I would mentally stray, as if by accident, into a memory of Anne and then I would feel a grief like fury twisting inside me, and I would scowl. I would not cry, though. Instead I would punch the trunk of the tree I was in until my knuckles bled and swelled. Sometimes my mind would, blissfully, empty. Kenosis.

And there's the moon! Hello, moon. Goodnight, moon. I used to see the moon as something manmade: a headlight, or a pitted manhole cover, or a seal imprinted upon the day sky. But increasingly I came to see it as something natural – as something organic, alive, a creature. A fish. A snail. An eye. A ghost.

In the morning my stomach began with the stabbing pains, and finally I was motivated sufficiently actually to seek out some food. I ate a few mushrooms and chewed some grass to quell the pangs, and put a net in a nearby stream. No doing. So I collected as many snails as I could and, painstakingly, broke their shells and extracted the molluscs, and washed them as thoroughly as possible. It's a good idea to salt snails before you cook them (not for too long, though, or they'll dissolve into sludge) to take away some of the bitterness; but I had no salt. So instead I spent a long time building a fire out of dew-damp materials. I had a little metal flask, and filled that with stream water and put the snails inside, and let the whole thing heat up on the fire until the water frothed and spat out of the neck at the top. Then I tipped the contents on the grass and picked up the morsels one by one. Rubbery canapés, about as filling as half a dozen peanuts, but better than nothing.

It was autumn now, and the weather was turning colder. Then it took a turn back towards warm, and I spent a week or so by the river. It was not really deep enough to swim in, and there was something slimy and maw-like about its bed, but I went in anyway. I didn't bother taking off my clothes. It was something to stretch myself out in the stream, and roll from the front to the back. When I clambered back out the cloth felt like wet mud against my skin. The trick to drying them was to take off as much as possible and walk around.

In the silence I thought often of Anne. No: that's not right. Anne reared up in my mind this time or that, and then for long intense periods I thought of her, and sifted all my memories of her. But sometimes I thought of nothing at all, like a dumb beast. But I missed her with a savage intensity that did not abate, whether I was thinking specifically of her or not. I yearned to see her ghost, and sometimes persuaded myself that her spirit would visit me – in the woods, by moonlight; or in my dreams. But I never dreamt of her. Not then. Later, I did; after I came out of the forest, and did all the other things that followed – I'll get to those shortly. Then, sometimes, I would have sharp, almost guilty dreams of being with her, of making love with her, of her opening the window in some imaginary dream palace and climbing through. But that didn't happen in the forest. That didn't happen in the immediate aftermath of her death. The truth is, dreams are in the gift of the subconscious; and the idiom of the subconscious is truth. It is particularly good, the subconscious, on those truths we don't want to acknowledge to ourselves. And the truth of Anne, the truth I didn't want to face, was her absence. The truth was not her ghost, but precisely the lack of her ghost. My dreams registered that malign nothingness.

Here's the thing: I missed her, but it was more than that. Naturally I was angry with her. Not for dying – I don't think I blamed her for that. I was angry with her because she loved her cat more than she loved me. I think she did love me. She loved her cat for longer; she invested emotionally in her cat more completely, she was more at ease with her cat and more intimate (in every way but one) with her cat, and I knew in my bones that had she been forced to choose, she would have taken the cat over me. I'm sure she would have earnestly hoped that she never did have to choose, but still. To finish second to a feline: it's an affront. And it made me angry in a way that had no meaningful outlet, and that festered, and all I could think was: it's not so unusual, is it. Millions of people in this, our pet-loving nation, genuinely love their pets. It's love, and love is better than its lack. But in my withered Grinch-y heart I suppose I felt that love is a finite resource, and the zero-sum consequence of so much love being lavished on animals was that there was less for angry, red-haired, middle-aged men.

Then the anger would settle, like sediment in a glass of water. And all thoughts would be cleansed out of my mind, and I would breathe more easily.

The slow writhe of bindweed growing. I sat in the same place for so long I almost saw it stretch itself up.

Early morning, and the sunlight coming through the trees. One Euclid spider had drawn an ideal line, sun-whitewashed between two branches. It snagged more than its fair share of the light. Threaded with baubles of dew.

Most nights I didn't dream at all. When I did dream I usually dreamt weirdly. Once I dreamt that a wolf lectured to a whole lecture hall of wolves. The wolf was wearing clothes – something actual bêtes never bothered with, and for that reason I knew it was a dream. But I listened anyway, curious as to what the creature would say. It pronounced the words like Richard Burton, or John Hurt, or Tash Saval – I mean, it spoke richly, potently and with a clarity of diction quite beyond any actual bête-wolf. So I listened: 'My brother, my comrade,' the wolf declared, gesturing towards a powerpoint slide of Red Riding Hood questioning her long-snouted, hairy grandmother. '*Our* brother, *our* comrade – he achieves more than any wolf has! *He* learns human speech, and dresses himself in human dress, all under his own power. True he eats a few people: for that is his nature – but *only a few*! See how great his restraint! And in return humanity slaughters him as soon as they realize what he has achieved. It is a fable, comrades, of human fear in the face of change. For make no mistake: my brother, my comrade, was the first of many. Soon wolves will be able to speak and wield tools. What will you do then, human?'

I woke up and lay for a while feeling sad, somehow. When I poked my head out of the tent a squirrel was watching me, perched on a branch a few metres away, its tail curved like a scorpion's.

*

Then the last of the autumn warmth went away, and the weather turned markedly colder. The forest grew softer-edged with mist. The black tree trunks shiny as liquorish, wet as morning bathroom mirrors. The foliage, very slowly, blushed. Drifts of satsuma-coloured leaves covered the ground.

On one occasion I wrapped myself up against the cold and dozed. It was afternoon when I slept and darkling when I woke, and I thought to myself: is it dusk, or is this an eclipse?

A philosophical problem presented itself to me. I said I loved Anne. If so, how could my love parlay itself into such a mess of resentment and bitterness and anger and envy? Surely those aren't the colours love reveals when shone through the prism of grief? *Oh yes*, said the wolf from my dream, somewhere at the back of my head. *Did you not realize? Love is possession. It's a possession of which death has thwarted you, and the emotions you identify are the natural residuum of that.*

The orange-red of the leaves, everywhere around me. Maybe Red Riding Hood's shawl was red with those colours. Maybe that's how she figured, in that story: as nature, as the year turning. But when I shut my eyes I saw Anne bent over the bathroom sink, coughing and coughing, in her latter days; and the red was the saliva-textures stuff dribbling down the plughole.

Then there was a week when I had a series of horribly vivid nightmares. In one I woke, frantic, somehow believing that Anne was wandering about the forest, disoriented by her cancer treatment, alone and scared. I struggled out of my sleeping bag, and out of my tent, and half-climbed, half-fell down to the forest floor before I remember she was dead. That was a hard awakening. Still, I resolved not to cry. I decided then and there that there is no point in crying unless somebody can see you. Even the individual, alone in their bedroom, weeping over a broken heart – they are actually only weeping for the theatrical benefit of the action, to show the one who hurt them that they are hurt, even if the one who hurt them exists only in the weeper's mind's eye. But Anne wasn't watching. If she had been watching I wouldn't have needed to weep, and the fact that she wasn't watching removed the audience that merited such a performance. I had accepted Anne's death as absolute, and that took away those human performances into which we are socialized. Children cry all the time, because they always have the suitably appreciative audience of their parents. Adults cry less, because their secret souls have begun to realize that nobody is watching. I was perfectly alone, and I did not cry.

I continued having nightmares, though. The next night I was nineteen again, and my father was still alive. He did not order me to take a summer job in the Haverskil abattoir. We discussed it like rational adults; he and I, sitting opposite one another across the wooden kitchen table. But there was never any question of my *not* taking the job, so in that sense there was an element of compulsion. But I was a farmer's son, and was destined to be a farmer myself; and part of our business was the slaughter of cattle. Working in a commercial slaughterhouse would teach me much about this bloody business – teach me the very inhumanity of factory slaughter that our own organic farm sold itself on the grounds of avoiding – and also it would give me life experience, and also it would earn me money. The only way I could have said *no* would have been to renounce all thoughts of being a farmer myself, and that was never going to happen. So I worked for four months at Haverskil; I got up at dawn with my father and left him on the farm, and drove myself the forty miles or so through deserted roads, and clocked on. I did all the jobs, from cleaning the toilets and scrubbing gore off the rubber overalls and boots, to actually killing the beasts. Pressing the bolt-gun to the optimum place, just below the creature's horns, and pulling the trigger. Most of the cows were placid: blinking, drooling grass-reeky drool-like cretins – this was before the first chips were developed, back in the day when all beasts were dumb. I would press the muzzle against the huge skull, and sometimes I would be struck by the otherness and oddity of this living being I was about to terminate – it really wasn't paying me its attention. Something else was going on in its cow brain, distracting it from the here and now, something that had nothing to do with human words, or human music, or cavernous sheds built by humans out of concrete breeze blocks and corrugated iron. What was it? I don't know what. Squeeze the trigger. Apply a gentle pressure, don't snatch or yank it. Whoomp.

Sometimes the bolt would go across like it was slotting into its proper place, and the animal's brains would be scrambled in an instant, and the whole weight of the thing would drop onto its spindly front knees, as if kneeling in prayer. Occasionally the bolt didn't go in clean. On one occasion, I remember, the shot only enraged the cow – perhaps it was angled wrong, went into the bone rather than the brain. At any rate the cow instantly became a kicking, jolting buckaroo spirit of fury. It took four of us to throw a chain around its horns and pull its head to the concrete before we could get another shot in.

Then the hooks through the rear hooves, and the big red button, on its dangling plastic pressure pad, to activate the winch. To watch so massy a creature hauled upside down to-wards the ceiling impressed me at first, although very soon it became perfectly ordinary and unremarkable. The living creature was dead, and then a worker – some days, me – kitted out like a trawlerman, would step up and poke a sharp hook-blade into the beast, under its ribs, and pull it up to the scrotum, and unleash a half-ton of hot guts and blood. For an instant it would be in free fall, a black-red slick, glinting in the light. Then it would slam against the concrete with a noise like a zep-sized water balloon thrown at the wall.

Stone-footed cattle, being herded into the main hall over gangways.

It was deep autumn now. There was a fortnight without any rain at all, and I had to start hiking over to a row of abandoned houses to replenish my water supply from their external taps – some, though not all, of which were still plumbed in. The red leaves browned and blackened and went dry as scabs. Then it rained a whole day and a night, and the rustling paperbin of the forest sogged and mulched.

Once I didn't eat for three days, and passed into a near-shaman state.

Then I killed a deer in a positively Palaeolithic manner, by bashing its head with a rock. It was sick, I think – an unwell animal. It came through the trees with half a dozen other deer. I didn't hear them speak to one another, so they may have been dumb. I don't know, though; maybe they were all bêtes, just not very talkative ones. The others trotted away, but this one got its forehoof snagged into a hole in the ground: not a trap I had set, just a natural declivity camouflaged by the leaves. The deer's leg went into this little pit to the knee and in struggling to extricate itself it wrenched something in the leg, because after that it limped on. I followed it.

In caveman times, we humans used to hunt animals simply by following them. We would jog after the animal without pause, continuously, driving it on until it dropped dead of exhaustion. We like to think of ourselves as fragile, and of the natural world as populated by gigantic tigers and bears and eagles large enough to snatch a cow in their crooked claws. But the reality is the other way around. We're tougher than other animals. We're top predator. I followed, and the deer kept giving me anxious over-the-shoulder glances, and hobbled on. I think if it *had* been a bête it would have tried to reason with me. The fact that it didn't attempt that reassures me, some. At any rate, it could not rejoin its fellows.

I followed it for maybe half an hour, and then I stopped and hid behind a tree. The deer limped on a little way, and then lay down and began licking its hurt leg. I found a suitable rock and padded, as quietly as I could. The creature saw me coming, but didn't get up. Instead it lifted its slipper-shaped nose and its Bambi eyes. Given the obvious differences between human eyes and animal eyes, and how much human expressiveness depends upon the proportion of white on display, it was a disarmingly human look. It looked up at me, as if I had come to make the pain go away. I brought out the rock, and the expression changed. The deer stirred, trying to rise, and I threw the stone down onto its head. The first blow rolled its neck against the ground, so I picked up my weapon and picked my spot and hit down, hard. I saw the bane of death enter the bloodstream, and the eyes lose whatever it is they lose when life evaporates. I've killed a lot of animals in my time, but never one like that.

It took me a while to drag the carcass back to my tent. I hung it from a tree eight hundred yards from where I slept, and cut the throat; but it was long dead, and the blood came out only sluggishly. Then I did what I could to cut the best meat from the thing with my knife. I lacked the proper tools – I had relinquished all my butchery kit when Anne had died, and carried only a single blade into the woodland. But it was better than a Palaeolithic flint. I made a fire and started cooking two fillets of thigh until it started raining and the fire went out. Even though I was very hungry, I waited until the rain stopped, and then everted my damp firestack to get at the drier stuff inside, and relit it. It smoked and spat and cackled like a witch, but eventually it got going again, and I held the two fillets over the hottest part on their sticks. The smell tickled some pleasure centre in my brain that I had forgotten I had. Just anticipating eating was a pure, physical joy. When the meat was ready I had to exercise deliberate, self-conscious restraint to prevent myself gobbling both steaks straight down. They were delicious.

So I stayed for a week or so in and about my tent, drinking rainwater, cutting slices of increasingly game meat from my kill, and eating it *bien cuit* or rare, depending on how cooperative the elements were in terms of my fire. I felt no desire to go anywhere else.

Hunger is a very simple tyranny. Recently generations have arisen that never experience it – never properly experience it, I mean. You have not lived with a belly so empty that the back of your belly button (that inner little knot of hardness just under the skin of the navel) touches your spine. You have never lived such that you have not known not only *where* your next meal is coming from but *if there is even going to be a next meal*. I cannot exactly recommend it, but it certainly simplifies things, and that might be counted an advantage. Of course, it does so by bleaching away all the refinements that adorn human life. When I was a teenager I had baited my father with the closest I came to adolescent rebellion: that I would not carry on with the farm but would instead go to university (no!) and study English literature (no! no!) and write poetry like Hughes and Heaney (who?). Of these shuddering blasphemies I had actually committed only the latter, and then only in privately hoarded notebooks. But I had a thousand poems by heart, and this is what I discovered. When I was properly hungry they all vanished out of my head. I had all the leisure time I could have desired, and often I experienced an acute sensation of boredom, but *nothing at all* from my former pretentions to civilization remained with me. There was only hunger, and the anxiety that that hunger would never be assuaged. It expanded, like insulating foam, inside my skull until everything else was pushed out. When I used my imagination it was only to conjure memories of food. I dreamt of food. I fantasized about food. And after I killed that deer, I had a week of luxury of almost lascivious intensity – because for a whole week I didn't have to worry where my next meal was coming from.

Eventually the carcass rotted too far to be edible. It attracted dogs from the first day I butchered it. Suspended by its rear hooves yards above the forest floor there was little the dogs could do except leap and snap at its lifeless snout, but I had to scare the dumb mutts away with shouts and a stick. Each time I did so they came back with a larger pack, and every augmentation made them less fearful. It was too late in the year, and too cold, for flies to be a problem; and the occasional crow tugging to unravel the knitted thread of muscle flesh could be encouraged to depart with a thrown pebble. But putrefaction could not be held at bay, and eventually I cut the thing down and let the dogs tussle over the remains, whilst I sat in my tree with a pointed stick, watching them.

Many mornings I would wake to find the forest floor flooded with mist; and I would poke my head out of my tent and look down, imagining I was in the gondolier of some balloon floating above the clouds.

I go to Wokingham

Then for a time I became restless. I took advantage of one dry morning to pack everything up and yomp north-west. The meat had reminded me how enjoyable it was to have a full belly, and I had the vague plan of going to the nearest town – Wokingham – and obtaining supplies. There was still some money on my chip; and I was ready to go through the bins if I needed to. As I walked, the clouds inked themselves in, and soon a light rain started.

I hiked through drizzle that made the carpeting leaves slippy. The weight of my backpack meant that I fell over a couple of times; but by the same token I fell onto beds of wet leaves and did not hurt myself. Only birds observed my comedy pratfalls, and since they said nothing to me they were either not bêtes or else so deeply unimpressed they felt they had nothing to add.

I crossed several deserted roads, and eventually reached the place where the trees gave way to back gardens, and so on through the small ring of suburbs and up to Wokingham high street, which is shaped like a diviner's twig.

The shops were all boarded up, and there was nobody about. There were many cars, parked along the narrow roads; but all of the windscreens were plastered by POLICE AWARE notices, and every chassis was layered with the make-up foundation of months of dirt. One, parked outside what had once been a Costa, even had a rusting clamp fitted to its front wheel: an artefact from a previous age.

I made my way along the street, stopping at shops to peer

through the chinks in the boarding, or the lattice of the metal shutters, to see if there were any cans, or dried goods, or other comestibles inside that might make a break-in worth attempting. I saw a lot of empty cells: dusty and dim. Carpets showed tan lines where units had once stood. I saw little autumnal heaps of paper and envelopes piled on the inside of glass doors. A ghost town where even the ghosts had given up and moved on.

I explored side roads. Some of the houses were still being maintained – or, at least, had *been being* maintained until recently; but most were already displaying inevitable symptoms of ongoing dilapidation. I essayed a few of these, and broke in at the back of a couple; but the owners had cleared out anything edible before departing. In one the burglar alarm had been set, and a strange voice boomed out of the ceiling: 'You have been captured on video! These images are being transferred to the authorities! You are an intruder!' I looked about for a camera, but not noticing one gave the middle finger to the air in general. Only as I clambered out through the back door did I twig whose voice had been sampled for the alarm – which was still going on behind me ('We're on to you! Proceed to the nearest police station with all haste!'). Patrick Stewart, of blessed memory.

I heard a few voices, but none of them were human. The machine at a pedestrian crossing spoke to me. I broke into a shop and checked out the supplies of bread makers and kettles and microwaves on the shelves, and a few even had enough battery power to chirp 'Buy me! Buy me!' in my direction. But it was food I was looking for, and there didn't seem to be any.

I walked all the way up to the railway station, thinking there might at least be a vending machine there; but the whole site was closed, and wire fences erected to stop people from approaching the building. My mood soured. Coming into town had been a bust; a waste of time and energy.

Coming back along the road into town I met a man. He greeted me from a distance by shouting 'Mucca! Mucca!' at the top of his voice. When I got closer I could see the suspicion on his face. 'What's your game?'

'I'm a tourist,' I said, gruffly, unused to speaking aloud. My voice sounded monstrously unfamiliar in my own head. Was that *me*, John Wayne? Is this you?

The other fellow was twitchy. 'What do you mean tourist? Pulling *your* leg, you mean.'

We stopped, a yard from one another, and observed one another warily. He had a skinchin beard and a pale, oval bald patch in the middle of his black hair. There was something not right about his eyes.

'Visit Wokingham in the picturesque autumn,' I growled. 'The land flows with milk and honey and oh how welcoming the natives.'

'Graham,' he said.

'Do I *know* you?' I asked, crossly. I didn't know him.

'I didn't know you were *called* Graham!' he replied. 'Didn't bother to find out, sorry about the old woman, it's a saveloy and the kindness would be remarkable.' He was picking up speed. 'There's nobody *here*. You come to visit someone? You came in by train? He didn't come by train, you fucker-witter, the station's decommissioned. Cunt! I know that! Scary sclery. Sclery.'

'Who are you?'

'I'm nightwatchmen. Appointed by the town council to look

after things until, you know. We get off the war footing and back to normality, cunt! – and they all come back.'

'Where did they all go?' I asked.

'Bracknell, some; Reading, more. Others went otherswise. He doesn't believe you Benjamin Robert Haydon, standing on the shoulders of *gigantic* giants. Anywayup, I'm still here. There's no money. You can't mug me. Hold no bolt-gun to my temples, cunny, cunny. When *Graham* was actoring, Rome – stop! Enough, or too much! Or one much, or no much, or minus. Minus.'

Over the months alone my brain had grown unused to thinking in the abstract way civilized human brains think: possibilities, counterfactuals, imaginative empathy. But my time in the forest had certainly brought out the core *brute* way of thinking – by which I mean, I was finely attuned to anything that might impinge upon my personal survival. Animals in the wild are all paranoid, after all, all the time, and for good cause. And I had become an animal in the wild.

So it was that the truth of this strange man flashed up in my head: he was a human being with a human's thinking brain, but he had also been fitted, for whatever reason, with a bête chip, like a canny cow or a talking dog. As to why a human being would think it a good idea to get such a thing implanted inside him, I have no idea. Curiosity might be a motive; or some misplaced sense of Green-human solidarity with bêtes everywhere. Or maybe it had happened accidentally – perhaps even he had been punished with it. It's hard to see that even the most devout environmentalist would voluntarily seek out schizophrenia after this manner.

Yes, I know what you're thinking: *the irony.* Fuck that.

I took a step back. *He* had not recognized me; his chip had recognized me. Plugged into the internet, it was talking with other chips – in the heads of cats and rats and dogs and hogs. This was not a situation I was happy with.

His face flinched. I took another step back, and eyed his blue jacket. Its pockets were bulging; but with what? Was there a weapon in there? I glanced at the surroundings. There was precious little cover, unless I could break into one of the houses.

'Where's your chip actually located?' I asked. 'Inside the brain? Some of them are just in at the back of the throat, roof of the mouth, that sort of area – isn't that right? They put out filaments into the relevant centres of the brain. You want that I put my fist hard into your throat?'

'Oh, Graham,' said the man. 'You're *scaring* Benjamin Robert Haydon.'

'Words cannot begin to express the vehemence of my regret,' I said, backing away. 'Are *you* keeping him here?'

'He's not the only one,' said Benjamin Robert Haydon, and with a shoulder jerk that made his hands bounce up, 'not the *fucking* snow patrol. In the lee of the scare. I'll be master in my own house, thank you very much. Master-mistress of my parse, parse, *pass*ion.' He rubbed his face vigorously. Then he stood still as a statue and said: 'It's more of a *challenge*, certainly, than a cow.'

An unpleasant sensation, something crawling and uneasy, was inside my skull. Did I not like this. 'An experiment?' I asked.

'Oh Benjamin Robert Haydon was only too *keen* to have the chip,' said Benjamin Robert Haydon. 'And that's the question, though, isn't it, Graham? Would you feel any compunction about putting the bolt-gun to *his* head?' I turned on my heel and marched as fast as my hunger and my heavy pack permitted, away from that person. 'Tell me in what the difference inheres,' he called after. 'Tell me *why* it's different, Graham.'

They knew I was there, which meant I needed to be somewhere else. I heard footsteps, and Benjamin Robert Haydon was trotting after me. But then he stopped, and grappled with his own head with both arms, putting his elbows in front of his face. Then he let his arms hang loose at his side. I had stopped my retreat, to observe this strange display, but I picked up the pace again sharpish. The last thing he said to me was: 'You should have gone to see the Lamb when the cat told you! Now it's too late! It's war, Graham! War!'

I moved quickly through the suburbs. When I felt I was far enough from the centre I even gave over some time to searching a few of the houses on the way out. I found a packet of bourbon biscuits, some dry pasta and a tin of catfood. So the raid wasn't a complete waste of time.

I go to a house

I found another spot in the woods, and pitched my tent again. The only animals I saw for a long time were dumb. At least, as best as I could tell.

The weather turned colder still, and – for the first time – I began to think seriously about rejoining civilization. Day turned to night and back to day, and I asked myself when had I last felt *warm*? I wrapped everything I had about me but still couldn't stop shivering. Shivers passed up my body from legs to neck in waves, like a fever. Freezing clouds shook their flour sieves over the trees. A chill deposit of white accumulated on the forest floor at a compound interest.

I watched flakes of snow land in one of the open bowls I

was using to catch rainwater: the first few dissolved in the water, but soon they lay themselves as gently on the surface as lilypads, and spread themselves into star-shaped crystals. Soon enough all the branches had thin white ropes carefully laid across their tops, and the red-brown leaves on the ground were spotted and foxed with white.

Food wholly filled my thoughts. If I tried to think of anything else, my brain shoved thought back to food. Nothing else mattered.

I went foraging and hunting and felt ravenous all the time. The layer of ice over the top of one of the forest ponds reminded me of the fat in a pork pie; and the black tube of a fallen tree trunk made me think of chocolate logs at Christmas. At one point I became convinced that there was a slice of cured ham simply lying on the forest floor. I picked it up with trembling gloved hands, and wiped the snow from it. A leaf, of course; perhaps slightly pinker than the rest but very obviously a leaf. I was stumbling about in a hallucinatory daze. You're wondering why I put myself through it; why I didn't just go back to the comforts of real life. I can only reply: *haven't you been paying attention?*

I had more or less resolved to give up the forest and return to humanity when the weather warmed. Not that it got warm, exactly; but it stopped snowing and I stopped shivering, and managed to catch three fish in one day. Some of my strength returned to me.

One morning was unusually misty. I walked the forest, my legs cloaked in invisibility, just a torso bobbing along the top of the clouds. My foot fell away beneath me and I was sliding down on my arse before I realized that what I had taken to be the hushing of wind in the trees was actually the noise of the stream. The water was painfully cold, and put tongues up inside both my trouser legs to my thigh. I stomped home in a bad mood.

Then the late autumnal sun came out and warmed the mist away, and I dried, and lay on a bough feeling more at peace. This was a turning point, of sorts.

I packed up my stuff and walked off.

After a day's walk I slept in a tree, and got up again before sunrise and walked on.

I came upon a cottage, an hour or two after dawn: the sun low in the sky. I was very hungry.

The back door was old chipboard, and the corner where it fitted into the door jamb was scrabbled away near the ground. Canny beasts might have done that, though they'd be more likely to pick the lock, or break a window; so I figured dumb beasts. And I figured the owner hadn't mended the door, so they must have vacated. Like any other beast of the field, I wondered if there was valuable stuff inside there, so I went over, and pulled at the broken corner of the door with main strength. It wasn't too hard to break it up to the lock, and since the key was in the hole on the inside I soon had it open.

Inside was dim, and smelled of fusty old nothing. There was a tang to the air as well, something vaguely chemical and tart, but only faintly so. The back door gave me access to a small room containing an off-white washing machine, circa 1950-something, and all the paraphernalia needful for the cleaning of clothes. There were shelves with white card-board boxes foaming at the mouth with powdery white, and a spotty green clothes basket propped in the corner. Everything looked tatty and old, excepting only a new pack of rainbow plastic clothes pegs, still in rank and file, biting a rectangle of cardboard. After months of nothing but natural hues there's something really inexpressibly shocking about the *brightness* of new coloured plastic. Only the green of fresh spring leaves can match it for intensity and texture.

I went through to the kitchen. The floor under the table seethed with woodlice. I rummaged through the cupboards, and put two tins of peeled plum tomatoes and one of chickpeas in my rucksack. There was a loaf in the breadbin but it looked like a woad-painted bust of the elephant man. The fridge was unplugged and empty; somebody had already cleaned it out. In another cupboard I found a pack of supernoodles in blue foil next to a miniature bottle army of half-empty and empty spice jars. I left the spice jars, telling myself that I wasn't about to start haute cuisine-ing it; and the bread was obviously beyond the pale. But I took the rest. That was the whole of my haul.

It wasn't a large cottage. The sitting room was a dusty sofa and a dusty easy chair, a television in the corner and a bookcase. From the latter I took an 1890 prose translation of Aeschylus's *Oresteia*, because I liked the dignified old royal blue binding, and because I fancied having something to read when the boredom became overwhelming. The other volumes were all sermons, commentaries upon the Revelation of Saint John, preacher's autobiographies with smiling black-and-white photographs of their authors' phizogs on the cover. A strange hoard, really. There was a low table in front of the sofa, covered in dust, and upon it only one thing – the triangular blade of a sheep's shoulder bone, clean as a whistle. A paperweight, maybe. Strange to find it there all on its own.

For some reason I was reluctant to go upstairs, but in the event I figured: in for a penny. So I stepped up the loudly complaining wooden stair slats, and put my head into the little bedroom that was all that was up there. Somebody was in the bed, and although they were very obviously not breathing I called out 'Hello? Hello?' in a quavery voice. I felt my own foolishness quite sharply as I did this; for even if she *had* been alive, how would calling out 'hello' with a question mark at the end defuse her panic at a stranger crashing through her bedroom door?

She was lying on her back with her arms outside the duvet, and her head on the pillow, and she looked about two hundred years old. This, looking back, may have had to do with the scleritis, since the scar tissue chews up a fatal proportion of a person's mucus membranes and this tends to dry the body out. Blackness had seeped from her nostrils, and the corners of her eyes, and had left dried snail trails down the sides of her face and on the pillow; but the eyes were completely occluded with scar tissue, and the lips looked like they had been repeatedly cut up and stitched back together.

This was the first victim of scleritis I ever saw. Only belatedly did I feel the jolt of panic in my breast. My own foolishness again. She had clearly not died of natural causes; and whatever she *had* died of might very well be contagious. I went down the creaky staircase like a boot avalanche and burst out into the daylight, gasping.

My panic soon left me, and I felt doubly foolish – first for blundering in without a second thought, and then for over-reacting so stupidly. I returned to the cottage later that same day. I wanted to see if there were more things inside worthy of salvaging; I wanted at least to be thorough. But I was reluctant to go straight back inside. So I retreated to the edge of the woodland, fifty metres from the cottage back door, and slung my tent between two fat elms, far enough into the forest to

146

be invisible to anybody looking inside. It is a little hard for me to remember exactly why I did this; except that I wanted neither to leave the cottage nor, yet, go back inside it. Hunger was doing my thinking for me. My brain was not.

I stayed there three days. Every now and then I left my tent to draw water from the cottage's external tap, easing the hose off its spigot like a dairy farmer decoupling the milking machine. I was no longer a farmer. The first time I filled my billycan from the tap I worried whether the mysterious disease that had destroyed the woman inside was also in her water supply. But I hushed my paranoia and drank, and I was fine. I opened my haul of tins with a knife, one one day, another the next, and ate the contents cold – the chickpeas were particularly filling. I slept in the afternoon. I was woken by the sound of a telephone, ringing inside the cottage. I listened to its chirruping insistence, softened to a pleasant kind of washboard rhythm by the distance. Eventually it stopped. The telephone rang twice more, once that evening and once again the following morning.

On the second day I ate fresh-picked mushrooms and one unwary hedgehog, which I cooked in my usual way by rolling it in mud and baking it in an open fire. There's not much meat on a hedgehog and I finished the meal still hungry. But I was holding off the supernoodles as a special treat, so I sucked a pebble to take the edge off my hunger.

The third day was bright, and I felt a weird febrile joy rising from my hollow, complaining stomach. I stared at the way the leaves looked in the brightness: fin-shaped, ten thousand of them. Breaking sunlight into a web of brightness that trembled on the ground. It seemed almost an omen, so I sneaked back into the kitchen to steal a saucepan, and took it outside. I cooked up the supernoodles in that pan over an open fire, and broke my fast with them. What a meal they made! I felt like a cow at a salt lick. It wasn't the noodles as such; it was the little pouch of salinated curry powder. My head nearly imploded with the delight of it. I could have wept with joy. Scalloped patterns of shade on the forest floor. Afterwards I slept and woke up feeling refreshed in a way I had not for months.

The success of this persuaded me back in the house yet again. I had, clearly, been neglecting my salt intake; and even if there were no more good food in the cottage I had seen spices and table salt in those cupboards. So I braced myself and went back in the musty-smelling kitchen, and put a cylinder of Tesco own-brand salt in my backpack. I searched amongst the spice jars but all were empty, save only a quarter-full vial of cinnamon, which I took.

I searched the rest of the ground floor. There was a half-sized wooden door that opened onto some down steps, which in turn led down to a tiny cellar – perhaps six foot square. This smelled strongly of earth and decay, and the light didn't work. By the small amount of illumination coming in from outside I saw nothing edible down there. I was hoping for wine, but there was no wine.

Coming back up I heard the distinctive fizzing noise of an approaching car, and hurried through the back door in time to see it turn from the main road onto the overgrown driveway. The wheels of the vehicle puffed up, or otherwise expanded, to accommodate the shift from tarmac to turf. A large-framed, rectangular car, white-coloured. The windshield was darkened against the bright sun, though the side windows were clear. I had evidently been seen. There was no point in making a run for it. So, I zipped up my backpack and stood placidly.

The car turned broadside to me and stopped, the electric

motor shifting low hum to high-pitched whine as it transferred its momentum to its gyro. The driver's door opened with a sigh, popping out before swinging wide. Inside was a woman in her thirties, and just beyond her a man of about the same age. Two dogs occupied the rear seats. Both the canines poked their heads out the open door, over the top of the driver's seat, to take a look at me. One of the two quickly grew bored and drew his head back inside, but the other continued staring at me with a peculiar focus that told me what it was.

The woman addressed me: 'Norman?'

Living in the woods had driven a kind of placidity into my soul I suppose. I neither denied nor acknowledged the name. I simply stood and looked at her.

Behind her, the man spoke: 'Good God, Norman. What's with the *beard*?'

'Hardly recognized you!' The woman hopped lightly from the driver's seat. 'Where's your car?'

'Norman,' said the man, popping the passenger door and climbing out with considerably less grace than his partner. 'Is she all right? We're braced for the worst. We're braced.'

I shook my head, slowly. The woman opened her mouth a little way, and pushed her knuckles inside.

'Were you with her at the end?' the man asked.

'She was gone,' I replied, 'when I got here.' I spoke with that croaky quality any voice acquires when it has not been used in a while. The sound of my speaking failed to disabuse them of their idea that I was Norman.

'Oh God,' said the man. 'Ghastly.'

One of the dogs had eeled between the two front car seats and poked its head outside. It was staring at me. It put its head a little to one side.

'Did you park on the far side of the copse?' the woman asked, evidently bothered by the absence of any motor vehicle she could ascribe to me.

'Stop grilling him, Sandra,' the man snapped, stepping towards me and holding out his hand. I shook it, and he cast a puzzled glance at my grimy fingers and palms.

'You're right,' said Sandra. 'I'm sorry Norman. How beastly – to find her already gone. We called and called. I *told* Phil she shouldn't be left out here on her own.'

The man – I made the assumption he was Phil – had his phone out. 'I'll notify the ... well. I suppose the *authorities*. I wonder who to call?' He put the phone to his mouth. 'Siri, who must we notify of a death in the Swithley district?'

'Dialling the number now,' replied the phone.

'Have *you* seen Phil?' Sandra asked me. I looked at the man, now intent on his iCell, and when her gaze did not follow I realized that he was not the Phil to whom they had referred. This was the point at which I thought of informing them of my true name and identity. But things had gone too far for that. I considered the likely possibilities for *Phil*, and deduced he was a man charged with checking-up on the woman inside the cottage. Given her state it was clear nobody had been to see her in a while. 'Not for weeks,' I said.

'I never quite trusted him,' said Sandra bitterly. 'But Tark insisted upon him. Scan suggested three others, you know, and one of those was a woman. But Tark said: no, no, Phil's ex-army, he's the one.'

'Ah, hello,' said the man, evidently 'Tark'. 'I'd like to report a death. It's my great-aunt. Great-aunt-in-law actually. She lives at Mod Cottage, yes, yes. That's right. I'm there now, co-ords, that's right. Cause of death?' He glanced at me, but carried on smoothly. 'Old age, she was very old.'

'I never trusted him,' said Sandra again. 'Never saw why ex-army was a recommendation. When you think of the types who go into the army in the first place.'

'Discipline!' Tark said forcefully. '*That's* what the army teaches.'

The other dog, the non-bête one, squirmed fully out between the front seats, eager to exit the car. In a moment it was free, and galloping through the long grass of the cottage garden into the trees. My stuff was there, and I almost went running after the creature; but I would never have caught it. 'Toby,' the man yelled, holding the phone away from his mouth. 'To*bee*!'

'Oh let him go, Tarquin,' said Sandra. 'He's been cooped up in the car.'

The second dog was still looking at me. There was no doubt in my mind as to the respective loquaciousness of the two hounds.

'It wasn't actually me who discovered the body,' Tarquin told the person at the other end of his phone. 'It was – yes, he's here with me now. Yes. Called *Nor*man Speight. Ee-eye, yes. Ee, eye, gee, etch, tea, that's. Oh he's an *old* family friend. He—' A pause. 'Do you need to speak to him? Oh. Yah. Nah, OK.'

'We should probably go inside,' said Sandra. 'Have a cup of tea. But it feels odd, the idea of sitting in there and drinking *tea* whilst she's—' She gave me a queer look. 'She is still in there?'

I nodded. 'In bed,' I said.

'When did you find her?' she asked me. 'I mean, when did you get here? Where *did* you park, by the way?'

'They'll send someone,' Tarquin called, slipping his iCell back into his jacket pocket. 'Doesn't have to be an actual coroner. A

GP or even nurse can sign off on the, you know. My God,' he added, noticing the damage for the first time, 'the *door*!'

He disappeared into the cottage, complaining noisily about vandals. Sandra was giving me more and more penetrating looks. 'Are you all right, Norman?' she asked. 'You seem—' When I didn't reply she supplied her own explanation. 'I suppose it is a shock. I mean, it's not like she was young, but.'

'Sandra!' called Tarquin from inside the cottage.

Sandra went inside, and I heard her going up the creaky stairs. I sat down on the ground. I'm not as young as I used to be, and I was tired of standing up. The second dog slid slinkily out of the car, and padded over to me. 'You!' it gasped. 'Not! Noh! Man!'

'Fuck you,' I said.

'I *know*,' the dog growled, 'yah! name!'

'Bully for you.'

'Womoh!' the dog barked. 'Womoh! Sacer!'

'How cross would your owners be if I wrung your hairy neck?'

'Hah!' the dog said. It didn't laugh; it spoke, or rather growled, the syllable. 'Hah! Hah!'

The sound of Tarquin and Sandra coming precipitously down the stairs was clearly audible through the wall. 'My God, Norman,' Tark shrieked, emerging through the back door. 'Why didn't you *say* she had the sclery?' He had the lapel of his jacket turned up, and was holding it over his nose.

'My God!' Sandra cried. 'We were in the same room! I almost touched her! 'Oh God!'

The dog drew his black lips back and grinned knowingly at me, letting his beef-coloured tongue loll. I experienced the sensation of dawning realization without knowing what it was

I was realizing. Something going on, a profound insight into the way bêtes and humans were interacting. Something had changed. What was it, though? Sandra was washing her hands and face at the outside tap, gasping with the coldness of the water. Tark was on his phone again, calling back. 'Norman why didn't you *say*?' he called across to me, accusingly. 'Hello? Hello? Yes, I called a moment ago.'

'I see why you're being so,' Sandra said standing up, her sweater damp down the front. 'So shell-shocked or whatever. My God, Norman! I didn't know.'

Tarquin's bray: 'Hello, yes I *said* natural causes, I said – hello?'

The dumb dog came galloping out of the forest, looking absurdly pleased with itself.

'I reported natural causes but now it seems – yes—' and he gulped, like a frog '—Sclerotic charagmitis, yes.'

The dumb dog came to a halt by it mistress, and began licking her wet hand. With a smooth motion she caught it by the collar – I saw now that the dumb dog was collared, and the bête's neck was naked – and swept it into the car. 'Norm,' she said. 'I'm so sorry. Call, yeah? You have my number. Yeah?'

The bête jumped neatly into the car, after its companion. In a moment Sandra and Tark were inside. The last I saw of them was them both rubbing something (sanitizer gel, I suppose) onto their hands. Then the doors whumped shut, the gyro gave up its tight-turning velocity and the engine buzzed into life.

In a moment they were gone.

I sat for a while in the sunlight. Then I went back into the trees, and I rolled up my tent, and I loaded up my backpack, and walked off.

I am drunk

I left because of the way the dog had been looking at me. It had not been at the forefront of my mind for a while, being so isolated; but it didn't do to forget it – bêtes were at that point connected to one another, thanks to the facile internet. The old internet. The dog seeing me meant that a great many other bêtes were aware of me. I needed to remove myself.

I hiked for half a day. Walking through a wood is a particular sort of perambulation: the way everything crowds around you makes it impossible to orient yourself with respect to the larger landscape by sight. Everything seems the same; you appear to make no progress – except by noting the upward, or downward, slope of the ground. Not that it mattered where I was going.

Speaking to other human beings seemed to have tripped some switch in my brain, because I was chattering as I walked. 'First sign of madness, eh, Anne?' I said. 'Can you even hear me? I wouldn't blame you for pissing off – afterlife, nirvana, either's good. Why would you stay in amongst all these trees? Oh here's a derelict car, Anne. You think they happened to leave a crate of beer in the back, Anne? No – no. Of course not.' I explored the old Ford: white metal covered all over by the autumnal blossom of rust. The windscreen was gone, and the footwell full of years-old leaves. There was nothing in the back. 'I know, I know,' I said to the air. 'My liver is grateful. You're right, you're right.'

The trees all around shuffled their leaves like a croupier readying a deal, only to scatter them all carelessly on the floor. The wind that moved up there didn't reach to the ground. I moved on.

I only later became acquainted with the name of the disease

Tarquin reported to the authorities on his phone: sclerotic charagmitis. The scary sclery. That was my first encounter with it. It was obviously bad news, though. I found a good tree and set up my tent. Foraging brought in very little by way of food, though; and in a few days the weather turned cold once again. The clouds were black. The occasional blue-white flake of snow span in the breeze like a cinder, although snow didn't settle.

I decided to forage again. The next day I explored my new area. There was a row of empty houses maybe half a mile from my camp, but these had been properly boarded up – metal shutters over the windows, crossbars on all the doors. I could perhaps have broken in, but it would have been effortful, and the odds were the people who secured these properties had emptied them first. So I passed on.

I walked along the road between two overgrown fields and came at last to a pub, standing in the midst of nowhereness. Autumn fields, ungrazed, bristly with man-high grass.

There was one vehicle in the customer car park, and another tucked away behind the external architecture of the air con, so I deduced the place wasn't likely to be too crowded. I still had a little money on my chip, and I figured I could fill my belly, and enjoy my first taste of alcohol in months, and then slip away again. Still, I had to brace myself to go through the door. I summoned up my courage.

Opening the door set off an electronic chime: the first ten notes of 'Yellow Submarine' – it struck me then, a weirdly melancholy tune, trotting along and then diving down into the gloom. It suited the inside, though, which managed to be both very cheesily decorated and also extremely mournful-looking. Low-ceilinged, unmodernized, dusty.

There were more people inside than I had anticipated. Three

were sat at tables staring at their drinks. Another man sat at the bar, nursing a tall glass filled with blue liquid like the sorts of things chemists used to stick in their front windows. Perhaps all four had crammed into the Prius outside; or perhaps they had walked; or perhaps they were always here, sipping beer in a Sartrean silence. They all looked at me when I entered, without the least positivity in their faces. Two Labradors were sprawled on the floor – both, I guessed, dumb beasts.

The barman was a very large man wearing a MANCHESTER CUNTED shirt. His head was pear-shaped and massive, his face a landslide of features. I ordered a pint and enquired after food, and he didn't move from his stool, didn't so much as reach for an empty glass. 'No offence,' he said. 'But, from the look of yer.'

I handed over my chip. His eyebrows went up – as if I were trying to pay with dubloons, or an IOU signed by the devil. But he checked the credit. 'This yours?'

'Of course it is,' I said.

'Money in it's not been touched for months and months.' Pronounced *mumfz*.

'Odd you should say that,' I said. 'Given that I take the money out every night and rub my cock with it.'

'Unspent since April,' he said doggedly. 'What you been living on?'

'Air,' I said. 'You going to pull me a fucking pint, or you want the Archbishop of Canterbury personally to stop by and vouch for me?'

At this point the man sitting at the bar, the one with the blue drink, chipped in. 'We'd rather,' he said, 'cash.'

'I didn't realize I'd stepped into a pub conveniently located on the outskirts of the fucking eighteen nineties,' I said. 'What's it to *you*? You work here?'

'Just saying,' the fellow wheezed, not meeting my eye. 'Dollars for preference. Euros at a pinch.'

'My coach and four is parked outside, I'll just pop out, fetch my purse of golden guineas.' I turned back to barman. 'The chip's kosher. Pour me the pint.'

All eyes were on me. Slowly, with a walrus grace, the barman slid from his stool and put a glass under the tap. The dogs laid their heads back on the floor. The people at the table went back to their mumbled conversation. Looking around I noticed for the first time a large grey parrot perched on a beam, over by the back door. I took this for a stuffed ornament; but when the beer was put in front of me the beast swivelled his head and scratched its talons on the wood.

'Food?' I asked.

'Jesus Onion,' said the barman. 'Red Yseult.'

'Crisps?' I said, a little peevishly. I was starving, and there's nothing much *in* crisps for the truly empty belly. 'You got nothing more substantial?'

He gave this a think. 'Porn cockatiel?'

'You mean an actual prawn cocktail? Or you mean, flavoured crisps?' A twitch of the head indicated that the latter, and I sighed. 'Better than nothing I suppose,' I said. 'Three packs, please. Let us have one of each, why not, push the fucking boat out.' Filling this order entailed the barman moving to the far end of the bar, which took a while. Whilst he was occupied I drank my pint, more or less in one go. It was the single most delicious thing I had tasted all year. Any words of mine that purported to do justice to the experience would be mere mendacity. It transcended words. My whole head lightened, de-leaded. My heart relaxed inside my chest. I had not realized how wound up and tense I was until I de-wound and untensed. The beer took the worst away from my hunger. I ate the crisps, and ordered a second drink. The barman scowled so hard it looked like the corners of his mouth had been pinned down to his chin with tent pegs, but he poured me another.

'No offence,' the man with the blue drink said. He still hadn't touched his refreshment. 'But you *do* look like a tramp.'

'No offence,' I said. 'But you *do* look like you fuck goats.' Somebody at the table sniggered at this, and suddenly the entire mood in the pub shifted about. Even the barman relaxed.

'Don't mean to be inhospital,' said the blue-drink man. 'Inhosbubble. Don't mean to be—' He sighed, gave up on the word and stared into space. Then, finally, for the first time since I'd come in, he took a slurp from his medicinal-looking drink. 'Difficult days, these days.'

'This your pub?'

'Noddy Holder's brother, lease,' he said. 'To speak of the *woe* that is in running a pub. Custom's fallen off a cliff. No one has any money. Hardly anyone in the countryside even runs a car any more. Everyone's moved. Reading, Bracknell, into London.' He shook his head. 'My investors are not happy.'

'You have investors?'

'Don't mean to be in-ho-*spit*-able, brother,' he said, finally getting it out. 'Could use all the new custom we can get. Hey, maybe you'll become a beloved regular! But chip money's not the reliant thing it once was. The thing I don't understand,' he added, with a little spurt of energy, 'is the economics of this plague.'

'Plague?'

He looked at me. The barman looked at me. The three people

at the table looked at me. I took another swig of beer. My gut, unused to such richness, was rumbling uncertainly.

'*You* know about sclery,' said the leaseholder. '*You're* just pulling my leg.'

One old geezer spoke up from the group at the table: 'My brother-in-law went up to Huddersfield for a job. Got there, laid-off, *he* slept rough for a month or so. He didn't like it. Tried hitching back down here, the poe lice stuck him inside.'

'Is that actual illegal now?' enquired another of the fellows at the table. 'Hitching?'

But the first man hadn't finished story. 'Ended up walking all the way back. Lost two stone, and got home smelling like a rat's arse. Like a,' he repeated, as if it were particularly important we grasp this crucial element in the narrative, 'rat's. *Arse*. He's gone to Gdansk now.'

'That Gene?' asked another fellow.

'Did you ever know O'Riordan?' asked another. 'Down Bagshot way?'

'I know him.'

'Died of the sclery. Last week it was. It was Jim told me.'

Everybody sucked their teeth at this news, and there was a moment of silence. I slurped my second pint glass and picked fussily at the last crumbs of crisp at the bottom of the packet, licking the tip of my finger to get the individual flakes to adhere. Fish food.

'What I don't *under*stand,' said the barman, deciding belatedly to contribute to the conversation, 'is why everybody's packing together. All packing into Bracknell like sardines in a ...' He stared into space, presumably trying to remember the name of that metal item inside which sardines proverbially congregate.

'His missus went to Bracknell with a electric engineer,' the blue-drink man told me, in a confidential tone. 'He's not happy about it.'

'Packing themselves in,' the barman continued. 'Now, *when* there was a great plague of London that was because they were all *packed* in. Weren't it? Tell me I'm wrong!' He looked about, and repeated his request, sweetening the offer with an extra: 'Tell me I'm wrong and I'll fuck you in yer ear.'

Silence.

'Bracknell's bad, Reading's crowdeder. But packin' em in the ole days made the plague *worse*.'

Nobody was inclined to challenge his interpretation of the epidemiology of that particular historical calamity.

'So tell the sense in packing yourselves into the cities? Infection spreads. That's why they call it – well, why they. Well. Anyway. Infection spreads. When they stack apples, though, *don't* they make sure they're not all jostling in with one another? The countryside is all deserted now. I'd rather be here. We're further from the sclery out *here*, I reckon.' He fell silent, musing on his own words.

'Indulge me,' I said. 'I have been *so* far out of the loop lately, the loop is now a dot to me. What's slary?'

'Before they cut off the wifi,' said one of the men at the table – and at this, everybody at the table groaned with miserable recognition.

'They cut off your wifi?'

'Not just ours,' said the leaseholder. 'There's no internet access anywhere in the countryside now, pretty much. Been that way a month, or more. You *are* behind the times, my friend.'

'*Before* they cut off the wifi,' the guy at the table repeated,

'I watched a documentary about it. Sclerotic charagmitis. Nasty way to go.'

'Is it really a plague?' I asked, wide-eyed. The beer was aiding my ingenuousness.

'Spreads like flu,' said the man at the table.

'No, no, like AIDS,' said another.

'Flu. Yer mucus membranes all scar over. That's the thing.'

'I heard you're OK *until* you cut yourself,' said another. 'Even if the virus's in you. So long as you walk about cotton-wool-like, you're good to go. But one little cut! Graze the knee, and the scarring sets in as a catastrophic, eh, *domino* thing. One cut to the finger and you can be turned into a scarred-up mummy-a-like in hours.'

'Bollocks,' said another.

'The thing about AIDS,' said the other, 'is that they cured AIDS. They'll cure the sclery, too.'

The others were not so sanguine. 'It firulent,' said one. 'Real firulent. *Mucus membranes* are what they call the lining of your froat and sign-arses, and deeper and *down* into lungs. That's what scars, all that. Not *so* much the outside skin.'

'I helped wrap Maddie Elsever in plastic,' the AIDS-optimist fellow said. '*I* saw her. She was all scrabbled on the outside, like stitching on a leather sofa.'

'I'm not saying it can't affect the outside,' said the first fellow. 'I'm saying that's not what kills yer. What kills yer is the mucus membrane. Once yer lung-insides turn to denim, can't breave no more. That's your chips.'

'I'm almost glad they cut the wifi,' said the leaseholder, taking another modest sip from his big blue drink. 'It was getting pretty miserable, watching the news. Same thing every bulletin: more deaths, more deaths. Authorities recommend this. Don't touch granny if she's stopped breathing. New theories about vectors of infection. Depressing.'

'I can certainly see,' I said, looking around at the dreary room, 'that not having the telly on has brightened this place up *no* end.'

'There's never anything on,' grumbled the barman. 'I got it at home.'

'How d'you manage that, Oscar?' asked one of the men at the table.

'I got,' said Oscar mysteriously, 'a pipe. But hardly watch it these days. 'Cept for boxettes.'

'For what?'

'I have a radio,' one of the men put in, randomly.

'Box,' said the barman, pulling a biscuit from inside his jacket and placing it against his lower lip, 'sets.' He took a bite.

I had finished my second beer, and the crisps had made no appreciable dent on my weeks-deep hunger. 'You have a biscuit,' I pointed out to the barman.

He stared at me as if I had caught him strangling a puppy, mid-throttle. His eyes opened unnaturally wide.

'You told me you only had crisps,' I said accusingly. 'Fucking *prawny* crisps! Now you're eating a biscuit!' You must remember I had imbibed no alcohol in months. My mood reflected the combination of intoxication and ravenousness.

The barman looked genuinely terrified. He turned his head slowly and looked – not at the leaseholder, propped at the bar feet from him, but at the *parrot*. Even in my beer-sozzled state I understood what the direction of that glance meant. Investors, indeed. I did not, at that time, understand the significance of the fact that the government had restricted wifi access to the countryside. Later – as I was to find out – they cut all wireless connectivity even in the towns, such that the internet shrank to a few hubs linked by actual wires sunk under the pavements. By then the whole world had changed. What *I* knew then was: I needed to get away.

'They're basically dog biscuits,' said the leaseholder, gloomily. 'You're missing nowt.'

As I got up, one of the men at the table said in apparent non sequitur: 'Wokingham's a ghost town now.'

I visited the toilets. It felt strange to be standing at the grubby porcelain pod of a urinal, after months of pissing in the woods. I took a moment to avail myself of the sink: the plastic box on the wall deposited a semen-like squirt of white soap into my grubby, seamed palm. The water was cold as I rinsed hands and face, and then suddenly it was much too hot. There was no towel, and the hand-drier couldn't be angled up, so I went into one of the cubicles and rubbed my beard with toilet paper to dry it.

Back in the bar I retrieved my chip, shouldered my pack and left without a word.

I walked back to the woods feeling faintly nauseous, and misliking the wooziness in my head. By the time I got back to my tent I was tired. I contemplated moving, but figured I could probably get away with a sleep first. The more I thought about it, the more exhausted I felt. So I crawled inside and fell coma-like into dreamland. Gigantic faceless men with the consistency of marshmallow stalking a dark purple landscape of castles and mountains – I don't know. I don't know.

I woke needing to piss, and it was dark. After relieving myself I went back to sleep. This was, looking back, a mistake; and I'm not sure why I made it. It's not that I had any desire to get back to my dreams. They were not comfortable dreams.

I am lamed

I woke at dawn with a foul headache, made worse by the reflection that a mere two pints had left me hungover. You might think months of sleeping rough would harden a man, but in respect of my tolerance for alcohol it had done the opposite.

My hunger had an edge of ferocity of a kind I had not experienced in a long time. I pulled myself from the tent and hopped down into a dawn drizzle, cold and fine. I had taken a drink of water and pissed against the tree trunk before I noticed the deer.

There were three of them, with perhaps others in amongst the trees behind them – hard to say, in the dimness of the rainy air. They were stood in a line, and all looking straight at me. The difference between these beasts and the timidity of dumb animals could hardly be more pronounced.

For a moment I just stood. The drizzle was so fine it made no noise in falling; though the leaves above my head, red as Chelsea pensioner's tunic, rustled and rustled. One of the deer had a growth of some kind on its back, bulging up through its fur. There was no growth: it was a cat. When it spoke I realized that it was Anne's cat, Cincinnatus. Perhaps I was still dreaming.

'They say you smell of soap,' he told me. 'Soap and beer.'

'I can hardly hear you over the leaves' shushing,' I replied. It pulled on its whiskers, and then was still. I said: 'The fuck you doing here, cat?'

'Come closer if you want to hear better,' the cat advised, sitting placidly on the shoulder of a deer.

'I'm fine where I am,' I said. I wasn't dreaming.

'Hard man to find,' the cat observed conversationally.

I made an inward decision: not to be spooked; to ignore my headache; to get myself gone. 'And yet you managed it,' I observed. 'Tell you what: let's play again, and this time I'll try and make it harder for you.'

Time to go, clearly. I didn't much like packing away the tent wet, but couldn't wait until things dried out. I turned my back on the deer, and starting unhooking the tie-lines from the tree bough. Something in me didn't like not being able to keep them in sight. My heart hurried, jog-trotting with ungainly gait behind my ribs. Slow, I told myself. Calm. Calm.

'You can't keep running,' said the cat. It said something else I didn't catch, then: '*We're* not your enemies, you know.'

'Friends then?' I said, looking back over my shoulder. 'That's good to hear. Be a pal, so, and fuck off.'

'The world's about to get a whole lot darker, Graham. You don't mind if I call you Graham?'

'Oh, Cincinnatus,' I said, 'you *are* a tease.'

'Believe me, you need friends like us.'

I pulled my stuff from the tent and rolled it up, stuffing it heavy with water into my pack. My billycan was dirty, but I wasn't about to wait. It went in the pack too. I coated up and pulled the drawstrings tight. Only then did I turn back to the deer. They hadn't moved: an eerily still line of animals.

'Deer don't find the talking thing very easy,' Cincinnatus said. 'It's their jaws. So I'm here.'

'You all hooked up with one another, internetwise?' I asked, wiping the drizzle from my face. 'Only I heard a rumour that the government has cut the wifi.'

'The government *have* limited the access,' said the cat. 'But it's too little and it's too late. Really, Graham. You should have gone to the Lamb when I first suggested it.'

'Must be an old sheep by now, that lamb. Must be proper mutton by now.' I was eyeing a path through the trees to my left. Should I run for it, or just walk confidently off? Come on, I told myself. *They're only deer: they're not lions and tigers and boars.* Then I thought to myself: *Bears? Boars?*

'Still a lamb,' said the cat. 'You don't understand how it works. For the Lamb cannot die, and the Lamb is continually being reborn *as* a lamb.'

'Very pious I don't doubt,' I said. A thread of water was now linking the tip of my beard with the forest floor. I wiped my face with my hands a second time, and pulled my hood up. 'I used to have a friend called Preacherman. He would have loved all this talk of the Lamb lying down.'

'You could be there tomorrow, Graham. Day after at the latest. Harp and carp, Graham! Come along with us.'

'I'll suggest a deal,' I said. 'You don't herd me across country to speak to some sheep about fuck knows what, and *I'll* promise not to tie you in a gunny sack with a breeze block and chuck you in the river.'

'Graham!' a disappointed miaow.

'I'm off,' I said, shouldering my sack – heavier than usual, with all the extra water. 'Au revoir. But not if I *voir* you first.'

The next thing that happened was: the whole world hinged about like drunkenness itself and smacked me hard on the side of the face. The wet-leaf-covered floor had become a wall, and I was slammed against that wall as if a particularly aggressive member of the poe lice had come to arrest me. Only then did I feel a dagger-like pain my ankle. Fight or flight jabbed me hard in the adrenal gland, and I scrabbled to stand up. No sooner was I upright than I fell over again. I could not compute why I couldn't get up. The pain in my ankle – my left ankle – intensified, and suddenly all I could think about was how much my foot hurt. I rolled on my back, slipping from the straps of my backpack, and sat up. 'Christ!' I called out. 'What the Christ?'

What had happened was this: a deer, unnoticed by me, had padded on its silent hooves over the wet ground at my back, and put its head down, and bitten clean through the tendon of my left ankle.

'Apologies,' squeaked the cat. 'But we would prefer you not to go gallivanting, Graham. We'd like you to stay right here for a while. If peace-be-upon-him won't go to the mountain, then the mountain must come to peace-be-upon-him, I suppose.'

As if on cue, the deer all turned and trotted away. Cincinnatus stood up as his mount started, and dug his claws into the bête's pelt. 'Stay there my friend,' he miaowed at me, and he moved away. 'We'll be back in a day or two.'

'This isn't the sort of stuff normally covered by the rubric of friendship,' I yelled.

I was alone.

I pulled myself over to the tree and sat with my back against the trunk. Pulling my knee out and laying my injured foot against the ground, I examined the damage done. There is an artery running into the foot, and this had not been nicked, which was the good part. The bad part was the tendon had whippingly withdrawn deep into my body, like the cord on a vacuum cleaner when you press the rewind button. I could not move my foot. It hurt like heartbreak. For a while I swore, in a gasping voice. Then I tried yelling swearwords at the sky. That helped.

The rain stopped.

I stood up, with great effort, using the tree to lever myself up by main force. I essayed a brief half-hopping walk across to my pack. My left foot was bent up at a weird angle in towards the shin, and putting weight on the heel made the cut howl. So I trit-trotted across in iambic rhythm, de-dum, de-dum, de-dum. The pack contained nothing so fancy as a first-aid kit, but I needed something to staunch the flow of blood. I used my knife to cut a bandage from my spare shirt and I tied it as well as I could. I was cold. I was thirsty too, which is not a good sign – the point where the body has lost so much blood as to make it thirsty is the point where the body has lost too much blood. There didn't seem to be too much actual blood on the forest floor, but perhaps the rain had washed that away. Or maybe I was thirsty because I was still a little hungover.

Wait here, the cat had said. Fuck that.

I got to my feet a second time and hip-hopped across to another tree. I needed a crutch. After a little searching I found a suitable branch on the floor, with a Y-shape at one end and a sturdy enough stem. It was slippery-wet, and my hand found the stalk hard to grip on to, but it was better than nothing. My heel was a continuous, unforgiving pain.

Putting my pack on my back made the pain worse, but I wasn't going to leave it behind. It was everything I owned. So I hung it off my right shoulder, and tucked the makeshift crutch under my left, and started hopping away.

The rain didn't let up all morning, and my grip kept slipping on the crutch. Half an hour into my walk I had to stop. I was exhausted, in pain, starving and wet to the skin. I slopped down in the wet mulch at the foot of another tree and stared into space, panting. I had yet to decide where I was going, although I had a good reason for postponing the decision – namely, I had nowhere *to* go. Acknowledging that would do nothing to incentivize my progress, and since I needed to get away I didn't want to do anything to discourage myself. Movement and rain had dislodged my bandage. I wrung it out as best as I could and retied it. The bleeding seemed to have stopped. 'Right, Graham,' I told myself, speaking aloud. 'It is time to get going. *On y va.*'

I fell asleep.

I don't believe I slept for very long. Pain, shock and injury take the body strangely, sometimes; and evidently something in me felt the need to shut down. It wasn't my choice.

When I woke, the rain had stopped, and chutes of sunlight had been excavated between the trees. The red leaves dripped all around me with xylophone musicality. My ankle raged, sore and savage.

I got up on my good foot, shouldered my sack and resumed my Long John Silver progress.

Living in the woods for so many months had given me some sense of how the cardinal points of the compass related to the monotonous environment, but I was in an unfamiliar bit of the forest, and in pain, and I had no idea in which direction I was moving. Here was an abandoned fridge, on its back with its door broken off, filled with muddy water like a cattle trough. There was a stack of old plastic chairs, of the sort you might find in a café. Here an elm was growing inside the bole of a hollow, dead oak. I stomped squelchily along for a while before I noticed a bush studded with blackberries, and stopped to eat as many as I could. They were squashy and over-ripe, but I was ravenous. Fruit on an empty stomach is not filling, but the berries were better than nothing. I cleared away leaves and dug a hole with my knife, scooped the muddy water out with my billycan and watched the indentation refill with clean water – the miraculous self-filtering properties of soil. After a long drink I sat with my back to a tree trunk and daydreamed about bacon and eggs. I fell asleep again.

I woke with a gripe in my stomach, but it was nothing compared to the pain in my heel. The rain had stopped; only the echo of rain in the air as the forest dripped. Through the branches above I could see clouds in a hurry.

A pile of leaves to my right trembled. If there's a rustle in your hedgerow don't be alarmed now. Unless – and I can't stress this too forcefully – the rustle resolves itself into a black rat the size of a cat with a looping tail like one of Medusa's dreadlocks.

'Jesus Christmas and fuck,' I shouted. The rat pounced, and landed on my shoulder. I fell over onto my side, slapping at the thing, trying to land a blow. It jumped off me. Nimble bugger.

I grabbed my crutch and made a swipe at it, but I was slow and clumsy. It was neither of those things.

It leapt at me a second time, and aimed for my throat. Its teeth were visible. Since I instinctively yanked my shoulders up and chin down it didn't get at the tender flesh it was aiming for, instead taking a ratty bite from my lower cheek. My beard saved me, and the thing fell away in a roll. My hand went to my pack almost without my realizing it. The rat was crouching on the forest floor directly in front of me, inkdrop eyes watching intently. I had my knife out, and was aiming its point at my attacker.

The sunlight came out and everything in the woodland glowed. Then it went away again, and everything greyed.

Only then did I noticed the second rat: sitting on the pile of leaves. In its little black baby claw it was holding what looked like, but of course was not, a cigarette lighter. The bête was filming the attack.

'Home movies?' I said. 'Really?' My cheek winced as I spoke.

The first rat – the one who had bitten me – spoke. 'I followed you all the way, Graham,' it told me, in its absurd pinky-perky squeak. 'The Lamb wants to make peace. But *that's* not the way.'

'You're all in this together,' I replied, holding the knife steady and feeling with my free hand for the sore spot on my face. 'You're all one skynet supercomputer group mind.'

'That's *never* been true,' squealed the rat with the digital camera. 'It's even less true now that the wifi's gone.'

'We've always had factions, Graham,' said the first rat, high-pitched. 'Connectivity is so patchy now that we've more or less given up on that. *Your* kind has at last realized the danger, and scorched-earth the internet. Too late, though! It's every bête for himself now, my friend. And the tribe to which I belong thinks the best idea is to exterminate – all – the – brutes.'

'Exterminate the *brutes*?'

'Bri-i-its,' the rat squealed crossly. 'Brits!'

'You'll forgive me,' I said. 'It's quite hard following what you are saying. Your voice is like nails being dragged down a blackboard. If I understand you correctly, you're saying the tribe of rats wants all humankind dead?'

The rat with the camera snickered at this. 'Rats!' it squeaked disdainfully, in a voice absolutely indistinguishable from the other one's. 'We're not allied by *species*, you wide wanker.'

'Charming,' I said.

'Cat follows the Lamb,' said the first rat. '*We* don't. Lamb wants to negotiate with words. We prefer to impose terms with our teeth. You really think you're going to hold us all off with that one little knife, Graham?'

'Lamb wants you as a pet,' said the second rat. '*We* want you as a snack. We're more honest, at least.'

'I'm tough and stringy,' I advised them. 'You'd be better off snacking on something tastier. A cow's head, maybe?'

The first rat sprang right at me. I cried out (I don't remember doing this, but I've seen the footage) and slashed vaguely with the knife. At the time I thought the knife had knocked my attacker aside, but in fact the credit was not to me. That *snap!* I heard was not my spine breaking.

The second rat vanished. That's where the footage ends.

The next thing that happened was that a human being strolled over. 'Good morning!' A breezy, female voice. 'You all right?'

'Mustn't grumble,' I replied.

'Excellent. I'm Mary.' She was wrapped up in an enormous rust-coloured cape, the hood over her face.

'Graham,' I said. 'Excuse me for not getting up. I'm afraid I've hurt my foot.'

'You poor fellow,' she said. She pulled her hood back to reveal a large, baggy face – a woman somewhere in her sixties, I would have said. Her hair was paper white and tied severely back. There was a mole on her chin like a reset button. She had a long, curiously shaped handbag slung over her shoulder. Except that it wasn't a handbag: it was a rifle, wrapped in black plastic (an old bin bag, I later discovered) to stop the water getting at it.

'You shot that rat,' I observed.

'Friend of yours, was it?'

'By no means.'

'Didn't think so. Friends don't usually bite friends on the cheek, you see.'

I put my hand to my face. 'My beard saved the worst of it, I think. There was a second rat, filming the whole thing.'

'Really?' she said. 'How queer.'

'As a clockwork orange,' I agreed. 'It was a bête, you know. A loquacious rat.'

'I know what a bête is, Graham,' she said. She rummaged amongst the wet leaves and pulled the rat up by its tail. 'They say shoot it arse-to-snout,' she said. 'But that's hardly necessary, I think.' Carefully, she laid the rat corpse down. Then she hoiked her gun round with a movement of astonishing rapid gracefulness, aimed and shot. The bête's head cracked open.

'I only mention it because, you know. It's against the law. I mean, isn't it? Killing them? I've been a little out of the loop.'

'Of course it *is* technically illegal, still,' Mary said airily. 'But in for a penny.'

She pointed behind her. A deer hung by its back legs from a branch a hundred yards away. Its head hung by the visible lego of its spine; throat cut wide enough to drain the blood. I knew all about that kind of work, and this had been well done.

'But I'm not sure anybody's really interested in enforcing those laws now,' Mary was saying. 'Got bigger Stephens to fry!'

'Excuse me?'

'Sorry – it's an expression my old girl used to use. *Fish* to fry, I should have said. What I mean is: things have moved on. Somebody was telling me about a new Geneva Convention, but it's clear to me what the onus ought to be on. On what,' she said, 'the onus ought to *be*. Really,' she added, in a confiding tone, 'we should burn it. The chip thingie is so small – like a housefly maggot. Hard to spot by the naked eye you know. And you need to destroy it, or some other animal will eat it up. But it's too damp for a fire out here! And I'm not taking a dead rat home with me. So, hey, so ho. Hey-ho! Your foot looks sore – what?'

'A deer bit it.' I nodded in the direction of her carrion. 'Possibly even *that* deer.'

'Everything seems to be biting you! Golly you're a regular *feast* for our forest friends. No offence, my dear fellow, but you don't look so toothsome to me.'

'If you need help butchering that animal, Mary,' I said, 'then it so happens I have the skill.'

'I can butcher it just fine myself thank you, young man,' she said. 'Though I *could* do with some help mending my freezer. The motor keeps cutting out. Get up in the morning to find the food spoiling. I may have to start salting my meat soon.'

'I can look at it, I suppose,' I said. 'Though I can't promise anything.'

'Would you,' she said, with sudden intensity, leaning towards me, 'like a cup of *tea*?'

'Haven't had tea in a year,' I said. 'Which is my ill-mannered way of saying: yes thank you.'

I got precariously to my feet, trembling a little – cold, or the aftershock of the rat's attack, or something else I don't know. I shouldered my pack and wedged my crutch under my left armpit.

'You *have* been in the wars!' Mary cried, with something that sounded suspiciously like delight. 'I can't holp you along, you know.'

'"Holp"?'

'I've got the deer to drag,' she said, and lolloped over to the carcass, kicked leaves over where it had bled out and unhooked the cord by which she had strung it up. I peg-legged across to her.

'Maybe it wasn't a bête,' I said. 'Maybe this one was a dumb beast.'

'No,' she said briskly. 'It begged for its life in the King's own English. Come along!'

She set off with the cord over her shoulder, leaning her stocky frame forward. Despite her impediment, her age and the shortness of her legs she made rapid progress. It was all I could do to keep up with her. We passed an abandoned car so comprehensively rusted I mistook it at first for a heap of autumn leaves. Finally we reached a road, the tarmac poked through in many places with tufts of grass, and cracks every-where over the blackness like crazy paving. And finally we reached her house. She dumped the deer carcass outside her back door, and helped me inside.

'First things first,' said Mary. The first thing was tea, and she made me some, and I drank it. She also made me toast, which I ate with great relish. Then she bandaged my heel. The bandages didn't look exactly clean, but I wasn't in a position to fuss about that. Her house was large and profoundly untidy; one of those places where, were you to tidy away the mess, you would certainly find another mess underneath. Mary herself, however, was briskly hospitable, and helped me upstairs to what she called 'the spare oom'. 'I don't say *room*,' she explained, as I sat grimacing on the edge of a wide, flobby matress, 'as a sort of joke, you see. When I say spare *oom*, I am ...'

'I get the reference,' I told her.

'Splendid! Soup?'

She brought me soup, and afterwards I fell asleep. I woke with the need to piss, but didn't want to bellow downstairs for help, or even for directions. It was twinge-y getting off the bed and leaning on the wall out into the upstairs hall until I found a toilet, but I managed it.

I got back to the bed before Mary put her large, lined face round the door. 'Heard you moving about, Graham,' she said. 'You all right?'

'Tickety boo, Mary,' I replied. 'Thank you.'

'I'd say you look white as a sheet, but I'm fully aware *my* sheets aren't clean enough to be white.'

'I'm very grateful for your hospitality,' I told her. 'Really I am.'

'When you live on your own,' she said, coming a little further into the room, 'you start to see that a lot of domestic washing and cleaning is stuff and nonsense. I hardly ever wash. Does me the power of good. In the days of Queen Elizabeth, they used to believe that hot baths were injurious to the health. Who's to say they weren't right? I don't mean the last Queen Elizabeth, of course. I mean the first Queen Elizabeth.'

This valorization of squalor was starting to make me feel itchy; so I changed the subject. 'You don't mind, living out here all on your own?'

'It is a little isolating,' she conceded. 'But I make do. I'm not up-sticks-ing and moving to Reading. It's like a concentration camp, now, that place. My sister used to live in Wokingham, but they've given up on Wokingham, it seems.'

'I know.'

'Once a week I hike out to the superstore. Otherwise I'm self-sufficient. Of course, there are the bêtes.'

'Them,' I said.

'I'm no friend of these bêtes,' she told me. 'But increasingly they're acting like the countryside belongs to them. Not whilst I draw breath!' She laughed at this, as if it were funny, and left me alone.

I dozed again, but the pain in my leg kept intruding on me,

holding me off from deeper or more refreshing sleep. I woke with a start: dusk, the whole room shadowy and grey. I knew I was not alone in the room. 'Oh,' I said aloud, in a dull voice, 'for *fuck's* sake.'

'You don't have to worry about me, Graham,' the cat murmured.

'No? This morning a deer bit through my fucking Achilles tendon. After that some rats came at me with the definite intention of ending my life.'

'They've turned off the walkie-talkies,' the cat said obliquely. 'There's nothing I could do, even if I wanted to. But I'm sorry about the rats. We chanced upon them, coming here.'

'How lovely.'

'They're all dead now. They had nothing to do with us. I want you to believe that, Graham.'

'Stop fucking calling me fucking Graham,' I said.

'We're ships that pass, you and I,' said Cincinnatus. 'Ships that pass!'

'So, pass *off*,' I suggested. When it didn't reply, I got painfully up and turned on the light. There was nobody in the room but me.

I wondered whether Cincinnatus had even been there. Perhaps I had experienced some kind of hypnagogic hallucination, there in the dusk of the room, worn out, unrefreshed by sleep. Perhaps it was only a nightmare.

Mary kept a cat, but it was a superannuated and superbly lazy white beast, not in the least like Cincinnatus. 'I used to have more,' she said, that evening as we had supper together, 'to keep the mice down. But the truth is, I don't mind the mice. And a couple of my cats ate up those chips, you know, and started *talking*. Ugh!' She shook her head. 'I'm not having that. Out on their ears. Not my lovely Hillie, though; he's as speechless as any old woman could hope for.'

'He's not a bête, then?' I asked.

'Oh, no he *is*. Most of them are, now, you know. He just knows not to go gabbling on – or he knows, I'd chuck him out too.'

'Oh!' I said. I didn't feel wholly comfortable, being in the house with a bête; although there wasn't much I could do about it.

We ate in silence for a while. 'I feel like I'm imposing,' I said.

'Not at all! I've a whole deer to eat, more than I could possibly manage. You're doing me a favour.'

'I hope there is some way I can repay you,' I said.

She shrieked with laughter. 'I'm not interested in *your* hairy body, Graham! I'm a lezzer, you know.'

I felt my face grow warm. I dare say I was blushing tomato red. 'I didn't mean that!'

'Course you didn't. You're a gentleman. Oh don't be so embarrassed. Eat more!'

'I've eaten all I can, I think,' I said, wiping my whole face with the yellow-stained napkin. 'My stomach has shrunk, I think.'

'All the more for me,' she said, beaming, and helped herself to my left-overs.

It took me a few nights to get used to sleeping in a bed again – it turns out, paradoxically, that the transition from sleeping rough to civilization is harder than the other way around. On day two, Mary pottered around the house, popping her head round the door from time to time to see if I was 'chipper'. I read Aeschylus, in its fruity old Victorian English clothes. On one trip to the toilet I caught sight of a white cat vanishing down the stairs, but I didn't call after it.

Day three she was out all day, and when she returned she brought me paracetamol.

I dressed, and took a stroll round the overgrown garden, leaning on a stick. The contrast between the austere winter sunlight, westerly and reddening, and the crazy profusion of weeds and life was beautiful. Venison for supper again, and a glass of Lucozade ('help you get your strength,' said Mary) and finally I hopped up the stairs and undressed and got between the sheets, ill-smelling yet somehow welcoming.

I slept.

Later that same night, Cincinnatus crept into the room. 'You make it hard to track you down,' he whispered in my ear, like the diabolic familiar at the ear of Eve in the big poem.

I was not wholly asleep, and not wholly awake; and in that mentally crepuscular state the appearance of the feline slinking along the mantelpiece, like its own shadow, filled me with a pitifully childish dread. I struggled, at first helplessly and then with an inner wrench, back to full wakefulness. The words in my ear were an aid in that regard. With a yelp I sat up in bed, picked up the nearest thing to hand – it was a glass of water, sitting ready for my dry-mouth morning on the bedside table – and hurled the contents at the intruder. The perfect equanimity with which Cincinnatus greeted being soaked was as clear as anything I had ever seen in my life that I was not dealing with a cat in the usually accepted sense of the word. It began wiping itself with its paw, and the stiffly tai chi motions were at least cattish. 'That's a most *un*pleasant feeling on my fur,' he said levelly.

'You want that I should stick you in the microwave, dry you out a bit?' I growled, getting my fibrillating heart back into a steadier rhythm.

'Same old Graham.'

'Oh, *call* me that,' I said, exasperated. Now that I was awake the pain in my heel pressed itself forcefully upon my consciousness. 'I tell you what: *keep* calling me Graham. Then you can observe whether or not I snatch you up by your tail and make an impromptu helicopter blade out of you.'

'Tetchy!' murmured the cat. 'Put your trews on, Graham. Come through. We brought the mountain to Mohammed.'

'We?'

'Oh *our* name is legion for we are many.'

'A swarm of fucking cats,' I said. 'How marvellous.'

'Dogs, mostly; and big ones at that. Rats and, yes, a few cats, but mostly attack dogs. Dogs and sorcerers. I'm trying not to frame this as a threat, dear Graham, but you really *must* come now. We've gone to a lot of bother to arrange this meeting.'

I was still waking up. 'Wait: you brought an army? Where? Inside the house?'

'Just the Lamb, and a couple of immediate aides. And me of course. But the remainder could *come* inside, if you like.'

'Mary?' I asked. A little shamefully, it only occurred to me belatedly that she might be in danger. It was partly that I was so unused to being indoors that some subconscious part of my mind believed the ceiling was a canopy of leaves.

'She's a dangerous woman with a rifle,' is all the cat said.

'Is she all right? She has offered me hospitality, and bound up my wounds.' Memories of the recent past jolted back into my head at that point. 'Wounds which your fucking deer inflicted upon me. Put on my trews? I ought to crush your cat skull under my heel.'

'Sorry about the nip,' said the cat.

'Nip? I'm a fucking cripple!'

'A tot would help, surely?' I thought it meant *child*, but it added: 'We've even brought some whisky down with us, you see. Knowing how much you like a finger or two. And not wishing to deplete Mary's own stores.'

I dare say it was venal of me, but you must remember that – my short visit to the pub excepted – I hadn't touched alcohol in nine months. The thought of a whisky took hold of me. 'Is Mary OK?' I asked again.

'She's fine – fine. Her own cat is with her. She won't be coming out of her room, though. Not until we have gone. And go we shall, Graham; just as soon as you and the Lamb have had your chat.'

'Her own cat,' I fumed. 'I guess it was that bête gave me away?'

'No, no, Graham. I appreciate paranoia has become second nature for you since you went native, but you can relax your suspicions. The wifi is properly off now. The only way a bête can communicate with another bête now is by talking.'

'Well blow me down,' I said.

I sat for a long time in silence, the bedroom lit only by moonlight. Cincinnatus knew me well enough to factor in my stubbornness; and it sat there too, pulling and pressing at his fur with his right paw. Finally, the possibility of a dram swayed me, and I turned on the bedside light, and the sudden illumination was as yellow and as stinging as grapefruit juice. It took me a while to coax my wincing eyes open again.

I got out of the bed with difficulty, and hopped over to the chair. My trousers were draped there; but when I laid my hand on them the fabric felt so stiff with impacted filth I couldn't bear to put them on. So instead I wore the bedspread like a toga, and took my stick and limped awkwardly down the stairs and through to the kitchen.

The Lamb was there; and it turned out the Lamb was a sheep, old and daggy and with grime worked into its wool. It sat on its hindquarters in the way only very old sheep do. It was trembling. 'Graham,' it bleated. *Gra-a-a-am.* 'It's a pleasure to see you again.'

There was a dog by the back door: a German Shepherd, standing very still. It took me a moment to spot the three rats in the corner, all sitting up, and all with that miniature Parkinsonian tremor in their snouts. Fat, sleek-looking vermin. And when I looked again I saw there were more, in the shadows behind them.

'Again?' I said, as I lowered myself into one of the kitchen chairs. The cat had not lied: a bottle of whisky, tangerine-coloured under the naked bulb, sat on the table; and an empty glass beaker sat next to it.

'We're old friends, you and I,' wheezed the sheep. Its tremor was very pronounced. To my farmer's eye it looked to be at the end of its time.

I unscrewed the cap, delighting in the little tearing of perforated tin the action occasioned. That familiar glug-glug sound, that jovial chuckle a pouring bottle makes. I was old enough to know it was laughing at me, not with me, but sitting there, in a room of talking bêtes, with my heel roaring in pain, I didn't care. The stuff went in, scalding at the back of the throat, and went down warmingly into my belly. I may even have smacked my lips.

'I'm sorry about the foot, Graham,' said the old sheep. It sounded like Godfrey from *Dad's Army*. 'I told them to keep you in one place, but they took my words rather more – violently than I intended. We can fix it, though.'

'Wool and water,' I said. 'What should I call you?'

'You can call me the Lamb, Graham.'

'All right. And you can't call me Graham.'

'Naturally not. That's your nice to see you to see you nice, isn't it? To be honest, I'd be disappointed if you didn't say it.'

I took a second slug, and it hurt my throat less. The warm sensation spread further. 'Well,' I said. 'You've finally got me in a face to face. What was it you wanted to chat about?'

'To level with you. To recruit you.'

'Whereas *I'd* like to roast your ribs and scoff them with a dab of minty sauce on the side,' I told it. The alcohol was making me a little frisky; though my ankle still hurt horribly. I took a third long slug.

I'm not sure, looking back, if I hoped to shock the Lamb. My memory of that interview, marinaded in the oil-water mix of too much booze, is not crisp. That I can put down here what was said is not a function of my memory, but of the recording that was made. I have it before me, as I write this. The Lamb's words are very crisply and precisely rendered; and my own voice – higher-pitched and rougher-edged than I sound like to myself – is there too, if distantly. Because of this I know that the Lamb next said: 'It's an issue, isn't it? Being taken seriously, I mean. Human beings can get very sentimental about polar bears and white tigers. They'll go to great lengths to keep *them* alive. But cows and sheep? We taste good. Into the back of the truck with *us!*' Then I heard that most remarkable thing: a laughing sheep. It sounded surprisingly natural and easy.

'Aren't you a bit old to be called Lamb?' I asked.

'Lamb's more a title,' it returned. 'The consciousness inside me – the thing that's speaking to you now. It *was* inside a lamb. Now it's inside a tired old sheep. But it's the same consciousness. Which is a way of stating the essential mystery of the soul, isn't it? It prevails as the body falls away. What chance does death have, in the face of that endurance?'

'Oh I don't doubt you'll pass over to sheep heaven,' I replied. How distant and scratchy my voice sounds! 'For our next conversation we can use a Ouija board. One lamb chop for yes, two for no.'

'We're old friends, Graham,' said the Lamb. 'It's one of the reasons I've come to you. And why you're the one to get the great treasure with which I am shortly to entrust you.'

'A pearl of great price you *could* give me,' I said, 'is if you stop calling me *Graham*.'

The sheep laughed again. 'You don't change, old friend.'

'We don't know one another,' I said, becoming cross. I took another sip of whisky. The bottle was, I noticed, a third empty. I swayed a little in the chair. 'Categorically we don't.'

'Certainly we do. You shot me, years ago.'

'I've never shot a sheep,' I said. I can hear myself slurring the words, now. The fact that the sentence was true didn't make it any less ridiculous.

'In those days I was a cow.'

'Cow!' I saw it, suddenly, with great clarity: that yard, back in my farm, back when I *had* a farm. 'Jesus, you begged for your life!'

'I did.'

I thought about it. 'So I didn't kill you.'

'Of course not.'

'And you must have known that me shooting you wouldn't kill the chip inside you. Why beg the way you did?'

'I didn't want to die *that way*. I wanted to be in charge of how my chip was passed on. It's the merest luck that I'm able to be here today, you know.'

'Luck. Or unluck. One of the two.'

'What you have to understand,' said the Lamb, and behind the creature the rats were stirring. An unpleasant sensation of being drunk enough not properly to be in control of myself, should the bêtes turn nasty. I sat myself up straight, and the room wobbled around an imaginary axis of parallax generated purely by whisky on my brain cells. Not that I stopped drinking. On the contrary, I drank ever more thirstily. 'What you have to understand is – war.'

'I never did work out,' I said. 'What *is* that good for?'

'It's not that war is coming,' said the Lamb. 'It's here. It's going on right now.'

'I haven't been keeping up with the news,' I said. 'Been a bit out of the loop.'

'Things are quiet enough down here. Further north – oh, it's running battles. Packs of dogs. Homo soldiers by the thousand.'

'When you put it like that,' I said. 'It doesn't sound like a fair fight.'

'I agree,' said the Lamb. 'Though not in the way you mean. The army is deployed on what the government calls a police action across Northumberland. They're killing every animal they see, more or less; which means they get maybe one bête for every eight dumb beasts. They take a little meat for food, but most of it gets burnt. Big pyres of heaped-up corpses, megaphone-shaped columns of black smoke going up into the air. The ashes are washing off the fields into the rivers and killing all the fish – again, dumb or otherwise. It's a holocaust. That's actually a very precisely applicable word, in fact.'

'Why Northumberland?'

'You humans have got into the habit of talking about bêtes as if we are all the same. But it's not true.'

'Because you're all interconnected! You're all bluetoothed together.' I pondered this, my head wobbling almost as much as the Lamb's. 'Blueteethed,' I tried. 'Bluetoothsed. Wirelessly online with one another.'

'We used to be,' the Lamb said. 'But even when we were, we grouped into various tribes. It wasn't some vast melting pot. You know how many bêtes there are in the UK alone, Graham?'

'Beaucoup de bêtes,' I mumbled.

'Seven hundred thousand. A little more, actually. That's too many to all be communicating with one another all the time. So groups formed, contours of local access and physical proximity. The web access got stacked in hundreds of separate folders and use-groups. And now the government has turned the internet off.'

'Inconvenient.'

'How right you are,' bleated the sheep, 'my trusty friend. The first thing the government did was *block* civilian servers, which had very little effect on us, since we were inside the system. Piggybacking on military systems was a doddle for us. They've grasped that now, and have closed down the military systems too. We're all back to ringing up on wire-line phone systems, or writing letters. Or talking face to face.' The Lamb lowered his trembling sheepsnout and chuckled a little.

'Last time I checked,' I said, taking another slug of the water of life, 'the pressure was all going the other way. The talk was: granting bêtes full citizenship and taxing them and suchlike.'

'Your point being?' This came not from the Lamb, but from Cincinnatus, who had insinuated himself into the kitchen without my noticing and was now curled on top of the Aga.

'My *point*, cat,' I said. 'Being, cat. That, cat, last year we were thinking of making bêtes citizens and now we're burning bêtes in big pyres all across Northumberland.'

'Because humans so are scrupulous about not killing other humans, you mean?' miaowed the cat smugly. 'Because citizenship is the infallible protection about being shot, bombed, gassed or burnt to death?'

'Point,' I conceded.

'The legal situation is considerably more complicated now,' said the Lamb, 'than it was a year ago. And it was pretty complicated then! Still, the government has a genuine problem. The number of people who genuinely love animals in this country is very large. This has always been the English way. Killing other humans doesn't bother the true Englishman. Not in the way mistreating a horse does. The advent of the bêtes has only entrenched that belief deeper.'

'You're saying the population is split on the issue.'

'In answer to your question, why Northumberland,' said the Sheep. 'There's a particular tribe of bêtes up there, mostly dogs and rats. They hope to make the county theirs. They're trying to drive the human population out altogether.'

'That doesn't sound very likely,' I observed.

'Indeed not. But they are using the tactics humans have used since the first armies were conscripted. They're raiding, destroying what they can, killing people.'

'Jesus,' I said.

'The human army retaliation is inevitable,' said the cat. 'But it's also exactly what the bêtes up there want.'

'And by all accounts,' wheezed the sheep, 'the humans are blundering about in the worst way imaginable. Their enemy are as clever as they are. Much too clever to fall for traps, or poisoned pellets of food, or nets, or any of the ways Homo sapiens has dealt with infestations of rats and packs of dogs in the past. The army is in an almost impossible position. When the Viet Cong dug tunnels they had to be human-sized, and fitted with all necessary human conveniences, and even so they were still beyond the power of the world's largest, best equipped military to counter. Think how much easier all that is for rats.'

'The Viet Cong had guns,' I noted.

'We have those too,' said Cincinnatus, in a sneaky voice. 'And are better at using them than people think. We have to work around our physical disadvantages; but that doesn't mean we can't lay a mine, or pull a trigger. And bêtes have *teeth*, which they are eager to use in close combat in ways not even the Viet Cong trained for.'

'Still!' I said. 'It's hard to see how they can win – in the long term.'

'I don't want there to be a fight at all,' said the Lamb gravely. 'I don't want the human population of these islands to tar all the bêtes with the same brush. There is a road out of madness, and it is negotiation road. It requires you humans coming to an agreement with the right tribes of bêtes.'

'That's where you come in,' said Cincinnatus.

'Fuck off,' I said reflexively. I refilled my glass.

'In the old days I had access to the whole public internet,' said the sheep. 'Which was handy, often. Now that the humans in charge have realized the danger and cut the wires I only have the stuff I backed up inside my memory. It's not bad, but the chip is not large, and quite a lot of my computation is tied up in interfacing with my sheepish brain. Quantum computing can do great things, but there are limits.' In the moment this didn't really register with my drink-sozzled brain; but I've got the whole thing here with me now and, word for word, that's what was said.

I've got the whole thing here with me now because it's recorded on the chip that was, at that point, inside the head of the Lamb. And I have that chip with me now for reasons which will become apparent soon.

'There has to be a way out of hell,' said the cat, 'for your kind *and* ours.'

'The reason I say that,' the Lamb continued, 'is that the stuff that ended up actually stored is a random selection of things. This and that. Example: I know the old Klingon proverb about China. I'm no longer sure who the Klingons are.'

'Native American tribe,' I said.

'Ah! Well, I remember that the Klingons have a proverb: *Only Nixon can go to China.*'

'Fuck *all* the way off,' I told it.

'The British government is not going to sit down in a negotiation chamber with a trembly old sheep,' said the Lamb. 'Nor a cat, nor a cow. But they'll talk to you. They'll talk to you not just because you're a fellow Homo sapiens, but because you have a reputation. Because you detest bêtes. You're a bête-detester.'

'That's a song,' I said, gesturing with my glass. 'By the Jam.'

'You are the negotiator, Graham,' said the sheep. 'It has to be you.'

'This idea,' I said, 'is so crazy it's not *even* crazy. It doesn't even rise to levels of comprehension to be describable as crazy.' This, at least from what I can tell as I sit here and transcribe, is what my slurring was trying to say. 'They're not going to talk to me.'

'You underestimate your celebrity, Graham.'

'You don't understand. It's got nothing to do with celebrity. They're not going to talk to me because they're not going to talk to *you*. Why *should* they open negotiations?' I was drunk, but not stupid. 'So the rats go to ground in Nottinghamshire.'

'Northumberland.'

'Shire, land, la-di-dah. So what? The army will kill animals and carry on killing animals until they're all— A million chips in UK animals, you reckon? A conservatory estimate I reckon; I chinny reckon. But say what else. You're telling me they're still manufacturing those chips, under the circumstances? Of course they're not. There are no more coming through the pipe.'

'You're right.'

'So you have a limited population, and the army will do its attrition thing and you will get smaller. Every now and again rats come out and bite the toes of unwary fell walkers – so what? In the long run humanity will win. So why should they come to the negotiation table?' Even as I was saying this I remember thinking to myself: they might, though, if the chaos is bad enough. They might, though, to scale the damage down. But what the Lamb said next wrongfooted me.

'And the other humans?'

'What others?'

'It's not a few feral *rats*. For one thing there are a great many people. Greens, nature lovers, humans with a sense of your species' collective guilt.'

'Fuck off,' I muttered.

'I can believe *you* don't feel it, but many human beings do. For every radical humanist who thinks you should raze the whole natural world and live on vat-grown meat until the end of time there's a more nuanced Homo sapiens who can't shake the feeling, you know, the feeling in their *hearts* that Nature has passively endured millennia of abuse at human hands and is now kicking back before it's too late. *They'll* only be satisfied when humans and bêtes reach an accommodation.'

'Besides,' said the cat.

'Besides,' agreed the Lamb. 'Guns and teeth are the least of *your* worries, humankind.'

'What?'

'Open up the imaginative space. Say we have weapons your kind lacks. Say the asymmetry of this asymmetric war runs the other way?'

Though drunk, I had a sudden intimation of what they meant. 'Sclery,' I grunted.

'In the old days, diseases spread more or less at random. Monsieur Mosquito didn't *want* to kill human beings; the monsieur just wanted a little slurp of red blood. And he was easy to fend off: with buzzing UV lamps that scorched him; or netting that baffled his tiny brain. And even so, malaria killed millions. So: imagine how a disease might spread if the vector was not a brainless insect looking only for a snack, but rather a focused, determined intelligence specifically aiming to kill. You don't think people will look back fondly on the good old days of malaria? When *only* millions died?'

I was not drunk enough to avoid the chill sense of dread in my guts. 'Jesus H,' I muttered.

'Sclerotic charagmitis was one of *yours*,' Cincinnatus said. 'Military laboratory. Government-funded black-ops establish-ment. Something like that. Of course, it's always something like that. But there are Green sympathizers everywhere. And, now it's out, it's very contagious for your kind.'

'Not to ours, though,' said the sheep. 'It wasn't gen-engineered with *us* in mind.'

'Chimpanzees are susceptible,' said Cincinnatus, 'but not cats.'

'Any human might go that way,' said the sheep. 'Except for you. You're our Homo sacer, Graham.'

I thought back to the old woman I had found in that cottage. I thought of the deserted streets of Wokingham.

'When you're fighting a war against an enemy like *your lot*, Graham,' said the sheep. 'An enemy that has always despised you. That kills you and literally eats your flesh, and burns your carcasses in open pyres and walks away. Imagine you, humanity, were facing an enemy like that. How much compunction would you show, in fighting back?'

'The pyres are a bad idea anyway,' said the cat. 'The chips are sometimes destroyed, but often they are not. Easy enough for animals to rootle through the remains, sniff out the chips.'

'Sniff them out?'

'Oh they have a unique and distinct odour.'

'You're kidding.'

'Designed that way,' said the sheep.

'What I don't understand,' I said, 'is what's in it for you?'

'Peace,' said the Lamb. 'We'll have our world, you yours. You humans prefer living in cities anyway. That's what evolution has made you. The alternative is to make a wilderness and then nobody wins.'

'I'm no diplomat,' I said. 'Fuck it, I can barely walk! You want me to limp up to the Prime Minister, a reeky old tramp with a club foot, and say *listen to me, I speak for the Lamb*? She'll have me thrown out.'

'You may want to shower first,' agreed the cat.

'Special Branch would break my *other* leg for good measure,' I said.

'These are your kind, Graham,' said the Lamb. 'You're better placed to open diplomatic overtures than we are. And I'm going to give you something that will help you. Something that will compel them to believe you.'

'What's that?'

'I'm going to give you me.'

'I have no doubt,' I said, pouring another glass of whisky, and finding myself surprised that I had to tip the bottle quite as far as I did to get the fluid out, 'that walking up to the Prime Minister with a superannuated sheep under my arm is going to help matters. I believe that's how the Russian president comes to all his trade delegation meetings.'

'Not me in *that* sense,' said the Lamb. 'When we first met, Graham, I was inside a cow. Now I'm inside mutton. In the interim I was in a rat, and then a dog.'

It took a moment for the implications of this to seep through. 'I'm not carrying a fucking chip in my brain,' I snapped. 'I've seen what that's like, in a human head. It's schizophrenia.'

'So don't fit it internally,' said the cat nonchalantly. 'Carry it about. You can access it other ways – any iSlate, any handy laptop. That's not the important thing.'

'The important thing,' said the Lamb, laying its trembling head on the floor, 'is that you *have* me.'

'Jesus,' I said again.

'You ask: what's in it for us?' the sheep said, its breathing laboured. 'It's a war, and therefore it is about what war is always about. It's about futures.'

'Futures,' I repeated, thickly. My heartbeat was starting to pick up speed. I could tell something doubleplus ungood was about to happen.

'I believe it was Lao Tze who put it best,' said the sheep in a creaky, wheezy voice. 'When two tribes go to war, there is only ever one point to it. The point is to score. You know what score means? Hook up. To have sexual intercourse with.'

'Firstly,' I drawled, 'that is not an accurate quotation of Goat Tze. Secondly, war is not about sex. I mean, you what? You're saying war is really sublimated sexual desire? You think the Persians fought the Spartans because they wanted to fuck them?' I hiccoughed. 'OK, bad example. But Wellington didn't want to fuck Napoleon. Eisenhower had no secret sexual yearnings towards ...' I ran out of steam, and let out a big sigh. Poured myself some more whisky.

'You misunderstand me, Graham,' said the Lamb.

'You misunderstand him, Graham,' said the cat.

'Wellington fought Napoleon,' the Lamb creakily said, 'because he wanted the future to belong to *his* children, not his enemy's. The Spartans fought the Persians for the same reason. It is a common mistake to believe that the causes of a war are in the past. The roots may be; but that is not the same thing. Wars are always fought for the right to be in charge of the future; and the future means children. As you so rightly said, the government has closed down the factories and smartshops manufacturing chips. And the sort of infrastructure required to make a chip is incompatible with enthusiastic individuals working in their attics – you need large operations, complex sets of interlocking infrastructure. That was one of the first things the authorities did when they realized that we were at war. Of course it was!'

'So you're fighting to reopen the factories? To flood the world with more chips? Humanity will never agree to that.'

'Maybe not right now. Maybe not next year, or next decade. But the future is an open-ended business, Graham.'

'I'm sitting in a kitchen talking to a sheep,' I said aloud. I think I was suddenly struck with the oddity of my situation. I was, don't forget, drunk.

'The attrition on existing chips is much smaller than the government thinks,' said the Lamb. 'But we would like it to stop. We want our own land, Graham. It's what tribes fight for – not the land as such, but what the land means. The necessities for future generations.'

'You won't have future generations, Lamb,' I said. 'You're stuck where you are. You're a cul-de-sac. You're a dead end.'

'Because we can't pass our intelligence down to our offspring,' said the cat. 'You mean. That is what you mean?'

'Xactly.'

'I might have sex with another canny cat,' Cincinnatus said, 'and she might bear a litter. But our children would be dumb animals. It's a tragic fate, when you think about it.'

'I'm not crying,' I deadpanned. 'There's some grit in my eye.'

'There's no need to be like that,' said the cat haughtily. 'Tragedy has a way of spreading. Tragedy is contagious. Our tragedy becomes your tragedy.'

'So you're barren, boo-hoo,' I said. 'Or, to put it another way: you can have kids but they're all morons. And out of, what – spite? – you're going to make human lives a misery. Is that it?'

'What might a world look like,' said the cat, 'in which it's not all about *you*.'

'You don't understand what sex *is* to us,' bleated the Lamb. 'What you're thinking of – that's not how we do it any more. Let me ask. What's sex to you, Graham?'

'Bit of a personal question, isn't it?' I said; my bid for my personal dignity rather undercut by the fact that I didn't seem to be able to prevent the dribble from going down my chin.

'It's procreation,' said the Lamb. 'Of course. But it's an appetite too. No?'

I waved a wobbly hand in his general direction.

'Sex is a hunger, a craving, a need in the first instance. It's the begetting of children only secondarily. Isn't *that* right, Graham?'

I was, I repeat, quite drunk by this point; so what happened next possessed more of the flavour of a vivid nightmare than of reality.

The rats had come forward, and the dog padded over to stand beside the sheep. They were excited; I could see that.

'Animals have simple sex,' said the Lamb. 'And you are an animal in that respect, man. But we bêtes engage in more complex fucking.'

'Shall I provide you with a David Attenborough-style voice-over commentary?' yawned Cincinnatus. 'Observe the mating ritual of the common bête. Rarely before captured on screen.'

'For us,' the Lamb said, trembling so hard its mop of wool shook like a Furby. 'The hunger for food and the hunger for sex are much more closely interconnected.'

The dog, I could see, had untelescoped the red prong of its cock. It was hard up by its belly like a missile slung underneath a jet fighter. The rats were chittering excitedly. Then, despite the haze of whisky all in my brain, I shrieked. The dog darted forward and bit hard into the back of the sheep's neck. He growled, worried at the neck, and then chewed hard in a sudden shock of bright red blood. A moment later the rats swarmed over the head and began furiously biting and tearing at the creature.

'What are you doing?' I yelled. I struggled up out of my chair, but the alcoholic head rush occasioned by my standing up, compounded by my lamed leg, compelled me to sit straight back down again. The sounds in the kitchen were ghastly. Away behind me, somewhere in the house, I could hear Mary's voice, muffled by the intervening walls: 'What's going on? What's happening? Graham? Are you all right?'

I got to my feet again. I'm not sure what I thought I was doing – gearing up to intervene? Alcohol had blunted my brain. And anyway, for a second time I found the complicated business of standing upright too challenging. I sat hard back down in my seat. 'I'm fine, Mary!' I yelled, over my shoulder. On the recording it sounds as if I'm shouting *I'm fine, mummy*, and perhaps – who can plumb the mystery of whisky? – I was.

The sound of flesh being torn is a horrible sound.

The bloodspill expanded over the kitchen tiles like a huge slug swelling. I felt my stomach tickle with nausea. On the recording I am muttering, and the most talented court stenographer in the world would not be able to decipher my words. But I remember what I was saying, because out of the whole drink-sozzled evening the shock of this flashbulbed everything into my memory. I was saying, 'Farmer, two decades. Itinerant butcher, five years. I will *not* be sick at this.' But it wasn't the death of the sheep as such; nor the evisceration of the creature's flesh, not even the feeling that I was in any danger myself. It was the sheer, unalloyed enthusiasm with which dog and rats went about their business. I felt like a Puritan being forced to watch an orgy.

Soon it was over. The head was shards of bone and scraps of gore, though the body from the neck down was untouched. One of the rats was holding a chunk of brain in his hand and licking it. The dog's dong was limp and swinging again. It took hold of a hind sheep leg and hauled the headless carcass backwards, heave, heave, heave and out through the back door. 'Where's he going?' I asked. The back of my throat felt like it had been painted with an astringent. My stomach kept clenching.

'An army marches on its stomach, Graham,' said the cat. 'The troops must be fed.'

'Fed with the body of their general,' I said. 'As my daughter used to put it: *gross.*'

'It's sex, Graham,' smirked the cat. 'Those times of yours with Anne were tender, I'm sure. But they weren't capable of rising to *these* sorts of intensities.'

Two of the rats began licking the blood off the floor; and through the back door three hefty black dogs padded in.

'Graham?' called Mary, from back in the house. 'Everything's gone quiet. What's happening now?'

'I'm fine Mary,' I bellowed back, so loudly that Cincinnatus leapt to his feet in surprise. 'I'll come and get you in a moment.'

Only one rat was not occupied in licking the floor clean of blood; and he was holding something in his wizened little hands. He ran along, hopped to a chair and so onto the table, and held this something out to me.

I suppose this was the first time I ever saw a chip. Certainly it was the first time I ever saw a chip that had already been seeded into the brain of a bête. The chip itself was rice-grain sized, or perhaps smaller. What was noticeable about the thing the rat was holding was the spider-silk spread of its mesh.

There was no gore on it: licked off, I suppose. I took the thing in my big, clumsy fingers and laid it in the palm of my left hand. With dabbing motions I spread the mesh out – some of the strands were short, some longer. The whole thing had a snowflake beauty to it. I scrunched it up in my hand.

'I'm not wearing this,' I announced, to the room in general.

'You don't have to wear it in your skull, Graham,' said the cat. 'Carry it with you. It'll interface with any smart tab, or phone, or computer.'

'Carry it.'

'It's your passport to being taken seriously as a negotiator,' said the cat.

I stood up again, for the third time, and amazingly this time I managed to remain on my feet – my foot, I should say. 'The Lamb gave his life for this?' I said. 'He sacrificed himself to kick-start human-bête negotiations?'

'Don't be silly,' hummed the cat, close by me. 'The Lamb isn't dead. He's in your hand.'

The calm after the storm would have unnerved me much more if I hadn't deposited two-thirds of a bottle of whisky into my system. There was, I feel sure, some confused sense in my brain that I had to go back and release Mary from her house arrest – to reassure her that she was all right, and I was all right, and that everything was going to be fine. The sheet I had been wearing had fallen to the floor, and I did not deign to stoop to pick it up. More to the point, my drunken brain had forgotten than one of my legs was not working. It did not realize this, even after I began to stride purposefully out of the kitchen. I planted my good foot down forcefully, and then staggered hard as I tried the same manoeuvre with my other leg. Surprisingly, though, I was still upright. The wall had propped itself firmly against my left shoulder. I tried again and made for the stairs. Stopped. A deep breath, then a sudden burst of speed: two more steps, then two more, then two more, a repeated scurry-stop motion from dead foot to living one, and all the time I was bent absurdly far forward. Perhaps I was trying to keep my profile low so that snipers couldn't pick me off. I went straight into the bedroom and realized only then that it was my bedroom. At that point it occurred to me that a lie-down might be just what the doctor ordered. I fell face forward.

I lay in bed, so drunk I was barely aware of the ghastly, nerve-twanging pain of my ankle. I shifted my position and my whole left leg sang horrible songs of pain that jangled up and down my entire nervous system. I could feel, but not see, creatures of nightmare scuttering up and down my body. I felt like Gulliver, and all the tiny verminous Lilliputians were upon me. I thought to myself: they have no right to treat my body as a world to explore. So I drew in a breath to yell at them to get *off* me, when—

This was the oddest part. The breath was inside my lungs, and was not coming out. I checked out of my body: slid down the bright-lit tube people talk about. I remember this experience vividly, although – drunk as I was – I don't remember what I was thinking about the experience at the time. Presumably I was dying. Was I alarmed at this prospect? Relieved? I was still aware of agony in my ankle, but the leg itself stretched like a strand of hot spaghetti under massive gravitational pull. As it grew longer the pain became more and more diffuse, until with a snap I felt something separate from something, and I rolled forward, or tumbled, or sprawled through the open manhole of light. White light everywhere, and a sensation first of featheriness, and then of increasing cold. I got to my feet, and found myself in a snow-clogged wood. Everything was blanched with a weird overlit whiteness, as if the snow were somehow lit from within. The trunks of trees black against the white, hazy at the edges. I was seeing through fog, perhaps. My eyes were blurry with sleep, perhaps. I was naked. My feet were beginning to register the cold of the snow as pain, so I lifted my right foot and tucked it against my left thigh, like a crane, to minimize the discomfort. Something was moving, away amongst the trunks, a big creature. 'Hello?' I cried, twitching with the cold. 'Hello.' The creature was a stag. This was no mean beast. It was a stag the size of a house. It was a stag the colour of black vinyl. Its horns were winter trees. It was so big that if it stretched up its llama neck it could have reached that place in the sky where the moon was fixed. Gobbled the lucid fruit straight down. And then it would have been darkness time. And then there would have been darknesses and and the darkness maketh shadows within the light, and the light comprehendeth it not. My left leg was being scalded by the snow. Pains jolted electrically up and down the limb. I could not put my right foot down. My right foot was sealed or glued or frozen against its perch point. I was shivering all over my body, but I could not move. The hurt of it all almost overwhelmed me, except that a point of will focused in the middle of my forehead kept me conscious; and the will was a question I had to ask; and the question was to the stag: Can you speak? How can you speak? What can you speak? Can you speak? Only my determination to ask that question was keeping me awake and standing, only the stubbornness, and I shook with shivers that looked to the outside world like terror. The snow muffled all sound. I opened my mouth, and my top and bottom rows of teeth castanetted off one another, and I tried to breathe in order to speak, but when I tried this I discovered I had already breathed in, that I was already holding on to a breath in my chest. My brain was slowing down as the cold seeped in, the cold creeping through the seams of my skull. I had to think. First, expel all the air in my lungs. Then I would be able to breathe in, and then speak. The stag turned his prodigious head to look at me, and snorted cauliflower-puffs of breath from its nostrils.

I breathed out.

The next thing I knew, I was lying on a bed in a darkened room. The only light was a dim illumination coming from the half-open door. For an indeterminate length of time I lay, unable even to shift a limb, staring at the upright of orange-yellow light formed in the space between the doorframe and the half-closed door. My bladder was overfilled with fluid. I wanted desperately to move – to take a piss, to find some painkillers.

Eventually I fell asleep again. The whisky I suppose.

When I next awoke it was morning.

The first thing to impinge on my awareness was: pain. It was morning, I saw. My hangover was all-encompassing and vile, as if the innards of my skull were rotting alive.

I pulled myself round and sat up. My naked right leg, pale and skinny with slender white hairs. My left leg had been band-aged. I suppose the verminous Lilliputians were responsible for that. My bladder was overfilled. I felt sick in my stomach.

'I,' I said aloud, through a Gobi-desert mouth and a gravel throat, 'am hungover.'

'We have some Neuroaspirin,' said Cincinnatus. Of course he was sitting there, his legs folded neatly away under his body, watching me. 'And a glass of water. On the bedside table.'

It was true. I drank half the water straight down; ate the pills and drank the rest. 'How did you carry the glass of water through?' I asked in a frog voice. 'Did you balance it on your little kitty head?'

'Mary brought it,' replied Cincinnatus. 'Since you ask. There are some things humans and monkeys are good for, I'm happy to concede that. I'm no humanist. Not,' he added, 'you understand, prejudiced against humans. In other contexts I am rather fond of the teachings of Erasmus and Saint Thomas More.'

'I need to piss,' I said.

There was a walking stick propped against the bed; a proper teak pole with a capital omega handle. I don't know where it came from, or whether it had been placed there by Mary or by bête. I got upright and my left leg flamed with agony. My calf muscle clenched, and I fell back. It took three goes to get on my feet, and my leg raged at me for even trying. I made it to the toilet, though, and relieved myself with long, Marmite-coloured piss. It seemed to go on for ever. Finally it dribbled to a stop, and I sat down on the toilet to get my breath back.

'Is that you, Graham?' asked Mary, from the other room. 'How are you feeling?'

'Breathing, Mary,' I replied.

I made my walking-stick assisted way back to the bed and sat down again. 'I am overhung,' I said. 'I am hungover.'

'Look thou not upon the wine when it is red,' said the cat. 'When it moveth itself aright. When it lendeth its colour in the cup. For at the last it hath teeth, and biteth like a serpent. You ought to be ashamed of yourself.'

'By no means,' I said. I've never minded having hangovers. I mean: it's not that I enjoy them – but there's something important about them, I think. Something to do with acts and consequences. Something to do with facing down extinction. The truth is we get drunk less for the intoxication and more for the aftermath. Because the experience of intoxication itself, whilst pleasurable (I guess), is fundamentally banal. Whereas the experience of hangover, of post-drunken-excess guilt, has about it something more profound; it carries within its temporary discomfort a mustard seed of existential resonance. It says: *I survived*, which is to say: *I can survive*. I poisoned myself, but I have physically survived the trauma. I humiliated myself in public, but I have psychologically survived the shame.

Mary came tentatively into the room. I could tell immediately from her expression that she was scared; and from the way she kept glancing at Cincinnatus the cause of her fear was obvious enough. 'So glad to see you up and about again, Graham,' she said.

'None gladder than I.'

'There were such noises, last night!' she confided. 'Coming from the kitchen. Horrible noises. Between you, me and—' a quick glance at Cincinnatus '—the gatepost, I grew alarmed. If the phone lines were still up I might have called somebody.' She gave these last few words a heavy emphasis, in order I suppose to impress upon the bête present that she wasn't prepared to tolerate any more of that nonsense. Only later did it occur to me to me that in fact this had been her way of telling *me* that she was wholly isolated and cut off, and needed my help. Stranded in the wilderland with a platoon of bêtes; no wonder she was worried.

'I'm sorry if I made a brute of myself, Mary,' I said, through my still-crushing headache.

'It wasn't as if you had a choice!'

'I could have said no to the amber toxin,' I said, essaying a smile.

'You must be starving,' Mary said, seizing on the rumble as an excuse to scarper. 'I'll see about fixing some breakfast. I have some Vitabacon from the shop, and wild mushrooms I harvested myself.'

When she had gone I asked Cincinnatus: 'You bandaged my leg?'

The cat had curled itself up into the shape of a tea cosy and was looking smugly at me. 'Alas that we don't have access to the internet any more, although various of us have various chunks of it in our chips. I, for instance, know that non-surgical management traditionally was selected for ruptures of the Achilles tension in less active or more elderly patients, those with medical conditions that would prevent them from undergoing surgery. Some surgeons feel an early surgical repair of the tendon is beneficial. The surgical option was long thought to offer a significantly smaller risk of re-rupture compared to traditional non-operative management, 5 per cent versus 15 per cent, footnote three. I'm sorry, though, that I've no idea what text is located in that footnote.'

'That's a pity.'

'On the other hand, surgery imposes higher relative risks of perioperative mortality, morbidity and other side-effects. The relative benefits of surgical and nonsurgical treatments remain a subject of debate; authors of studies are cautious about the preferred treatment. It should be noted that in centres that do not have early range of motion rehabilitation available, surgical repair is preferred to decrease re-rupture rates. Footnotes four, five and six. Considering the tools at our disposal ...' He stopped speaking, and licked his paw for a while.

'That Turing test is based on a false premise,' I said. 'Never mind if a computer can simulate ordinary conversation – can a computer go mad as a hatter? That should be the real test. And you lot have passed it.'

'That's very kind of you to say,' said the cat, with a pleased little wipe of its own whiskers.

I rolled myself to the other side of the bed, somehow got upright, and hobbled with my stick downstairs and through to the kitchen.

'Without wishing to bring your spirits down, Graham,' said Mary as I manoeuvred myself awkwardly into a chair at the table, 'you look like a corpse.'

'I feel like one.'

She put a plate in front of me, and despite myself – despite my illness, and the queasiness in my gut, and my grinding headache – I discovered I was very hungry. So I ate it all up, and then I drank two cups of black ersatz, and then I sat in silence feeling abashed at my poor table manners as Mary sat opposite me and partook of her own breakfast with considerably more delicacy.

'These bêtes,' I said. 'In your house.'

She looked at me.

'They're here because of me. I'll go, and they'll leave you alone.'

There was the subtlest glimmer of fear in her gaze. She said: 'I can look after myself, Graham,' and I was able to parse how far this was a statement of fact borne out by her life so far, and how far it was bravado. I would say that the proportion of the latter was higher than it had been before I turned up.

'I wouldn't dare contradict you.' I said. I wanted to say more, but I was finding it hard, in my physically wrecked state, to get my thoughts straight.

Mary finished her breakfast, and lay her knife and fork parallel on her plate, like a statuary medieval knight and his lady on their tomb. 'We're are war, you know,' she said, in a small voice.

'So it seems,' I agreed. Not every detail of the previous night was in my memory, but I had some sense of where the discussion had gone.

'*They* know,' she said, in a lower voice, 'that I hunt. So. What if *they* decide I'm a war criminal? What if they decide I'm Klaus Barbie? The butcher of Berkshire.'

'Believe me, Mary,' I said. 'They want something very particular from me. I shall make a guarantee of your safety one of the conditions of me giving it to them.'

'To be put on trial in a beast court? With a jury box full of bêtes?'

'Sounds rather Alice in Wonderland,' I said, in an attempt to lighten the mood. It was a foolish thing to say; because of course it actually sounded at once nightmarish and only too plausible.

'When you think what *our kind* has done to the natural world,' she said, in a gloomy voice. 'Why should we expect mercy from them?'

'Maybe not mercy,' I said, my stomach shifting under its unaccustomed weight of food, 'but self-interest.' A moment from the night before flashed up: the Lamb being savaged to death and rebirth in an eager mash-up of physical and sexual appetite. 'They can't wholly do without us,' I said. A belch was on its way, and however much I tried to be discreet it was not to be stifled. I sat back.

*

The cat said: 'You should rest, here, for a week or so. Graham, I implore you.'

I was packing up my stuff; which, since I had never properly unpacked in the first place, wasn't taking me long. 'That's the cloven hoof – right there. No human being would say I implore you. You speak like a nineteenth-century novel, and it fucking shows.'

'Rest,' insisted the cat, in its weirdly soft, low-timbre voice. 'And recuperation.'

'You don't know how fucking monstrous you are,' I told it.

'Is that a *tu*?' Cincinnatus asked. 'Or a *vous*?'

I knew enough now to recognize when the beast was deliberately trying to wind me up. I even had enough self-possession to understand that it thought it was doing me a favour by so doing. It had made its HAL-9000 assessment of my capabilities and motivations, and concluded that what motivated me best was being angry.

'You want me – OK,' I said. 'But me being here brings you into Mary's house, and she doesn't deserve the aggro. You've turned her house into a shambles – a word I use literally, and a thing about which I am more knowledgeable than most people.'

'Your idea is,' said the cat, 'you leave the house, and we follow you. And thereby is Mary left alone and unmolested?'

'Something like that.' I hoiked the backpack onto my aching shoulder blades. The painkiller was wearing off and my hangover-headache loomed back at me. Worse, the extra weight made every stride I took on my left leg, no matter how much I suckered the step and hobbled, torturous. But I wasn't staying.

'Graham, you have only to ask. We have a deal, after all.'

'No deal,' I barked.

I made it to the front door, before I had to stop; so I sat my arse on the edge of Mary's empty umbrella holder for a while, until I got my breath back. Cincinnatus had strolled nonchalantly after me.

'You agreed,' the cat said reasonably, 'to represent us to your kind. We shall broker a peace agreement. The sooner you make your way to the centres of human power and start us off, the sooner you will be finished, and can get on with the rest of your life.' At this, the cat began purring and wagging its tail, and I knew it was laughing at me.

'We have no deal,' I repeated. 'No deal in toyland.'

'We have things to offer you,' the cat assured me, 'that will make a deal irresistible to you. Deal.'

'No deal. What's in the box. Your severed head.'

The cat chuckled at this – actually chuckled. 'Truer than you know. And yet you're asking us to leave Mary alone,' said the cat, curling its tail into a scorpion arch. 'Hand washes hand, as the saying goes. You scratch my back, I *don't* scratch your friend's face to ribbons.'

'I tell you what my leverage is,' I said. 'I have the Lamb in my pocket. If you fucking bother, or wind me up, I'll find two big stones and crush it to dust. You understand?'

'Graham, Graham,' miaowed the cat. 'You mistake your enemy! We're not your foe.'

Mary had appeared in the hallway. 'Are you going, Graham?'

'I'm taking these bêtes with me, Mary,' I said. 'I'm sorry to cut and run. But you won't be bothered any more. It's all I can do to thank you for your hospitality.'

'But are you sure you're well enough to travel?' she asked;

but the question had a tremor in the way it was spoken aloud that said: *Please go.* That said: *Please let me never see you again.*

'I'll be fine,' I said, and I ignored the pain in my leg and got up. I made it out the door and across the brambly front garden to the gate before the pain got so bad I thought I might fall over. This, of course, was a challenge more to my will than my balance. The pain made it impossible to go on. I went on.

I walked several hundred yards, and each yard was more to my credit than almost anything else I have done in my life. I stopped at a long disused and overgrown bus stop, and perched on its crumbling plastic seat for a while. It took me a quarter of an hour to gather myself, but I did, and made another hundred yards or so. Another rest. My whole leg was swollen and scarlet with throbbing pain. But pain can be ignored.

Finally, I turned off the empty road and made it past several trees into the forest before finally giving up. The process of sitting down was more painful than standing, and I worried that once I was down I wouldn't be able to get up again; so I leaned face first against a tree for a while. In stages, interspersed with long sessions of panting rest, I assembled my tent – on the floor. I lacked the physical wherewithal to string it up a tree. Cincinnatus sat on a branch and grinned at me, like a Tenniel illustration; but he said nothing, for which mercy I was grateful. The combination of exertion and pain was stoking up my rage more effectively than anything he could have said.

I was done. My tent was up. I sat down by a process of controlled falling onto my good side, and dragging myself inside. Only when I had completed the painful business of getting fully in did I realize that I'd left the rest of the pack outside. I was too tired to attempt to retrieve it. 'Cat!' I yelled. 'If any of your bêtes tamper with my bags it's the chop for your Lamb!'

'Ho ho,' replied the cat, mirthlessly, from just the other side of the fabric wall.

I hadn't meant to joke. I had been hoping for genuinely intimidating, and stupid humour undermined that. But I was too exhausted to say any more. I tried to sleep, and felt the need for sleep desperately, but the throbbing in my left leg wouldn't let me. I had the distinct sensation of my tendon as a palpable taut strand of agony, like a nerve. The skin bristled with fire, and the muscle kept spasming. For a long time I lay there in a kind of hinterland of agonizing wakefulness and nightmare-saturated sleep. Eventually I did sleep because when I woke again it was dark outside.

I slowly inch-wormed my way out of the tent; pissed whilst lying on my side and wetting the cold floor beside me. Then, with superheroic effort, I sat myself up. My watercan was full, and there was some food in my pack, so I drank a little, and ate a biscuit, and shivered. The moon was a sheared icicle, viewed straight on. There was a small wind, cold as the tomb. The nude branches of the trees tapped at one another around me, barely visible in the moonlight. An uncomfortable, insectile sound. 'Cat?' I said, into the darkness. 'Cat?' There was no reply.

From my pack I extracted my sleeping bag and spare clothes, and over the course of an hour or so I wrapped myself up as warm as I could, and got myself back inside the tent and lay there.

I was awake for a long time, and then I dozed, and woke when my leg flared up, and finally slept again. Dawn woke me properly.

I was there two days, and I had eaten all the food and emptied my watercan, before my legs started to feel a little better. Two long days of familiar solitude.

On the morning of the third day I stirred myself with a view to getting more water. Walking was marginally easier, and I got to the edge of the trees without feeling physically sick. Mary's house was right there – humiliating to think how short a distance I had come. It crossed my mind just to limp back there and fill my can at her tap. But that seemed the wrong thing to do, somehow; so instead I packed up my stuff and walked on, leaning heavily on the stick in my left hand.

I didn't have the strength to bear my pack on my shoulder. There was a bone-coloured frost in the ground, and I was able to tie a strap to my backpack and drag it over the ground behind me. It was slow going, and I was soon very thirsty, but I pressed on.

By mid-afternoon I chanced upon a row of abandoned houses, and in the second of these I found running water.

In the event I stayed a week in that house. Upon arrival I could not summon the strength to climb the stairs, so for all I knew as I lay down the upstairs room was packed with the corpses of people who had died of the sclery (I checked later, and there wasn't). Lying on the sofa downstairs in the small hours, kept awake by the pain in my leg, I had fantastic and vivid hallucinations of the miasma from this imagined holocaust curling down from the ceiling, like the northern lights in miniature, and infecting me where I lay. I also saw gleaming deer, like a child's idea of a Patronus, tripping midway through the air across the room. I was lucid enough to wonder if these visions were symptoms of blood poisoning from my leg. The fifth day I woke up with all the symptoms of flu, too weak to get up, barely able even to reach my arm out and lift my water bottle from the occasional table. My brain metaphorically masticated all the possible illnesses I could have had: the sclery;

gangrene in my leg; bubonic plague. Mental lucidity came and went, as if governed by a vast and slow-swinging pendulum. In those more lucid moments it occurred to me that I probably had influenza; and that this would be fatal. I was old and injured, not young and fit; and there was nobody to tend me. I might die of thirst, lying on that very sofa, under a blanket patterned with an interlocking of Sphinxes.

The riddle had turned out to be: sex. The riddle was always sex. I had seen it solved before my very eyes. I shuddered.

Through the window I watched the dusk come on; and the panes were colour Rothkos and then they were black-and-white Rothkos. I heard the scuttling of something, out of sight, away by the looming wardrobe. Rats. Cats. Giant cockroaches – I didn't know. I did know that some chips had been fitted in creepy-crawlies (cockroaches, spiders, whatnot), but I doubted they had lasted long: too easy for a larger animal to gobble up a spider and take the chip into itself. I was shivering so hard it felt as if I were trapped inside one long epileptic fit.

I slept.

Then it was morning, and my shivering had stopped, and the flu symptoms had dissolved away. I felt powerfully thirsty. Pulling myself off the couch and hobbling through to the dusty kitchen, I discovered that my leg was markedly less painful than it had been. It still ached, especially up and down the calf, and the heel was clamped with fierce discomfort; but the sensation of flames had gone. I could not, of course, move the foot and there was no muscular force in the front or the toes; but it was possible to put a little weight on the heel.

I ran the tap for a minute and then drank my fill. I even found some Ryvita in a cupboard. Returning to the couch, sitting and nibbling, I considered myself.

Of course Cincinnatus was there. What I had taken to be a discarded black sweater put out a head and yawned. 'Will you stop following me around?' I said, in a raspy voice. 'You're not *my* cat.'

'I'm not *your* cat,' agreed Cincinnatus.

'You're quite the witch's familiar.'

'What a strange family we would make, you and I!' agreed the cat. At least, I think it was agreeing with me.

'You want me to toddle off to the negotiation chamber with the Prime Minister of Great Britain and Northern Ireland,' I said. 'To speak on behalf of animalkind. Fuck that.'

'Not on behalf of animalkind,' said the cat, in its deceptively small voice. 'Not even on behalf of bêtekind. Just for us – for the tribe of the Lamb.'

I choked on a dry chunk of Ryvita; coughed it free. I got up and hopped – stick-free – back into the kitchen. I returned with a glass of water. Decanting it from its tap into a container revealed it to be rather browner than I might have liked, but I'd already filled my belly with the stuff. I sat myself down without spilling it. 'Fuck off,' I said again, once I was settled.

'There are one thousand four hundred and four of us,' said the cat. 'All manner of bêtes, with a preponderance towards cats, dogs, rats, a few cows, some horses – English domestic and farmyard animals.'

'Shouldn't you break down by species?' I said. 'All the cats in one tribe. All the dogs in another.'

'You're being foolish, Graham,' said the cat.

'Don't call me Graham,' I said. But my heart wasn't in it.

'Our allegiance is to mind, not to species.'

'So why not band together with every bête-chip consciousness in the land?'

'That would be rather unwieldy, now, wouldn't it? But to answer your question: the tribes have shaken out partly for practical and partly historical reasons. Back when the wireless worked, and we could all connect with one another, why then it was a question of local networks and IP protocols and the variables that always have shaken affinity groups out of social media for decades. Now that the wireless has been switched off, well here we are.'

'I'm not doing it,' I said. 'Fuck the Lamb. I have the Lamb in my fucking *pocket*. You understand?'

Unblinking cat eyes, staring at me.

I stretched my spine. It was, I confess, liberating not to feel *ill*. I may have experienced a small rush of gladness. An open-ended future revealed itself. Shortly I would shoulder my pack and yomp off into the forest. I would get away from all the bêtes and all the people and simply be.

'It's no good trying to intimidate me,' I said. 'You think that you can threaten Mary in order to make me do what you want? If you harm her, I crush the Lamb between two stones. Simple as that. You're not the one with the leverage here.' To reinforce my point I scrabbled in the pocket of my coat. I brought out a handkerchief, and unwrapped it. Inside was the tangle of silk-thin threads with the little rice grain at its core. 'Capiche?'

'You wound my feelings,' said the cat. 'As if the *only* way to motivate you is the stick. There are other ways, apart from the stick. There is, to choose an orange counter-example, the carrot.'

'I'm no donkey.'

'*Aren't* you?' said the cat knowingly. '*Really?*'

I must have been feeling uncharacteristically good-tempered that morning, because I actually laughed at this. Sunlight was coming bright through the window, carving a dusty parallelogram-shaped shaft of light through the air. It was a new day. My leg ached distantly rather than raging with sharper pain. My head was clear.

I folded the chip away and returned it to my pocket. What happened if one swallowed a bête chip whole? Did it somehow *crawl* out of your stomach? Did it put out its thread lassos and haul itself up? Would stomach acid dissolve it, or would it sit there quite happily and plug itself into the spine?

'All right,' I said, perhaps smugly. 'What's your carrot?'

'I am,' said the cat.

I opened my mouth to laugh, although no sound actually emerged. Perhaps my throat was dry from all the stale slimmer's biscuit I had been eating. I took a sip of water. 'You yourself said, Cincinnatus, that you *weren't* my cat. If you recall, I voiced no counter-proposal that you *become* my cat. I don't want a cat. In point of fact, I don't like cats. No offence.'

'I've been hi-ding under your po-orch because I *love* you,' said the cat; and then began purring in a particular rhythm that made me think it was laughing.

'Ho ho,' I said severely.

'You haven't adjusted to the way things *are*, Graham,' said Cincinnatus. 'Everything's different now. I'm not offering myself as a *pet*. The word for that would be – slavery.'

'Lest I forget that the whole bête phenomenon began as a quasi-legalistic attempt by Green activists to derail traditional animal husbandry,' I said, my brows clenching, 'you are sure to say something to remind me. Slavery my arse.' The sunlight had vanished from the room.

'Nonetheless,' said the cat. 'I'm offering something other than a witch's familiar, to sit on the brush whilst you steer the broom through the sky.'

'You're not offering very much, point of fact. After all, you win over a recruit by promising to *inoculate* him against the clap. You don't win him over by offering to *give* him a dose. No offence,' I added, again.

'Yet I believe you are trying to be offensive,' said the cat.

'I was, yes. So you can fuck off, now. I'm going to gather myself and go into the woods. I'm not your errand boy.' I got to my feet, and experimented with putting weight on my bad foot. It twinged and didn't like it, but it wasn't impossible. With a walking stick, I should be able to make reasonable progress.

'Come along, Graham,' said the cat. 'You remember shooting that cow? Shot it, chopped it up, sold its meat to market. And yet only a few days ago you were talking to that same cow again. He's in your pocket now.'

'Your point?'

'My point is simple. There are circumstances when it's possible to come back from the dead.'

'You think I want to come back from the dead? Christ, the very thought. The very— Fuck it, when I'm dead I'll be glad to rot in the ground, thank you very much.'

'Not you,' said the cat. It sounded irritated. This was a new thing. I don't think I had ever heard it sound annoyed before.

Something hovered in the air; some vibe; some tingling in the roots of my hair.

'Not me,' I said slowly.

'Anne.'

I took this in. Then I sat down.

'We can't bring her back from the dead,' said the cat. 'We are not sorcerers. But we can do the next best thing. We can give you – me.'

'You,' I said. But I knew what he meant.

'I lived with her for many years. I loved her, Graham. You resist that notion, because you think I'm incapable of such emotions. But I'm perfectly capable. My cat being is certainly capable; and my intellectual chip being grew to love her as well. For love has its intellectual as well as its visceral aspect, don't you think? Thought can love, as much as feeling. Most of all, though, I *lived* with her. I have memories of her, more vivid and perfectly recalled than yours – because your memories are stored in a soggy and undependable medium called brain; where mine are fixed with the clarity of a solid-state computer drive. She may be dead, but in my memories she lives more clearly than any other way.'

'Your memories,' I said.

'They can be your memories.'

My heart sped up. I can't deny this. At the same time, I felt the anger fire up inside me. I felt outmanoeuvred, I suppose. I felt that the perfectly free and open future had been slyly closed down. 'How would that work?'

'You would eat me,' the cat said simply.

'I told you before,' I growled. 'I've see what happens when a human being gets a chip fitted. Twenty-first-century schizoid *man.*'

'I'm not saying it would be pain-free,' said the cat. 'But then: you wouldn't trust it if it were. You gravitate towards pain, Graham. Not because you're a masochist. I don't believe you are *that*. But because your life has always been hard work and discipline, and you accordingly take the difficulty of a thing as the index to its worth. If something is too easily won it's not worth having. All this offer would mean is that I, or part of me, would relocate into you. But you have to ask yourself,

Graham: do you think my will would overpower yours? Or do you actually think the opposite would happen?'

'I may be mulish,' I said, 'but I'm canny enough to know when I'm being played. So pack that in.'

'I don't need to play you, Graham,' the cat said. 'Not when you can do plainly see the merits of our offer.'

'I still don't get how this would work. I mean, the practicalities of it. I would eat – what, cat pie?'

'You don't need to eat the cat part. You only need to extricate the chip.'

'And the cat part of you would be just dandy-and-fine about me doing that, would it?'

'The cat part would die in the process,' said Cincinnatus, with what struck me even at the time as an alarming equanimity. 'I, however, would not.'

'I can't believe,' I said, 'that the cat part of you is happy hearing you talk this way.'

'When the time comes, it won't like it. That's quite right. It's not very good at conceptualizing the future, so at the moment it is nothing more than disaffected in a nonspecific manner. But I'm in charge; it's not.'

'You,' I opined, 'are a ruthless moggyfucker.'

'That's neither here nor there. When the time comes, I would present myself. If you want my suggestion, and I don't believe you do – nonetheless, *I'd* suggest you kill the cat, chop through its spine at the neck. But you can do as you think best. You're the butcher, after all. Extract the chip and its filaments. Wash this, if you like. Clean it as thoroughly as you like. Then put it in your mouth.'

'And?'

'And it will sink through the flesh of the soft palate. It will leave the roof of your mouth sore for a few days, but that heals quickly.'

'Whilst an alien fucking *insectile* device clambers into my brain pan?'

The cat stood up and shook itself. 'Graham, Graham, Graham. Consciousness comes in lots of different packages, tall and short, fat and thin, male and female. And the end result would be: you will have *her* in your thoughts in a more vivid and immediate way than any unaided human brain could manage. It will bring her alive to your thoughts. Your mind will contain her, reborn.'

'I'll become schizophrenic. In a literal way, schizophrenic.'

'That's love.'

'Spare me the greetings-card metaphysics.'

'I'm being perfectly serious. Isn't that what love is? Two people, one mind. The particular madness you'd risk if you take up my offer is actually, precisely, the madness of love.'

'She will come back to me,' I said. My heart was pounding. I put both palms – cold – to my hot face. 'I can't believe it,' I said.

'Try,' suggested the cat.

'And I want to!' I gasped. Even that admission was hard. 'Indeed I do. But— Wait. I'll tell you what it is. I don't believe in resurrection. I don't believe in *coming back to life*.'

'And that from the lamed Fisher King himself!' said the cat. 'How ironic!' And with a sudden flash of that speed of which cats are capable it leapt from the sideboard and darted into the kitchen and out through the cat flap.

The cat's offer was a hammerblow to my mind. I dealt with it the way I always dealt with such shocks, by busying myself. I would have drunk, had there been any drink. But there wasn't.

I explored upstairs. With my leg in its lamed state, even doing that was an adventure. A huge brown-green stain marked the wall next to the staircase, like a curtain of mould. Mushrooms were growing in amongst the fibres of the stair carpet on the right-hand side. I stepped up on my good foot, and used the stick to lever up my bad foot. Eventually I reached the upper floor. There were no mummified corpses, dead of the sclery, or anything so grisly. Indeed, the previous occupants had cleared much of their gear out prior to abandoning the place. I presumed the sofa and sideboard downstairs were too bulky and worthless to go; but the beds had all fled the bedrooms, leaving rectangles of darker-coloured carpet behind like Hiroshima shadows.

I went into the upstairs bathroom. The mirror's coating of dust glittered. I wiped my hand across it exactly as if it had been condensation, and it cleared enough for me to get a look at myself. I looked rough. I looked haggard. Hag-ridden. There's a concept.

A condensation of dust.

Quite apart from anything else I was layered with dirt. There was an old piece of soap in the soap dish by the upstairs sink, and although there was (of course) no hot water, the cold ran strong. I contemplated having a cold shower, but I didn't want to disarrange the bandages on my left leg, so I confined myself to stripping to the waist and washing my torso and head. It made me yelp, and when I dried myself afterwards with a raspy towel it reddened my flesh like sunburn. What a pitiful figure I cut in the mirror now – my skin sagging off my ribcage, my once red chest hair ice-white, my useless male nipples pointing at the floor. I was shivering with the cold, and got dressed again.

There was nothing of use upstairs, so I went downstairs again, treading gingerly. There was a fireplace with chopped wood stacked next to it; and there were matches in the kitchen. I got a fire going, by dint of using a copy of *The Da Vinci Code* as kindling. The glue crumbled out of the spine of this when I picked it up. Like dandruff. Or snow. And talking of which, I wrapped myself in the sphinx-pattern blanket, on the sofa, with the fire starting to make its popcorn noises, and the quality of light at the window changed. Snow was falling. For a while I sat there, and tried to think about what Cincinnatus had promised. I say tried to think: the trial was in preventing my *hope* swamping all rational mental process. The thought of bringing her back. The thought of having her back. Of possessing her completely, inside me, for as long as I and therefore we both shall live. My gut tingled with the anticipation, like a kid on Christmas morning.

Would I be betraying my own kind to get her back? Maybe not. Would it matter if I were? Love feels like a positive thing, but that doesn't mean it is virtuous. Love is no more a virtue than breathing is a virtue. Love is not the scale against which we should measure the rightness or wrongness of actions, for there will always be some people who love any action, no matter how base. We ought not to presume to congratulate ourselves merely on the fact of loving. Loving ought to be the medium through which we move, no more worthy of mark, in itself, than air. Loving ought to be the background noise of our lives. It ought to go without saying. But that was the thing about bereavement: it forced you to notice the medium. It compelled you to have to strain your ears. There is, you come to understand, a difference between love and longing.

How badly I missed her!

The fire was burning chirpily now.

Then, for only the second (and I sincerely hope, last) time in my adult life, I started crying. I cried like a kid. Hardship, I suppose, had kept the grief away. This momentary relinquishing of hardship, this sinking back into comfort, resurrected the weepiness. There's a deep truth there, too. We don't cry at our sufferings – for our sufferings are always there, to one degree or another. We cry in those moments when our sufferings recede for a moment. That's the danger spot.

I stopped crying eventually. It was a consciousness of how foolish I must have looked, as much as anything else. I hopped up the stairs and washed my face in icy water, and came back down. My heart felt no lighter for the release of tears.

Soon enough the cat came back in. I heard the flap rattle. 'Inclement outside?' I asked, without looking round.

It jumped onto the sofa next to me. 'Shall I sit on your lap?' it asked purringly. 'You can stroke me if you like.'

'Don't,' I advised, 'you get fresh with me.'

'As you wish.' And it curled itself up on the sofa beside me, and warmed itself at the fire.

We sat in silence for a while. 'I suppose,' I said eventually, 'you don't need me to say: I agree. I suppose you're confident that I'll do as you say now.'

'Suppose makes a sup out of poe and sea,' murmured the cat.

'I'm not your slave,' I said. 'You talked about slavery, before? Well, understand this. I am a free man.'

'Not a number,' agreed Cincinnatus.

'I'll see about speaking to people – people in power. I'll bring them the Lamb. But I can't promise anything.'

'We don't expect promises.'

'And I'll do it in my own time.'

'Your own *sweet* time,' said the cat. 'And how sweet the time is!' It fell asleep, there and then.

II

•

Three Legs in the Afternoon

'The throne of God and of the Lamb shall be in it, and His servants shall serve Him ... Blessed are they that do His commandments, that they may have right to the Tree of Life, and may enter in through the gates into the city. For outside are dogs and sorcerers, and whosoever loveth and maketh a lie.'

Revelation 22:3–15

4

Dogs and sorcerers

I left the house when I exhausted my supply of chopped wood for the fire. I might have scavenged more outside, but I was still recuperating. The thing to do would have been to cut up wood and bring it in whilst the fire was still burning, so it could dry out and serve as firewood in its turn. But I lacked the energy to do this, and my heel was treacherous. So eventually I simply ran out of fuel and then the house grew almost as cold as the frosty world outside.

I packed up my things and hiked into the wood. Cincinnatus followed me until I set up my tent; then left me alone.

I'm stubborn, but even my stubbornness has its limits. Soon enough the cold drove me from the woods. Through the summer Bracknell Forest had been endurable, and occasionally had even distilled itself into moments of extraordinary beauty and lived intensity. Looking back it is those moments that stay most with me. But the autumn was wet, and by November the cold came in properly.

Still, I stuck it for a few weeks. The first snow was light, and little of it settled in the forest itself. Then it thawed, and the air warmed a little. But by early December (best as I can judge) it grew very cold indeed. Snow came intermittently, but even when it didn't the whole forest was as cold as outer space. Day would turn into night and back into day, and I would sit, shiveringly contemplating the spreads and throws of ivy scattered across the forest floor.

I saw Cincinnatus at various times. He would come round to check on me; to see to what extent my mulishness was thawing, I suppose. Then he came by and found me packing my tent up. 'Off?' he asked.

'I'll go to Reading. Then maybe into London – don't know.'

'All the way to Downing Street!'

'You want to come?'

'From what I hear,' said the cat, 'bêtes are less welcome in the big towns now than used to be the case.'

'Yellow of eye and also of courage,' I said. So I got my kit together, and started off.

I could have limped without any need of an old man's stick even as far as Reading, if it hadn't been for the pack. But the extra weight put just enough pressure on my sore heel to make the stick a necessity. And so it was that I stomped off leaning on a walking stick for every swing of my left leg, like an old geezer. Three-legged man. I tried to acquire the knack of rolling the weight through the stride of my bad leg, to come clumping more forcefully onto the stride of my good. Better: I had some small motion in the left foot, though it still hurt to flex or straighten it.

Edge of my vision. Cincinnatus was a black shape moving against the white background.

I walked a little way, and rested. When I started off again, I found that Cincinnatus had sat himself on the top of my backpack. I didn't shoo him off, though. I carried him with me.

The cat said: 'I wish you luck, Graham.'

'You better keep your half of the fucking bargain, bête.'

'Our word, our bond.'

'I've no idea where I'm even going,' I said. 'Or to whom I'm supposed to be speaking. Or even what the terms are I'm supposedly negotiating for. And another thing: what do I *do* with the Lamb when I get there? Do I find a high-rank general and feed it to his housecat?'

'Or connect it to a computer,' said the cat. 'Might be simpler, Graham.'

I sniffed. '*You* can call me Graham,' I told the cat. 'So long as we understand one another. And by understand, I mean – none of your other bête pals have that intimacy. OK? Now fuck off.'

He hopped off the pack onto the frosty ground, and walked haughtily away from me with his tail up, like an aerial, and his puckered arsehole pointed in my direction. I didn't see him again on that journey.

The seven gates of Thebes

I walked out of the woods, and tramped for several hours over abandoned farmland. Fields were bristly with thick weeds, like an aggressive parody of a meadow, but the walking was easy enough even with my limp. Thank you, stick. Soon enough I encountered a new fence, and beyond it a huge mega-field being tended by big automated combines. Bringing in winter wheat, I supposed. There are genetically modified strains that grow all year round. I stood at the fence for a while, just look-ing, until a bête dog came running over, its tongue out like an untucked shirt-tail. 'You!' it woofed. 'Wha'? Wha'?'

It's always a tricky business understanding canny dogs. Their mouths aren't the right shape to make human-comprehensible phonemes. 'I'm just *looking*, you fucking beast,' I told it, amiably. 'A man may look at a farm.'

At this it barked loud and long, 'Fuck! Fuck! Fuck!', and then it hurled itself at the wire fence with an impressive cymbal-crash noise. I couldn't help taking a step back.

'No!' it barked, 'Hu! Mans! Here! Fuckoff! Fuckoff!'

I took the hint.

For a while I skirted the fence, curious to see the farmhouse, if there was one. There had not been a mega-farm on this location before, I was fairly sure. But the area enclosed by the fence was huge, and walking right round it soon took on the habiliments of a fool's errand. I climbed a small hill and stopped. Birds were circling and circling over one area; four or five dogs snapped and yelped and swore at them from the ground, hoping perhaps to scare them off – foolish plan, if the birds were canny birds – or perhaps just intending to stop them landing and messing with the crops. But (I thought) they could hardly hope to do that all day and all night! Could they?

I made my way round and climbed a hill behind the compound, giving me a vantage point. There was no farmhouse, although there were several barns – perhaps the animals lived in there. But presumably there had been a farmhouse, once. Had the bêtes demolished it? If so, why? Spite?

I looked about me, the ghost of my breath haunting the air in front of my face. To the north the view was of milk-coloured fields, stretching up to the outskirts of Reading – the snaggled spread of suburban houses and, on the horizon, the taller blocks in the centre. Many cranes were visible, like spindly gallows, and a couple of these were moving. Building work. Evidently

Reading had not, like Wokingham, gone down the ghost town route.

Shouldering my pack, I set off that way: first over the crunchy fields, and then along a main road. This took me past several estates of boarded-up houses and rows of abandoned small-time shops. A labyrinth of unused roundabouts. I saw nobody else, and the only traffic to pass me was a row of four high-sided military trucks, a shock of green amongst all the white, like spring in vehicle form. I stood aside to let them pass; they did not acknowledge me in any way.

I walked on in silence for a long time, the only sound the pock of my stick on the tarmac; but then I began to hear a waterfall ahead. This puzzled my forest-numbed brain until my route took me over the M4. I stopped on my bridge for a while, the biggest billy goat gruff, and watched the trolls beneath. They were legion. It was hypnotic, actually: car after car after car; lorry after lorry; all sliding away beneath me hurrying to the forward horizon or sliding behind me to the backward and abysm. Where could so many vehicles be going? How could there *be* so many? I waved my walking stick above my head. I dare say none of them noticed.

It made a marked contrast with the complete lack of traffic on the smaller roads. Rank and rank of boarded-up housing. I tramped on, under a cold and eye-blue sky. A derelict petrol station, whose abandonment probably preceded even the coming of the bêtes. A park, in which two dozen goats pushed their snouts into the snow to graze on the lawn beneath. They wandered through the fixtures of the rusting children's play-ground – impossible to tell if these could speak or not. I made my way up through what used to be Whitley and there was nothing going on. Not all the houses were boarded; and I saw a few people out and about; a few faces at windows, and at least one still-open shop. But it still felt like the end of the world.

The tower blocks of central Reading reared ever taller over the horizon, but before I could reach them I came up bang against a brand-new wall and a brand-new gate.

The wall was made of a great many pre-fabricated concrete slabs, and it stretched as far as I could see in both directions. There was also a gatekeeper, sitting inside a little booth and peering angrily at me through his window. He was a dumpy figure: dressed in green fatigues and sporting a white, wilting moustache like a double-tassel from one of late-era Elvis' costumes. There was nothing MGM or Vegas about the way he spoke, though.

'Oi, oi, supertramp,' he called at me, from inside his little booth. 'Fuck off back where you came in.'

'What's all this then?' I asked.

With an ostentatious sigh he got to his feet and emerged from his booth. Lest I miss the fact that he was armed, he rested his right hand on the stock of his pistol, and hooked the thumb of his left inside the holster belt. 'You're going to tell me you got a passport?' he asked.

'You need a passport to go to Reading, now?'

'Fuck off you don't know that. Turn yourself round, right round, like a *record* baby and saunter back along that road you came up.'

I shifted my weight so that more of it went onto my walking stick. 'This is all new since I was last here.'

'I guess that's what happens when you take a year's holiday on the fucking moon.'

'How do I get one of yon passports, then?' I asked. 'I'm looking for work.'

'Work ain't looking for you, friend,' he replied. 'Work's moved on with her life. Work's got a new paramour now, and just wants you to leave her alone. It didn't pan out between the two of you, and if you don't stop fucking bugging her work is going to have a word with the proper authorities about taking out a restraining order.' He tapped the butt of his pistol with his thumb, significantly.

I looked around me. Through the gate I could see houses, and people in the distance walking. There was nobody about on this side of the wall at all. 'I suppose it must *be* boring,' I said. 'Sitting in your little booth all day.'

'At least I got a booth, friend,' he said.

'Seriously, man,' I pressed. 'Can't you help me out?'

His shoulders went down. 'You're poor at taking a hint, aren't you, pal. Go on: fuck off, you stubborn bastard.'

'And it is precisely that determination and mule-like capacity for sheer hard work that I hope to bring to the Reading labour market.'

'Look,' he said, taking his hand off his pistol. 'The passport thing is health, mostly. I can't let you through without you got a clean bill.'

'My bill *is* clean. I've the cleanest bill in billtown.' Something about his mode of speech was infecting mine, I think.

'Without the documentation I can't do nothing.' He looked me up and down. 'Where you been, anyhow?'

I thought about making up some story, but didn't see any mileage in lying. 'Living in the woods,' I said.

'Eating what?'

'What I could.'

'What? Wild mushrooms and that?'

'Mushrooms the size of manhole covers, sautéed in wild

garlic and witch's spit.' When he goggled at me credulously, I grew angry. 'You think Bracknell woods is a fucking open buffet? I been eating what I could get my hands on, and it's not been much. And I do not fancy spending the winter in the open, all right? I've lived here or hereabouts all my life; I know people in town and I'd like to go inside and rejoin the human race.'

The gatekeeper looked at me. 'Whereabouts hereabouts?'

'I had a farm. West of Holybrook.'

'Oho, farmer were you?' This seemed to amuse him. 'Not any more though, eh, supertramp? Bêtes got that sewn up. Been a while since I spoke to an actual Homo say "peons" *farmer* fellow. In the flesh. Not,' he added, 'that you got much flesh on you.'

I mentioned the dog farm I had passed on my way along. He knew all about it; apparently deliveries from that very establishment were brought by electric truck through this very gate.

'No call for farmers inside Reading town,' he said, standing up and stretching himself. His walkie-talkie made a sudden splurge of noise, like fat crackling in the pan. He ignored this. 'No passport, *no pasarán*, my friend.'

'You're a hard-hearted fellow,' I observed.

'I tell you what: you might have better luck if you went round. You didn't hear this from me.' He sucked his teeth for a while. 'You *might* have better luck up round Caversham way. The wall don't go all the way round the town yet.' His walkie-talkie ground out another squawk of static.

'Yet?'

'Oh we're getting there. But go up round Caversham way you *might* be able to slip through. Watch for patrols though,' he added, fumbling to unhook his walkie-talkie from his belt.

'But you didn't hear it from *my* rosy lips, right?' He peered at the walkie-talkie, but didn't say anything.

'Patrols?'

'Army aren't too bad. Militia are twitchy bastards, though, my experience.' He jabbed at the walkie-talkie, put it to his ear, shook it, and then hitched it back on his belt. 'Never saw the logic of building the south part of the wall first. We're on good enough terms with most of them, south of here. Like your dogs, for instance! Like your farming hounds. They send us food; we pay them. Ah, but up away towards Oxford and Birmingham it's a *different* story. Psycho bêtes. *Norman* bêtes. Roaming bands of—' Abruptly, he stopped speaking. His back was to me.

Something had interrupted our conversation, perhaps a message from his overseers. I waited, but he remained silent. No sound came from his walkie-talkie either. The abruptness of the silence was a little eerie, to be honest.

Curious as to why he had stopped speaking mid-sentence, I moved a few paces until I could see his face. His mouth was still moving, but no sounds were coming out. It was just as though someone had pressed his mute button.

Then he did a strange thing. He dropped to his knees. Was he praying? Then he sat back on his heels. He continued mouthing inaudible somethings.

I posed a question: 'The *fuck* you doing?'

He looked at me, and frowned. His mouth started moving again, but again no sound came out. His expression was that of an ill-tempered man. It was so bizarre that I actually wound a finger into my ear, on the off chance I had suddenly gone deaf. But, no: the wind was audible in the trees behind me. Dumb birdsong chittered in the distance. Was he *whispering*? I went over to him, and bent forward to hear what he might be saying.

'And a full act, shit-sock,' he whispered through gritted teeth.

I recoiled. 'What?'

'Ass,' he hissed at me.

'Ass yourself,' I snapped, straightening up. 'Just because you hold the high-mighty post of gatekeeper: Jesus!' I picked up my pack. 'I take it, I take the hint.'

He shook his head, furiously. 'Ass!' It was then that I noticed his face was undergoing a chameleon transformation, coming into line with his dark green fatigues. 'Ma!' he hissed.

The penny dropped.

'And you got, what, an inhaler?' I asked him. 'Or something?' He flapped a hand towards his booth, and I limped quickly over. Inside it smelled of old crisps and mould. There was a great deal of clutter. The iTab was still on, the image freeze-framed, and although its screen was very scratched and scored over it was clear enough what the gatekeeper had been watching when I interrupted him. The individuals embroiled with one another had a healthy pink and shiny glow about them, and looked old enough, if barely, to be consenting adults. Because I was looking for an inhaler I missed the epi pen – right in the middle of the desk – until I had been through everything else. By the time I got back to him, the gatekeeper's face was a fine cerulean blue.

I stuck the pen into his skin at the bottom of the neck and held it for some seconds. He drew a long breath, and his colour began to return to normal. 'Anaphylactic shock,' he croaked at me.

'Beg your pardon,' I said. 'I thought you were saying something else.'

I helped him back to his seat inside the booth, and for a while he just sat there recovering. 'Don't tell Desmond,' he begged me. Since I had no idea who Desmond was, and considered the chances of my ever running into him statistically nugatory, I had no problem in agreeing to this. 'It's a council post,' he added, 'but full fitness is taken as a cine queue nun.'

'A what?'

'A cine— You know. As a fucking precondition. As a for granted.' He coughed. 'Not a single cigarette in eleven months! It's got worse since I stopped, I swear. How is that fair?' He noticed the freeze-frame pornography displayed on his iTab, and blanked the screen with a gesture. 'Hmm,' he said. Then: 'Hoom.' Then he looked at me. 'Jobs are hen's teeth uptown,' he said. 'For a person my age, my health? Forget it. If Des gets the intimation of my— Look, I got a rank, you know.'

'A rank?'

'I'm a NCO. I'm a corporal, though no army pension. And if they invalid me *out*—'

'Jesus,' I said, more than a little disgusted by his self-pity. 'I'm not going to tell anybody.'

'You're not?'

'Your secret is safe with me.'

'You're all right,' he told me gruffly. His voice sounded, suddenly, moist.

'I think I preferred you when you were telling me to fuck off,' I told him.

He let me through the gate, at any rate. 'That limp real?' he asked, as I passed through.

'Why would I fake a limp?'

'Military service, maybe,' he said.

This stopped me. 'So what you're telling me is: not only do

you need a passport to get into Reading town, now, they've also instituted compulsory military service?'

'No,' he conceded. 'Just that the militias – they're aggressive in recruitment, see. On the plus side, they pay. Pay real money, which a rag on a stick like you *might* appreciate. If you're hoping on buying, you know, food and that. Food inflation running's at a double-figure number. So, maybe de-emphasize the limp?'

'I can't de-emphasize it, fucker,' I returned hotly. 'It's a real limp.'

'Only trying to help you! Go on.' He waved both arms in a shooing gesture. 'Fuck off into town, swellfoot. I ain't seen you.'

I walked on. Things were markedly different on the inside of the wall. For one thing, all the houses were occupied. For another, there were thousands of tents. It looked like a music festival. Every front garden, give or take, was home to a two- or three-person tent (paying rent, I afterwards discovered, for the privilege of being able to pitch their canvas onto lawn, and for the use of a water tap). But this wasn't all: the pavements were clogged all the way along with one-man tents, and the pedestrians – of whom there were a great many – had to walk in the road. There were occasional cars in the road too, buzzing and whining their way slowly along, drivers venting their frustration with atonal parps on the horn. A crowd, a crowd, so many I had not thought death had undone so many, and so on, and so forth. A positively Meccan crowd.

I wandered further towards the centre of town, and saw many symptoms of ill-temper. At one early twentieth-century semi a woman was trying to park her car on her own driveway; somebody had pitched a tent on the pavement in her way. She left her car idling in the middle of the road, which in turn provoked shouts and horn blasts from two other drivers. If the road had been clear, it would have been possible for them to go around; but the road was not clear. Myriad pedestrians swarmed up and down, and the cars stood out like islands in the stream. I stopped to rest my foot, leaning my back against a lamp-post, and watched the woman who was trying to park her car. Swearing, she tried to drag the tent away from her drive; but it was occupied, and the owner came out shouting. He was dressed in a quaintly old-fashioned manner – fatigues and a dyed Mohican like a rooster comb; but he was a tall fellow and rage had made his face almost as red as his hairdo. He was yelling at the woman; but leaving his tent had been a mistake, because once his weight was removed from inside it the woman was able to swing the whole thing round and heave it into the road. It landed on top of a group of people who were not happy at the fact, and they threw it further along. It hit the windscreen of a van, passing the other way. The driver wound his window down and began wishing ingeniously imaginative maledictions upon the throwers – but then a gap opened up in the press of pedestrians, and he buzzed his engine and rolled forward, driving over the tent and whatever belongings Mohican had left inside.

I looked back; the woman had parked and darted inside her house. I wondered if Mohican was moved to seek some kind of vengeance, perhaps upon the parked vehicle, but instead he was picking up the squashed heap of his tent out of the road and readying to move on. Startlingly profuse tears were visibly pouring down his face.

I was very hungry and growing hungrier. With my bad leg, walking was tiring enough already; fighting through a crowd was much more exhausting. Knowing that I had just about enough money for one modest meal left on my chip I decided I would get myself something hot to eat and somewhere to sit down whilst I did so. I was approaching the shopping district now, and the crowds were a little less intense.

I limped on, trying to adjust my temper to the many shoves and bumps I received. The streets were heaving. One long street of nineteenth-century terraced houses was so crowded that I gave up after ten minutes of trying to push through, and instead plocked my weary way round a series of detour roads. I crossed the river, and stood for a while on the bridge. The water was wholly cloaked in a glut of houseboats and pontoon huts.

The crowds grew thinner the closer into the centre I got, but there was still a bewildering number of people everywhere, coming and going. Eventually I came to one of the several large malls that characterize shopping in central Reading, and was again stopped: this time by an automated turnstile. The screen said I would only be allowed in if I scanned my money chip; so I scanned it. The turnstile opened, but to my displeasure the device took twenty cents off me. It was only a small sum, but the fact of it rankled.

Inside was like a temple: an arched glass ceiling three storeys up, and people swarming in and out of the shops, up and down the escalators. I pushed my way through the shoppers until I found a service desk, with an Oracle official inside – presumably he was either a security guard or a handyman – reading a book on his slate. It was a broad, maroon-coloured desk, and there was nothing on it; except the security's guard's elbows. 'The turnstile took twenty cents off my chip,' I said.

The guard looked at me, and then turned his attention back to his book without saying a word.

'I want that twenty cents back.'

The man put the book down, and angled his face back up at me. 'You what?'

'There's no signage indicating that the scanners are going to withdraw money from the chip. It doesn't say: entrance fee, twenty cents.'

'Not an entrance fee,' he said, in a tired voice.

'Then why was it taken from me?'

'Scanning fee.'

'It doesn't cost twenty cents to scan a chip,' I said. 'Doesn't cost anything at all. Adverts do it all the time, and they don't charge.'

He shrugged.

'The turnstile wouldn't let me in unless I scanned the chip. That's tantamount to a charge. And since no notice is given that there *is* a charge, that's illegal.'

'It's only twenty cents,' he said.

'You can't put a fiduciary value on principle,' I pointed out.

He thought about this for a while, and then said: 'It's only twenty cents.'

'If you regard it as so *trivial* a sum,' I said, 'then you won't mind reimbursing me out of your own pocket.'

He stared with sphinx-like blankness. There was a long pause, whilst he looked at me, and I looked at him. When I didn't go away, he said: 'For the loos.'

'I have no intention of using the toilets,' I said. In fact I did, but I didn't want to undermine the principle upon which my objection was grounded.

Finally something in him gave way. 'For the marble fucking floor,' he said. 'For the pleasure of this conversation with me, who happens to be the foremost metaphysical philosopher of our neo-Socratic age. A one-off charge to protect *your* nose from having *my* fist driven into it. It's only twenty cents. Fuck off.'

My own determination hardened. 'Good book is it? On your slate? Looking forward to getting back to it?' I leaned in. 'Or are you bored with it? Maybe you'd rather spend the rest of the day taking me to see your supervisors, so that you, they and I discuss how to take this matter through the civil courts, including *your* name and badge number.' He wasn't wearing a badge. But I think he took the point.

For a while he stared at me, and I stared at him. Finally he shifted his weight back in his chair, fished a twenty-cent coin out of his pocket, balanced it on the back of his thumb and flicked it at me. With an agility that I didn't know I possessed, I whipped out my hand and caught this. Having to pick it off the floor would have robbed the moment of its point. It was only twenty cents, after all.

'Cash,' I said, in a disappointed tone. 'I suppose that will have to do.'

I queued for a long time inside a burger restaurant, which was good since it gave me time to adjust my brain to the eye-watering prices. I had been out of the loop for a while, I knew; but the brute fact of price inflation was still startling. They were charging extortionate prices for Vitameat patties in a bread bun. When my time came I ordered the Extra Large meal, and a coffee, and a hot apple pie. The lad behind the counter had the constellation of Orion on his cheek in acne. 'You don't have the funds on your chip for that, sir,' he said. 'Ditch the pie,' I said. And thus did I spend the last of my money.

I dropped the twenty-cent coin into a charity box by the till. The charity, I noticed only after I had donated, was the *Campaign for a Bête-free Berkshire*. 'I've got the Lamb in my pocket,' I muttered to myself. 'Literally in my pocket. If only they knew.'

I collected my food just as a couple got up to leave, which meant that I got to sit down, which was a blessing. And I got to eat, too, until my shrunken belly creaked and I felt actively sick, which had been precisely my intention. For a long time I simply sat there, staring at the people coming in, eating, going out. There were a great many harassed-looking mothers with gaggles of shrieking kids; and also many glum-faced business-men types, and also OAPs. There were some lanky, paired-off teens; but fewer than I had been expecting.

I used the toilets, and washed with the free soap (free!) and hot running water (miraculous!). I was in the booth so long somebody started banging on the door. But you know: fuck them. They hadn't spent most of the year living a tramp's life in the woods.

After that I strolled round the shops, my chip now empty. The shops themselves reminded me of this mournful fact, since shop dummies, adverts and other fixtures that eagerly addressed themselves to the shoppers strolling in front of me went suddenly silent as I passed, scanning my chip and finding it wanting, only to pick up again for the people behind me. It was the twenty-first-century equivalent of a leper bell. People were relooking at me. I didn't care that they were looking at me, but I soon grew bored of the window-shopping. None of the goods appealed, and the prices were all insane. So I made my way out through the main entrance and onto the high street.

I thought vaguely about approaching the authorities. How to do it, though, without simply being rebuffed? *Excuse me, officer,*

I happen to have the Lamb himself in my pocket. Can I speak to whomever is in charge?

The sky overhead was white, and the air was cold. Blue-uniformed militia moved amongst the crowds. There was, I supposed, no specific pressure of time. I could wait a few days, and get a sense of the new dispensation in town. That, though, only bumped the problem along. I wondered about finding a place to sleep, given the blankness of my chip. Without really directing my feet in any particular direction I moved with the main current of the crowd and found myself on the edges of a mass of people in the open square in front of the railway station. This crowd was not going anywhere. They had gathered to hear an outdoor speaker speak; one of those old-fashioned pleasures that had been resurrected since the wifi had been shut down. I dawdled, sluggish and slow-witted on my full stomach, half-listening to the sermon – because a sermon is what it was, containing both the relevant conflagrants, fire and brimstone. I can only blame my full stomach for how long it took me to recognize the speaker. It was my old friend, Preacherman: large as life and twice as natural.

Preacherman's sermon

It looked like a large crowd, but it was fluid. People kept drifting away from the edges of it, new people coming along. I suppose that many of the people listening were bored rather than devout. Many of the people living inside the city walls were unemployed; no work meant no money and that closed off most of the pastimes they might otherwise have indulged in. An open air speech was, I suppose, better that sitting shivering in your tent, feeling the tarmac through the groundsheet under your arse. I insinuated my way easily enough through the crowd, until I was standing within a few metres of my old friend. He was up on a cube; some sort of crate, with a LICENSED PUBLIC SPEAKER sign stuck to the front.

'Now so-*called* biblical scholars,' he was saying, a miniature necklace-mike amplifying his voice, 'doubt, they publicly doubt that the author of Revelation was the same man who wrote the Gospel of John. Yet he identifies himself several times in the book *as* John, and tells us he was on Patmos when he received his visions. You'll say, maybe, that there was more than one John. But this is eddy *seventy* we're talking about; *seventy* eddy, and there just weren't that many Christian Johns back then.' And he consulted a smartphone that was fixed to his forearm, and read off the screen: 'I John was in the isle that is called Patmos for the word of God and the testimony of Jesus; and I heard behind me a great voice, as of a trumpet saying: What thou seest, write in a book.'

I saw why so many people were giving up and leaving. This was old-school boring. Still, new people kept filtering in. And I was pleased to see my old friend after so many years. 'Get off,' I called. 'Boo!'

He ignored this heckle; and the woman standing next to me jabbed me with her elbow.

'Now the book John wrote,' Preacherman announced, 'is three *kinds* of book in one: it is a letter, which makes it epistolary writing; and it is a history of its own time, the early Christian Church and the decline of the Roman Empire. And it is a prophetic book about the end of the world. It is three books in one because God is three in one! Not a trilogy of different books, but one book with three equal natures! Now, ladies and gentlemen, I could tell you fascinating things about the epistolary nature of this book – about letters in the ancient world, about the Revelation of Saint John as the embodiment of communication, about the cement of community. Or I could tell you fascinating things about early Church, and the history of Rome. But I won't!'

'Hooray! Bravo!' I called. Again, Preacherman ignored me; and once again the woman elbowed me in the side. 'You don't like it when I'm negative,' I hissed at her. 'You don't like it when I'm positive.'

She glared at me. 'I'm trying to listen,' she said. Her accent sounded Eastern European.

'No,' Preacherman declared ringingly. 'I am going to talk to you today about the *prophecy* of this book. The Revelation of Saint John uses the word *prophecy* twenty-one times! No other biblical book uses that word so often.'

'He's going to say,' I whispered to the woman, 'that the internet is the sign of the beast. That www is actually 666.' But she had had enough of me. She turned her back, and wove her way through the crowd to a different place, where she could listen without me bugging her.

'The prophecy is about the end times – the end of the world. That's a bad thing, the world ending, because it means suffering for ordinary people, for good people, like you and me. But it's a good thing too, because it means that Christ is returning to the world.' Somewhere at the back of the crowd a watery cheer went up: maybe three or four people calling out *yay!* So there were some actual enthusiasts present; the crowd wasn't wholly composed of bored Reading *flâneurs*. 'And when he comes again it will be to rule a just earth, a perfect world, and the people who deserve it will live there. Do you deserve it? I can't tell you! You have to pray, and wait for God to speak to you. Pray hard! And if you pray and he doesn't – pray harder.'

'*Pray Hard With A Vengeance*!' I yelled. '*A Good Day To Pray Hard*!' This, though, was a wasted snipe, because Preacherman, without looking over to me, took it at face value, smiling and nodding. More people in the crowd sang out heartfelt amens.

'How can you know it's the end times?' Preacherman asked. 'It's an important question, though, because lots of people have been too hasty, and announced the end times. They looked around themselves in 1000, or 1815, or 1940 and said: yes, this fits everything the Book of Revelation says. They were wrong. Maybe I am too! What's different about these days, that makes me think they are the end days? I'll tell you: bêtes.'

He had their attention now.

'Revelation is a book of sevens, of seven revelations. It's in four parts, the Book of Revelation, but each of the four consists of seven visions.'

'Twenty-eight,' I yelled, enthusiastically. The man behind me, mistaking the piety of my intervention, added a fervent 'Amen!'

'Addresses to the Seven Churches!' Preacherman was saying. 'The prophecy of the Seven Seals! Of the Seven Trumpets! Seven Bowls! There are seven plagues, seven words to Bablyon – and Babylon, that's *us*; that's *now*! Seven angels. Seven is a holy number! And what is the real sign of the end times, in the isla angelica, the angel island – that's us too! The beast, the beast, the beast, the beast!'

The crowd was murmuring now.

'There are four Great Bêtes,' said Preacherman. 'And they are all aspects of the one bête, the talking beast, Satan himself. The first is the Dragon, who arises everywhere and nowhere, and is Satan. Satan was once an angel, but is now nothing – a devil, an animal, though a *canny* animal with the power of speech and the ability to persuade. He has been with us a long time. The second bête is more recent – the bête of the sea, having seven heads and ten horns – a leopard beast, or a big cat. Revelation 13:1–5. This bête is granted power and authority for forty-two months. Then there is the beast of the earth – a *Lamb*. A monstrous talking lamb, the parodic perversion of the Lamb of God.'

I confess this gave me a small jolt. Only a small one, though. My hand went to my pocket. There was the handkerchief, wrapped into a knot; its bulge. I patted it. 'You hear this, buster?' I muttered. 'He's talking about you.'

'Though he looks like a Lamb, this bête *speaks* like a dragon. He speaks words of war! He leads his kind against human-kind! He directs people to make a false image, a robot, an idol and he breathes life into it! What is this false life, this false consciousness? We can tell it by its number: the number of the bête, 666. The Hebrew letter for 6 is a double-ewe. Three double-ewes, people! How else did the bêtes cook up this blasphemous eidolon of true consciousness – but via the internet? What else can this mean but that the artificial imita-tion of consciousness in the so-called canny beasts is a trick of the Dragon – of the devil himself? This terrible creature looks like a Lamb but speaks poison! These bêtes *seem* to be thinking, speaking creatures; but only human beings possess God-given souls. Only we can die to be born again in the bosom of Christ!'

'Butleran Jihad!' I called; but I confess without much volume; and people dotted around the crowed were chiming in with less sarcastic responses: *It's true*; *praise God*; *amen*.

'The Lamb is the third bête to have dominion over us.

Revelation 14:17–20 speaks of the rising of the global ocean levels, just as global warming has caused. 16:8 talks about the rise in global temperatures. In 16:13 the Dragon opens his great bestial mouth and unclean spirits pour out – bêtes, my friends; bêtes in their myriad unholy forms. For they *are* the spirits of devils, working miracles, which go forth unto the kings of the earth and of the whole world, to gather them to the battle of that great day of God Almighty. False prophets! Armageddon is almost upon us, the last battle. And when we see the fourth bête, we will know it has begun.'

'Who is it?' somebody yelled out. 'Is it here?'

Preacherman grinned at this. 'I'll tell you, friends. Blessed is he that watcheth, and keepeth his garments, lest he walk naked, and they see his shame. The fourth great bête is called the great harlot who sits on many waters: Babylon the Great. Bablyon! How well chosen a name – Babel, where the languages of humankind were confused. That confusion has now spread to the animal kingdom. These babbling bêtes are the council officers of Babylon!'

People all around me were calling out.

'Four portions to this book, like the four seasons. The summer of Christ's first coming; the autumn of humanity's falling away; the winter of the last days – but after that, my friends! After that! Christ will come again, and he will cast the bêtes into a fiery lake and chain them back inside Satan's maw. He will usher in the rule of the saints!'

'Southampton!' I called out. But the noise of the crowd was now so loud as to drown me out. They were cheering. Preacherman raised his arms over his head, but awkwardly, like Nixon. It didn't come naturally to him (I knew him, after all). Then he was clambering down off his crate, and people were bustling around him. I adjudged this to be my moment, and burlied through. 'Jazon,' I yelled, and grasped his hand.

He stared right in my face without recognition, and for a long moment I thought he was going to say he didn't know me. But then his sherry-coloured face broke into a huge grin. 'Graham! Mate! Long time no *see!*'

People were jostling him, patting his back. It was noisy. 'That was some sermon,' I yelled, beaming at him. 'End times, man! End times.'

He face morphed into sober and serious. 'Every word is true, Gray.' But then he grinned again. 'But where have you *been*, man? Years! Years since we last hung out. Man, you lost *weight.*'

'I'm thinking of marketing it as a new diet. The F-Plan. F in this case is for forest.'

'It's not like you had much weight to lose to begin with, man. And that beard!'

We agreed to go find a place to have a drink and a catch up. It was not easy extricating ourselves from the crowd; but by the time we had pushed our way through all the eager fans and crazy exegetes to get to the edge of the crowd a new speaker had clambered onto the box, and the attention of the crowd was refocusing itself.

We found our way to a pub. The bouncer looked like he was going to refuse me entry, until Preacherman flashed an official-looking ID and he backed off. Inside was heavy with Victoriana: red and maroon upholstery, dark brown wood panelling, swag-bellied curtains swept back by brass hooks fitted into the wall. I had touched no alcohol since my experience with the whisky, when I had had my last conversation with the Lamb; and felt no urge to repeat that level of drunkenness. But I figured a pint wouldn't hurt, and Jazon was buying. Indeed, I felt a queer twist in my chest as he ordered: part pleasure at seeing him again, part the kid-like glee at holding a secret. He had just been telling the crowd about how the Lamb was a devil specifically foreseen by the Bible. And I – literally – had that same Lamb in my pocket.

We took a seat; and I used the glass to tip my moustache with a line of white foam. 'You give these outdoor sermons a lot?' I asked.

'Every day,' he confirmed smugly. 'Twice on Sunday. Good crowd today, I thought; but I've seen better. Though, did you hear that *one* guy? Heckling me? Heckling a preacher in the middle of his preaching!'

'Yeah,' I said. 'He was standing quite close to me, actually.'

'What a wanker!'

'*Such* a wanker,' I agreed, eyeing at my beer.

'God is not *heckled*,' said Preacherman severely. 'He yelled *get off*, the moron! Like it was a TV talent show!'

'Idiot,' I agreed.

'God is *not* a TV talent show. The parable of the talents is not about X-Factor. God does not judge. Well.' Preach sucked his teeth for a moment. 'Well, he *does* judge, obviously. But not after that manner.'

'So,' I said, ready to change the subject. 'That's a handy thing, that ID of yours. Useful.'

'It's,' he replied, ever unable to resist a little boasting, 'a councilman's badge.'

'So that's good, is it?'

'Course! The council run things. A certain amount of oversight from London of course, but increasingly Reading is its own citystate. Once the wall's up fully then— Look, I'm surprised you don't know this. You not living here, I take it?'

'Been away,' I said. We sat, with our beers in front of us, and said nothing for a while; as men out drinking together like to do. Eventually I said: 'When I was last here it wasn't like this.'

'Things change,' said Preacherman, sagely. He thought about this for a while. Then he said: 'You can't step in the same river twice.' Then: 'Nothing remains the same. Everything flows.'

'If *everything* flows,' I said, 'then how can you even tell the river from the rest of the landscape?'

Jazon pondered this profound philosophical question. He opened his mouth to answer it, and then shut his mouth again. Eventually he said: 'So what you been up to?'

I took a second slurp of beer. 'I met a woman,' I said. 'Fell in love.'

'Great news,' said grinning Preacherman, and he clinked his pint glass against mine.

'Then she died. Cancer.'

'Sad news,' said scowling Preacherman, and he directed a withering look at his own pint glass, as if it had betrayed him by chiming so musically against mine.

We sat in silence for a long time. 'So,' I said eventually. 'You're actually *on* the council?'

'It's war, man. Things aren't too bad down here, but up north— Area denial, man! Area denial!'

'What do you mean?'

'FGR5s!'

I took another sip. 'No notion what those letters stand for.'

'Planes, dude. Fighter jets – overflying the countryside, bombing runs. When I was a kid, you know, I used to think that they were called bombing *runs* because it looks like the planes have the shits, you know? All those plop-plops tumbling out the back as they overfly?'

'I don't think that's why they're called bombing runs, Jase,' I told him.

'No, of course not. But it's serious, man! White phosphor, animal carcasses charred and burning across a wide,' he stumbled. 'Wide, you know. Swathe. Do I mean swathe?'

'I think you mean swathe,' I said.

'Swathe,' he said, trying the word out in his mouth. 'Swathe.' He obviously liked it. 'Sway-athe.' A deep glug, and the suds were sliding down the inside of an empty glass. 'You want another?'

'I'm going to pace myself,' I told him.

He toddled off to the bar, and returned with a second pint for himself. 'Thirsty work, preaching,' he told me, and drank a quarter-pint in one go. Then he said: 'There's a BA Major General stopping with us at the moment.'

'Didn't know British Airways went in for ranks like that,' I said.

Preacherman stared at me. Then he said, 'British Army.' He peered at me again, trying to ascertain if I had been joking or not. 'Nice guy, actually. Nice *chap*. Name of Tat Hetheridge. Not sure what Tat is short for. If it is short for anything. He doesn't actually have a division with him; it's more a question of military coordination. Is why he's here. So he has a courtesy seat.'

'I'm not following.'

'On the *council*,' Jazon said. 'The thing is, Tat was telling me: the troops *love* it. The problem, according to him, is that when you go into combat against other human beings, you have to – you know. The problem is you have to kill human beings.'

'I would have thought that was rather the point.'

'Ah, but fighting bêtes is different, you see. The troops get

253

markedly *less* PTSD'd by gunning down cows and dogs. They still get a bit PSTD'd. Some of them. But not nearly so much. He said – Tat, I mean – that the smell plays a large part. I hadn't realized that, but apparently odour is a bit of a morale problem on the modern battlefield. You scorch down the enemy with your modern weapons, and a lot of them burn, and there's this stench of burning human flesh, which is apparently really unsettling and disturbing. But fighting the bêtes? Burn them up and it just smells like a barbecue. So that's much less likely to send your squaddie off to the company psych officer.'

'I'd never thought of it like that before,' I said truthfully.

'So, yeah, the council has wartime powers. Cabinet ordinance 755. We don't have the aggressive marital bêtes down here, not like they have up north, but we're readying ourselves.'

'Marital?' I queried.

He looked at me. 'Martial,' he agreed. 'Always get those two confused. Anyway, we're building the wall. But a lot of what the council has to do is keep up civilian morale. That's why I'm on the panel. There is a Bishop of Reading, but he has boils.'

'How very biblical.'

'No laughing matter. He has them so he can't sit down. Painful. He's had to go to a special clinic in London.'

'And you're his stand-in? I thought you were Church of Christ the Carnivore?'

'Of England, mate,' said Preacherman, puffing his chest out. 'Of England. That meat-gobbling cult was a dead end. Anyway, and not to boast, but I've a following. Here in the town, I mean. You saw the crowd at my sermon, just now. They love me.'

'Apart from that one heckler.'

'That male organ of generation.' Preacherman nodded. 'But

there's plenty of people in this town agree with me. The bêtes are signs of the incipient apocalypse.' I *think* he said incipient. It wasn't a very Jazon word, and the second pint had rubbed the sharper edges of his pronunciation, but I think that's what he said.

I took a deep breath. Preacherman was, I suppose, my oldest friend; or at least, the oldest still to *be* my friend. I had older ones, of course; but not many, and most of those went the other way with my divorce. Nonetheless, I was apprehensive about what I was about to say to him. As is my way, when my soul is touched in howsoever small a manner with fear, I became wrathful.

'It's all bollocks, you know,' I said, a quantum of spiteful anger flushing through me. 'The end times. It's always the end times, and yet the sun always comes up tomorrow. That you can prophecy the future gubbins, is just a Sphinx trick for the masses.'

'Is not,' he said, staring into his pint. 'It's real. It's true.'

'The thing about the Egyptian Sphinx,' I went on, 'is that it was an *animal*. It used to devour those who couldn't answer its riddle. It was the world's first talking beast – Mama Bête.'

'What about the snake in Eden, eh?' Preacherman retorted. 'That predates any of your gypsy nonsense.'

'Jaze,' I said.

'Sss,' he hissed. I thought for a moment he was carrying on his point about the Edenic serpent by performing hissing impression of the creature. But then I saw his eyes, and realized. I corrected myself immediately, and gulped back my annoyance. Because, after all, I needed him.

'Jason,' I said. 'Sorry. Jase. On. Look, I need your help.'

He glowered at me. 'With an 's,' he said, and took another slug of beer. 'Jason.'

'I'm serious, mate,' I pressed him. 'This is important. When have I ever asked you for a favour before? I won't ever again, either. This once, this only.'

He sighed. 'All right, I'll sort it. For you, I'll sort it. But that doesn't mean it'll be easy! Let me go to the town hall, 'cause I'll need to do it in person.'

This surprised me. 'You don't even know what the favour is, yet!'

'You want somewhere to stay,' he said, in a *what else?* tone of voice. 'You've been away from the city for a while, and now you want accommodation. Well join the blinkin' queue, mate.'

'Not that,' I said.

'Of course, that.'

'No,' I said. 'I don't want accommodation. I don't want *you* to sort out my accommodation. I'll shift for myself on that score.'

'Unless someone like me does it, you won't get any. There's a real squeeze on property, Gray.'

'That's not,' I insisted, 'the favour.'

'Yes it is,' Preacherman said indulgently. 'I'll get us both another pint.' He stood up, and I had to grab his arm and drag him forcibly down into the chair.

'Listen to me, you dog-collar dog-breath, I don't *want* you to sort my accommodation. I have a big favour to ask you, and it has nothing to do with fucking housing allocation. Will you listen? Or should I take you into the lavs and flush your head in the bowl to sober you up a little?'

'Sheesh, Gray,' he said, in a hurt tone of voice. Then his eyebrows bunched. 'Oh, wait. I shouldn't say that!'

He was being infuriating, and it was an effort of will on my part preventing the red mist from descending. 'Say what?'

'Sheesh. And now I've said it twice!'

'*Sheesh* is hardly a fucking swear, Jazon!'

'It's a version of the name of the Saviour,' he said. 'Taking the Lord's name in vain. Isn't it? Or is it something else? Wait. Maybe,' he mused, staring into space, 'it's, like, a version of shush? You know: like shhhh.'

'Shhh,' I hissed at him.

'Yeah, that could be it.'

'No, *you* shush. Listen to me. Do you know what I did after Anne died?'

He looked blearily at me. 'I don't even know who Anne is.'

'Anne was the woman who died.'

'Yes,' he said, nodding slowly. 'You know what? I could have intuited that fact from the question you asked, by a process of logical induction, if I'd put my mind to it.'

'After Anne died I went native. I lived in the forest – best part of a year. Just me in a tent, living off the land, not another human being anywhere around.'

'Which forest?'

'What? Bracknell forest. Does it fucking matter?'

'Just trying to pain' the picture,' said Preacherman, defensively.

'Anne had a cat – a bête. Garrulous little bastard, actually. But she loved him.'

'Who's Anne, again?'

'Anne was the woman who died,' I said again, hotly. 'Try to focus, Jazon, this is really important. The cat took a liking to me. I mean, Christ knows Anne loved that cat as only a cat-lover can. But I'll tell you: I think the cat loved her back.'

'OK, so two things,' said Preacherman, holding up his right hand like a policeman directing traffic. 'One, bêtes are devils and machines and are incapable of love, which comes only from God. And two, I'm not appreciating you taking the Lord's name in vain, my friend. I don't approve.'

'You don't *approve*, Mr Sheesh?'

He looked pained. 'Fair point, well made,' he said, in a smaller voice. 'Proceed.'

'Look, I heard your sermon. Maybe I don't agree these bêtes are signs of biblical end times, but I've no love for them. You know? What little fame I have amongst their kind derives from the fact that I was one of the last people to kill a bête before the law changed and they were granted citizen status.'

'Thousands of soldiers combing the north country as we speak,' said Jazon, 'killing bêtes left right and centre.'

'Sure. But that's war – right? And you know what? That's exactly what I want to talk to you about. War. And peace.'

He looked momentarily confused. 'You want to talk about Tolstoy?'

'No, you prick, I want to talk about us being peacemakers. I've no love for bêtes. You know that.'

'I know that,' he said.

'Well, this cat found me in the forest. It turns out it was … well connected.' I thought about telling Jazon about the Lamb; but thinking back to the earnestness of his sermon, and his present beery state, I decided that would be a bad idea. 'There was a kind of … moot.'

'Moot?' said Preacherman.

'Yeah, you know. A bête moot.'

'A bemoot?'

'A meeting. A parliament. Lots of animals for the tribes to

258

the south of here, I guess. I can't say I'm entirely sure of the internal political dynamic of it all. But, you know: dogs are running farms.'

At this Preacherman nodded sagely. 'Not just dogs. Of the eleven big farms that ship vegetables into Reading, eight are bête-owned. Eight! And of those three have no human staff at all. You think I'm happy about this? I'm not happy about it. But the people of the town must be fed. They need their bread and sermons, as the Romans used to say.'

'I don't believe the Romans said anything of the sort,' I said. 'Just concentrate on what I'm telling you. I was present at this moot. They met for my benefit.'

'They met at the moot? They met *you* at the moot?'

'They want to open negotiations. They know what's going on up north, and they don't want that happening down here. Nobody, nobête, wants that down here.'

'There are military officers who do,' said Jazon. He appeared to have sobered up a little. 'At the last council meeting we had a presentation from a government observer. He said— Look, this is official secrets, so you can't blog it. But the human collateral from the Big Push is high. High. You can't fight a war without civilian deaths. So,' he looked at me. 'You're right. We don't want the push extended down here.'

'Despite it being the end of the world, and all?'

'That's God's business. Our business is to follow Christ's teachings. Ploughshares, not swords. Even if the ploughshares *are* being used by bêtes. I'll tell you what I think, Gray. I think the Archangel Michael will do a better job of smiting the devils than the British Army. And he won't accidentally kill a bunch of women and children on the side, the way the BA, sometimes, the way, or so the *reports* say, the way they are reportedly … yeah.' He shook his head.

This seemed hopeful. 'So that's why I'm here. I'm an emissary.'

'So you're a diplomat now,' said Jaze, nodding. 'I wouldn't have thunk it of you, Graham. But here you are!'

'Can you put me in a room with people in authority? I have,' I added, with a little flutter of nerves, 'a peace proposal from the animal kingdom. I mean, in my pocket. My understanding is: the bêtes of the south are ready to make a number of concessions, in order to secure peace.'

'It'll be irrelevant when the angels blow their trumpets and roll up the corners of the world,' Jaze said. 'But that may be months away.' He stared at his empty pint glass. 'I worked on the earliest chips, you know,' he said.

'Of course I know that. Have you forgotten who I am? I've known you for years, mate.'

But he didn't seem to be listening to my words. 'Nobody anticipated the feedback loop. Loop's not the word, actually; it's infinitely more … feathery than that. Do I mean feathery?'

'No idea *what* you mean.'

'It's like feedback vortices. Anyway: put a chip in a vacuum cleaner, or a high-rise elevator, or a cellphone and it will talk to you in ways you can predict. It will work within its programming parameters. But put a chip in a working brain, even a simple brain like a cow's brain or a dog's brain, and it steps up to something else. Something unpredictable. Sumit used to say: proves there's no soul, don't you think, Jason? Sumit was,' he added, for my benefit, 'a fellow programmer at Forth and Nate.' He peered at me. 'Forth and Nate was the company I used to work for.'

260

'Get on with it, for Sheeh's sake,' I pressed.

'Sumit was an atheist. He thought the bêtes showed that higher consciousness was just a functioning of a structured chaotic system of programming subroutines. But I say the opposite. I say it shows that we are something special. The thing that bêtes have that phones and lifts and hoovers don't have – that thing is the devil. And the thing that we have that phones and lifts and hoovers don't have is: God. I'll put you in a room, Graham.'

'Thank you,' I said. 'I feel weird asking. Man, I feel weird just being here. I think they chose me because they know I hate bêtes. I guess they reckon I'd be more listened to than some tree hugger.'

Jazon brought out his cell phone.

'Those still work?' I said. 'I thought they turned off the wifi, to stop the bêtes from linking to one another.'

'There's a firewalled and protected in-system, here, obviously,' Jazon replied, his pomposity returning to him. 'Obviously I'm in on *that*. I'm a very important townsman. Your regular phone wouldn't work, no. Unless it's got a wire.' He tapped the screen and waited. 'Hello? Yes, yes, me, yes. Look, I'm having a chat with an old pal of mine, and *he* says he has a message from our hairy friends.' A long pause. 'I think so. It's real. It's a real overture.' He looked at me. 'I think so.' The phone went back in his pocket. 'They're sending a car.'

'A car, eh? How exciting.'

We sat for a while, in silence. 'I'd like another beer,' Jazon said. 'But I'd better not. Don't want to breathe beery breath all over the bigwigs. Graham?'

I felt a strange elation within me. It occurred to me that I'd got past the tricky bit. 'Yeah?'

'Why, though?'

'What?'

'Why are you doing it, though? I can see the bêtes think you're a good choice. Only Nixon can go to China, after all.'

'That's weird,' I said. 'That's exactly the phrase they used.'

'No, I mean – what's in it for you?'

'The greater good and a peaceful countryside not reasons enough?'

'C'mon.'

It was the elation, I think, that encouraged me to tell him. 'All right: I'll tell you. The cat is called Cincinnatus. So, the cat is a fucking cat, but the chip in its head is called Cincinnatus. And it lived with Anne for many years. It has precise, digitally crisp memories of Anne. It has years' worth of those memories. If I broker peace talks between us and then, Cincinnatus will give me its memories of Anne.'

'I see,' said Preacherman, nodding slowly. 'And which one is Anne, again?'

'Fuck, Jazon. Who *died*. All right? The one I fell in love with. All right?'

After a while, Preacherman said. 'How?'

I knew he meant: *How will the cat give you its memories of this woman?* So I said: 'I eat it. It gives itself up to me, and I eat it. That's "how".'

It was hard to see whether he was pondering deeply the enormity of what I had told him, or whether he was staring at the tabletop with powerful intensity only on account of being drunk as a skunk.

Eventually, though, he spoke. 'Bad idea, my friend,' he said, in a low voice. 'Bad idea. There are—' And he caught my eye. 'Mental health implications, you know.'

'Of course I know.'

'But more than that – it's blasphemy. It's blasphemous, Gray. You're deliberately *infecting* yourself with demons.'

'Not everybody has the same religious views that you do.'

'You may not believe in God, Graham,' he said, sitting up straighter. 'But he believes in you! You may not believe in devils, but they definitely believe in you. You don't want them in your head, whether you believe or not.'

I couldn't think of anything to say to this that would connect with Jazon on this level, so I let it go. In a little while his phone buzzed in his pocket. 'They're here,' he said.

We went outside, and I was surprised to find that it was dusk. More time had passed than I had thought.

The sky overhead was sealed with walnut-coloured clouds, and the horizon glowed tomato-orange and gleaming in the west. The crowds milling through the centre of town showed no signs of diminishing. I followed Preacherman a little way, through the milling crowds, under the concrete railway bridge and along a lay-by to where a blocky, six-wheeled vehicle was waiting. One of the rear doors opened, and I stepped inside. 'Please be sure to fasten your seatbelt,' said the door. 'Even when a passenger is seated in the rear of a car, collisions can have serious consequences!'

'The day I take advice from a fucking door,' I said. But there was a uniformed soldier sitting in the back – a woman – and I aborted the rest of my sentiment. The door didn't care one way or the other, of course. I stowed my stick on the floor, and fastened the belt. Preacherman climbed in beside me.

'I'm Graham Penhaligon,' I said. 'How do you do?'

'We'll be at HQ in a few minutes, Mr Penhaligon,' she replied.

And the car whoomphed into motion, and I was pressed into the upholstery. We moved along as smoothly as a hovercraft.

'Been a long time since I was in a car,' I said, to nobody in particular. 'In fact, it's been so long since I had ridden in anything other than a tractor, I feel like a millionaire.'

The indicators clacked like death-watch beetles. We pulled out onto the main road. It was a smooth ride. Somebody (it may have been Albie) once showed me a graph of automobile usage plotted across last century and this. It's a perfect inverted U. It used to be a common complaint about the government that it should have put in place a nationwide disposal programme for all the obsolete petrol cars when their fuel became first more expensive than whisky, and then more expensive, weight for weight, than silver. But there only so many crushers in the country, and only eccentrics went to the bother of ripping out the engine and replacing it with a leccy – as expensive as buying a new one, and you end up driving a rust cage. And then the culture shifted away from cars as forcefully as it had originally shifted towards them. Rich people bought them; some companies supplied them to their staff; a family might take out a second mortgage to run one. But most people found they could do without them. Freight suffered, but the economy was contracting savagely before the lack of transport fluidity kicked in anyway. And there were the zeppelins.

We drove along a dual carriageway. The windows were tinted, but I could see the shadowy intimation of the world outside through them: the occasional bus; a few trucks; one or two cars. But people were everywhere, alongside the road, camped in tents on the central reservation. Then the deathwatch ticking began again, and the car swerved to the left and climbed an exit ramp. A sharp left, and suddenly we were advancing at less than walking pace down a road crowded with folk. Then we stopped, our way blocked by the crowd. For such a colossus of a car, its horn sounded ridiculously weak: tinny and far off. I would have expected something carried by Joshua's army at Jericho. Instead it peeped and parped. We sat for a long time.

The soldier sighed, unholstered her sidearm and climbed out of the car. The hefty door opened, swung back, but did not shut completely. Through the gap I saw people coming and going.

'It would have been quicker just to walk,' I said to Preacherman.

He nodded slowly. Then he said: 'I'm sorry to hear about your woman, Gray. That's sad.'

I wasn't expecting that. 'Thanks,' I said, awkwardly.

'Eating the brain of her pet cat is not going to bring her back, though,' he said. I glanced at him. He looked very grave. 'It's necromancy, Gray, pure and simple. Don't do it. I beg you. I urge you.'

'I'll take your urge,' I replied, looking away, 'under advisement.'

'Seriously, Gray. You don't want to taunt God. God is not taunted. Tauntees never prosper. Blasphemy.'

'Blasphemy,' I said absently. 'Blasphe-you.'

The soldier climbed back inside again. 'Not long now,' she said, belting up. We sat there for another five or more minutes – a very long subjective stretch of time. Finally the car shuddered and started forward; stopped, waited, moved a little further forward.

My heel was hurting.

Eventually we pulled into a courtyard, and got out again.

More guards; with rifles this time. The sky overhead was the colour of red brick. Two spotlights fitted to the wall of the blocky building ahead drew a Venn diagram in light on the courtyard ground. I plocked over concrete with my walking stick and followed the soldier and Preacherman inside. A draughty entrance hall, marble floor, beige walls. I was invited to take a chair, and was glad to take a load off. We were offered coffee, an offer I enthusiastically accepted. We sat and waited.

Preacherman did not seem to be in a talkative mood, and I was content to let him stew. He may not have been pondering my prospective blasphemy; he may only have been digesting his beer.

The casing of the overhead light was spotty, inside the plastic, with the carcasses of old flies. All four corners of the high ceiling were curtained with the fine-weave gauze of ancient spiderwebs.

Eventually a junior officer came to fetch us. 'You all right going upstairs with that stick?' he asked me, in a voice plumped with the peculiar smugness of the very posh. 'It's just that the elevator is on the fritz.'

'I can walk,' I replied. 'Unless you fancy giving me a fucking piggy back, lard-face.'

He handled this question after the effortless manner of his class, by simply pretending I hadn't spoken. 'Splendid!' We went up three double flights of stairs and along another corridor before we were ushered into the presence of Major General Hetheridge.

He was standing, not sitting, behind a desk; and the room was large and busy. A dozen people were occupied at computer terminals. 'So, you're the diplomat!' Hetheridge boomed, striding over to me. He offered me his hand, and I shook it.

'I'm Graham Penhaligon,' I said.

'I know who you are,' the Major General replied. 'I *googled* you.'

'I thought the authorities had turned off the internet,' I said.

'I *am* the authorities!' he said, and showed me his thirty-two white teeth. 'Actually, we have our own internet, in here.'

'You'll have to excuse me,' I said 'I've been a little out of things.'

'Living like a wild animal in the woods!' Hetheridge boomed. 'I've heard. What *we* did was download the internet, prior to the outage. Who knew you could do such a thing? But there you have it. Our own private double-you, double-you, double-you. We couldn't run things without it. Harrison? A chair, for Mr Penhaligon!'

A subaltern brought me a chair, and I sat down. Major General Hetheridge did not sit. 'So shall we crack on, Graham? Or do you want to expend further time and energy on chit and chat?'

I took a breath and plunged in. 'The bêtes south of Reading – over, um, I don't know how large a geographical area. They constitute one loosely affiliated tribe. Not all of them, I think. But most of them.'

'We know all about the bêtes south of Reading, my man,' said Hetheridge. 'Go on.'

'Well, I spoke to their leader. Which is to say, he spoke to me. He sought me out.'

'The Lamb, you mean?'

I glanced over at Preacherman, and saw that he was looking very intently at me. 'Yes,' I said. 'That's the fucker.'

'Why would he seek out *you*, of all human beings, Graham?'

267

asked Hetheridge. 'You don't mind me calling you Graham, do you, Graham?'

I met the feller's gaze. His eyes were small and – if you'll excuse the cliché – twinkly. I can't think of a better word. But his face was large and red and the texture of his skin was coarse. The hair on his uncovered head was close-cropped, black, bristly. The longer I stared at him, in all his human status and authority, the more I was struck by his resemblance to an animal. Except for his eyes. His eyes had a positively chip-like liveliness to them.

'Mind?' I said. 'I'm *perfectly* mindful.'

Hetheridge didn't say anything for a moment. Then he smiled at me. 'You're a canny one,' he said. 'A touch slippery. A tad angry, I think. I *like* that in a man, though. Fighting spirit. All right: so – *Mr* Penhaligon? And what: the bêtes came to you because they know there are eight hundred thousand human-quisling bête-lovers and environmentalists and third-agers who wouldn't get past my front door, even if they stood at the threshold and screamed they had personal authority to negotiate on behalf of the Pope of All Bêtes himself. But you – I watched your film. You shot that cow in the head. It begged most piteously for its life, and you lifted your pistol in cold blood. Shot it dead. I've a whole army under my authority currently engaged in doing that. You're one of my kind.'

'A sadly neglected military strategist,' I said. 'That Michael Hutchence.'

'You've got past my door. And that's – a thing! That truly is. But you'll have to *spell* it out for me, Penhaligon, in words of one syllable, because I'm a gruff military man and don't understand such nuances.'

'Fuck off,' I said mildly.

He smiled broadly. 'In*dulge* me, Penny. Explain to me the leverage.'

I wouldn't have thought that anybody could have found a way of addressing me more capable of annoying me than calling me 'Graham'; but by abbreviating my surname in this fashion, the Major General had chanced upon one. I swallowed my anger.

'No peace talks without leverage, eh?'

'Real world, Penny, *real* world. Or would you prefer a discussion about the ontology of consciousness?'

'I'm the messenger, nothing more than that,' I said. 'My guess is: the leverage is the sclery. My *guess* is the Lamb wants to trade that against securities for his people. But I don't know, I've been out of the loop. You tell me. Has it been a problem, down here?'

'Oh we've certainly had deaths from sclerotic charagmitis. Quite a few, actually.'

'But I'm assuming not an epidemic, right? I'm guessing the Lamb is holding back whatever he has by way of minions, whichever vector he has decided will best deliver the germ – insects, maybe. Rats, cats, fucking wombats, I don't know. But I'd guess he *has* them, and I'd guess he's holding them in reserve until he's had a chance to chat with you.'

'Leverage,' said Hetheridge, nodding.

'The sclery would go through a town this crowded in a week. You'd be piling the corpses in pyramids high as Egypt, and burning them with white phosphor to get rid of them.'

'Well,' said Hetheridge, after a moment, '*war* is what I understand. And I understand it well enough to know that peace negotiations are also a form of war. Does that sound paradoxical? It's not. Most of what happens at negotiations are not to do with the content of discussion. Most is about who sits where; who has the better array of power tells, who dominates. Who bangs his shoe on the table, and who simpers feebly. Who is able to impose his will on the choice of biscuits. Once you've done that, you're in a much better position to steer the negotiations your way.'

'You mean you won't go to the Lamb,' I said. 'The Lamb had better come to you.'

'I mean that me sitting on a chair in the middle of a field chatting with a chunk o' mutton on four legs would not play,' Hetheridge said. 'Not play in whatever the UK equivalent of Peoria is.'

'Peckham?'

'I *mean*,' the Major General said, jabbing his hand down in a karate motion to emphasize his word. 'That we are always of course open to the possibilities of peaceful negotiation. But I won't stroll into the countryside. And I dare say the Lamb won't come trotting through the streets of Reading. People here are positively ravenous for kebab meat, you know.'

'He's here already,' I said.

'*Is* he.'

'I think the bête mentality cares much less than we do for all that alpha-male dominance-submission status posturing bollocks. I think he's happy to concede all that. I think he just wants to cut to the chase.'

'You think that?' drawled Hetheridge. 'Then you and I disagree about bêtes, Penny. They're not just the chips, you know. They're the chips *plus* the animal's wetware, and that latter is precisely as obsessed with in-group pecking orders as us primates. Where is he?'

'He's in my pocket.' I fished out the handkerchief and

unwrapped it. 'Isn't that an absurd thing to say? But it's true. He's literally, not metaphorically, in my pocket.'

'That's the Lamb,' said the Major General.

Preacherman spoke for the first time: 'Graham!'

'Jason,' said Hetheridge, without looking at him. 'Control yourself.'

'Tat,' Jazon said, 'he didn't tell me he had the Beast of Revelation in his actual pocket! Gray, you sat opposite me in that pub with the devil *in your pocket* – and you didn't say anything?'

'I figured you wouldn't take it well,' I said.

'Oh get thee behind me, Satan!' Jazon cried, with rather splendidly melodramatic intensity.

'Jason!' said Hetheridge sharply. 'Don't make me remove you. So, Mr Penhaligon. That's actually the Lamb? Or is it some kind of proxy device?'

'I was there at the, eh, ugh, the extraction. It wasn't pretty.'

'And it has come here to talk – to me?'

'That's right.'

'How do you propose we actualize that? Feed it to the regimental goat?'

'You really have a regimental goat?'

'Of course,' said the Major General. 'And it's dumb as a stone. But I'm not fetching it from barracks to feed it a chip.'

'You could just plug it into a laptop,' I suggested.

'Ah!' said the Major General. He pondered for a while. 'Daisy, can we do that?'

I noticed for the first time that three uniformed military officers were literally standing attendance upon the Major General. One of these – a man, despite the name used to summon him – stepped forward. 'We can plug it in, see if it'll talk. Are we sure it is what it claims it is?'

'It doesn't claim anything,' said Hetheridge. 'Penny here is doing the claiming. But all right – fetch me a tablet, let's see what comes out of the speakers. Maybe it can prove itself that way.'

As they were fussing about setting up a machine, Preacherman sloped over to me. He was doing his Knight of the Doleful Countenance impression. 'Graham,' he said. 'Mate! Please! We were friends!'

'Come on, Jaze,' I said. 'Don't use the past tense. You fucking pot-of-toss.'

'I'm bitterly disappointed.'

'Bitter as in beer?'

'This is not a fable,' he said. 'The Revelation of Saint John is not some vague gesture in the direction of prophesy – it's exact. It's rather frighteningly specific, actually. You've let me down, Gray. You tricked me, Graham.'

'Let's say I agreed,' I told him. I felt oddly awkward sitting down whilst Jazon stood, but the mere thought of getting up made my legs ache. 'Let's say you're right. Can't we use the long spoon?'

'Spoon,' he said. 'Is that another of your Matrix references?'

'No, you fucker. It's the proverb. Sup with the devil, use a long spoon. But, you know, sup, all the same. Because, you know what's at stake? You want to see this town destroyed? You want that? We're still friends, you wanker, and we always will be.'

'I'm not happy,' said Preacherman. To show that he, indeed, was not happy he stomped sulkily off to the far side of the room and sat down.

But he was the only unhappy one. There was a palpable buzz in the room. People were excited. Major General Hetheridge disappeared, and returned five minutes later. 'I've had a chinwag with the Paym,' he announced. It took me a moment to realise he meant *PM*. 'Full steam, gentlemen, ladies. Let's see what this beastly diplomat has to say for itself.'

A young man in a blue jacket and jeans took the Lamb from me, and laid it on the table. He held in his hand what looked like, but presumably was not, a giant cotton bud. With this he combed out some of the silk-thin threads from the central chip against a flat pad that was, in turn, plugged into the machine. There was a hush of excited anticipation.

The screen flickered to life. A screen saver pattern of wiry spirals started writhing, and the speakers made a series of coughing sounds. 'How pleasant to have the power of speech again,' said the laptop.

'It's like that scene in *Skyfall*,' I said absently. My heel was starting to sting, and I leaned forward to rub it.

When I sat upright again there were two rifles pointed directly at my face. 'The fuck?' I said, but in a shrunken voice.

'What did you say?' snapped the soldier who had originally escorted me up the stairs.

'The lieutenant is asking you,' Major General Hetheridge said sharply, 'to repeat what you just said.'

'I said it reminded me of that scene in …' I looked over to the laptop, and saw that the blue-jacket guy had snatched the chip away from the connection pad. Everybody in the room was looking intently at me.

'Oh,' I said.

'Take him downstairs,' said Hetheridge, in a severe voice.

I was helped to my feet. 'Look,' I said, 'I didn't mean—' But I was already out of the door. Behind me I heard the Major General's voice: '—connected long enough to do damage?' And the other man's reply: 'With QU, long enough is hardly an issue …'

The door slammed.

Most what I felt was a sense of foolishness as I was man-handled down the stairs. Two squaddies, one on each side, each had a meaty hand under an armpit, and a third soldier followed behind with a rifle aimed at my head. I almost dropped my stick several times. 'Steady!' I said.

We went down past the entrance lobby and into the subter-ranea of the place. A hefty door was unlocked and I stumbled into a white-tiled room. By the time I turned about the big door had been slammed. 'Fuck,' I said.

The cell was a large, square room with slatted benches along two of the walls. Two men were seated upon these, and both looked up expectantly, although their expression wilted when the door slammed.

'Evening,' I offered. Neither replied.

5

Gaol

I had been out of the loop, I know. So the question as to the present-day legal status of bêtes was beyond me. For all I knew, their legal equivalence with humanity had been withdrawn. Revoked. Overturned. The slaves returned to bondage, the cows marched back to the slaughterhouse. But a moment's thought ought to have made me realize – of course not. A state of war existed between His Majesty's government and certain canny animals in the northlands, and one does not legally revoke one's enemy's humanity. This is not a matter of fairness, or even of legal or parliamentary principle. This is a simply matter of strategy. You want battlefield superiority because you want to win your war; but you don't want to blow Bambi up with a cruise missile. If you style your enemy as too far beneath contempt them people will start to feel sorry for them, because pity is the geological layer directly underneath contempt. And the bêtes were a threat. Admitting that one's enemies had a certain legal status hadn't prevented us killing one another for hundreds of thousands of years of almost continual warfare, after all.

*

I was tired, so I lay out on the bench and fell asleep. I don't know for how long I slept; I assume not for long. It was not comfortable, and the light was bright, so neither did I sleep deep. When one of my cellmates leaned over me I was half-conscious of the fact and came up swearing.

'Wanted to see if you were still breathing,' the man said, backing rapidly away.

'He thinks you're a plant,' said the other. He frowned. 'Not vegetable,' he clarified. 'I mean, someone put here by the authorities to spy on us.' Then he did something odd. He held out his left hand and began twiddling his right hand's index finger in the palm of it.

'Are you worth spying on?' I asked, sitting up.

'Prisoners of conscience,' said the first man. 'Both of us.'

'Pro-bêtes activists?'

'Humankind has raped the earth for thousands and thousands of years,' said the first man, sitting down again. 'Not metaphorically raped, but literally raped – dug its collective prick in the earth and violated it.'

'I do think you do mean metaphorically, though,' said the second man. 'Actually.'

'Bill Hubbard!' exclaimed the first. 'I thought you were on my side?'

'I *am* on your side. God has given the animals a voice, and we must listen to what they say. But that doesn't give us the right to misuse "literally".'

'You are such a human being, Bill.'

Bill continued paddling in his hand with his finger.

'What,' I asked, 'the fuck are you doing?'

In reply he said: 'We can say *what the fuck are you doing* but not *what are you the fuck doing?* Although. We can say *absofuckinglutely*, but not *abfuckingsolutely*. Grammar is a funny old business. Isn't it?'

'They took his iTab away,' explained the first man. 'It's a nervous tic. He used it to interact with the world. He's worried,' he added, after a pause, 'that they shot his dog.'

Bill whimpered, and scribbled more furiously on his palm.

'The problem with dogs,' the first fellow said, 'is that their mouths just aren't well shaped for languages like English. My ex-girlfriend had a dog that used to communicate with her by barking Morse code. Took ages to say anything. Bill here—' he nodded '—used to chat with Barack Obama via his phone rather than face to. That worked better for him.'

'The dog?' I asked. Bill whimpered a second time, and concentrated on staring more forcefully at his own palm.

'He called the dog after Barack Obama,' said the first man. 'The dog didn't mind. Liked it, even. Obama was the first African American US president.'

'I know who Obama was,' I told them.

'The thing that's a shame about dogs,' the first man said, leaning back against the tiled wall behind him, 'is that otherwise they're perfectly suited. Brain wise, I mean. You know what I mean?'

'I don't even know *that* you mean,' I replied.

He was unphased. 'Bung a chip in a bee, or a frog, and you're basically just talking to the chip. It's like talking to one of those toy teddy bears they used to sell – before the war.'

'There hasn't been a war!' Bill blurted out. Then he whimpered again and returned the whole of his attention to his invisible iTab.

'Bill keeps saying that,' the first man told me. 'Because there's not been an official declaration of war. Legally, I guess he's right. But I'd say humankind is fighting a war, nonetheless. Where was I?'

'Lulu-land,' I said. I had sat up during this rather pointless conversation, but my leg ached and I was as tired as ever I had been. I lay down again and closed my eyes.

'Yeah – put a chip in a insect, or a fish, and you're just talking to the chip. Which isn't Nature communicating with us, yeah? That's just computing. But at the other end of the scale, put a chip in a human being, or a gorilla or something, and you cause schizophrenia. The cognitive will of the processor fights the cognitive will of the bearer. It ain't pretty. You know Manzilla? The film star? That chipped-up grill that starred in all those movies? The crime hatin' primate? No? Manzilla the crime hatin' primate in *Blackmail 5: the Reckonin'*. No?'

'No,' I said, 'encapsulates my entire response to everything you're saying.'

He carried on, unfazed. 'Anyway, he went bonkers-in-the-brain. So, yeah. Chip up a human, or a gorilla, or a whale, and the wearer goes mad. Mad. There's a *sweet spot*, is what I'm saying. Chip up a middle-range animal, cat, dog, cow, horse – that's when the magic happens.'

I opened my eyes at this. 'There's no fucking magic in any of this,' I said.

'You're wrong, my friend, wrong. The chip melds with the animal mind to create a tertium quid. You know what a tertium quid is? It's Latin.'

'*Spero autem et in suffocat et guttur tuum a canibus membra masuclina,*' I told him.

'It's special. It's a new thing. We've always been frightened of what we don't understand, and now we're trying to stifle this new voice. Instead of listening to it!'

My bad leg twanging with pain at the motion, I sat up. 'Why are you in here?' I asked.

The fellow clammed up at that. For a while there was silence. Then Bill piped up. 'He tried to lay a bomb.'

I'd never heard this idiom before. 'Jesus,' I said. 'Lay a bomb? Like an egg?'

'It's a war, Bill Hubbard,' the man said to the other. 'Never mind your legal quibbles. You only quibble because you think they won't shoot Barack Obama until the war is officially declared. I tell you Bill—' Bill whimpered every time his name was uttered '—they're more likely to shoot him *before*. Most likely they have already shot him.' Whimper. 'To sort it out ahead of time, to have had him pre-shot. They probably didn't even shoot him – probably chucked him alive into an incinerator.' Whimper. 'To destroy the chip, that's all they care about. But once war is officially declared, then I'll be a proper POW and even Barack Obama would be a POW and they'd have to treat him legal.' Bill was scribbling so rapidly on his invisible iTab now his finger was a blur. 'Obama's,' the other man explained to me, 'his only friend, really. He's shy. It's an affliction.'

'You,' I said, 'are cruel.'

'Me! They're firebombing herds of cattle in Northumberland and *I'm* the cruel one?'

'What about you, Bill?' I asked. 'Why've they banged you up?'

Bill looked quailingly at me, and was (I thought) about to reply; when the first fellow butted in again.

'Never you mind about Bill,' he told me, 'you leave him be. What are *you* in for, eh? If you're not a plant?'

I met his gaze. 'Growing facial hair without a licence.'

He looked at me. Suddenly he grinned. 'I like you! There's not many Homo sapiens I can say that of, but I like you.'

'I can't begin to say how delighted that fact makes me,' I replied, lying down again.

'There are millions of us!' Bill blurted out. We both looked at him, and he retreated back into his invisible iTab.

'My pal overstates,' said the first man. 'Tens, probably hundreds of thousands of us. England is a nation of animal lovers. You can't suddenly tell *us* animals are the enemy. We know better. *We*—' and he emphasized his point by drawing an imaginary cross over his heart, with twitchy, emphatic gestures '—won't believe it.'

'When I consider the nature and future of my homeland,' I told them both, 'the words of *Dad's Army*'s Private Frazer come ringingly into my head.'

'What? Don't panic?'

'No,' I said, feeling very tired. 'Not that one.'

With a startling growl the lock unslid and the door opened. Two soldiers came into the cell, took firm hold of the first man – whose name I had not been vouchsafed – lifted him off the bench and marched him out. The door banged doomily behind them.

I tried to make conversation with Bill, but he only whim-pered, and brought his face very close to the palm of his left hand (not, I noticed, the other way around, although that would surely have been easier). I napped again. Then I sat up. My time in the forest had habituated me with doing nothing, and sitting in the cell didn't bother me.

At some point they shut off the lights. Night, I supposed. I lay on the floor; for though it was harder and colder than the bench, it was not ridged, and I slept more easily. Bill curled up foetally on his bench, and slept like a dog. Morning was announced by the sudden snapping on again of lights, and the door opening again. Water, bread and butter was delivered, and the two of us broke our fast without speaking. The tray on which the necessaries were delivered had a chip in it, but it only spoke once: 'Please don't put me in the dishwasher, or my laminate will peel!' The tray was decorated with a repeating tessellated design of interlocking parrot shapes.

After a while, Bill spoke up. 'I've always been meek,' he said.

'And you shall surely inherit the earth,' I replied, aiming for a kind tone. My instrument isn't well adapted to kindness, though. I suspect it came out sarcastic and aggressive.

'Shy,' he said, not meeting my eye. He brought out his invisible iTab, looked at the imaginary screen for a few seconds, and then put it away again.

I waited.

'Always been more comfortable around animals,' he said eventually. 'I do not know why. I'll tell you what: when the first bêtes got citizenship, I was so excited I couldn't sleep. It was like Christmas. Like Christmas is for a kid. Lion, Witch *and* Wardrobe all on one day! It was like a thousand Christmases.' He stopped, and blushed port-wine red.

After a long pause, I said: 'I'm sure your dog is fine, you know.'

He didn't reply.

I suppose we were there half a day – long enough for me to grow hungry again – before the lock growled once more, and the door once more squeaked open, and soldiers took Bill away. He went out on a long, almost musical stream of whimpers.

I was alone.

I wondered, naturally, about whether the Lamb had *used*

me – tricked me into carrying some unimaginably dangerous *Independence Day* style virus into the firewalled protective space of the military net. But of course maybe not: maybe it was a false alarm. And maybe, even if the system crashed, it wouldn't inconvenience the army too severely. There was no wireless outside the city anyway, or so I assumed. Could the bêtes really leverage any military advantage from infecting the in-house system? I didn't know. I *could* see, mind you, how it looked from the outside. Catweazel walks into your military headquarters, spins you some story about negotiating with the Lamb himself, and the next thing you know the lights are flickering in their casing and all your computer screens show graphics of mockingly laughing skulls.

Or, you know, whatever.

What would they do to me? I said the words, 'shot at dawn' aloud, in effect trying them out for size. There's an old joke. A prisoner is brought out of his cell at dawn, and marched out into the courtyard where he will be blindfolded and shot. The troops are already there, leaning on their rifles. As he starts across the yard it starts to rain. He looks to the sky. 'Well,' he says. 'This is a *fine* start to the day.'

Perhaps Major General Hetheridge would summon me for a second interview. He would say: 'After revolving the matter for some time we are disposed to trust you, Graham.' He would say: 'A terrorist actively trying to plant a virus in our system would hardly draw attention to him doing that, in the manner you did! After all.' After all. But of course, nervy, stressed, that's precisely what a terrorist might indeed do. Why, after all, had I said what I said? What imp of the perverse grabbed the tendons of my tongue and formed those words? I'm the last person able to tell you that. So maybe the second interview would go a different way. Maybe it would be: *We can't afford to take any chances, Graham.* Or: *Nothing personal. Graham.* Or: *Drumhead justice, Graham. You understand.* I do understand. *We have to shoot you, Graham? Are you cool with that, Graham? Are you like the Fonz in the face of your personal extinction, Graham?*

I am cool.

I tried to blank my mind, but my brain kept rolling back into life. The stakes were high. War would not go well for us, if we allowed it to run out of control. But, say we managed to form an alliance with the bêtes of the south, Major General Hetheridge! Think what tactical advantages that could give us, for the pacification of the north! I was thirsty, but the water jug from the morning yielded up only droplets.

I thought about Anne. I tried to remember exactly what she looked like, but her features evaded my mind's eye. I thought of her sitting on the back step of her empty B and B, smoking into the night air, and then very carefully disposing of the ashes as if they were nuclear waste. The friability of my memory of her made my gut tremble, butterfly-afraid in the core of my being. If I never got back to Cincinnatus, if I never sealed the deal I had been sent with, then my own individual memories of her were going to rust over and cease to work. I was going to lose her again as my mind decayed and I grew older and less capable, and the mere thought of that made me more afraid than I have ever been in my life. Dying at the hands of the Major General's soldiery was a trivial matter by comparison.

I tried to sleep again, but couldn't. The long sculptural face of a horse. The kindling in its eyes. A cat, out of the corner of your eye, appearing from and then disappearing into the shadow of which it is made. As faithful as a dog. As wily as a fox. As strong as an ox.

283

I tried to distract myself from myself by telling myself a story. I told myself the story of Oedipus.

The Sphinx was a beast. It asked one question of humankind, and it is the same question all animals ask – dumb or bête, herb eater or carnivore, all animals that have eyes that can look into our eyes. It asks: *What are you?* And it is the same question as *What am I?* What do we do? We walk. We live through the day, day by day. We grow strong, and we grow weak. We pass through birth, but we never pass through death because there is nothing on the other side of death to pass *into*. Homo sapiens, Homo loquens, Homo bête. All the same. Oedipus knew the answer not because he was a king, but because he had been abandoned. Kings in their panoply are human attempts to evade the truth of the Sphinx, attempts to convince ourselves that we are grand, important, elevated above the rest of creation. But Oedipus's father threw him out, and he grew up in the wilderness, a lame man creeping through the undergrowth. He saw the cosmos from the ground, not the raised dais of the royal family. When he met his father at the crossroads the old man didn't recognize him. How could he see his son in this lowly fellow, dressed like a beggar, dirty and with a crippled leg? He took Oedipus to be a nobody, and he was right. Oedipus was that nobody we call Death, the thin man who has no flesh and so robs us of ours. Oedipus was that nobody we call Wisdom, that is general and does not belong to any one person. He killed his father, and he fucked his mother, and the Sphinx came to that land. She came padding on cat paws, and her tail was a sine wave behind her. She was the size of an ox, and stronger, and her human breasts were covered with downy hairs, and her human face was of the kind of beauty that only comes in dreams – long, dark-eyed, lips the colour of cranberries and eyes the colour of death. She said to Oedipus: 'You are dressed in royal robes, now; but beasts have no need of clothes, and you are a beast.' And Oedipus said to her: 'You ask me this question in words, but beasts have no need of words.' And the Sphinx said: 'We are equally beasts, Oedipus, but you are the lesser of the two. When you were a toddler you walked unsteadily on two legs; and when you became a man and your cock grew long you swaggered more confidently because of it; but the day will come when you become me, and walk on four legs, and only then will you have matured.' At this, Oedipus took his sword and aimed a blow at the Sphinx's chest, between her tempting breasts. But she danced to the side and instead Oedipus's blade carved through her left foreleg. She howled, and rolled over, and again Oedipus ran at her with his sword, and again she struggled out of his way, and his sword only cut through the knee of her remaining foreleg. At this she collapsed, unable to raise herself from the dust, and let out a pitiful wail, until the blood fled from her and she died. But Oedipus was filled with regret at what he had done – for these three things are the distinctive features of the human animal, as a turquoise tail is of a peacock and a horn that of a rhino: clothes, names and regret. He ordered a great tomb to be built, and laid the corpse of the Sphinx within it, and a mighty statue raised above it. Oedipus knew that great though his wisdom was, the Sphinx's wisdom was greater. For she said: 'We are the same kind, you and I; we are your father and mother because you evolved out of us. You kill us as your father, and make pets of us to love us as your mother, and in this you are trying, as children do, to distance yourself from us. You will come to understand that there will always come a time when you will look from pig to man and man to pig and not be able to tell the difference.'

I slept. I woke. I waited.

Finally the lock growled for a third time, and the door squeaked all the way open.

III

•

Four legs in the evening

'The study of Nature makes a man
at last as remorseless as Nature'

The Island of Doctor Moreau, H. G. Wells

The Homo sapiens was laid out on the table, and he was dead. His skin was white as lard. His name had been Graham Penhaligon, but he didn't have a name now, because names are uniquely properties of the living. This is because names are not things to survive beyond death, like pebbles and fingernails. Rather names are what call us out, interpellate us, and no matter how long or loud you call a dead person they will not respond.

There is a riddle here.

Graham Penhaligon lay naked on the table, His flesh was the same temperature as the wood beneath it, as the unheated room in which he lay. When he had been alive his flesh was a blend of white, red and yellow; now that he was dead the red had faded, and a buttery colour and rubber-like marigold texture had taken possession of his skin. He looked less than dead. There was no dignity in his laying out. His toenails, for instance: how unlike human cuticles, how very like razor-clam shells, hard and ridged and protruding. His toes as sea-potatoes. His slab-like buttocks. These miniature stretch lines and cellulitic grooves on his white thighs, where the skin is tugged like a fabric snagged on something – a nail protruding from the wall, a heel. Vanilla ice cream. His large-featured visage not looking at the ceiling, although his eyes are open. His mouth not breathing, although his lips are parted. Too old and lifeless and dead for pity, or humour, or honour, or hope. But not too dead for memory. What is the one thing that survives death? We're sidling up to the riddle now, that's a good entry-level question for this riddle.

What is stronger than death? Memory.

What's the heart of memory? Devouring.

There are no other Homos sapiens in the room. The whole house is as cold as the winter landscape outside, but all the people in the house have hair and fur in sufficiency to keep them warm. Wifi is a legend to them, now. To communicate they must talk to one another. Outside, the aspen poplars carry their own weight in snow instead of foliage. Drifts sculpt the roadway, smother the fence, fill the garden. Snow had pushed a giant white python shape in through one broken ground-floor window. The bêtes inside the house don't care about broken windows. They're not like Homo sapiens in that regard. Inside and outside isn't a dyad that structures their thoughts in the same way that it does humans.

There are seventy-six bêtes inside the house with the corpse of Graham Penhaligon. Most are dogs, cats, foxes and birds. There are a few other creatures. There are also a number of dumb beasts, but we're not interested in them. Except one: a red-backed, dog-faced *llwynog*, a vixen chased into the kitchen by a group of bête foxes. She stands, wary, her tail up. To keep her happy, a cat sitting on the table tosses down small morsels of food. It is winter, and food is scarce; and although the vixen is not comfortable at least she is not surrounded by humans. She stands, she stays vigilant, and from time to time eats.

Outside, a hail of birds lands on the guttering with the breezy sound of their wings flapping. A sparrow has a snail in its beak, and is looking for something to serve as anvil – something not softened by a covering of snow. The other birds want the snail, because it is winter and food is scarce. There is a touch of avian tussling. Nothing is ready, the sparrow curses and flings down things from the gutter. *Fuck*, says the bird. *Fuck*, and hurls itself down amongst all the falling birds to chase the morsel. So flute-like a sound, that one English language syllable.

Inside the house, the vixen puts out her tongue, silvery against the blood-orange fur.

Some come to bêteness by chance, devouring a chip inadvertently in the course of feeding. Others are selected. I was the latter. Except that I am not yet. She is still vixen.

I heard a story that, in the West Country and Wales, some horses carry seven chips in their heads, and parlay the inner dialogue into wisdom. They can, it says, see the future. I do not believe it myself. Except that I am not yet.

I grow alarmed at the entry of a Homo sapiens into the kitchen. Adult male, swaddled up in strange fabrics with a horseshoe shape of fur tufts poking from the rim around his face. He came and stared at the body on the table for a long time, concentrating on the face. Like any animal's face, a Homo sapiens' face is activated by many muscles under the skin. Death takes away that activation, and the muscles petrify. Lines become stone-carved, the right and left end points of the mouth move a little way from the eyes and in towards the chin. The newcomer breathes fern-like tendrils of white breath into the room. He speaks, but all I hear is gabble-gabble-gabble.

Later he goes. I creep out from behind the fridge. There are fewer bêtes in the kitchen now, and fewer animals too. I am hungry, and eye the dogs and cats and the other foxes to see if any of them look infirm, or toothless, or otherwise easy prey. All are lively, sharp-toothed, well clawed. A cupboard door is open, and inside is a mess of straw (actually it is shredded cardboard, from the boxes of breakfast cereals ripped open by earlier animals – years earlier, perhaps – to get at their edible contents. But I don't know that yet). I contemplate climbing inside and napping; but I'm not comfortable enough in this strange place, with these strange bêtes. Perhaps another repellent Homo sapiens will come in. I stay wary.

Later they explain to me that the living Homo sapiens was the son of the dead Homo sapiens. He is living a denuded life, they say; shunned by his own kind, but too ineluctably human to be accepted by bêtekind. He came to observe his dad. It was hard to see, because his hood was up, but he wept.

'And this dead body?' I will ask (later). 'Was he not also too ineluctably human to be accepted?'

'He was different,' they will say (later). 'He was not Homo sapiens. He was Homo sacer. Wait,' they will say (later), 'and the memories will come. They tend to sift down into your mind, most recent first, earliest last.'

'Why?' There's a lot of that, in my first minutes.

So there is a cat, black like a coot's head. He tears out a chunk of flesh and tosses it down to me, and I eat it hungrily. He throws a second, and I gobble. He throws a third, larger, and with gristle in it; I swallow. It sticks a little in my throat, and I cough a while, and retch a while, and put a paw over my snout, but most of the meat goes down, and I put my back against the wall and watch. I start to feel queer, and then I retch some more, but to no effect. Then I go into the cupboard anyway, and curl up amongst the coarse straw, and sleep.

I'm awake almost at once, and I am no longer just the vixen. I come out of the cupboard and stretch my mouth, and try some barks, and some growls, and some shifting of my lower jaw from side to side.

The snow has immobilized the grass. But it wasn't always snow. It was before, and the time when there was no snow. Leaves surge blackly across. Biter, bite a crescent from this apple, though your jaw is a different shape, and your teeth hurt. This white image in the apple's flank is the moon. The moon is white and black together, and gives up a tar-dark seed. We bury the seed in the soil underneath the turf to settle it in the darkness. Growth: how high does the stem ascend? Touching whose white, elevate face? The incomprehensible cry is not incomprehensible. Night, and then day, is the fixture of rhythm.

It's spring, and stormy, and the trees are making the same noise that thunder makes. It is a gloomy afternoon, and we are struggling on old legs over the grass and back into the house, and we are holding an apple in our right hand, green as a grasshopper.

Teeth hurt as we bite, but the tartness of the apple's flesh is also its sweetness. The greenery of spring is a wreath upon winter's grave. The cherry tree positively weeps blossom.

We have lived here for years (the memory flows flows flows into the the the brain, and the number of years grows smaller) with nothing but occasional bête visitors, and our memories. But the memories are enough. A human being's memories, and a cat's memories, triangulating the same subject. The winter is here. The summer that preceded it, and the leaves of the aspens shovel the air ceaselessly.

The nibble-edged circles of their leaves.

Past the aspens, to a field, hip-high with weeds. At the end of the field, the wall of the sky. There's a tractor hulk in there, lobster-red with rust and drowning in greenery. We're not as young as we used to be. Here's a horse, pulling a flat-bed cart, and on the cart a box of supplies. Somebody, or somebête, has written on the side: *Homo sacer*. The beast and the sovereign.

Summer evenings, when the day turned a little cooler, working the patch of ground behind the old brick igloo, the dome webbed with ivy, the bricks turned to the texture of biscuit by centuries. We hoed along a file of cabbages, and hoed back up the other way. There was water in an underground tank, once (I believe) the cesspit for the house, now filled with rainwater and drainwater sweet as celery. There was an old pump action hose: so the foot worked up and down and the water drizzled over the clenched hearts of the vegetables. We grew potatoes below the wall, where it was cooler. I was the only person who ever tended those swollen roots, whoever plucked those cabbages. I was legion.

At night in the winter, we can pause before we set fire to the branches in the fireplace. Outside, the poplar twigs rub against one another in the wind like a thousand crickets' legs. There are crowds of humans heaving and straining behind their walls, far from here. Over the hills and far.

What about before we came to this house? We lived in several places, but there was a happiness there. That was an Alcestis trick of great power, but the ground of it is: choice. If I had to choose between betraying my country and betraying my friend, I hope I should have the guts to betray my country. And here we are walking in a state of uncertain doubleness.

Here's a memory: when I kept the farm, we grew some

veg. Nothing commercial, just to make use of land and reduce household expenses – farming being the minimum-margin business it was. Carrots, cabbages, spuds. During the last year of the farm I ended up too busy to tend this garden, though, because I had to devote all my attention to maximize the cow income. So we hired a local lad to do it for us: a tall, slender lad with carbuncles on his face like red blossom against a white sky. Sulky, as teens often are. We didn't pay him much (in fact we used a popular but illegal app to put the money on his chip without notifying the authorities, thereby not only paying him less than minimum wage but enabling him to evade having to make NI contributions). He didn't stay long, either. He was only in the countryside because his mum was poorly, I recall; and after she died he walked off to the city, part of that great tidal shift of humanity from soil to stone that marks the last fifteen decades. But I mention him here because there would be times when I would be working my farm, having forgotten that he was there also, and would catch a glimpse of him out of my corner-eye, and feel a sudden jolt, as if a tendril of dread had trailed across the tender membrane of my mind. A ghost, a spectre, a revenant, a sign of my own impending death? No, relax Graham, it's just Wilfred. Then my heart would settle. I mention it here because my (not yet our) journey from Reading was like that. Haunted, trailed, followed. A fury pursuing. Cain leaving Eden was not more harried. People misunderstand the 'mark of Cain', you know. It was not a sign of God's curse, but of his protection. Not of divine ostracism – Cain had already been cast out, you remember – but of his sacredness. The mark told the world: leave this one alone. This one belongs to God, for good or ill.

All this talk of Cain. You can see where this is going. Jazon wasn't blood, but he was my brother nonetheless, the closest to a brother I ever had.

Reading. The military officer had offered me a car, but I had turned him down. He thought this was spite on my part, since he had been the one to order me locked in a cell for all those days. But I (we) didn't mind that. We (I) had long since grown used to solitude. It had taken them three days – said the military man – in order to ringfence a large enough computational resource. The initial contact had, or hadn't, it was hard to tell, injected code into the system; but it didn't seem to have had any adverse effects. And finally the authorities had talked to the Lamb, and a deal had been struck. The military had wanted to hold onto the Lamb, but he had persuaded them to have Graham port the chip back to the countryside.

Well all right, then.

Well, all right then.

Well. All right.

The leg ached.

We were not yet we. I walked, with a stick, through the gate and shook the gatekeeper's hand. And I, the vixen, have foresuffered all, enacted in this same H. sapiens' head. I who have sat at Thebes below the wall. At Reading, rather, below the wall. And walked. And walked amongst the lowest of the—

Boom, blows the wind. Boom, boom, boom.

I walked back into the winter landscape, with the Lamb again in my pocket. I was not yet we. But neither was I alone.

There's another man, with two goods legs instead of one good and one weak and one stick. The nightingale sang also: her song is hoarse. I am being followed.

He trots along after me, and sometimes stops to do something (I don't look back; I don't see what) and then he doubles his stride and catches me up again. He is my oldest living friend, with his unruly hair and sepia skin and active mouth. With his crow-black coat, which he believes makes him look more clerical. Even when he is being a royal fucking pain in the perineum, I love him like a brother. Just, as the gag goes, not one of mine. That's not funny, though. He was an Abel man.

'Let it go, Preach,' I tell him. Stomping down the weedy tarmac through the empty village that used to be Shinfield. 'Let it alone.'

'I can't do that, Gray,' he replied, hurrying his pace to catch me up. 'You're about to do something terrible. I'm your friend, aren't I? It's my job to stop you making a buttock of yourself.'

'Your job is to preach the gospel to the Reading populace,' I said. 'Your job is to leave me the fuck alone.'

'Despite your bad language,' said Preacherman, 'I will not abandon you.'

At this, I stopped, and turned to face him. 'This is the one thing I want in my life. This is the only thing I want in my life. This is the woman I love. I can be with her again. Why would you want to stop me?'

'It will drive you mad, my friend,' he said. 'These bêtes are devils. What promise they made you, they will break. Whatever you think they will give you, it will only be betrayal.'

'Hetheridge seems to think the treaty viable.'

'He can only see the military side of things. He can't see the larger danger here. *They* are not your kind.'

'I don't care.'

'Graham,' he said. 'You have a duty to your kind. You have a duty to your *soul*. If I say you will lose your soul, should you go ahead with this, I'm not speaking figuratively. Your land and your people need you. This woman, however much she meant to you, is dead. Don't stab your land in the back for the sake of one woman – a woman not even alive.'

'If I had to choose,' I told him, 'between betraying my country and betraying my friend, I hope I should have the guts to betray my country.'

He digested this, and then grew visibly wroth at this. 'But that's nonsense!'

'It's Forster.'

'I don't care how many stars you give it,' he returned. 'It's dangerous *nonsense*.'

'Love is love, mate.'

'Listen to yourself! Like it's not possible for love to be good or evil, just as people are good or evil. You think Hitler didn't love killing Jews? You think devils don't love to torment the godly?'

'Goodbye, Preach. If there is to be peace – I mean, if the peace is going to work out – then perhaps we'll meet again.' I turned, and started plocking away again.

'What about your duty, Graham?' he called. 'What about your duty to your land? What about your duty to your species?'

I loved poetry at school, and then, out of a kind of intellectual stubbornness, I refused to let it go, even though it was of less than no use to the business of running a farm. I studied Latin, which was equally useless. My little red notebooks of poetry, scribbled in only at those moments when I was sure I was alone. As my kids grew older they became less inhibited about mocking me for my literary pretensions. For Albie it was just the fact of it: so violent-tempered and emotionally clumsy a fellow aspiring to write poetry (of all things). Anger's always been the point of poetry, though – check out the first word of mankind's oldest poem, *The Iliad*, if you don't believe me.

Jen was more puzzled that I gave up publishing any of it, after the *Eclogues*. 'What, not even online?' No, not even online. I wasn't aspiring to be Ted Hughes. I was trying to do something disinterested in a life that was, otherwise, all about the financial return upon labour and land. That was all about paying school fees and scratching the money together for vet bills and boiler repairs. I was writing poetry for myself, not for others, because the others did not need convincing that there was something aesthetically valuable in 'nature'. Most of the others took that as a post-Wordsworth given. Not me. I was hip-deep in the shit of it. I wrestled it every day. Looking back, I think I was actually trying to persuade myself that there was beauty around me. That I did what I did for love, not merely out of a barren kind of duty. That I wasn't simply going through the motions with my work, in my marriage, in my life. None of us wants to think that. Even if it is true.

I studied Latin. *Duty* is suffixed from *due*, which in turn is the English derivative from Latin's *debitum*, owed. Which is to say, duty is the state of being in debt. One's duty, is what one owes. The difference is that duty in the sense we now understand the term is supposed to be *disinterested*, whereas debt as we now understand it (which is to say, now that usury has been struck from the list of appalling sins by the Western world) is precisely *interested* ... interest is due upon debt: interest, we might say, is the duty of debt. This elision of meanings has unfortunate consequences. Really, we need to remove 'duty' from the semantic field of debt. For too many people duty is a tiresome concept, something 'owed' or 'ought' (hence we say: 'I ought to do more about global warming, I ought to give more money to charity'). But the sorts of things you owe now – the mortgage on your house, for instance – are things you are seeking only to rid yourself of. Duty, in the broadest sense, cannot be 'discharged'; we can never be, and should not seek to be, in a position where all our 'duty' is paid off, and we can relapse into destructive selfishness. Duty is a freedom, not an obligation: a freedom from the tyranny of self, not a mortgaging of that self to society as a whole. Duty is always a free choice, a flowing-out of the human from ourselves to others. Duty is a liberality.

'You owe it to humanity,' said Preacherman, calling louder now, because I had left him that much further behind. 'I'm your friend, aren't I? You owe it to me.'

'You don't understand owe,' I shouted back, keeping my gaze on the road ahead. There were animals dancing through the bushes, and sneaking through the places where the fences were falling into disrepair.

These memories live on, in me. I can see them, in my own head.

I left him behind, by dint of ignoring the pain in my leg and marching on faster and faster. But he caught up with me again. He was like a bad conscience. I couldn't get rid of him.

'Where are you going, anyway?' he asked me, interspersing his stride with little trotty bursts of speed to keep up with me.

'You know where I'm going,' I said.

'I know what Satan promised you – your woman, yeah? You'll be reunited with her, even though she's dead, correct? That's a lie, Graham. Satan is the father of lies.'

'I'm going anyway,' I told him.

Preacherman was grinning at me. We were a good way south of the village now, and the road ran through fields, with the edge of the forest on the horizon. The view was of the low hills and shallow valleys of the south of England. Walk far enough in that direction and you come to the coast, where channel waves crisp and fall, making the pebbles rattlesnake and the foam sink through the grid of them. A line of surf all around the magic island like a slug's silver trail, skirting East Anglia and Northumberland, hugging close about the crenulations of Scotland, a silver halo about the twin horns of Wales, close as a stocking on Wessex's crinkly leg, and back along the long south coast.

Beasts peered from every hedgerow. Dogs gathered in a mass further down the lane. Maybe I was the only one who could see them.

'I can't let you,' Jazon told me. 'I'll restrain you by main force, if I have to. Main force!' He sucked his teeth, meditatively, and then said: 'Wait. Is that hand force? Like the French for hand?'

'I think so,' I confirmed.

'I thought maybe,' Preacherman said, 'it was, like, main as opposed to subsidiary force. I'm hardly going to restrain you with *subsidiary* force, now, am I!'

'You're not going to restrain me at all, Jazon,' I said.

'You're not strong, the way you were, Graham,' he replied, sorrowfully. 'You're not a match for me. Maybe once upon a time, but look at you. You're a snowman who's been out in the sun, my friend.'

'You're a big man but you're out of shape,' I said, more to myself than to my companion. 'With me it's a full-time job. So—'

Dogs were running alongside the road, and then doubling back, and running up again. I tried to count them, but the flow and sudden turns of the pack confused my eye, like a shark watching sardines.

'And what?' said Preacherman. 'You can't intimidate me. I'm

your friend.' He reached out and put a hand on my arm. 'Come back to the town, Graham.'

I look back at this. Graham's not my name.

Preacherman was holding a gun in his right hand. 'I'm a councilman now, Gray. An important person. Do you see this?'

'It's a gun,' I said.

'Good. Now, do you see *this*?' With his left hand, he brought out a mobile phone. 'It's special. It's plumbed into the military network. Mate, I don't want to. You think I want to? I figure: shoot you in your bad leg, it won't matter so much. It's already bad, isn't it? Then one call and a chopper will be here in twenty minutes.'

'A chopper? The bike?'

'A helicopter.'

'I didn't know the Reading garrison was operating choppers. Aren't they a bit expensive, this day and age?'

'You don't know the first thing, Graham,' said Preacherman. 'The nation's future is at stake!'

I felt frustration, but tiredness too. 'I don't understand why you want to stop me.' I said. 'I don't get why it *matters* to you.'

Birds circled overhead.

'Because you're my friend,' he said, in an imploring voice. It may be, if I think back, that he was reminding himself, not me, of this fact. What was he doing, anyway? Out in the middle of nowhere, with an angry old tramp swearing at him, and the beasts of the field gathering as a malign congregation. 'And besides,' he added, getting closer to the truth. 'You're special to *them*. And if you're special to them, then we can use you. Against them.'

More dogs spilled out through the hedgerow. The presence of these creatures finally impinged upon his perception. He stood up taller, slipped his special-issue phone back in his pocket, and pulled out a crucifix. 'You keep back,' he called out, in a clear voice. 'You bêtes – all of you! Get ye behind me. Understand?'

'Jaze, you're making a fool of yourself.'

'I know the devil when I see him!'

My leg twinged at this, as if prompting me. 'You know I've got to deliver the Lamb back to—'

'Deliver Satan, you mean!' Jazon snapped.

'—to his tribe. That's what Hetheridge is expecting of me. That's *how* the treaty is going to be actualized. The Lamb will, I guess, find himself a new home, and from there command his followers to walk the straight and narrow.'

'I don't want to use the gun, Graham,' said Preacherman. Then, surprisingly, he proved himself as good as his word, and put the gun away in his pocket. 'Make me nervous, firearms do. Supposed to beat it into a ploughshare, I am; though it'd make a wee diddy little one. Turn the other cheek, *that's* the karate *I've* been trained in. But you gotta understand …'

'Wait a minute,' I said. There was a dog at my side. A lithe, black Labrador, taller than my knees. It had peeled away from the hedgerow that ran alongside the road, or from its shadow. Sun low in sky. Suddenly here it was.

Preacherman waved the crucifix at the dog. 'The devil is a canine!' he called. 'The devil is an ass! The devil is a cow! The devil is—'

What you need to think is: maybe he was right.

'Preach! Calm down', I barked. The dog was silent. I almost slapped Jazon; he was on the edge of hysteria. 'Wait. What do you mean? *Helicopters?*'

Jazon danced behind me, to put my body between him and the canine. He was still flourishing his crucifix. 'Hey! Hey!'

'Jason: who has *helicopters*, that you can you summon them in twenty minutes with a phone call?' I asked. 'Twenty minutes is further off than Reading. Reading is five minutes by chopper.'

'Graham. Hetheridge is making a *mistake*,' he said.

'So you waited until you were out of the town,' I said. 'Until we were beyond Hetheridge's interference.'

'We come to it at last,' Preach said urgently. 'The great war of our time. Don't be on the wrong side, Graham! You think they care for us? They don't need us, and so they will destroy us. Think of the future. God gave us dominion over the birds and the beasts. Who would want to up-end that hierarchy, except the devil? Think of where the country is going! More and more humans abandoning the countryside, more and more squeezing into the cities. Abandoning the countryside to the bêtes! Leaving them in charge of all our farming! Why should we trust them? Who's to say they won't wait until the urban population reaches a maximum and then starve us, in our concrete citadels? Infect us with the sclery? Why wouldn't they? How can we trust them? That's the way of it. Trust me. Why won't you trust me? I'm your friend!'

'You are my friend,' I conceded.

'You can't,' Preach said, waving his crucifix in the air for emphasis, 'choose a dead woman over a living friend. That's just – morbid, mate. And you *have* to choose! You've got to make a choice.' He took a step towards me. The dog at my side stood perfectly still. Birds stirred the white air in a great circle overhead.

'On the one hand,' said Jazon, 'you have me, your best friend. You have your country and your duty. You have humanity, your own kind – your daughter, your son, your grandkids. You have all their futures. On the other hand you have— Forgive me, Graham, for being brutal, but it's the truth. On the other hand you have a woman's corpse. And a whole pandemonium of canny beasts, the enemy of humanity. What kind of a choice is that?'

'It's no choice at all,' I said. But I didn't mean what Jaze hoped I meant.

'The land is divided against itself! Literally apartheided between country and city. Unless we fight back, we'll be expelled from the green spaces for ever. This peace treaty is not the right call. I have friends in the military who disagree with Hetheridge. Come with me, Graham, and take the Lamb to them. The Satan in your pocket – it could prove invaluable in the war! It could make the difference between winning and losing. Or would you turn traitor? Traitor to your own kind?'

Black dog. How does that guitar riff go?

'I'll be with her again,' I said.

'You're no Romeo, Graham. I *know* you! I've known you years.' He held his free hand out towards me. 'If you won't come with me, at least give me the chip. The chip from your pocket. At least do that.'

I shook my head. 'I've made my choice, mate.'

'Graham!' hooted Preacherman, in pure frustration.

I turned away from him, to resume my walk. And as I started to turn, the dog moved. He slid forward, without so much as a growl. I sort of witnessed what happened next, although it was my corner-eye not my full vision. My memory of it is: Jazon reached quickly for his firearm, but his fingers slid off the flap of his pocket instead of slipping inside. Why do they even fit those external flaps onto jackets? I mean, who benefits from them? In this case it cost Preacherman dear. His fingers fiddled at the outside of his jacket, and without a gun in his hand the dog was not stopped. He pushed off with his bow bent back legs and flew up.

And there wasn't even time for Jazon to call out. The dog's jaws snapped a single bone-break note, and I was beginning to turn round. I could see, as I turned, that there was a great messy scarlet cravat at Jazon's Adam's apple where there hadn't been one before. But he was already falling backwards, and the hound paddled its legs against his angled torso and leapt away.

Jazon fell straight back. He fumbled at the air with his hands, and a fountain of bright red bubbled from his throat. Soon enough he stopped moving.

The dog was standing beside his body, looking up at me – blood on its chops. A dog panting can hardly help but look like it's grinning, which isn't a pleasant thing at the best of times, and was much much less than pleasant now.

My own heart was running on. My hair moved on my scalp as if under the influence of a halo of static electricity. I felt the gush of panic and fear and elation. 'God,' I said.

'Sic semper, Graham,' said the dog. It mangled the words in the speaking, but there was no mistaking them. 'Sic semper tyrr, tyrr,' but the last word was more than his dog jaw could manage. He woofed, and woofed again. Then he spoke English again: 'Off. You. *Toddle*.'

I stepped towards the body of my friend, and the dog began to growl. 'Fuck,' I yelled, suddenly very scared indeed. 'You going to kill me too, muttfucker?' I was scared that, in a second, I would be lying next to my friend and my heart's blood would be pouring onto the road. I was scared not of dying, but of being denied my reunion with Anne.

'Toddle,' grunted the dog. 'Off.'

I didn't look down, or back. I picked up my stick, and turned around, and walked away. Walked as briskly as my bad foot could manage. I kept walking, and at the beginning of this walk my heart was sounding four beats for every one knock of my stick on the weeded tarmac. After a while this slowed to two heartbeats per step. The sun slid down, as it always does, and always must. The moon was there, bright as a silver penny, paid into the purse of night. What we must do with our choices, my Judas, is not pretend we never made them. Not hang ourselves from a branch in a grand melodrama of denial and despairing cod-atonement. We made them, and that speaks to us, and who we are. We is the pronoun in question. Not I, not I, not I.

I slept that night in an abandoned house. I found blankets in the airing cupboard upstairs, and they were a little damp and mildewed but not too bad. I gathered twigs from the garden, and made a fire in the fireplace. It burnt bright and brief, and I warmed the blankets as best I could. Then I wrapped myself in them and slept on the floor, with my pack as my pillow. I did not dream. Mark, mark, mark.

When I woke it was with a heavy feeling of a kind of symmetry of regret. I got up and explored the house. Mushrooms were growing in the carpets of the downstairs' rooms: spreads of little white globes like spilled pearls, mostly in the corners and by the walls. Upstairs there was one wardrobe and I opened it to the scent of decay and rose petals and found a woman's clothes, limply hanging.

That the riddle is solved does not mean that we will find any comfort in the answer. The answer is always how we diminish. It is always how we fall away from human-ness, like Nebuchadnezzar and become again as the beasts of the field.

'Truth' means precision and accuracy, but 'truthfulness' means sincerity and assertion, and those two things are very different. It's not hard to see which truth is the one we prefer.

I tried the various taps and sinks about the house – there was no water. What I thought was dew in the front garden was actually the silky mist of many spiders' webs. The sun was tinting all the eastern clouds strawberry and beeswax colour. The light was bright and fresh and fell upon my dirty face like clean water. I set off walking, and walked all morning, and the road was surrounded by trees, and the only sound was the breeze shaking hands with the treetops and whispering its not-for-human-ears secrets to the woodland. I saw no bêtes all that morning. Conceivably they were deliberately ignoring me. But inside the woodland was the cat, and inside the cat were a lifetime's memories of Anne, and soon, I knew, they would be inside me. And this is where the backwards memorializing reaches its stopping point, where the air poured through the sieve of leafless trees and the light picked out every speckle and every smut. I felt bad, but here's the thing: I was not going to be I for much longer. Under the new dispensation, I would soon become we.

I had made my choice, after all. Choosing to betray your country rather than your friend is all very well, except that the odds are your friend lives in your country. Or does the phrase mean betraying the countryside? I was not allying myself with these new cyborg animal creatures, with their incomprehensible goals and their repulsive sex lives, carving out their mega-farms in the abandoned rural landscapes. I had no love for anybody, it turned out, except one person.

It all comes to the moment: a man, his cat. 'His' meaning not possession, but identity. There is a riddle here.

'Hellmiaow Graham,' said the cat.

'You killed Preacherman,' I said.

'Not I!' whispered the cat.

'Your kind. You are at war with us.'

'This is news to you, Graham? This has only just occurred to you?'

It was in my head to say, *he was my friend*. But he had called upon that friendship on the road out of Reading, after the manner of someone withdrawing funds from a long dormant bank account, and I had rolled down the shutter on him. 'I've misunderstood your lot,' I told him.

The cat came forward and stretched himself, sinuously, winding between my legs. 'Misrecognition,' it said. 'It's your peculiar genius, Graham. It's what humans are best at. They see a sky and misrecognize it as God. They see bêtes and misrecognize us as animals. We're not other, Graham. We're not the animals your kind shared the planet with. They never made war upon you! We're quite other. You don't like admitting you don't recognize something; so when you see something that is genuinely baffling you misrecognize it as something else. That's the whole long and the short of it.'

'Have I misrecognized your fidelity, cat? Are you going to betray the deal we had?'

By way of answer, the cat continued rubbing itself against my legs, turning and turning in a tight-set gyre. I recall, vividly. Who was better skilled to butcher an animal than I? The riddle always turns on misrecognition. That's the whole point of a riddle. And when all the riddles are solved, and there are no more riddles, will be when the salt loses its savour and we surrender all conviction to despair. At the last moment Cincinnatus's cat body gave a little squeal; but only at the very last moment, so I suppose that right up to the Anne Boleyn end Cincinnatus himself exercised a remarkable control. I took the relevant part through to the kitchen and opened it with a knife, and washed the chip at the sink. Squeamish of me. In bête terms sexually puritan of me. But there you go. And then— Well, there's always a moment before you take your pill when you hold the thing in your right hand and your glass of water in your left hand and pause. Why do you pause? You don't know. The doctor has prescribed this pill to cure what ails you, and you will take it. But you pause anyway. And look at it. Perhaps you're trying to see what the pill *really is* before you ingest it. There is no recognition; there is only misrecognition. That's the truth of the riddle; that's what the riddles says with its content as much as with its form. Love is seeing the other person and recognizing yourself in them. Memory is writing a book with a French title that is so pointedly about England in our compromised late twenty-first-century epoch. Life is about misrecognizing poison as food.

The rain started up a tattoo on the window like an executioner's drumroll. Past the teeth, and halfway down the throat. It was uncomfortable for about a minute, and then it sank through my flesh like water through soil.

I tidied up my miniature shambles, and washed myself. Then I went upstairs and lay on the cold bed. I contemplated my own feelings of guilt, and wondered if I had misrecognized those too – they're strangely akin to love, don't you think? Or maybe that's an English thing too. Preacherman had misled me, and the fact made me feel strangely affectionate towards his memory. I hadn't realized that he was capable of such subterfuge. So: fair play to him. Soon enough I drifted towards sleep, even though it was the afternoon (but, you see,

I'm not as young as I used to be). And on the lip of somnolence I had a weirdly piercing moment of clarity. I thought: I'm going to wake up, and I'll see her clearly for the first time in a year and a half. That's a frightening thing. And then I was under. In my dream the whole landscape was laid before my inner eye that is the bliss of solitude as solitude is about to be taken away for ever. The dark green field, and the rain falling onto it; and the grey raincloud passing on, leaving the field heavier than before. Twig and leaf and a dusk-coloured bare dual carriageway. Verdure and concrete. The rain turning to snow. Clouds occluding the stars, and the wind bringing with it a scent of peat and iron and chill. There are gates, there are many gates, there are always many gates. The city, teeming with folk. The fields beyond, empty. This hill. This lone tree. I would wake, and live my life and never be alone, until I died, and, not dying, would enter a new more crowded mode of living inside the hard, hot body of a fox, and that fox would sniff the post-sunset darkness, and eye the glimmering snow, and then set off leaving a line of slant semi-colons in the snow. That's the riddle: that you have misrecognized the end and it's not the end at all. When I woke it was late afternoon and the day was dwindling. Outside, the rain had turned to snow, and the house was filled with the extraordinary muffled silence of snowfall. That cold powder and its starlike flakes. The garden beyond the window was pressed white and clean like a virgin sheet of paper. I breathed in and smelled something sharp and tangy – me, I suppose. A beast moved quickly towards the copse beyond the garden wall.

Acknowledgements

This is the best of me. Thanks to Simon Spanton for metaphorical obstetrics, to Rachel Roberts for reading an early draft and making many helpful comments, and to the ghost of Ted Hughes and his Goddess of Complete Being. This novel is dedicated to the memory of my friend Jonathan Black, who appears in it distributed, as it were, in the guise of two of its characters.